REDEEMED

BITTER HARVEST BOOK FIVE

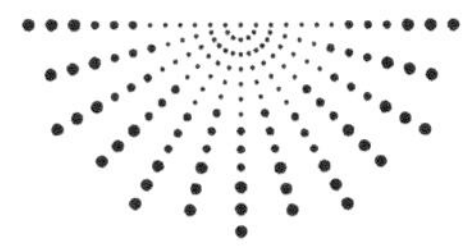

ANN GIMPEL

Edited by

KATE RICHARDS

CONTENTS

REDEEMED

BITTER HARVEST, BOOK FIVE

Dystopian Urban Fantasy
By
Ann Gimpel

Copyright Page

All rights reserved.
Copyright © February 2018, Ann Gimpel
Cover Art Copyright © July 2018, Sly Fox Cover Designs
Edited by Kate Richards
Copy edits by Diane Eagle Kataoka
Names, characters, and incidents depicted in this book are products of the author's imagination or are used fictitiously. Any resemblance to actual events, locales, organizations or people living or dead, is entirely coincidental and beyond the intent of the author.
No part of this book may be reproduced or shared by any electronic or mechanical means, including but not limited to printing, file sharing, e-mail, or web posting without written permission from the author.
ISBN: 978-1948871419

A runaway spell is the most dangerous weapon of all.

Alpha for the few remaining Sea Shifters, Leif's been playing fast and loose with death for years. Plagued by a poisoned ocean, treacherous sea gods, illness, and bad bargains, he's learned to roll with the punches. Setting ancient antagonism aside, he joined a group of land Shifters, pledging both his help and that of his pod.

A vulture shifter, Moira embraces her life on *Arkady*, a small polar cruise ship. She faces problems—ones that may kill all of them —but at least she's free. No more sneaking around hiding from Vampires and not having enough magic to shift, courtesy of short rations and toxic air.

Leif yearns for Moira, but Sea Shifters don't mate with their land cousins—ever. Besides, they have their hands more than full. Not only is there no time for love, there's barely space to breathe as they wend their way through a volatile obstacle field littered with demons, hostile gods, and ancient horrors bent on their destruction.

MAGIC UNDER FIRE

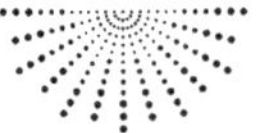

*L*eif swam lazily next to *Arkady* with his dolphin pod spread around him. He could have moved twice as fast as the ship, and then some, but he couldn't keep up that pace all day, every day. Four of five whales paddled nearby. They'd rendezvous with the fifth when they were closer to the Siberian Arctic. Two-and-a-half days had passed since Ketha's transformation back to her human body, and they'd just crossed the equator. Normally temperate, the central Pacific was far colder than he'd expected, but it went along with the weather as a whole being chilly and unsettled. Nothing like Antarctica or New Zealand, but different enough for him to suspect Earth would never fully recover from the Cataclysm's onslaught.

Times like these, though, when he cut cleanly through water that was clear of toxins the Cataclysm had pumped out for ten years, the simple joy of movement filled him with hope.

And then reality intruded.

They were so few. Fourteen sea Shifters. Fifteen land Shifters. Nine humans. An unknown number of the fair folk had promised their aid, but who knew how long their memories were? Poseidon, god of the seas, had ordered him and his sea Shifters to halt their northward journey. Leif defied him, a decision cutting them off from a potential source of aid. He slapped the water with his tail. In his secret places he was nearly certain his liege had switched sides, but he had no proof. Only instincts honed over his five-hundred-year lifespan.

Leif had stopped trusting Poseidon long before his surprising edict to turn the ship around. The sea god, along with his consort, Amphitrite, had stood by and done nothing while nearly all the sea Shifters died, victims of poison spread by the Cataclysm. Nothing worse than the song of a dying whale. Multiply it by a thousand or more, and his soul was permanently riddled by sorrow.

Perhaps whale dirges were the lynchpin that had been Poseidon's undoing. If he'd opened his magic to darkness, evil may have blotted out the haunting laments.

Leif had been nearly dead himself when the Shifters aboard *Arkady* reached out to him and his pod. The land Shifters had no idea how desperate his plight was, but once they found out, two veterinarians had worked like hell to cure the parasitic infestations choking the life out of him and his people.

Leif exhaled in a shower of salty water. He felt better than he had in a very long time. The crippling pain that used to soak up all his attention was gone, and he felt like cavorting in the surf. If he'd been in his human body, he would have shaken his head. Being in the water at all was an indulgence, but he'd herded his group into the sea to take a break from endless battle planning going on throughout the ship.

They were at least two weeks away from Wrangel Island, their objective in the Arctic, but he agreed with Viktor, *Arkady*'s captain and a raven Shifter, that they needed to leverage every advantage they could.

"What do you think will happen next?" Lewis, another dolphin Shifter, swam near enough to talk. Their vocal chords were similar enough to human, they didn't require telepathy to communicate.

"After we reach the Arctic?" Leif focused one laterally placed eye on the other dolphin.

Lewis sputtered around a mouthful of briny foam. "You actually believe whoever's masterminding this isn't going to strike long before we get that far?"

Leif's small, artificial window of peace frittered to nothing. "If the ship's journey to date is any indication, I'm surprised we haven't run into some other atrocity already. What's it been? Nearly three days since we left the Solomons. Three days of harmony, tranquility, goodwill—"

Lewis batted him with a flipper. "Spare me your cynicism." He shook himself, and water flew everywhere. "I'm apprehensive. I like to have backup plans."

"Rather difficult to finesse when we have no idea what will crawl out of the ether next," Leif countered. "I don't expect any more Kelpies, but beyond that, the field is wide open. For all we know, the Cataclysm spawned some new breed of monster we have yet to meet."

"Aren't you Mr. Cheerful?"

"You brought this up," Leif countered. "You are right about one thing, though. Playtime is over. Spread the word, and I'll see everyone back on the ship."

"If I spend too much more time in my human body, my hide will shrivel," Lewis groused.

Leif didn't answer. Hundreds of years ago, sea Shifters and their land kin had played by the same rules. Land Shifters always had an easier time hiding their dual natures, though. Far simpler to conceal themselves in a forest, turn into a wolf—or a coyote or a bird—and join a local pack than it was to swim into the ocean and shift in plain sight of boats and fishermen. The rise of the Church meant his kind faced persecution. Torture. Hangings. Burnings. So they'd taken to the sea for greater and greater chunks of time.

When the Cataclysm hit, many hadn't shifted to their human forms in decades. And then there'd been their ill-conceived bargain with Witches to augment their magic in exchange for a stud service. Who'd have guessed it would turn into a death sentence for the Shifter unlucky enough to be picked as a sperm donor?

"I thought you said playtime was over." Lewis prodded him with a flipper.

"It is. I got lost thinking about how we ended up like we did."

"Not much value in that. It's a bloody miracle any of us survived." Magic turned the air around him shimmery and iridescent.

Leif summoned his own power and shifted right along with the other dolphin. They ended up dripping water on *Arkady's* broad quarterdeck. Viktor kept the surface clean enough to eat from, but he'd never complained about their sloppy transition from sea to ship. The damp marine air glowed and pulsed as the other dolphins and four whales shucked their oceangoing bodies.

All the dolphins had names beginning with L for convenience. Their dolphin names would have been impossible for humans to pronounce. At the time Leif proposed that small concession—since they had a better chance passing for human if they didn't lapse into sea speech—the whales had told him to stuff it. A corner of his mouth twitched. That little episode occurred at least a century before the Cataclysm. He'd always thought it strange none of the whales challenged him for the alpha position, but none ever had.

"We were hoping for a few more hours in the water." One of the whales pushed past a pair of dolphins and planted himself in front of Leif. He stood at least six inches taller and was impossibly broad. Fair hair was already beginning to curl as water dribbled down his body.

"Maybe we can catch some surf time tomorrow." Leif latched onto the whale's dark-eyed gaze, staring him down.

The whale twisted water out of his thick locks. "This has the stink of a meeting. Where and when?"

"You're assuming the one taking place round the clock on the bridge ended," Lynda broke in. Another dolphin shifter, black hair eddied around her, framing high cheekbones and violet eyes.

"The bridge is as good a guess as any location," Leif concurred. "Say half an hour?"

The whoosh of wings caught the edges of his sensitive hearing. He looked up in time to see a good-sized, black vulture swoop from one of the upper decks. It dive-bombed their group, cawing like a mad thing.

Lynda snorted laughter. "She gets to play. We should do more of that. It's good for us."

The vulture made another pass, flying low and veering off scant moments before impact. Leif made a grab for her, but she tossed her tail as she made a ninety-degree turn. "Moira!" he called.

"Who else?" she countered in telepathy. Unlike him, her vocal chords weren't conducive to speech in shifted form.

Ketha bustled out one of *Arkady's* many doors and onto the generous expanse that took up a portion of Deck Three. Brown hair shot with red and gold hung loose to her waist, and she shielded golden eyes—a throwback to her wolf bondmate—with one hand.

"Goddammit, Moira! Get down here."

Still shrieking with delight, the vulture obligingly swerved hard left and headed straight for Ketha, landing on her shoulder and digging her talons in for balance.

"Ouch!" Ketha thumped the flat of her hand across the bird's talons, but Moira didn't uncurl so much as one of them.

Sensing a story lay behind Moira's appearance, Leif aimed his words at Ketha. "What happened?"

"We were deep in tarot spreads, or the other women were. I was working with my glass trying to get it to give me something other than the past."

"The tarot was contradictory," Moira said, clacking her beak a time or two for emphasis.

Ketha angled her head and eyed the vulture. "Patience never was your strong suit."

"Never claimed it was." Another beak clack.

"Anyway," Ketha went on. "One minute, Moira was at a table with Tessa and Zoe. The next, she jumped to her feet and bolted from the room. Right after that, I heard her yapping in vulturese, so I'm betting her clothes are in a heap on the floor somewhere."

"When what you're doing isn't working," the vulture inserted in a sing-songy tone, *"do something different. Sitting on my ass for another three hours begging the cards to cooperate isn't my style."*

Leif smothered the smile that hovered in the background. He liked Moira. She was outspoken and gutsy. Beyond that, her acres of black hair and liquid dark eyes were lovely, as was her delicately boned face sprinkled with a dusting of freckles. Her lush lips were always rosy, and she had a way of licking them that made him want to replace her tongue with his own. She stood medium height, and he'd spent surreptitious moments taking in the curves of her breasts, hips, and ass. She had a fine ass, high and round and made for a man's hands to grab.

His cock began to swell, and he cut off his line of thought fast before his arousal became noticeable. He angled a cascade of his long, thick hair to provide better cover for his nether regions, but no amount of hair could conceal a full-blown erection if his unruly appendage got totally out of hand.

Ketha drew her mouth into a frustrated line and made another effort to displace Moira's talons, with no success. "How about making dinner? Is that more up your alley? It would free Aura and Zoe to spend more time with the cards."

"Sure. I'll lose myself in the galley. Probably for the best. Maybe the cards decided to cooperate after my negative energy left." Still cawing, the bird launched hard off Ketha's shoulder.

She stifled a yelp and rubbed the place the bird had been. "How can a bunch of feathers and hollow bones weigh so much?"

"I heard that!" Moira punctuated her words with a hearty squawk.

One of the whales approached Ketha and inclined his head. "I am not as skilled at scrying as the whale waiting for us in northern waters, but what happened when you tried to coax a vision out of your mirror?"

Ketha drew her brows together and exhaled raggedly. "It's different than before the wickedness that yanked me and the whale Shifter out of *Arkady*. Then I ran up against a blank wall. This time, when I instructed the mirror to show me the future, something that's already happened popped up."

"Not good," the whale muttered. "It's a time inversion."

Alarms tolled in Leif's mind, and he switched to his third eye, the one allowing him to view the world from a psychic perspective. Glowing bisecting lines formed. Some vertical. Some horizontal. Ley lines, they carried the world's magic, concentrating it in key locations. He stared at them, assessing their integrity, and bit back a startled exclamation.

"What?" Several voices, including Ketha's, asked almost in unison.

He held up both hands, fingers spread in front of him. "Do. Not. Panic." Leveling his gaze at everyone, he repeated, "Do. Not. Panic," knowing the injunction was aimed at himself as much as anyone.

Lynda rolled her eyes and made come-along motions with one hand. "Fine, oh fearless alpha. What did you find?"

He shuffled through palatable explanations but couldn't come up with anything, so he stood straighter and muttered, "Magic is weaker than it was last time I looked at the ley lines."

"How much weaker?" Ketha demanded, followed by, "Never mind. I'll look myself."

"I don't know how much weaker," Leif answered, but she'd shut her earth eyes and was deep into her own assessment. "These things aren't easy to quantify. It's a sure bet, though, that if our magic isn't as effective, neither is theirs."

"I wouldn't be so sure about that," one of the whales said

"I agree," Lewis broke in. "I never believed the dark ones sucked power from the same trough as us."

"You make us sound like pigs," Leif protested.

Lewis shrugged. "Sorry if my analogy offended you. It's not the point, though. If something has laid siege to our power, you can bet an ugly surprise is right around the corner."

Ketha opened worried-looking eyes. "You won't remember Rowana. She died before we met up with you, but she discovered small chewed places at the convergence of some of the lines. It looks to me like whatever started that destruction is still working on it, and it's finally had an effect on how much magic is available for us to tap into."

"Probably why the tarot wasn't cooperating. Or your scrying," Leif said.

"Exactly what I'm thinking. Crap. We do not need anything extra to stumble over. I'm going back upstairs. I'll tell the women to conserve their efforts. Only one tarot spread at a time. While they're working on that, I won't do anything with my glass."

Leif nodded and glanced around the grim-faced group. "A staged approach may help. If there's only so much magic, rationing it so it only has to do one thing at a time should maximize its utility."

Ketha ran across the deck, vanishing inside the ship.

"Turns out us coming out of the water when we did was prophetic," a whale muttered.

"Yeah. I wish I could disagree, but it rings true for me," Lynda said, adding, "I'm headed for the clothes locker. See all of you upstairs."

"Before you leave," Leif called after her, "have any of you checked the ley lines lately? Last time I looked might have been New Zealand, and I'd like a more recent comparison if anyone has one."

"I drew power from them during the Kelpie attack," a whale said. "Didn't notice much of anything other than the augmentation I needed was there for me to tap into."

Leif glanced at a sea of shaking heads. "Thanks for trying. See you in a little bit."

It wasn't cold, but a shudder tracked down his body, his earlier arousal forgotten. Who could be sabotaging their magic? The damaged ley lines couldn't be accidental, and whoever was behind the problem had clearly been chipping away at them for a long time. Months from the sound of things.

He hunkered beneath a bulkhead near the door his pod had taken as they filed inside. Five minutes would give him time to think. Besides, with everyone crowded around their clothing locker, he wouldn't be able to get close to it anyway.

He catalogued what he knew, which wasn't very damned much. The assault on their magic had been subtle, so subtle it had mostly gone unnoticed until today. Rowana, the eagle Shifter he'd never met, may have sounded a muted alarm, but the other women hadn't been worried enough to check the lines regularly.

Balling one hand into a fist, he brought it down on the deck. Pain had a stabilizing effect, forcing him to narrow his roiling thoughts. The way they were bouncing around, he'd never make sense of anything, let alone figure out what he needed to do next.

One fact smacked him squarely between the eyes. It would take a hell of a lot of magic to erode the ley lines—even more to do it so delicately as to go largely unnoticed.

Could Poseidon possibly be behind such an undertaking?

Leif played the possibility through his mind, but it seemed remote. Poseidon had magic to burn, but it was an in-your-face kind of power. The sea god had never been a cloak-and-dagger type, mostly because he lacked the incisive elegance required for subterfuge. When he'd gone after the Kelpie, staff swinging, it epitomized his approach to almost everything. Hit fast and hard and ask the tough questions afterward.

If there was an afterward.

If not Poseidon, then who?

Leif slumped lower, resting his naked butt cheeks on the deck. When the answer came, it was so obvious, he cringed. Amphitrite. In her own way, she was far stronger than her consort, and her magic held both grace and refinement. She was more than capable of taking a chink here and there out of the ley lines, siphoning power to augment her own while leaving less for Shifters and others who relied on the lines for their ability.

Soon after Leif had entered into the bargain with the Witches that was almost his undoing, Poseidon had cuffed him, cussed him out, and called him things far worse than stupid without offering to cast even one spell to aid the sea Shifters so they could nullify their pact.

Furious at his liege's patronizing condescension, Leif had hurtled out of the royal dwelling intent on losing himself in the sea. He'd no sooner found his dolphin form than Amphitrite joined him. Nereids swam next to her, sending glowing contrails through the sea's murky surface.

He ground his teeth together, the memory of that day still engraved in his memory. The queen of the sea had apologized for her consort, but once she was done, she'd invited Leif to share her bed. Nonplussed, he'd blundered through a refusal. He hadn't totally given up on Poseidon coming to his senses and aiding the sea Shifters. Sleeping with his wife would certainly put the kibosh on any possibility of assistance.

With a knowing smile on her ageless face, Amphitrite said her invitation was open-ended, and she'd encouraged him to give it some thought. The Nereids had flashed breasts and tails his way before the whole convoy disappeared as quickly as they'd arrived.

Fury swept through him. Had Amphitrite been skimming power even then? Or was this something new? A little trick she began experimenting with after the Cataclysm struck?

He raked wet hair out of his face. If it was Amphitrite, he had an idea. One that would send a nasty magical shockwave boomeranging back in her face the next time she had the temerity to dabble in what didn't belong to her.

"Magic belongs to all of us."

His dolphin's voice reverberating through his mind shocked Leif, and he shot to his feet. "You never talk with me when I'm human. And you're using English. I had no idea you spoke anything but our sea tongue."

A low chuckle tickled the corners of his consciousness. *"How could I not know your human language after sharing your mind for centuries? When we spent most of our time in my body, there was no need to speak during the rare occasions you were human, but we seem to have reached a turning point."*

Leif sent warm thoughts winging inward. "I agree about magic belonging to us all, but what would you have me do to stymie her?"

"If you set a trap, it will snap shut no matter who's meddling. Right?"

"Maybe. If it's someone from the darker side of things, it might roll off them without much effect, but it should protect the ley lines from further degradation."

"It might be enough." The dolphin paused. *"We must do everything we can to ensure Poseidon and Amphitrite survive. Our power is rooted in theirs, and if they fail..."*

The dolphin stopped there, but it didn't have to say any more. Leif understood. Suddenly, the task stretching before him grew far more complex. Cutting the sea gods off at the knees wasn't an option. No. Somehow, he had to convince them to return to their proper roles. Protection, rather than extracting what they needed without a thought to their subjects.

Weariness crashed over him as he made his way inside. The lower corridor was empty, and he dressed fast. The sooner he laid his thoughts out for the others to pick apart, the sooner they could come up with a plan.

Regardless, they had to move fast, before magic to summon even the simplest of castings ran through their fingers like sand through an hourglass.

2

SOMEONE WANTS US DEAD

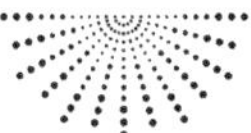

*M*oira Miller flew through the porthole she'd left open and shifted back to human in a deserted cabin. *Arkady* was large enough to house around seventy passengers and fifty crew, which meant a whole lot of unoccupied space. After storming out of the thwarted tarot reading on the bridge, she'd run down two flights and picked the first empty cabin she came to on Deck Four.

Ketha had been absolutely correct about her clothing lying in a heap. Clucking imprecations to the air, Moira sorted through the tangled mess, hunting for her panties. Her fit of pique had run aground, and worry eclipsed fear. She'd heard the conversation play out between Ketha and the sea Shifters. Their conclusions about the ley lines made perfect sense and sent ice chips skidding down her spine.

She finished dressing and left the cabin, intent on doing as Ketha had requested and getting a meal together. Her stomach knotted painfully. Food was the last thing she wanted, but everyone else was probably hungry, and a meal would do her good. She shouldered into the dining room and crossed to the galley door, entering the compact space with its gleaming stainless-steel surfaces and appliances.

Her vulture grumbled, squawking incoherently. Bad moods were its norm, and she didn't bother to question it. After a side trip into the pantry, she worked mostly on autopilot as she grabbed things for supper. Guilt burned. She'd known about the damaged ley lines, but had she bothered to check them?

Moira dumped dehydrated food into bowls, covering the desiccated bits with water to plump up. "None of us checked," she muttered, but spreading blame beyond herself didn't make her feel any better. After she poured far too much salt into one of her bowls, she dragged a stool close to the counter and sat.

She had to find a balance point, a place where her usual equanimity would return. What the hell was wrong with her? She'd survived a decade in Ushuaia by living in the moment, not getting too far ahead nor wallowing in what they should have done the moment the Cataclysm hit.

Turned out they would have been well served to locate transportation and drive north before the barrier became impenetrable, but they'd guessed wrong. Thrown the dice and lost. Not that sitting out the Cataclysm would have been any easier even if they'd managed to traverse South America to its northern coastline. She gripped the edges of the wooden seat beneath her, squeezing hard to force a different focal point.

Like many of the other female Shifters, science was her home base. A geological engineer, she'd spent years working hotspots around the globe where she predicted how earth materials would behave under stress. Her job had encompassed geology, mining, and civil engineering with its emphasis on building sound structures. Ones that wouldn't collapse the first time a stiff wind blew.

Lured by a generous offer from an international mining corporation, she'd ended up in Wyoming. Once there, she'd discovered the resident Shifter packs and extended her stay for a month because she enjoyed the other women so much. When they'd invited her along on a junket to harness the power of an eclipse in Ushuaia, she'd been delighted and informed the company waiting for her in northern Tibet she'd arrive a week later than expected.

They'd groused, but she had skills they needed, so they'd told her to come as soon as she could... Moira untangled her fingers from the stool and went back to her dinner preparations. She sampled the over-salted bowl and grimaced before tossing its contents in the garbage and starting over.

What would have happened if she'd been in Tibet when the Cataclysm hit? The whole country was plagued by deep, unstable fissures, some extending into magma bubbling beneath the Earth's crust. It was why she'd been hired. To come up with a fix before huge chunks of the landscape fell prey to quakes or slides, taking expensive infrastructure along with them.

Her trip backward in time settled her. She couldn't do much about Tibet. Who knew if it was anything beyond a pockmarked landscape rivaling the moon at this point. But she could do something about the ley lines, beginning with checking them a few times each day. Between her and the other women, they'd come up with a fix, a way to repair the damage to their primary source of magic.

Shifter power—her brand, not what the sea Shifters tapped into —was linked to the Earth. Ley lines fused with earth at every vertical juncture. While magic's precise mechanism defied efforts at quantification, she'd always assumed the lines extracted what they needed from the Earth. Precisely how that worked in the middle of the Pacific Ocean was murky, but the lines probably extended to the sea floor.

If they did, perhaps the sea Shifters did tap into their magic. She'd have to ask one of them about it.

A casserole and flatbread took shape as she tried out possible approaches to the ley line problem, recognizing they'd have to pick one and run with it. If they did anything as sophisticated as A-B split testing, they might run out of magic. And then they'd be screwed and at the mercy of whatever had them centered in its metaphorical crosshairs.

"Maybe not so metaphorical as all that," she mumbled and pushed pans into the waiting oven.

"Feeling better?" Ketha strode through the swinging galley door.

"Not really. I heard that part about the ley lines crumbling. Or their magic, anyway."

"It's kind of one and the same." Ketha narrowed her eyes. "When we limited ourselves to a single tarot run, it did yield information."

Moira's stomach lurched, and she turned to face Ketha. "Are you planning to tell me? Or did you make the trip down here to ensure I understood my negativity was what ruined the cards?"

A shocked look etched into Ketha's face. "I know I can be a bitch, but—"

Moira waved her to silence. "Don't mind me. We're all edgy. Hell, I had to throw away an entire batch of beef stroganoff. Enough to feed twelve. Because I stood over it pouring salt into the water while I stewed about the ley lines."

"Eh, it's okay. We have plenty of food after all the raiding we did in Invercargill."

"Not the point." Moira ground her teeth. "We can't make any mistakes. We have to get this right."

"Tell me something I don't know." Ketha sucked in a noisy breath, her nostrils flaring.

"The cards?" Moira crooked two fingers Ketha's way.

"Yeah. Them. Nothing unexpected. Not really. We head into great darkness, our future uncertain, yet there were a few rays of hope."

"Any clues on timing?"

"Soon."

Moira crossed her arms beneath her breasts and resisted an urge to tap her foot. "Soon as in?"

"Who knows?" Breath whistled from between Ketha's clenched teeth. "We need to get a handle on those ley lines. See if we can repair enough damage to ensure we don't run out of power mid-casting."

"It's what whoever is behind this wants. I figure they've been planning a strike for a long time. Maybe years."

"But how could they have even known we'd be slogging through the ocean?"

"Too literal, sweetie. Take a few steps back and look at the big picture. Unless we're dealing with a malevolent version of Merlin, with his soothsaying skills, all they did was lay the groundwork, figuring the Cataclysm would yield at some point. When that happened, they wanted to be ready. Didn't aim to deal with any further threats."

"So they hunted down every source of magic they could find and began whittling away its integrity?"

"Something like that."

"But what if the ley line problem is linked to wickedness loosed by the Cataclysm? It's kind of my working hypothesis."

Moira considered it as she trudged to the oven and opened the door. A quick peek told her dinner was done, and she transferred the pans to the counter and met the other Shifter's intense golden eyes.

"I was assuming there was a third entity in play, but I could be way off base. We've run into so many different types of evil since we left Ushuaia, and none of them were related to one another."

"Isn't that the truth? Vampires march to their own drummer. So did that dark mage who'd taken over King George Island."

"Don't forget the Sirens or the sea dragon or the Kelpies or Ceridwen." Moira tilted her head to one side.

Ketha rolled her eyes. "What are you? The scribe of doom?"

"I want to make damn good and sure we never forget any of what we've run up against." Moira closed her teeth over her lower lip. "Sooner or later, we'll find a pattern, and it will help us plan. So we'll be stronger and more effective when we get to Wrangel Island and the main event."

"Mmph. Hope you're right about that pattern. When I left the bridge, Leif was deep in conversation with the other sea Shifters and Viktor. He sent me down here to see if dinner was ready."

"Vik wants to pick through the possibilities and select our course over dinner, huh?"

Ketha twisted her hair behind her head, knotting it into a loose bun. "My guess too." She tilted her head sideways, and magic shimmered. Not much, though, and not for long.

Moira rolled her shoulders back. "You just told him to come on down, right? Using as little magic as possible."

"Hey. Maybe you could be our Merlin stand-in," Ketha joked and picked up one of the pans with a hot pad. "I'll help move our supper into the dining room."

Moira ferried food and silverware and plates, so everything would be ready. Her mind spun a million miles an hour. Viktor was their captain, but did it give him power to make decisions that extended beyond *Arkady* and their nautical route?

What if she didn't agree with the group consensus? Moira chewed her lip. This was why she'd preferred working alone in a consultant capacity. She drew her own conclusions, wrote up her reports, and let the chips fall where they would. By the time the government or corporation that had hired her chose a path, she was long gone, and she never heard how things had gone unless they went very well—or very badly.

She glanced around the empty dining room and skirted tables on her way to the door.

"Where are you going?" Ketha called.

"Bar," she replied over one shoulder. "Want anything?"

"An entire bottle of Scotch would be wonderful, but ill-advised. How about one of those nice red wines from Invercargill?"

"Sure thing." Moira pushed through the door and started up the stairs, expecting to be like a salmon swimming upstream, but no one blocked her way. They might have taken one of the ship's other stairwells, but the one she was on provided the most direct route to the dining room.

Taking a hard left once she reached Deck Four, she traversed the long corridor leading to the bar. A cozy space, it consisted of several table-and-chair combinations, all of which were bolted to the floor as a stopgap against rough seas.

Karin was already there, in search of her own bottle. Or more likely, one she could share with Daide, her fiancé. The other Shifter straightened, and Moira got a good look at her. The corners of her mouth twitched. "You should have shanghaied that faery. We could keep her in abeyance for kisses as a hedge against growing older."

Karin laughed. "I don't believe it works that way. Dryad kisses must be spontaneous and freely given or they won't erase the ravages of age."

Moira crossed the bar and gave Karin a quick hug. "You look amazing. I've never seen you with black hair, and your skin is perfect. Damn if it doesn't glow."

Karin rolled her copper eyes, about the only part of her that hadn't changed. "I cut Daide off when he waxes enthusiastic about my dip into the Fountain of Youth, and I'm cutting you off too. I feel exactly the same."

"Yes, but it's so rare when something good happens—"

"Stop." Karin's voice was stern. "Don't tempt fate by inviting it to make your observation a self-fulfilling prophecy."

Moira rooted in a crate and withdrew two bottles of ten-year-old Cabernet. "Do you actually believe that?" she asked after she'd straightened.

"Yes, I do. Otherwise, I wouldn't have wasted my breath."

Moira closed her teeth over her lower lip and took a chance. "How can you?" she demanded. "You're a doctor. Trained in scientific method just like me. Since when do idle words shape the future?"

Karin pursed her lips into a tight line. "Scientific method requires we leave no stone unturned."

Heat rose from the zippered neck of Moira's long underwear top. "Unless the words in question are part of a spell, I fail to see how—"

"Doesn't matter." Karin cut her off. "Let's join the others in the dining room. If the goddess grants us grace, choices we make this evening will keep us alive."

Moira watched the wolf Shifter stride out of the bar, moving quickly. Karin and the other female Shifters had all made Wyoming their home. Moira had been the only transient, and while the others had always been nothing but warm toward her, nonetheless she'd never truly felt like part of their tight clique.

Until that ten-year stint in Ushuaia where they'd formed an unbreakable alliance aimed at protecting humans and evading Vampires. Realizing she'd been rooted in place, she followed Karin's route out of the bar. The sound of voices reached her long before she dropped two decks to the dining room level. Ketha hovered just inside the door, and Moira handed her one of the bottles of wine.

"Thanks."

"You're welcome." Moira made her way to a table where Zoe and her husband, Recco, were already seated, digging into overflowing plates. Irish to the core, Zoe was a redheaded coyote Shifter with compassionate hazel eyes. Recco had been a Vampire in Ushuaia, but magical intervention turned him, Viktor, Juan, and Daide into Shifters. Recco's bondmate was a wolf, just like Karin's.

"Come sit." Zoe patted an empty place next to her.

"You just want my wine," Moira teased.

"Aye, that too."

"We'll guard it for you while you get yourself some dinner." Recco grinned. Darkly striking, he had black hair, liquid brown eyes, and a movie-star-handsome face marked by the high cheekbones and defined chin characteristic of Native tribes. He and Daide became friends in veterinary school and practiced together in Ushuaia for twenty years before the Cataclysm changed everything.

"Thanks. I'll do that." Moira plunked the wine on the table and went to fill her own plate. She still wasn't hungry, but food and rest were her best hedges against magical depletion. With whatever was chewing up the ley lines still loose, she needed all the help she could get.

She'd just sat down when Leif cruised past and asked, "Mind if I sit here?"

"Happy to have you," Recco said and waggled the wine bottle. "There's a glass left."

Leif shook his head. "I don't drink. None of my Shifters do."

"Why not?" Moira asked.

"Doesn't play well with our physiology," Leif replied. "Not much of a window between feeling good and getting sick."

"Would tend to put a damper on things," Zoe agreed in her soft brogue. "Sure and 'tis a good thing you don't hail from Ireland."

Leif settled into an empty seat and tucked into his meal. "I wasn't so far away as all that," he said after he'd swallowed a few mouthfuls.

"As in?" Zoe arched a reddish brow.

"I was raised in the hill country north of Carlisle. At the time, borders were fluid, and it was sometimes part of England and sometimes part of Scotland."

"I thought sea Shifters were born in the sea." Moira drained her glass and wished she'd brought an extra bottle down from the bar.

"That would be true in modern times, but I was born during an era when there was little difference between us and you."

Moira bit back the obvious question, which was how old he was. Such things weren't polite, and didn't matter since Shifters sometimes lived for a thousand years. She had a feeling the whales lasted longer than that.

"Here's to the British Isles." Zoe raised her wine glass, and Leif clinked it with his tumbler full of water.

Viktor strode to the front of the room and clapped his hands to get everyone's attention. "Humans are welcome to remain, but you might wish to take your meal and retire to the other dining room."

Boris stood. Tall and slender, he shook black hair out of his eyes. "What are you going to be doing?"

"We have a problem with the source of our magic," Viktor replied. "We'll be brainstorming solutions."

The zoologist from McMurdo stood too. Middle height and barrel-chested, he had dark, shaggy hair and brown eyes. "Aside from the fascination factor, I vote to remain. If your solution goes south on you, it's probably in your best interest for us at least to have a ballpark idea of what's going on." He sat back down.

"My thoughts too," Boris said as he sat. "We're all in this together, which means we don't split into human and magical camps."

Viktor's green-eyed gaze tracked around the room. Tawny hair fell below his shoulders, and he wore his usual black pants and black top, covered by a vest he hadn't bothered to zip. "Open discussion, people. Get your thoughts out there."

Leif set down his fork and turned his chair so he faced the front of the room. "I believe Amphitrite might be behind this."

Viktor spun his hand in a circle, encouraging Leif to continue.

"When Rowana first noticed the damaged ley lines, didn't she conclude someone had been tapping into them for a long time?"

"Something like that," Ketha spoke up.

"Places where the lines bisected held chewed aspects," Karin added. "Like a rodent had taken to them and selected a bit here and another there, but never too much in any one spot."

Leif nodded, a solemn expression on his face as he regarded the group through blue eyes. He'd braided his gray-green hair, and it trailed over his shoulders in many small sections.

Moira respected his knowledge and his standing as alpha in his Shifter pack, but she took a good look at him for the first time. He was a damned attractive man with his high, unlined forehead, square chin, and straight, white teeth. His body drew her too. Broad shoulders tapered to narrow hips and a rounded ass. When she started imagining what he'd look like once she'd divested him of the clothing hugging him like a second skin, she brought herself up short.

For one thing, if anyone was looking, they'd be able to read her thoughts. Her cheeks grew warm, and she wished again for more wine. She'd barely thought about sex during their time in Ushuaia, but with Ketha, Aura, Zoe, and Karin newly mated, the very air vibrated with pheromones, making it impossible not to be impacted by them.

"Why do you think it's Amphitrite and not Poseidon?" Viktor asked.

Moira glommed onto the question, hoping to mute her lust with an overlay of logic.

"Poseidon's not canny enough to pull off something like that," Lewis answered in his British accent. "Powerful sod, but anything subtle is beyond him."

"Same conclusion I drew," Leif agreed. "Regardless of who's behind raiding our power, though, I came up with a way to stop them. Or at least slow them down."

Settles one thing, Moira thought. *Their power springs from the ley lines too.* Intrigued, she leaned forward.

"Before you launch into solutions, does anyone have any more data to add to the mix?" Viktor asked.

"Nothing new," Ketha replied. "The lines are in worse shape than they were when we last looked about a month ago. We're not sure how much worse, but if the current trend continues—" She mimed slicing a finger across her throat.

Moira winced at the dramatic gesture and wished it weren't quite so true.

"Come on up here." Viktor motioned to Leif. "Let's hear what you have in mind—and how much it will cost us."

The corners of Leif's well-formed mouth twitched. "What makes you so sure it will cost anything?"

"Because even green as I am when it comes to Shifter magic, all power has a price. That was even true when I was a Vampire, but less so. Blood smoothed over a whole bunch of rough spots."

"Feel like going back?" Leif started for the spot Viktor stood.

"Bite your tongue."

Ketha punched the air in his direction. "Good thing you came up with the right answer. My wolf was ready to take on your raven in armed combat."

The humans sported a variety of alarmed looks, but Ketha made soothing motions with both hands. "A joke." She projected her voice. "It was a Shifter joke. The animals don't operate like that."

Moira turned her attention to her cooling food. If her mouth was full, it meant she couldn't talk, couldn't contradict Ketha. The animals most certainly did "operate like that," but the humans didn't need that tidbit of intel.

Leif reached Viktor and turned to face the room. "My idea is quite simple," he began.

3

MEET STEALTH WITH STEALTH

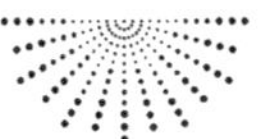

eif took a swallow of the water he'd brought with him to buy himself a moment to think. Talking openly about how magic worked in the presence of humans ran against the grain, but these were desperate times. The humans had thrown in their lot with *Arkady's* Shifters, knowing full well what they were. In truth, the five from Arctowski hadn't had much choice since a dark mage blew up their home and was running amok after his genetic atrocities were destroyed. The four from McMurdo were another situation entirely; they could have remained at McMurdo but had chosen to leave.

"If you're hunting for a more palatable explanation, don't bother," Juan said from a nearby seat. His blond hair was drawn into a queue, and his green eyes radiated shrewd intelligence. A mountain cat Shifter and Aura's husband, he and Viktor had operated a polar cruise service before the Cataclysm. *Arkady* was one of two ships they'd owned. The other, *Gavrill*, had pitched up on rocks off Argentina's southern coast at the Cataclysm's front end.

Leif smiled sheepishly. "Yeah, that's exactly what I was doing. All right. Here's my idea." He took a measured breath. "We pick two or three spots where the ley lines are quite weak and chop away more

25

of their infrastructure. Enough to alarm Amphitrite if she's the one behind this. While we're in destruction mode, we also plant magical markers."

"What will they do?" Viktor asked.

"Two things," Leif replied. "They'll act as a homing device, so we can hone in on the miscreant, but they'll also pack a nasty wallop. Rather akin to a powerful electrical shock. Because our sneak thief will be linked with the ley lines, however briefly, their distress will reach us, and we'll close in for the kill."

"I've always considered myself a pacifist," one of the women from McMurdo called out, "but I'm all for murdering whoever's behind this."

"Hear, hear," some of the other humans chimed in.

Their support warmed Leif, but also worried him. He hoped to hell they wouldn't do anything stupid. A rash move that would require a diversion of magic, which was spread thin already, to rescue them.

Karin frowned, stood, and moved toward the front of the room. "There's a downside. A big one."

Leif nodded. "Aye. The price Viktor alluded to. I know. We'll have to be damned careful. There's barely enough juice to power our spells as things stand. If we take too much, we won't have any magic left to deal with the bastard once we catch them."

Her frown deepened, and she drew her brows together. "How about a staged approach?"

"What do you mean?" Leif asked.

"We designate a B Team. They'll dive in and shore up the lines the minute we have the target in our gunsights."

"I like it," Leif said, trying not to sound too bloodthirsty. The humans in the room might have lived through the Cataclysm, but they didn't have animal forms where they killed and ate their prey. While they'd offered a staunch vote in support of violence, who knew where they'd actually stand when faced with the grisly reality.

And then he reminded himself most of them had stuck around

through the episode when he and the other Shifters killed the Kelpie. The Scottish water demon had transformed back into a horse in its death throes, and Kelpies held an unearthly beauty as horses. If the humans were going to revolt, that would have been the time for it to happen.

"If we did select a B Team," Viktor said breaking into Leif's thoughts, "they'd have to be some of the strongest of us."

"Agreed." Karin nodded once, sharply. "It will be a get in, do your stuff fast, and get out endeavor."

"May I ask a question?" Ted, Boris's partner, got heavily to his feet. As fair as Boris was dark, he was quietly competent and not much rattled him.

"I don't see why not." Leif crooked two fingers.

"The way I'm envisioning these ley lines, they traverse the globe, not just the area we're in right now. And they're kind of like longitude and latitude lines. Is that correct?"

"Close enough," Leif said.

"First off, just because the lines are damaged here, does it mean they're damaged in other spots?"

Karin exchanged a glance with Leif before she answered, "Probably. Since we unearthed fragmented lines in Antarctica and also here, it suggests the problem is widespread."

"Is it similar to a bushel of rotten fruit where once one piece rots, the ones next to it do, and so on?" Ted pressed, still working to flesh out his understanding.

"No," Leif replied. "The ley lines are self-repairing to a point. It's why none of us noticed the damage until Rowana looked." Ted wore a puzzled expression, so Leif went on. "It takes a lot for the lines to get to a tipping point where there's no going back. To the best of my knowledge, it's never happened. Something like that would have been noted in our Shifter histories."

"Exactly," Moira chimed in. "The lines can be reduced to a state where we can't tap into them anymore, but that doesn't mean they're on the edge of fading into nothingness."

"Only that we are," Karin muttered sourly.

"Yes, the lines would eventually cure themselves," Leif muttered. "With or without us. I'm not sure how amenable they'd be to providing a magical assist to the darker side of things, but it's at least theoretically possible."

"Are they sentient?" Ted asked.

"In a manner of speaking," Leif replied.

"What does that mean?" Ted persisted.

Leif blew out a breath. It was a reasonable question, but not one he had a ready answer for. "They hold magical energy," he began, "and it resonates at a frequency our personal magic recognizes. It's what allows us to tap into the lines' wavelengths."

"So anyone with magic could use them as long as they knew the proper frequency and wavelength? Sorry to beat a dead horse, but I like to understand. If it's tied to electrical theory, we could generate the frequencies artificially. Would the ley lines know the difference?"

Leif looked at Karin, who shrugged. "Not something that's ever come up before," she said.

"You asked for a reason," Leif said. "What was it?"

"If it's just a matter of a certain frequency, we can help. If those electrical pulses have to originate from a magical source, we won't be much use to you."

"We'll figure it out while we're cutting deeper into the lines," Leif said, followed by, "If that's what we end up doing."

"Discussion?" Viktor raised his voice to make certain everyone heard him.

Moira stood and walked to where a whiteboard hung on one wall. She snapped up a colored marker and began to draw a diagram, talking as she went. "Essentially, this is a two-stage process." She pointed at a set of intersecting lines she'd drawn with little lightning bolts around them.

Switching colors, she marked Xs at three junction points. "Some of us will hit these exposed spots and make them weaker, while laying traps in what's left of the junction points. Once it's done, we wait."

She drew another identical grid next to the first one, duplicating the Xs. When she was done, she went on. "The B Team will have to be ready to roll round the clock, which argues for at least four of us. We can take twelve-hour shifts. If the trap activates, whichever duo is awake will dash in and institute as much of a fix as we can."

"And the other part of Team B will show up as soon as we can roust them," Viktor said.

"Yeah. Four might not be enough. We're going to have to work damned fast with minimal magic to keep the lines usable," Leif said. "Plus, we'll have one pissed off thief on our hands."

"Once we identify him, I figured we'd drag him back here," one of the whales said. "We can ride herd on him—or her—better with more of us."

"What if there's more than one?" Juan asked.

"We'll figure it out then," Leif replied. "There are too many unknowns to plan for every contingency."

"All right, people." Viktor clapped his hands together twice. "Who's doing what?"

Moira erased what she'd drawn and made three columns on the whiteboard. She labeled them Destroyers, Team B-1, and Team B-2.

"Put me down as Destroyer and Team B-something," Karin said.

"Me too," Ketha cut in."

Leif thought about it. More than two as Destroyers made stealth much harder to maintain. "All right," he called. "Ketha and Karin can boobytrap the lines. I'll volunteer for one of the Team Bs. Three more will give us three on each leg of the B Team."

"Me," Moira said.

"And me," Viktor spoke up.

Ketha shook her head. "Nope. Not you. The ship needs you."

Viktor opened his mouth to argue, but Daide made his way to Karin's side. "I'll help."

"So will I," Zoe said, her usually thoughtful expression set in grim lines.

Moira shifted names around and ended up with Karin, Daide, and Ketha on B-1 and herself, Leif, and Zoe on B-2. "Nice work, folks." She tapped the board. "Here are the assignments."

"Thanks for your assistance," Viktor spoke formally.

Leif probed with magic, concerned Viktor was furious Moira had inserted herself into a role he considered his. Relief rattled through him when he found only gratitude. And worry. No wonder Ketha had fallen in love with him. He was wise and kind and smart about picking his battles.

Everyone went back to the remains of their dinner. Leif finished the cold scraps scattered on his plate and watched Moira surreptitiously. She ate quickly and methodically but with the easy grace that marked everything she did.

He waited until she was almost done before catching her eye. "You're quite skilled at that," he said.

She glanced up. A startled expression crossed her face. Dark brows winging upward like bird's wings suggested she'd been deep in thought. "At what?"

"Managing groups of people."

She shrugged self-consciously. "I did it for a long time. It's kind of second nature."

"What did you do where you managed people?"

She set down her fork. "I'm a geological engineer, but it was people who hired me, not rocks, so I needed group management skills."

"What do geological engineers do?"

A small, pleased smile formed, easing her worried look. "It's been a long time since anyone's asked me about myself. I managed chemicals and rocks and the Earth. Maybe managed is too strong a term. I explored their capacity to destroy things men wanted to maintain."

"And instituted preventive measures?" He lifted one brow.

"Something like that. How about you? I understand you've been in the sea for maybe the last couple centuries, but how about before then?"

The dining room was emptying out. Zoe sent a meaningful glance skittering his way and winked at Moira. "How about if the three of us meet in the bar in half an hour to plot our B-2 strategy?"

"Perfect," Leif said and sent a reassuring smile Zoe's way. She nodded pleasantly and walked out of the room, arm in arm with Recco.

Leif glanced away. He should take the time to craft strategy, but he wanted to get to know the woman sitting across the table from him better. Much better. Admitting it to himself was a surprise. Before the Cataclysm, he'd assumed he'd find a mate someday. Many possibilities had graced his life—and his bed—but none felt quite right, and he'd angered more than a few women. After a dolphin Shifter screamed she didn't give a crap that he was her alpha, he was still a self-centered, egotistical bastard, he'd kept to himself—until the disastrous bargain with the Witches.

After that, he'd wanted to hide in one of the wrecks littering the ocean floor and never resurface, but his duties as alpha meant he put his game face on and plowed forward. After the Cataclysm struck, survival was everything. Sometimes he rebuked himself for not encouraging his people to produce more young, but they'd have been the first to die in the face of a toxic ocean and scarce food.

"I'm not going to pry." Moira tilted her head to one side as she regarded him. "You don't have to tell me anything."

"It's not that. Your question got me thinking—about a lot of things. The world I was born into was far different than this one. Even pre-Cataclysm."

She offered an encouraging smile but didn't say anything. Perhaps she understood leaving things open ended would loosen his tongue, make it easier to share details about a life he'd almost forgotten.

"Shifters tended to live in our own settlements toward the front end of the sixteen-hundreds. A few of us put down roots in towns, but the Church was gaining power, and they hated us. Labeled us abominations and didn't miss a chance to fan the common folks' hatred and fear.

"I lived along the coast northwest of Carlisle on the shores of the Irish Sea in a group comprised of both land and sea Shifters." Sadness tugged at him as images from his youth marched across his mind.

Moira must have picked up on his mood because she said, "I'm sorry."

He shook his head. "Don't be. Those first two hundred fifty years were easy. Despite skirting churchmen and their irrational reaction to us, we were happy. It's always been easier for you land Shifters. You can hide in a forest, shift, and no one is the wiser."

"I see the problem," she murmured.

"Compounding it was we're prone to spontaneous shifts when we're young, making it almost impossible to conceal what we are when we're in the midst of a mad dash to the nearest water." He blew out a tight breath. "The world grew smaller—and faster—with the advent of more efficient means of transportation and communication. By the middle of the nineteenth century, it was clear we needed stronger magic—and a whole lot more time in the sea."

"Hence the deal with the Witches." Compassion rimmed her expressive eyes.

"Exactly." Leif was relieved he didn't have to describe that catastrophe. She already knew plenty about it.

"Apologies in advance if this is indelicate, but how did sea Shifters earn a living?" Without waiting for him to reply, she continued, "We've always worked at some type of trade, if our histories are to be believed."

A smile tugged at the corners of his mouth. "Remember the rings I gave Zoe and Aura for their weddings?" At her nod, he went on, "Men have gone to sea for hundreds of years, which means untold numbers of wrecks. The maps denoting them miss well over half."

Her eyes kindled with understanding. "You scavenged for coins and gemstones."

"We did. And sold them. Always more than enough to go around."

"Clever."

Her approval warmed him, but more talk would be pure indulgence. "We should probably head upstairs."

Moira's mouth thinned into a concerned expression. "This ley line thing will happen fast, huh?"

"Yes. It has to. If we wait, we won't have enough power left to pull it off." He stood and waited for her to get to her feet.

Latching a hand beneath his arm, she leaned close. "Thanks for trusting me."

"Thanks for caring enough to ask." He stacked their empty plates and silverware. She let go of him, picked up the glasses, and they walked everything to the kitchen, piling them in one of the sinks.

"We should wash them, but I don't want to take the time right now," she said.

"It's quite low on the priority scale," he agreed, not giving voice to his next thought, which was none of them might be left to worry about whether a few dishes remained unwashed.

He reached for her hand, and she laced her fingers with his. Touching her felt awkward, yet right in a way that baffled him. He didn't try to dissect his contradictory emotions as they walked out of the empty galley and across the equally empty dining room.

"We need to launch this tonight, don't we?" she asked, a catch in her voice betraying her anxiety.

"We do. As soon as we have a bombproof plan in place to insert those trackers into key ley line junctions."

"Ketha and Karin are resourceful. Bet they've already got it nailed down."

"Not without input from the rest of us." Dismay ratcheted

through him along with knowledge he shouldn't have spent the last quarter hour chatting with Moira. His first duty was to his pod. Nothing had changed about that.

He drew his hand out of hers.

"Did I say something wrong?" She trained confused dark eyes on him.

"Not at all. It's not you. It's me. For a minute, I forgot myself."

"I don't understand."

He took a deep breath, not wanting to slam the door on his developing feelings but also not seeing any alternative. Leif avoided touching her, Instead, he augured his gaze right into hers.

"My first duty is to what's left of the sea Shifters. I'm their alpha, but you know that. I truly enjoyed our conversation, but—"

"You can stop right there." She cut him off. "I get it. I'm not a sea Shifter." Without waiting for him to reply, she spun on her heel and raced up the stairs, leaving him staring after her with his mouth hanging open.

Desolation swept through him. Her rejection had the same sting as the female dolphin who'd catalogued his faults.

"Pull yourself together." His dolphin's voice thundered through his skull.

"I'm trying," he told it and trudged up the stairs. As he walked, he cleared his mind of everything but the plan he'd developed. This was his scheme, and a damned dangerous one at that. He had to do everything in his power to make it work. If they failed, they were all dead men.

4

TRAPS SNAPPING SHUT

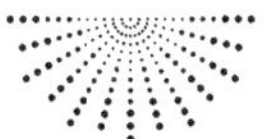

*M*oira castigated herself for being a fool. For about half a second, she'd let herself believe Leif was interested in her, but he was just lonely like all the rest of them. Except maybe more so in his case since he'd presided over the deaths of thousands of his kin—and nearly died himself.

She pulled the tattered edges of her hurt feelings together, determined to move beyond her disappointment. All he'd done was talk with her. He hadn't made promises and not delivered. Nor had he lured her to his bed, and then told her to get lost.

A major challenge stared them in the face. One that required her full and complete attention. Now wasn't the time to be a prima donna and indulge in anything other than her very best efforts as a Team B member. She winced. She'd placed herself and Leif on the same team on purpose. Maybe she could swap places with Daide or Karin—

She shook her head. No. She'd leave things as they were. Leif's distressed expression had been genuine when she'd told him to shut up. Moira winced again. His pod probably never offered him anything other than respect. She needed to adjust her attitude. Immediately.

She strode into the bar and crossed to a table where Zoe and Recco sat. "There you are." Recco smiled and stood. "I was just leaving." His smile faded. "Take good care of Zoe. Do not come back without her. Or better yet, include me on the team."

Moira exchanged a pointed look with Zoe, who nodded. "Since it's all right with your wife, I'm good with it," she told Recco.

He scooted back into his seat. "Thanks."

"Don't thank me. It's better this way. If we have problems, I won't be the one explaining what went wrong to you."

"That was blunt," Zoe muttered.

"This whole endeavor is blunt," Moira countered and slid into a chair next to Zoe. "I'd love more to drink, but it's not a good idea."

"Same conclusion we came to," Zoe said.

"Where's Leif?" Recco asked.

Moira scanned the doorway. "Right there." Despite her resolution to be strong, her heart fluttered oddly at the sight of the sea Shifter alpha. Maybe it wasn't anything beyond sexual heat, but whatever it was, she had it bad.

He nodded briskly and strode across the room to their table but didn't sit. "Have Karin and Ketha announced their approach?"

"Not yet," Zoe replied.

Moira scanned the bar, locating Karin, Daide, and Ketha on its far side. Viktor wasn't around, which meant he was probably on the bridge making certain *Arkady* didn't stumble as she sailed through the moon dark waters of the central Pacific.

"I'm going to check in with them, and then I'll be right back," Leif said.

Zoe waited until he left and then placed her mouth near Moira's ear. "He's very nice."

"Not going there." Moira shook her head.

"Why not?" Zoe persisted. "I saw the two of you talking. Looked mighty cozy to me."

"Don't mind my wife." Recco bent his dark head closer to theirs. "She's drowning in marital bliss and wants to share the joy."

Zoe snorted and muttered, "Spoken like a man with a perpetual hard-on," in Gaelic.

Moira chortled and tried not to wish for her own perpetually erect cock, standing by to service her.

"What'd you say?" Recco demanded.

"Women's secrets," Zoe replied.

"It was very complimentary to your prowess in bed," Moira said, hoping they could change the subject before Leif returned. The last thing she wanted to bat around with a man she was salivating over was sex talk.

As if he'd tuned in to her thoughts about him returning, Leif strode back across the bar. "I'm sending one of the whales with them," he said without preamble. "I was concerned about too many Shifters ruining the stealth factor, but they can work so much faster with three of them, it makes sense to do it that way."

"What will they be using for magical markers?" Recco asked, adding, "Sorry if it's a stupid question all of you know the answer to, but I like to understand how things work."

"He's coming with us," Zoe explained to Leif.

"All right. I'd assigned a dolphin to the first B team and another to this one as well. I'll tell him we have a fourth."

Moira read between the lines. "I'm guessing Ketha and Karin ran into some problems choreographing how they'd manage their role."

"Their timing was more of an issue than anything. With three, one can plant markers as soon as the other two have eroded the filaments a little more. To answer your question"—he directed his words Recco's way—"when the markers are disturbed, it will set up an oscillation through the ley lines. Since we'll be monitoring them, we'll know and snap up our thief red-handed."

"Wonder where that expression came from?" Recco mused.

"Och, sure and it came from old Scotland where the guilty party still had blood on his hands from murdering or poaching game." Zoe smiled brightly at her husband.

A blast of magic sparkled through the bar from the far side of the room. "They left already?" Moira had a tough time choking out the words.

"Yes." Leif's reply was terse. "Sooner the better. The first B Team is on duty until nine tomorrow morning. We need to get some rest between now and then."

"Where will we meet?" Zoe asked.

Leif scrunched his brow in thought. "Sorry to intrude on your newlywed bliss, but we should all bunk in the same spot. In case the first team is called to respond, and we're needed to back them up."

"Or to ride herd on whomever we catch," Moira muttered.

"By that token, all Shifters should remain close. Good thinking on your part." Leif offered an approving nod.

The flutter from before raced through Moira again. She put a lid on her longing before anyone picked up on it. He may have enjoyed talking with her, but he had no interest in anything further. He'd made that abundantly clear.

"Either this room or one of the dining rooms would do," Recco said.

"I vote for the bar," Zoe spoke up. "'Tis a wee bit more comfortable."

"I'll get us blankets and pillows," Recco said, "unless you need me." He quirked a brow at Leif.

"No. Go on. I'll let everyone know we're staying here." Leif walked to the front of the bar. "All Shifters will remain here until our mission is complete. Make yourselves comfortable but stand ready to react when called upon." He didn't raise his voice, but every head in the room swiveled to stare at him.

"Ted and I will remain here with you," Boris said.

"Us too," Sasha, another Arctowski refugee, spoke up. Bald and with a thick Russian accent, he'd been part of a Soviet scientific team stationed at the Polish research base.

Moira assumed the *us* referred to Diana and Nora, the women they'd rescued from Arctowski.

"If they're staying, so are we," the McMurdo zoologist said.

"Yeah, can't see hiding out in my cabin and missing all the action," one of the women from McMurdo chimed in.

Moira considered telling the humans this wasn't their war, that they'd only get in the way, but they wore such earnest expressions she didn't have the heart to dismiss them. Besides, Shifters had always held somewhat of a patronizing attitude toward humans, and she'd just experienced up close and personal what being dismissed felt like.

Yeah. Not very fucking good.

She turned back to Zoe. "Are you ready for this?"

The coyote Shifter shrugged. "Nay, but what choice do we have? If we do nothing, our power will gutter and die like a candle suffocated by its own fat."

"Not a very appetizing image." Moira unclenched her jaw. None of this was pleasant. "The worst part for me is even if we come out on top, the breaks between onslaughts are brief."

"Aye. True enough. 'Tis grateful I've been to Recco. He has a practical side, and it keeps me from drowning in a flood of doom-and-gloom scenarios."

Moira lowered her voice. "I have no idea what's wrong with me. I spent twenty years traveling from one nasty hellhole to another. And that was before I got stuck in Ushuaia. If not for the Vampires, my time there would have been almost enjoyable—in comparison with a lot of places I've worked."

Zoe patted her arm, her hazel eyes softening with compassion. "'Tis been a long haul. Sure and it never occurred to me I'd never see my home in Ireland again. Had I known afore I left, I may have turned down that visiting professorship in Wyoming."

"None of us knew." Moira drew her brows together, thinking. "Maybe that's the hardest part. The not knowing, and the living on the edge of a precipice." She took a breath. "No matter how hideous my jobsites were, I knew I'd leave and go home to lick my wounds before I volunteered for one more Third World assignment."

"Where was home?" Zoe asked. "Not sure I ever knew."

"You didn't," Moira replied. "Nor did anyone else. I didn't see any percentage in talking about the past after it became painfully clear we were trapped at the south end of Argentina. It's kind of like not thinking about food when you're starving."

"Aye, except you can't help it. Do you mean to tell me you never dreamed about potatoes swimming in butter or a nice, thick piece of meat when we were living on rats and kale in Ushuaia?"

"Of course, but I did my damnedest to redirect myself." Moira rolled her shoulders back, aware of tension sitting between them like an unwelcome block of granite. "You'd asked about home. I have a house east of Seattle, on the northern edge of Lake Washington. I was never there much, but it was a special place. Other Shifters lived nearby."

"Bet the humans didn't know." Zoe grinned.

"Nope. Why would they? We look just like them, and enough forest stretched on all sides, we could shift and remain hidden from prying eyes. If they saw me, they simply assumed I was one more vulture on the hunt for carrion."

"Where do you want us to be?" Recco was back, a duvet tucked beneath one arm along with two pillows.

Zoe's eyes lit with love as she glanced at him, and Moira battled jealousy. She wanted someone special in her life too. Never mind the feeling was small and petty and unreasonable. Never mind she'd spent her entire adult life alone. She gave herself a good, swift mental kick in the ass.

Zoe slid out of her seat and joined her husband. "We'll be over there." She pointed. "You should be near us."

"How near?" Moira couldn't help the resentment beneath her words.

"Close enough we can map out how we're going to put the ley lines back together in the quickest possible time without ending up fried to a cinder like poor Rowana."

"Got it. Be right there." Moira was grateful for the relative darkness in the bar and hoped no one would notice her face. Judging from how hot it felt, she must have turned bright red.

After a final, longing glance at the well-stocked bar—she could drink all she wanted later, assuming there was a later—she walked to Leif and told him where they'd be before joining Zoe and Recco.

"Good thing you mentioned Rowana," Moira said and settled on the floor next to Zoe "I hadn't exactly forgotten her dragging herself out of that magical pit by hanging onto the ley lines, but it wasn't in the forefront of my mind, either. How will we work with the lines if we can't touch them?"

"I've been thinking about that," Recco said. "And Zoe and I talked about it. Remember, I was in that pit along with Ro and the other three women."

"So was I." Moira spat out the words. She'd made a huge effort to block out the incident that had killed Rowana. The eagle Shifter saved them by sacrificing herself, and Moira still felt guilty and responsible she hadn't done more. Her eyes burned with unshed tears; she blinked them aside.

Leif strode to the corner they'd staked out and sank onto his haunches, keeping distance between himself and Moira. At least it's what she thought he was doing, but she could have misinterpreted how he'd positioned himself.

"Sorry to interrupt," he said, "but we need to cover something. The ley lines pack quite a wallop with their electrical load, so touching them directly won't work. Before they left, Karin and Ketha developed an oblique way to address the problem, and my whale Shifter added to their strategy with ideas of his own."

"We were just talking about that." Moira nodded tersely. "Recco and I were there when Rowana grabbed the lines to forge a way out of the dark mage's enchantment."

Sadness creased Leif's forehead, and he said something in the dolphin's tongue, a series of bleats that radiated sorrow before switching to English. "I am sorry I did not get to meet the eagle Shifter. She had courage, that one."

"Aye, that she did," Zoe agreed.

"I argued with her," Recco cut in. "Told her I should go first, but she said my magic wasn't strong enough, grabbed the lines, and shouted for us to follow her."

Leif extended a hand. Moira felt the zing of magic, and a blue-white nimbus formed around his spread fingers. "Tap into my power," he instructed. "Feel what I did, how I've protected my hand. This won't shield you forever, but it should be enough for us to weave the shredded filaments back together. We won't have to do all of them. Even a small percentage will encourage the lines to repair themselves."

Moira opened her magical reservoir and linked to Leif. A shock ran from the top of her head to her toes. By the goddess, his magic was strong. If this was what was left after he'd severed his ties with the Witches, what the hell had it been like before?

Setting her amazement aside, she delved into the underpinnings of what he'd done. The thought of her flesh smoking and burning from the inside out and sloughing off her bones like Rowana's had done scared the crap out of her. Rowana had known she was signing her own death warrant. Moira only hoped she'd be as brave as the eagle Shifter when mortality stared her in the face.

We will do what is required, her vulture spoke solemnly, and Moira silently thanked it for its steadfast presence. It was usually dour and critical, but maybe that went with the territory.

Magic shimmered around Leif's hand. "Did you all absorb this casting? I don't wish to squander power unnecessarily."

"Aye," Zoe said.

"Yeah. I'm good," Recco seconded.

"Me too," Moira murmured. She loved the feel of Leif's magic and didn't want to let go of her connection to him. It soothed her, reminded her of a time when the world wasn't teetering on the brink of annihilation.

The glowing halo snuffed out abruptly as Leif withdrew his

power. "All right. Now, we wait, but I have a feeling this will play out fast."

"Why?" Moira wanted to dig as deep into the dolphin shifter as she could, understand how his mind processed information.

Leif set his jaw in such a tight line a muscle danced beneath one eye. "If Amphitrite is behind this, she ran through a lot of magic during the Kelpie attack."

"But she did nothing," Zoe protested.

"How much power does it take for you to guard a secret?" Leif countered.

Understanding kindled in Zoe's gaze. "Aye, a lot if the person in question is in the midst of others with magic, but I wasn't paying any attention to her."

"Never occurred to me," Recco admitted. "But then why should it have? She's a goddess, and I'm still in awe such things are other than the purview of fairytale books."

"I did look closely," Leif said. "At both her and Poseidon. He knows there's no love lost between us, and that I don't trust him."

"What'd you find?" Moira asked, almost not wanting him to answer.

"Poseidon was the same way he always is. Tap the surface, and you find a pissed-off liege, who's annoyed as hell he has to do anything beyond snapping his fingers before the world falls at his feet fawning over him."

"How about her?" Moira urged.

"Aye, since she's the one you suspect," Zoe cut in.

Leif hesitated and looked away. It was dim in their corner of the bar, but Moira thought a flush spread over his well-formed cheekbones.

He tossed his head back, chin tilted at a defiant angle. "The queen of the sea made it clear long ago she'd welcome me to her bed. I recognized her invitation for the snake pit it was bound to turn into and declined her offer."

The white-hot dart of jealousy that had pricked Moira receded. She'd been ready to tear Amphitrite limb from limb but recognized she was being foolish, reactive rather than deliberate.

"Because of that," Leif went on, speaking stiffly, "I took care to be subtle about my incursion into her mind. Didn't want her to misread my presence as interest that had suddenly blossomed."

"And?" Recco crooked two fingers Leif's way.

Leif shrugged. "And, nothing. I didn't find a thing, but I also didn't dig very deep. The absence of even surface thoughts led me to believe she was shielding herself very carefully."

Magic flashed, hot and bright from across the room. Ketha, Karin, and the whale stepped through a portal that glowed with a purplish haze.

Leif sprang to his feet and hurried to where they stood. All three gasped like landed fishes, blowing hard.

Moira scrambled upright, as did Recco and Zoe. Everyone hastened toward the gateway. It winked out just as Moira reached it.

"We did it," Karin announced.

"And in the nick of time," the whale broke in. "If we'd been even half an hour later, we might have lacked sufficient power to pull this off."

"It was bad enough," Ketha added, "we shored up the ley lines in a few key spots. To ensure we'd be able to return to apprehend our thief."

Moira inhaled raggedly. Switching to her psychic view where she could see the ley lines, and traveling to the dimension where they lived, were two entirely different things. It was like a world within a world where Earth was wrapped in the lines that maintained its integrity. Humans felt the backlash when they did stupid things like set off atomic bombs that blew gaping holes in the ley lines' warp and weft, but they had no idea what they'd tampered with.

Daide hurried to Karin's side and wrapped a protective arm

around her shoulders. "Proud of you," he murmured close to her ear.

"Be proud later," she shot back. "Keep an eye on those fucking lines. You're the only one on our team who doesn't need breathing space."

"My coyote and I are on it," he reassured her.

Nervous energy nagged Moira, making it tough to stand still. Latching her hands behind her, she paced from one end of the bar to the other. The time for talking was past. Either their trap would work, or not. Even if it didn't, a group of them would still need to patch the lines. Unfortunately, they'd be providing a fresh source of magic for whoever they were trying to catch too.

Nothing to be done about any of it. She cast a sidelong glance around the bar, drawn to Leif's palpable energy.

"Karin! I think I felt something." Daide's words held excitement edged with trepidation.

Moira clamped her jaws tight. If he was right, this had played out far quicker than any of them assumed it would. She hurried to where Karin and Daide stood in the middle of a tight knot of Shifters.

"Yes," Karin said. "They fell for the bait."

"On my way," Leif yelled. "Who's with me?"

"But we had a plan," Karin protested.

"You're too depleted to return so soon," he told her.

She didn't contradict him, just rattled off a string of numbers. "These are the coordinates where we planted markers."

"I'll go." One of the whales stepped forward.

"And me." Moira stood tall. Maybe she was a fool, but her magic was as robust as any of the land Shifters, except maybe Karin or Aura. Ketha was strong, but in a different way that powered her seer magic. Besides, her power was as diminished as Karin's.

Shifter power was synergistic; Moira's would potentiate the sea Shifters' gifts.

"Are you certain?" Leif cast worried eyes her way.

"Yes. Let's go." Moira summoned magic to forestall further discussion. She and her vulture would make this happen.

Power boiled around her, and she sprang through a portal along with Leif and the whale.

5

UNFAMILIAR MAGIC

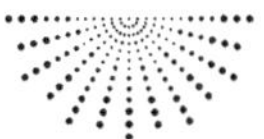

*L*eif would have preferred almost anyone but Moira. He was worried he'd chose protecting her over their duty, and it couldn't happen that way. The air thinned as it always did in the paths between worlds, and he reflexively slowed his breathing. It wasn't unlike what he did as a dolphin to make his air last for long periods underwater.

Lights flared around them. White. Green. Violet. He slitted his eyes against the glare. Who would they find at the end of this undulating funnel? More importantly, would they have enough magic to corral whoever was siphoning power and ravaging the lines?

He extended his arms. The whale grasped one hand, Moira the other. Her grip was warm and enticing, but he couldn't think about her now. Not in that way. Any diversion from absolute focus and none of them would make it back to the ship.

"Get ready." He ground out the words as he sensed the passageway thinning around them.

With a final gush of violet tinged with blue, the funnel he'd summoned opened into something out of a science fiction nightmare. An elongated cavern stretched as far as he could see. It

47

would have been pitch black if not for the glowing ley lines stretching before them, some parallel to the spongy dirt floor, others extending upward beyond the line of his vision.

A startled intake of breath from Moira suggested she'd never been here before, but he didn't waste breath asking.

The whale grunted. "Fucking place never changes. No matter where you enter it."

"I don't get it," Moira muttered. "I thought someone would be here. I checked Karin's coordinates, but—"

"Look with your third eye." Leif switched to his psychic view and scanned the cavern. Nothing jumped out, so he did it again, taking more time. A flicker of energy sparked but dimmed almost immediately.

"Focus about twenty feet down the third aisle over," he instructed, switching to telepathy. Someone had to be here, cloaking themselves. Maybe it meant they couldn't reach beyond their ward to listen to mind speech. He hoped so.

"Yes." Moira sounded jubilant and tugged on his arm. *"Let's go."*

"Safer from here," the whale said.

Leif agreed with him. He gathered power from Moira and the whale, pleased by how the slightly different version from Moira gave theirs a boost. Once he had enough, he powered a seeking spell and heaved it right at the suspicious spot.

A globe took shape, shattering with a high-pitched squeal that made his ears hurt. Amphitrite rose from a crouch and faced them squarely. She curled both hands around the ley line nearest her.

Leif would have fallen back a pace if he hadn't been firmly latched to Moira and the whale. Incandescence from the lines spread from the sea queen's hands up her torso and down her legs until her entire body pulsed and glowed.

"She's draining our power source," Moira shouted and jerked harder on his arm.

"At least the female among you has brains." Amphitrite drew her lips back from her teeth in a parody of a smile. She glowed brighter by the minute.

"Why aren't you burning to a cinder?" Moira shot back.

"I'm a goddess. I have power you can only begin to dream about."

"If you have so much power, why'd you switch sides?" Leif growled.

"Who says I did, dear boy?"

Tinkling laughter drove what felt like hot nails into his brain, and he gritted out, "It's obvious you plan to sabotage our efforts. Why else would you drain our magical source?"

Amphitrite squared her shoulders; sparks shot from her like miniature lightning bolts, zinging around her robed form. "You let all that alpha crap addle your mind. You're collateral damage. Nothing more. Nothing less. The only side I've ever been on is my own." She skinned her lips back from her teeth. "Best of luck getting out of here."

The light around her grew until Leif had to shut his eyes. Even that wasn't enough to block it out. Brilliance seared his corneas.

"She's leaving," Moira screamed. "We have to stop her."

"We can't. She's gone," the whale snarled as the light faded to a sickly glow from the depleted ley lines.

Leif opened eyes that felt gritty and tender. He disentangled his hands from Moira and the whale. About the only thing he'd been right about was the identity of the power thief. Beyond that, he'd miscalculated rather badly. Not only about the extent of the goddess's power, but about her motives. Apparently, he'd deluded himself when he figured she'd be so devastated about being caught, she wouldn't put up much of a fight.

He sucked in a tight breath. "I am most humbly sorry—" he began.

Moira made a chopping motion. "Don't waste words on apologies. We have to repair enough of the lines for us to get out of here. I didn't like her parting salvo. Nor do I like the looks of the lines. They're flickering as if they're ready to die altogether."

The whale bent and let a hand hover over the nearest line. It pulsed weakly, and he straightened, his rough features folding into a frown.

Leif wanted to check for himself, but any unnecessary expenditure of power was a very bad idea. "What'd you find?" he asked the whale.

"There wasn't much left when we got here," he grunted. "That sea bitch siphoned so much, I'm amazed she didn't explode."

Leif had known the whale for a long time. "You're walking around my question."

The whale nodded. "Because I'm working out what we have left to leverage, and my reasoning is running in circles."

Moira cleared her throat. "We shouldn't remain here. Not long, anyway. At least according to the lore, the borderworlds sap our ability to reason." She knelt and focused intently on a horizontal line. "Look."

Leif crouched next to her. "What am I looking at?"

"Follow this line as far as you can see. It's not evenly depleted. Some spots hold more power than others."

He narrowed his eyes and examined the line. It took two passes before he saw what she did. "You have sharp eyes. I'd never have noticed the differences."

"They are subtle," she agreed. "Credit my vulture. Raptors have very precise vision."

Hope flickered deep in his gut. They needed power to get back. They also needed power to repair the lines. In their current state, the ley lines didn't contain enough juice for the three of them to teleport back to *Arkady*. Draining their power repairing the lines would only exacerbate the problem.

Maybe there was another way.

They weren't starting from bedrock, not if they could control the better parts of the lines and urge them to partially heal the other sections. It was a sound idea—one that didn't require an output of magic from them—but could it happen fast enough?

"What are you thinking?" Moira asked.

"Two variables are in play," he responded. "One is how fast the lines will recover. The other is how quickly this place will sap us."

"So the lore books were correct?" Moira angled a brow into a question mark.

"Yes, but not in a straightforward manner," the whale replied. "There's an interplay between how strong we were to begin with—a highly individual measure—and the power inherent in each borderworld. We can survive on many of the borderworlds, but the longer we stay, the harder it is to find the will to leave…"

As the whale droned on, Leif tried out and discarded possible approaches to their dilemma. Moira had been correct about their stay on a borderworld being dangerous. By the time the lines had recovered enough to power a return trip, he, Moira, and the whale might be sunk into the lethargy created by too much time away from Earth. They'd lose their ability to reason, but it wouldn't matter since a corollary was they'd stop caring about anything beyond making a new life on the borderworld.

He'd been in a similar spot before and barely escaped.

The folks back on *Arkady* must be frantic, but none of them would have enough magic to launch a rescue effort.

"If we can encourage the heathier parts of the lines to work on the gutted ones—" Leif began.

"Exactly," Moira jumped in.

"But how can we do that without sucking ourselves dry?" the whale asked, apparently not the least bit annoyed at having been interrupted.

"I've been working on it." Leif inhaled deeply, all the way to the bottom of his lungs, blew it out, and did it again. They'd have one shot at this. *Ideas?* he asked his bondmate, but the dolphin didn't answer.

"Are you certain we don't have enough magic to teleport ourselves out of here?" the whale asked. "It's my assessment, but you sometimes view things from a less conservative perspective."

"Quite certain," Leif answered in almost the same breath as Moira.

She added, "Teleporting isn't as easy for me as it is for you. In fact, it's not easy at all. I burned through far too much magic getting here." She screwed her face into a determined expression. "Maybe you two could leave, though. I'd wait until the magic recovered somewhat, and—"

"Not going to happen," Leif growled.

"We are not leaving one of our own behind," the whale concurred.

Moira angled a pointed look at both of them. "This isn't exactly the time for chivalry. Do you suppose we could talk with the lines? Sorry, but I'm shooting in the dark. All I've ever done is view them, and from Earth, not from wherever we are now."

"Not talk in the manner you mean, but there may be a method to communicate with them," Leif said and settled on the packed earthen floor of the cavern. It felt warm beneath his haunches, and the warmth gave him hope the entire cavern was interconnected.

"What are you doing?" the whale asked.

"Sit next to me. Stretch out your legs so they connect with the cave floor. You too, Moira."

She sat, legs splayed in front of her. "Now what?"

"Quiet your mind. What do you feel where your body is in contact with the floor?"

"What am I supposed to feel?" the whale muttered.

Leif smothered annoyance. Whales were always literal to a fault. "I'm not sure," he replied, holding a neutral tone. "Maybe nothing, but we won't know until we try. I'm guessing this entire structure is intertwined, which might mean the ley lines and the floor and walls and ceiling—"

Next to him, Moira wriggled from side to side. When he looked, he saw her sliding her pants down her legs. She caught the angle of his gaze and shrugged. "Better contact with the ground." She toed her boots off and pushed them aside before removing her trousers the rest of the way.

Long legs, shapely with muscle, stretched before her, and Leif felt his groin tighten. Before his arousal developed a life of its own, he said brusquely, "Probably a good idea since I'm not feeling much of anything this way."

The whale muttered in their sea tongue and pushed his pants aside. He wasn't wearing footwear. None of the sea Shifters did. "Never saw much use for clothes in the first place," he added in English.

Not trusting his anatomy not to respond to Moira's nearness, Leif dragged hair over his shoulders to shroud himself. He'd considered cutting it now that he was spending so much time as a human, but maybe this was a good argument for keeping it knee length. To maximize what little power they had, he extended his hands and the others gripped them.

He shut his eyes and concentrated on the warm, uneven surface beneath his legs and buttocks. Minutes ticked past, and he was close to telling Moira and the whale they'd have to come up with something else when the slightest flutter tickled the back of one thigh.

It was so subtle, he might have imagined it, so he forced himself to remain completely still, his mind empty of expectation. Holding a quiet mind was growing easier, which unnerved him. It represented the beginnings of the borderworld sapping his will. He recalled the other time that had happened, and his blood chilled at the memory.

Stop. Do not go there.

Leif inhaled, picturing the ocean and his ability to remain submerged for long periods of time. He parceled air to his body slowly, much as he did when he was a dolphin. Somewhere between the second and third breaths, he felt the same flutter, this time against his other thigh.

Moira tightened her fingers around his hand. Did that mean she'd felt it too?

He waited, focusing the entirely of his attention on breathing. It was like the magic of this place was testing him, and he didn't want to spook it. If the cavern and ley lines were sentient, it must have infuriated them when Amphitrite showed up and helped herself to what didn't belong to her.

What had his bondmate said? *Magic belongs to everyone.*

Cautious, he let the phrase run through his mind. The response was instantaneous, and the flutter beneath him turned into a staccato tide. "Magic does belong to everyone," he said aloud.

"Was there ever any doubt about it?" Moira trained her intense, dark gaze on him.

"I feel movement beneath me," the whale said. "What should we do next?"

"Reassure it we mean it no harm," Leif replied.

"What is *it*?" the whale asked and shook his big, shaggy head. "I do better in the sea."

"You do fine here," Leif reassured him. "It's different from what we've grown used to is all. *It* has to be whatever powers at least this borderworld, maybe more of them as well." He tightened his grip on the whale's and Moira's hands. "Let me try something."

"Hurry," Moira urged. "I'm starting to like it here, which isn't good."

Leif gathered energy from the other two Shifters and collected his thoughts before speaking. The undulation beneath his legs hadn't lessened, and it gave him hope the force behind the ley lines might listen to him. The whole idea was so esoteric, he stumbled wrapping his mind around it. Because it was a losing battle, he stopped trying to force their current situation into any of his previously conceived ideas about how magic and the world worked.

"I apologize for Amphitrite," he said. "She may be a goddess, but it doesn't give her permission to steal from you."

Beneath him, the earth warmed still more, so he forged ahead. "We are very sorry for harm you've sustained." He paused, hunting for words. "Parts of you are stronger than others. Can you work with them to heal yourself?"

A booming, crashing noise rose around where they sat. Leif opened his eyes. If he'd just signed their death warrant, he'd face it squarely.

"Where?" Moira muttered. "It's asking where."

"How do you know that?" the whale asked.

"My vulture told me." She pushed to her feet and walked carefully between two sets of lines. "Here's a stronger place." She pointed. "Another sits over there."

One more boom was followed by several lesser rumbles. Moira kept going, index finger extended as she identified spots the ley lines weren't as badly damaged.

The whale leaned close. "Maybe this blending of abilities isn't such a bad idea after all."

Leif eyed him. "I had no clue what the entity sitting behind the lines wanted. Neither did you. If we'd had one of the wolf or coyote Shifters along, they may not have, either."

"The goddess takes care of her own."

"I'm assuming you're not referring to Amphitrite."

The whale made a disgusted, snorting noise. "If I ever lay eyes on her again, I'll—"

"She's immortal," Leif cut in. "Naught we can do but our damnedest to stay out of her way. Poseidon too. Although, I got the impression there's no love lost between them."

"Aye, she was quite clear about being on no one's side but her own." The whale nodded thoughtfully.

Leif scrambled to his feet, wanting to keep Moira in sight. The cavern's only light came from the ley lines, and they'd dimmed to perhaps half what they'd been when he arrived. Moira stepped over a line, ducking to avoid the one strung above it, and continued her mission. At least, she was walking back toward him.

The whale stood too and dragged his trousers up his legs. Leif did the same. The skin-to-earth contact had at least snagged the cavern's attention.

Moira strode to him and bent to retrieve her clothing. "Now we wait," she said as she dressed.

Leif stared at the lines, but they didn't appear any brighter. "Do you have any idea how long—?" he began.

She shook her head, cutting off his flow of words. "The others back on *Arkady* must be desperate. I'm certain they've tried to come after us by now and discovered they don't possess enough magic."

"The same thought occurred to me," Leif said.

"Nothing we can do about it," the whale cut in.

Moira knelt and slid one foot into a boot, which she then laced, following it with the other one. Remaining in a crouch, she shaded her eyes with a hand and focused intently on the lines nearest them. "I keep thinking I shouldn't hold my psychic view open since it utilizes magic, but I don't want to miss anything, either. Does that look brighter to you?" She angled her chin to the right.

Leif walked in the direction she'd indicated, close to the next horizontal line over. A pulse began at the far end of the line, slow and undulating like a sea snake emerging from hibernation. By the time it passed him, continuing where the line crossed through the cavern's wall, it was followed by another.

Faster this time.

After a few more pulses, the line brightened considerably.

"Does that mean we can leave?" Moira asked. Tension zinged through her words, betraying her nervousness.

"Not yet," Leif cautioned. "Look. More of the lines are joining suit."

A pattern lit as intersecting lines began to glow. It was beautiful and mesmerizing. Blues and greens and reds and violets blinked and flashed.

A heavy hand fell on his shoulder. The whale squeezed hard. "Better not to look," he rasped.

Leif tried to close his eyes, but he couldn't stand to shut out the glory unfolding before him. It sang to him, pulled him, made him long for a life he'd never have again. One where the sea hadn't been tainted by the Cataclysm, killing almost all the sea Shifters.

"Goddammit." The whale moved in front of him, grasped his other shoulder, and bodily turned him around.

"Thank you," Leif muttered.

"What just happened?" Moira sounded confused—and worried.

"It's how the borderworlds hang onto us," the whale said. "We invited the energy in when we were sitting in the dirt. Whatever the driving force behind all this is took it as our consent."

"For what?" Moira's words held a strangled edge.

"To remain forever," Leif answered. While he still could, he reached deep, assessing his magic. It was recovering along with the ley lines. Was there enough to power them out of there?

"If we don't go soon…" The whale left the rest of his thought unspoken.

Leif stood straighter. "Agreed. Our magic is recovering, but so is the mage or god or whoever maintains this place."

"Won't we piss it off if we leave?" Moira closed her teeth over her lower lip and moved closer to Leif and the whale.

"Probably, but the longer we remain, the more possessive it will become." Leif exchanged glances with the whale, who nodded once tersely.

"Get between us," Leif told Moira. "We'll include you in our casting."

He was grateful when she wrapped an arm around them both and didn't argue or insist she wanted to try this on her own. Their escape would be close, so close they might end up in the airless void between worlds.

"Are we all of one mind?" he asked.

"Is there any choice?" she mumbled.

"Yes," he told her. "If we remain here, we'll at least be alive. If we run out of magic between here and *Arkady*, we'll all die."

The arm she'd threaded through his hardened into an iron band. "We have to try."

"Yes," the whale agreed. "We do. Being alive on a borderworld is no life at all. We may as well be dead if we remain."

Leif didn't respond. If they lost the battle in Siberia, the survivors—if there were any—would probably end up on a borderworld. Nowhere else left to go.

"Open your magic to us," he told Moira. "We will draw from it, but do not deploy it yourself."

"I understand. Let's get on with extricating ourselves from this place."

Leif launched a channel that encompassed Moira and the whale and let magic boil through him. Once he thought he might have enough, he summoned a spell to teleport them back to the ship.

6

A WHOLE LOT OF UNKNOWNS

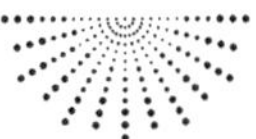

*M*oira unlocked the channel to her magic and abandoned control over what would happen next, which wasn't easy. She'd always been a major control freak. One of many reasons she'd chosen to work alone whenever she could. No one to argue with about how to do something, and if that something didn't work out, she didn't have to deal with recriminations as she introduced plan B.

"You're a master at turning your shortcomings into virtues." Her vulture smirked.

Despite the seriousness of their predicament, the corners of her mouth twitched. She didn't know whether to scold her bondmate or strangle it; the bird rarely missed an opportunity to dish out criticism. Magic surged around them, turning the air blue-white, the color of many of Leif's workings.

Electricity pricked at her skin, and the fine hairs along her arms rose. Usually, magic held soothing elements, but not this time. She wanted to help, but the only way to do that was by making sure she didn't engage in a kneejerk reaction and protect her magical center by tossing up wards.

The specter of dying in the void between worlds mocked her.

She was strong, knowledgeable. Leif had made a mistake not allowing her to control the feed of her power—

"None of that." The vulture was back.

Moira felt its peculiar brand of energy clamp around her, watchful and ready. Even if she lost it and panicked, her bondmate wouldn't allow her to do anything to interfere with Leif's spell.

It bubbled and boiled, thickening the air around the ley lines. The bizarre light show intensified. This time, captivating enough to draw her in. Since she held onto Leif and the whale, it seemed safe enough to look. Red diamonds merged into blue circles and thence into greenish diamond shapes.

Tension bled out of her. The kaleidoscopic effect was reassuring, soothing. What a silly goose she'd been to—"

A sharp blow centered on her midsection almost unbalanced her, and she started to pull away from the men.

"It wasn't them." The vulture enunciated each word as if it spoke to a child. *"Empty your mind. Don't watch. Don't think."*

Irritation surged, driving the dreamy trance state aside. *"You can't order me about."*

"I can, and I will if your misplaced attention threatens everyone's survival. Breathe deep. Pretty soon, there won't be any more air."

She knew better than to ask Leif or the whale anything. Lines of strain carved deeply into both their faces. Even with magic thick enough to touch, they remained in the cavern.

Why wasn't the spell working? Did they not have enough spirit to carry it off?

She was still employing her psychic view. She cut it off to funnel a little more energy to the men's efforts. Once she'd returned to her earth eyes, the macabre dance laid out before her vanished, the lines merely glowing ropes again. She inhaled raggedly and held it. She hadn't freed up much. Would it help?

Leif changed incantations to one she knew. Even though she wasn't imbuing her words with magic, she chanted along with him and the whale. Between one breath and the next, the cavern walls exploded, and they hung suspended in the same void she remembered from their trip there.

Leif and the whale continued to chant, so she did too. She wanted to ask her bondmate if this was a good sign or the beginning of what would be a short, downhill slide to death and oblivion, but she was afraid of its answer.

Instead, she said, *"Maybe you should leave while you can."*

"Too late for that."

"No, it's not," Moira urged. *"All the borderworlds are linked. You could return to the animals' world—"*

"Not going. It's a coward's path. Save your energy."

Her eyes prickled with unshed tears, and she wasn't the crying type. Her lungs were starting to burn, and she dragged her jacket over her nose, hoping to capture some trapped air molecules. She tightened her hold on Leif and the whale. *Come on,* she urged without words, trying to convey hope and belief through her touch.

Her magical reservoir, what there'd been left in it, was emptying fast. Not being able to breathe would only hasten the process. She tried to remember how long it had taken them to get to the borderworld when they left *Arkady*, but sentient thought was departing fast.

Deep in her mind, the vulture fluffed its feathers, standing at attention, beak opening and closing. The small clacks blatted through Moira's head, sounding like a small-caliber weapon. Nothing soft or fuzzy about her bondmate.

Leif and the whale struggled to breathe, their rasping pants growing louder by the second. Their methods for conserving oxygen were far superior to hers, but they were working much harder than she was. At least so far, she was dead weight. Along for the ride.

Moira gritted her teeth. Now wasn't the time for negativity. Or a place for her to decide she had to establish control over her power. A bitter laugh rattled out, sounding like not much more than dry grass rustling. No more power left to worry about.

Her head spun.

Would the dark, airless void win after all?

A slurping, sucking noise told her Leif had harvested the last of her magic. She wanted to tell him it was all right. That he'd tried his best, but she could barely form the thoughts, let alone the words.

Thunderous crashing shrouded her. Probably the beats of her dying heart, loud in her ears. Water closed over her head, cold and salty. She must be imagining it. No water in the space between worlds. Her lungs seized. She had to breathe. Air. Water. None of it mattered anymore.

Leif dragged his arm out of her grasp. So did the whale.

Shit! They were abandoning her.

No. They're dying too.

Before she could dissect any other aspects of the spectacle unfolding around her, an arm closed around her neck, pulling her upward. Leif. What the hell was he up to? She inhaled reflexively, choking on water rushing into her lungs.

"Do not breathe!" Leif's voice in her mind was stern.

But once she'd let go of her iron control over her body, it wanted to breathe. Had to. Even if it hastened her death.

He hauled her upward until her head broke into air. Blessed air. She choked and sputtered, coughing and spitting out salt water.

"Moira." He transferred his grip to beneath her arms, keeping her upright. "We made it."

She blinked stupidly. Daylight. A weak sun floated overhead. Another spasm of coughing racked her, and she started to shiver. Cold from the water soaked through her clothing, leaching all the warmth away.

"Boat?" she croaked. "Where?" More coughs as her lungs ejected water.

"Not far."

A flicker of motion caught her attention, and the whale swam closer. He'd had enough power to shift, and Moira was happy for him.

Shift. I can shift...

But then she remembered how depleted her magic was. Down to bedrock. Another spate of breathless coughing convinced her shifting was out of the question.

"I'm going to help you climb onto the whale," Leif said.

She eyed its broad back, assessing how on earth she'd manage to remain astride it. Nothing to hang onto. "Easier to catch a ride on you," she gasped out.

"I'm in the same boat you are. Not enough magic to shift, but I swim better than you, even in my human form."

Moira let Leif turn her until she faced the whale. He boosted her until she slithered on top. She tried to sit but lying down was more stable.

"She's there. Get moving," Leif said, presumably to the whale.

"Thank you for doing this," Moira said.

"Thank me once we're back," the whale replied.

Leif's form cut through the water next to them. Moira had questions. Lots of them. How had they escaped? She'd been certain they were goners. Leif had said the ship wasn't far, but what did that mean? When she scanned the horizon, all she saw was water. How did he know where the ship was if his magic was too depleted to shift?

She recognized self-defeating thoughts and yanked them out by their roots. This wasn't a time to get too far ahead of herself. It was one of those occasions where she had to become firmly entrenched in the moment. She'd been in dicey situations before, but never without her magic.

Waves washed over the whale, each one seemingly colder than the last, even though she realized it was impossible. The whale's hide was thick and slimy. The thick layer of blubber beneath guaranteed not a sliver of heat made it through to warm her.

Shivers racked her, making it hard not to slip into the sea. Her teeth chattered. If she could move around, she might warm up, but it wasn't possible. Spray from the whale's blowhole joined the other water, but at least this latest infusion was warm. She edged closer to the hole, hoping for more of anything warm.

"How are you doing?" Leif asked.

"Okay," she replied not liking her role as weak link in the chain. "Um, how far away is *Arkady*? You'd said close, but..." The distant roar of a motor reached her.

A Zodiac.

It had to be. Nothing else out here. She edged across the whale to see Leif grinning up at her. "You heard it, right?" he asked, his grin widening. "Telepathy requires almost zero magic. I employed it to ask for help."

She smiled back. "Yes, I heard it. Most welcome sound ever."

"I'm hurt," the whale sputtered. *"I've been ever so careful to swim straight and level."*

"You've been amazing," Leif praised the whale. "But having anyone on our backs is unnatural. It can't be comfortable for you."

"Pfft. Barely noticed her." The whale still sounded out of sorts.

"I'll talk with the whale." Moira's vulture cawed.

"Thank you. Try to be nice, please."

"I'll choose how I am," the bird retorted, and then added, *"Another half hour or so, and we'll have enough magic to shift."*

By then, Moira heartily hoped they'd be back on the ship and she'd be standing under a shower set to scalding. Her bondmate could fly all she wanted to after Moira had warmed up.

The thrum of the motor grew louder. When she risked lifting her chest off the whale's back, she saw the Zodiac closing fast with Juan standing at the helm. No one else was with him. At first, she wondered why, but her still-not-firing-on-all-cylinders brain pieced things together. The raft must travel fastest with a lighter load.

"Thank you for your magic." Leif angled his head her way. "We couldn't have escaped without it."

Moira made a dismissive gesture and nearly slid off the whale.

"Hell, we almost didn't make it with my magic. I felt when you drained the last of my power."

"I joined it with the last of mine," Leif said. "I kept what the whale had left in abeyance. Good thing."

She tried to keep her teeth from chattering. "It was close."

Leif nodded, a solemn expression on his face. "So close I didn't think we'd survive."

Her ability to evaluate events and come up with conclusions was returning. "We did…all that…for nothing."

"Not for nothing. Amphitrite knows we're onto her. It will either make her more cautious, or much bolder." Before Moira could reply, he went on, "We know more than we ever have about the energy behind the ley lines."

Air swooshed from between her chattering teeth. "Like it's out to get us?"

"No. It has an affinity for our energy. It's why we can tap into the lines for our magic. The lines care about us. They're drawn to us. It was why they didn't want to let us go." He flipped onto one side and continued to talk. "Before this, I assumed the ley lines were part of the making of the world."

She searched for a logical extension to his reasoning but couldn't find one. "And now?"

He drew his brows together into a thoughtful expression as he continued to swim without apparent effort. "Someone very ancient, maybe the first one to wield magic, created them. Obviously, I have no way to be certain about this, but if I'm correct, we just met evil's opposing force."

Understanding spilled through her. "Like Vampires hold darkness in opposition to Shifters' light." At his approving nod, she went on. "Everything requires an opposite or it will cease to exist. It's what they taught me in magic school."

"It's true, but don't you see?" Wonder and hope illuminated his handsome face, turning it into a thing of beauty. "We forged the beginnings of an alliance with someone—or something—that can help us close the fissure in Siberia."

Moira wanted to believe him. If he was right, it would add to her peace of mind, but he'd made several assumptions that didn't quite jell. "We must have pissed the thing off when we left. Beyond that, if it's so powerful, why doesn't it march up north and deal with the fissure on its own?"

"You're envisioning it with a body. What if it's spirit?"

The question caught her off guard. "There's a whole lot we don't know."

"Indeed." He smiled crookedly. "The beginnings of wisdom are recognizing your limitations."

Her vulture cawed and hooted. Moira wanted to tell it to shut up, but it had her dead to rights. She'd never been one to accept anything that stank of boundaries. Neither had the bird; it was where she'd learned that strategy.

The Zodiac chugged close, and Juan cut the engine. "Jesus, but I'm glad to see the three of you," he called across the few feet of surf between them.

"Thank you again," Moira told the whale as she slithered off its back and swam to the Zodiac. Juan angled his body across a pontoon and gripped her arms, dragging her into the raft.

"How about you?" he asked Leif.

"I could swim alongside, but I'd appreciate a ride." Without waiting for Juan to help him, he pulled himself up a rope hanging over the side and scrambled into the raft.

The whale swam ahead, exhaling briskly through his blowhole.

Juan engaged the engine. "There are clothes in that drybag." He pointed.

Moira made a dive for it, but then stopped to craft a plan of attack. She was wet to her skin, which meant it would make sense to dry off before putting on fresh clothes, but she didn't want to strip in front of the two men. The Zodiac picked up speed, and she hunkered in the bottom to avoid as much of the windchill as possible.

Leif joined her, digging through the bag and extracting a pair of thick pants and a zip-up jacket with a hood. "What? No towels?" he joked with Juan.

"Hell, you're lucky you got that much. You wouldn't have if it weren't already in this raft. As soon as Ketha and Karin picked up your message and sounded the alarm, I was gone. Not that I'm being critical, but how the hell did you end up so far from *Arkady?*"

Leif turned away, offering her privacy to change. It solved her false modesty problem, and she started with her sodden boots, pouring water out of them once she got them off.

"We were lucky to escape at all," Leif said, his tone mild. "I'm amazed we even hit the right ocean."

Moira had divested herself of her wet pants and underwear and was partway through working a pair of blessedly dry insulated pants with a warm, fuzzy lining up her legs. "How far away is the ship?"

"Five miles. Aura wanted to come. So did Ketha and Karin and Zoe, but I told them I might not have enough fuel to ferry a loaded raft that far—and back again." He stopped to take a breath. "Once you'd been gone nearly an hour, we grew concerned. The women tried to launch a rescue mission—"

"But discovered they didn't have enough magic to carry it off." Leif finished Juan's sentence.

"Exactly. And then all of us were a whole lot more than worried. We were afraid we'd never see any of you again. The sea Shifters were crying—the women, anyway."

Moira settled into a warm jacket and zipped it to her chin after snugging the hood into place. She'd wrung what water she could out of her hair and piled it atop her head. One item missing from the drybag was socks. She hefted one Arctic Pac boot, considering whether to put it back on, and decided she'd wait until they were closer to *Arkady*. The boots were heavy and wet and clammy.

Leif was just now changing. She tried not to look, but it was a losing battle. Not that she hadn't seen him naked whenever he emerged from the sea, but this was different. Maybe because this wasn't a transition from dolphin to man, but a man removing his clothing.

She gave herself a good, mental shake. What kind of sex-deprived slut was she? Just because she hadn't been laid in a decade was no reason for her breath to hitch and her throat to grow dry at the sight of his muscled legs and broad, shapely shoulders.

"Well?" Juan's question broke into the lust-riddled swamp her mind had turned into. "What the hell happened? More specifically, why'd our plan turn to shit?"

Leif zipped his trousers and shrugged into a jacket, letting his long, curly hair trail down his shoulders. What she wouldn't give to bury her fingers in his glorious mane and slash her mouth across his well-formed lips. Her nipples pinched into buds that had nothing to do with being cold. Heat slicked her nether regions. Moira wrenched her gaze out to sea, hoping no one would look at her too closely. *Arkady's* bulk was just coming into view on the horizon.

Home. They were almost home, or what passed for it these days. Gratitude welled, displacing the sexual heat.

"Are either of you going to answer me?" Juan looked from one to the other of them.

"The short version," Leif began, "is Amphitrite was the power thief, but she's stronger than I ever imagined."

"No shit," Moira cut in. "She grabbed hold of the same lines that killed poor Rowana and soaked in juice like it was mother's milk."

"Once she'd drained enough of the ley lines' magic to trap us"—Leif picked up the tale—"she left. Her parting shot was something like, good luck getting out of here."

"So what then? You waited for the lines to recover?" Juan spun one hand in a circle.

"No. We found a way to communicate with whoever controls them," Leif said, followed by, "I understand you're curious, and I fully get how worried everyone must have been, but this discussion needs all of us."

Juan's nostrils flared. "You're right, of course."

"Not sure about the *right* part," Leif replied. "This mission added to our collection of unknowns, but we learned things too."

Moira blew out a weary breath. Now that she wasn't shivering anymore, she understood how wiped out she was. A "collection of unknowns" was quite the understatement. "At least the ley lines should recover enough to power our magic," she muttered.

"Another plus," Leif agreed. "And all because your vulture figured out how to communicate with whatever drives them."

A triumphant cawing rose in her chest. She opened her mouth and let it roll out. Both men started to laugh.

"Guess your bondmate liked the compliment," Juan said once he'd stopped laughing.

"It adores shit like that." Moira grinned. A glance told her they'd reach *Arkady* soon.

"It deserves accolades," Leif said solemnly. "Without its help, we'd probably still be there."

He didn't have to add forever to his statement. She understood. "My bondmate is brave," she said. "I told it to leave when it was looking like we were going to die in the place between worlds, but it refused to go."

"And see? I was right. I knew we'd make it back, and my assessments are always correct."

Moira ground her teeth. The vulture's way of bludgeoning her with its competence had grown old over the years. Still, it had been a hero today, so she muttered, *"Thank you,"* in hopes it would mollify the bird, and it would stop singing its own praises.

"Clearly, you've left more than a few things out"—Juan's tone was pointed— "but I can wait." He guided the raft to the bottom of the gangway.

Karin and Ketha hovered on the small platform with Karin's black medical bag between them. Ketha grabbed the ropes and tied the raft off to cleats. Moira felt the heat of Karin's gaze as the doctor scanned her from head to toe with magic.

"I'm fine. Or I will be once my magic recovers," she said brusquely to cover her wellspring of emotion at being cared about.

"I'll follow you to your cabin and just have a look-see for myself before I pop you in a hot shower," Karin said.

"How come you're not worried about him?" Moira jerked her chin in Leif's direction.

Karin chuckled. "He's a sea Shifter, or did you forget that little fact? The ocean is his native environment, but it's not yours. Now, get moving before you fall on your face."

"The whale returned a little bit ago. I'm so glad you're all right." Ketha smiled warmly. "I'll see you once you've had some food and rest."

"Shoo. Get moving so I can put the raft away," Juan said, followed by, "I'll bring all the wet clothes inside with me."

"Is my pod inside?" Leif asked Ketha and Karin.

Ketha shook her head. "No. They retreated to the sea once they got worried about you. The whale never did come aboard. He's in the sea with his kinfolk."

"I'll join them there," Leif said. "My magic has recovered enough for me to shift. See all of you inside around dinnertime."

"I'll let Vik know," Juan said.

A perverse part of Moira wanted to hang around and watch Leif strip out of his borrowed clothes, but a wiser part powered her out of the raft and up the gangway with Karin clucking behind her.

A flash of magic carrying Leif's signature told her he was back in the sea.

They crested the gangway, and Karin trotted after her across the deck and through a door. "What happened on the borderworld?"

Moira stopped and turned to face the wolf Shifter. "I thought you wanted to assess me for injuries. If your ulterior motive is to pick my brain—"

"Get moving. I'll find out soon enough."

Moira plodded forward, grateful no stairs stood between her and her cabin. "Juan mined for details too," she said. "Better to tell it once to everyone and be done with things."

To her credit, Karin retreated to doctor mode, only leaving Moira once she'd assured herself nothing beyond time and rest were required to set things right.

"Thanks for the house call," Moira called after her, but the door swung shut on her words. Smiling to herself, she dropped her clothing in untidy piles on her way to the shower.

7

HATCHING PLANS

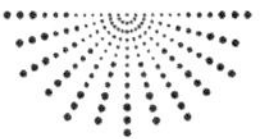

Leif sat in a quiet corner of a vacant cabin on Deck Two. Soon, he'd have to join the others for dinner. His pod had cooed and fussed over him until he'd ordered them to stop. One thing his absence had accomplished was establishment of a line of succession. Lewis would take over as alpha if something happened to him. Everyone had agreed on the plan, which was a great relief.

Back before they'd joined with *Arkady's* Shifters, he'd been certain all of them would be dead within the next month or two. It made no sense to plan for who'd take over if none of them were left. At least he finally understood, in an uncomfortably up-close-and-personal way, why the king and queen of the sea had abandoned them. The partnership had been one sided and existed only in his mind, not theirs.

Amphitrite had her own agenda, one she probably hadn't bothered to share with her consort. Leif dragged the heels of his hands down his face as he worked to force a logical pattern out of everyone's subterranean motives. It didn't help that Moira kept popping into his mind with her wild black hair and keen dark eyes.

Even so little as allowing his attention to drift her way set his

73

blood alight with need. He wanted her, but it ran far deeper than the erection pressing into his belly. Something about her independence and incisive mind made him want to be more than just her lover.

Far more.

If he could move past his ambivalence about being attracted to a woman who wasn't a sea Shifter—a huge *if*—he wanted her as his mate. Giving up on sorting through Amphitrite, Poseidon, and the ley lines' guardian, he considered how such a pairing could possibly work. Sea Shifters may have mated with their land kin centuries ago, but such marriages had ceased when his kind took to the sea for longer and longer periods.

He rolled out of his hunched position in a corner of the bunk he'd perched on. Thinking about Moira was a waste of time. Precious time when he had to hone his focus on survival. Besides, the vulture Shifter probably wouldn't be interested in joining her life with someone who loved the sea. It was far from her preferred element. That had been obvious when they'd ended up stranded a long way from the ship.

She'd been a decent sport, but she'd been cold, and he'd recognized her attempts to tamp down panic as water soaked her clothing, dragging her down. He'd done his damnedest to instill confidence, and he'd told her not to breathe. Maybe he hadn't said it soon enough, because she'd sucked water into her body anyway, flooding lungs that weren't designed to process anything except air.

He'd been relieved beyond words when he got her head above the surface and she'd choked and wheezed. If she'd been unconscious, he'd have had no good way to clear the water from her lungs since his magical center was sucking fumes. His fallback position was the whale, who still retained some of his power, but it hadn't been necessary.

He stretched his hands in front of him, flexing his fingers as he forced his mind back to how they could take advantage of what they'd discovered on the borderworld. He'd carved out this little island of solitude to make sense of everything, and he hadn't made much progress.

Where had the ley lines come from? What was the original purpose to stringing them around Earth? What manner of being was the guardian? Would that entity help them defeat evil? The malevolence he'd seen blazing in Amphitrite's silver eyes left no doubt the ley lines would be one of the first casualties of war. Given that, an alliance with the guardian made sense, but how could they raise it to engage in dialogue?

"Yeah," he muttered in the clacks and bleats of his dolphin tongue. "Lots of questions, but no answers."

He wasn't under any illusions the land Shifters would know any more than he did. Their magic was weaker.

"You make assumptions without facts to back them," his dolphin spoke up, startling him. Leif waited, but his bondmate didn't add to his statement.

He screwed his face into a frown. The dolphin rarely said anything, which had to mean Leif's assessment of the other Shifters was incorrect. He thought about what he knew from his limited time on the ship. The land Shifters' magic seemed to be evenly split between Shifter and bondmate, and the animal bondmates acted independently, even when the pair was in human form. Moira's vulture jumping in and saving the day by communicating with the guardian was one example, but he'd seen others.

"Thanks." He directed the word inward.

"Our magic is complementary," the dolphin reminded him.

"And different doesn't mean weaker. Do you know how the ley lines came to be?"

"No. They've always existed."

"I think not," Leif countered. *"I'd always assumed they were part of the warp and weft of the world's makings, but after today, I'm not so certain."*

"Some of the land Shifters' bondmates are very, very old. Ask them."

It was a good idea. And if that didn't work, maybe one of the animals could retreat to their borderworld and scare up someone who had answers. He switched to his psychic view, gratified when ley lines formed immediately, lines that appeared far healthier than they'd been prior to their mission to trap the power thief.

"There you are." Viktor stood in the doorway of the cabin where Leif had sequestered himself.

"Here I am," Leif agreed, engaging his earth eyes as he met Viktor's direct gaze.

Viktor narrowed his green eyes and stepped inside the cabin, pulling the door shut behind him. Tawny hair spilled down his shoulders, and he wore his usual black pants, black stretchy shirt, and black vest. "Anything you'd like to talk about, mate? Before we're all together, that is?"

Leif nodded, straightening from his crumpled position on the narrow bunk. He understood. Viktor was requesting an alpha-to-alpha conversation. Despite the land Shifters not designating alphas, Viktor was the *de facto* captain of this ship. It was a whole lot like being an alpha because he was responsible for the wellbeing of everyone aboard.

"Go ahead. Sit." Leif glanced at the room's only chair.

Viktor settled into it, not saying anything.

"Mostly, I have a lot of questions," Leif said.

"About?" Viktor angled a speculative look his way.

"The ley lines. I'm starting to think they were an afterthought, rather than part of the planet's underpinnings."

"What difference would it make?"

"A lot. Clearly, someone—in this case Amphitrite—isn't concerned about Earth failing if she bleeds the ley lines down to nothing."

"Say more."

Leif marshaled his thoughts, not an easy task since they pinwheeled around his head in crazy circles. "It's like a building where you assumed something was part of its foundation, but it may not be after all."

"Got it. If the ley lines aren't critical—for anything beyond fueling magic wielders—short-circuiting them long enough to fuck with us might be in the other side's best interest."

"Something like that, although this is all esoteric since I have no idea if I'm right or not. I've always believed Earth is sentient and the ley lines a part of its intelligence."

Viktor frowned. "Maybe both are right. Earth can keep chugging along without the ley lines, but it won't like it."

Leif raked his hands through his hair shoving it over his shoulders. "We should head for the dining room before we fall off the end of the Earth into chaos theory."

"Chaos theory, huh? That's obscure as hell."

Leif shrugged and got to his feet. "It's not new. It dates to Poincaré's work in the 1880s. I exited the ocean from time to time before the Cataclysm hit, and I've always been drawn to unusual ideas."

"Thinking outside the box makes you a good leader."

Leif shook his head, his mood growing somber. "You're offering me way too much credit. Not reacting fast enough almost killed all my people. If it weren't for you…"

Viktor clapped him across the shoulders. "No going back, mate. Come on. Bet by the time we're done eating, we'll have a bunch of directions to choose from."

Leif hoped so. His plan to come up with a few fertile guidelines hadn't borne fruit. "Thanks for coming to check on me."

Viktor pulled the door open and motioned Leif through ahead of him. "I do the same thing when I'm sorting through something."

"Hide out?"

"Something like that."

The welcome smells of cooked food met him as soon as they exited the cabin, and he smothered a grin. He'd adapted to a human diet far quicker than he'd anticipated. At first, he'd choked down prepared food, but that phase hadn't lasted long.

He ducked through the dining room door with Viktor right

behind him. The raven Shifter moved around him, heading for where Ketha sat near the front of the room. A spate of bleats and clacks welcomed him, and he nodded at his pod where they'd gathered off to the right, taking up three tables. Food sat on platters and in bowls on the tables, so no need to make a trip through the galley.

Leif scanned small groups scattered through a dining room that could hold triple their number, hunting for Moira's dark head. He chided himself. What he needed to do was join the other sea Shifters and do a better job corralling his disorganized thoughts.

Easier said than done. Where was she? Had the seawater she'd inhaled created damage he hadn't suspected? Worse, had illness dug its claws into her from her stint in the water? He balled his hands into fists, pressing his nails into his palms to get hold of himself. Shifters never fell ill. He was being stupid. And he needed to move beyond his attraction for the vulture shifter fast.

He might miss something critical while part of his mind was occupied yearning for the impossible.

Lewis had left his seat and strode toward him. "Is everything all right?" he asked in their sea tongue. Straw-colored hair stuck out at crazy angles, and his gray eyes radiated concern. None of them were spiffy dressers. Lewis had mixed green pants with a shirt in clashing notes of green and red.

Leif nodded and followed the other sea Shifter back to their table. Someone had poured him a mug of hot, bitter black tea and he took a sip, grateful for the immediate lift it provided. He accepted dishes as they were passed his way, taking a little of this and a bit of that, not hungry but recognizing the need to fully replenish his magic.

"You're not acting like someone who just spit in Death's face," a whale observed. Like all the whales, he looked like a stuffed sausage, body spilling around clothing much too small for his Neanderthal build. Fair hair cascaded down his barrel chest in corkscrew curls, and his blue eyes held keen intelligence.

"Leave him be." The whale who'd come with him to the borderworld made a chopping motion. His shirt was open, revealing a thickly haired chest.

"If I'm quiet, it's because I'm considering how best to proceed." Leif kept his voice low. "Sometimes one avenue rises above all others, but this time I'm having trouble finding any path at all."

"We trust you'll do what's best." Lynda smiled encouragingly. Her black hair had been braided, and her violet eyes shone with compassion. She must have borrowed clothing from the land Shifters because a lovely, embroidered teal tunic swathed her upper body.

"I appreciate the vote of confidence, but—"

She shook her head, cutting him off. "None of that. We move forward. Poseidon's balls, Leif. All of us were so ill, it's a miracle we can think at all."

"Thanks, cousin."

Lynda made a face. "Our kinship is one of our many problems. Those of us who are left are too closely related to mate."

"Let's see if any of us are even alive after Siberia," the whale who'd come to the borderworld spoke up.

"Priorities?" Lynda quirked a dark brow.

The whale nodded.

Maybe because he hadn't done as good a job as he'd thought banishing Moira from his consciousness, Leif felt her distinctive energy enter the room. He couldn't help gazing at her as she stood framed in the doorway. Her face was blotchy from being asleep, and unbound hair fell to waist level in a riot of curls. Navy-blue pants hugged her slender hips, and a multicolored fuzzy jacket hung off her shoulders, covering a white long-underwear top. The points of her nipples were visible through the thin fabric.

His body reacted immediately, and he directed magic to obscure his desire and confusion—in case any of the sea Shifters were paying close attention to him. The last thing he needed was a barnacle load of crap about how mating outside his immediate genetic circle was forbidden.

Karin hurried toward Moira, and Leif eavesdropped shamelessly as the wolf Shifter said, "I was getting worried about you."

"I overslept. Told my vulture to wake me, but it's not around. Must've returned to the animals' world."

Karin hooked an arm through hers. "Come on. Food's still warm, or on the warmer side."

A corner of Moira's full mouth twisted downward. "Whiskey?"

"After you've eaten." Karin eyed her sternly.

Moira rolled her eyes. "Yes, Mother."

"Better." Karin grinned, and the two women walked to the table where Daide, Aura, and Juan were seated.

Over the next quarter hour, everyone finished eating. Leif was grateful for the respite. It gave him an opportunity to regain the upper hand and block the lissome vulture Shifter from his thoughts.

Viktor rose from his seat and walked to the rostrum at the head of the dining room. Turning to face everyone, he nodded at Leif. "Join me."

While Leif made his way to where Viktor stood, he continued, "Our task this evening is to get every single possible idea out on the table. Nothing is too far-fetched. We're stronger as a group, so don't hold anything back."

Leif faced the assembled mix of Shifters and humans. "That goes for our human companions as well," he said. "A lot of brain power resides in this room."

"Thanks!" Boris called from where he, Ted, and the other three from Arctowski sat.

Ketha stood. "I finally saw bits of the future with my glass." She strode to a whiteboard mounted on the wall behind the rostrum. Once there, she snapped up a colored pen and began sketching. What emerged were three intersecting spheres with what looked like lightning bolts shooting through the points they overlapped.

"These places"—she tapped the lightning bolts—"maintained

their integrity despite the darkness around them. I couldn't see far enough ahead, but what I did see suggested we could glom onto their energy and use it as a tool to defeat the dark places."

Ted shot to his feet. "At the risk of being overly literal, where is the fissure in respect to the spheres?"

Ketha's mouth twisted into a rueful expression. "I asked my glass the same question in a whole lot of different ways, but it didn't yield anything beyond what I drew."

"Any idea what the three circles represent?" Viktor asked.

Ketha shook her head and gazed at the assemblage. "Aura? Any prophecies, unfinished or otherwise, come to mind?"

Aura stood slowly. "Maybe. First, though, I want to hear from Zoe, Tessa, and Becca."

Zoe got to her feet. "Aye, sure and we were busy with the cards casting tarot spreads."

Ketha spun an index finger in a circle. "Don't try too hard to interpret, just—"

"Let me tell this my own way." Zoe's brogue was clipped. "Tarot is naught if not interpretation."

"Sorry. I guess I'm edgier than I thought." Ketha held a hand up, palm facing outward.

"Aye, we all are," Zoe muttered.

Recco left his chair and joined her, draping a supportive arm around his wife's shoulders.

She leaned into him briefly, but then ducked from beneath his embrace and stood straight. "The cards were as equivocal as I've ever seen them."

"Yes, but that's a good thing," Tessa called from her seat.

"'Twas positive in that the cards didn't say we were doomed. Nor did they predict victory. My impression was we would rise or fall directly predicated on the decisions we make and our efforts. If we choose wrong, we're probably doomed. But the option is also open for us to choose right."

"We face a level playing field," Leif said. "My people have never done much with tarot cards. The difficulty of maintaining something like cards in an ocean environment is daunting. My read of your divination is we have a better chance than I'd hoped against whatever holds the fissure open."

"'Twas my take as well," Zoe said and turned toward Aura. "How does this feed into a prophecy?"

"Nicely as it happens," Aura replied. "I was vacillating between two possibilities, but this one is a better fit." She cleared her throat and her gaze hazed over. Leif assumed she was accessing memories, and her next words clinched his impression.

"As the other land Shifters know, the duty of pack historian is passed like a baton—or torch—from generation to generation. The previous historian is usually still alive but wanting or needing to move responsibility for the task to younger, fresher blood. Although our histories exist in written archives, the information is also handed from one historian to the next in oral form."

Aura stopped to take a deep breath. "The first unfinished prophecy deals with the beginnings of the world. Bear with me while I relate the tale. Once upon a time, there was no time and no gods. No man walked the surface of the land. But there was the sea, and where the sea met the land, a mare was born, white and made of sea-foam. And her name was Eiocha.

"From an oak tree that grew in the land sprouted a plant. This is where Eiocha gave birth to the first god, Cernunnos. Cernunnos mated with Eiocha and begot more gods. The gods were lonely because they did not have anyone to command or to worship them, so they created the first man and woman, as well as other animals from the wood of the oak tree. Giants, too, were born from the bark of a different tree that Eiocha hurled into the water."

Juan moved to Aura's side and handed her a tumbler. She drank deep and continued. "The gods squabbled. Eiocha was worried about the integrity of their magic, so she dropped out of sight for long years. When she returned, she told the assemblage she'd created an infinitely renewable source of magical power that crisscrossed Earth."

Leif nodded to himself. So the ley lines were an add-on, created by one of the first gods. "Does she still appear as a horse?" he asked.

"I'm getting there," Aura said. "In truth, I'd forgotten about this prophecy until earlier today."

"Maybe it hid itself from you until you needed it," Leif countered.

"Anything is possible. Let me finish. There's not much left. No one has laid eyes on Eiocha since the time she told her fellow gods about what I assume were the ley lines. Cernunnos loved her and tried to follow her, but she eluded him."

"Do you suppose she's the guardian?" Moira met Leif's gaze from her seat at a nearby table.

He glanced at Aura. "What do you think?"

"It's likely. Let me get to the prophecy part, which is that Eiocha will awaken and reappear when need is great. I'm a bit confused about the awaken part because it suggests she's been in some type of trance state all these years."

"It's a Celtic myth," Karin said. "Do you suppose Eiocha will respond to Gaelic?"

"Hang on," Moira said. "My bondmate is back. Let me ask it." Moments dripped by before she nodded, a solemn expression on her face. "Yes and no. My vulture only heard one word, and it was in an extremely archaic form of the language. It reminded me, though, that the guardian understood me when I walked along the lines talking as I pointed out the stronger spots."

"The guardian, whether it's Eiocha or another, wanted to keep us in the borderworld," Leif muttered.

"That was how we interpreted things," Moira said, "but what if we were wrong?"

"I'm not seeing how we could have been," the whale who'd been with them said.

"Maybe the guardian knew how close we were cutting things

and was trying to hold us in place to let our magical reservoirs gain more strength," Moira suggested.

"This is great. Keep the dialogue flowing," Viktor encouraged.

Leif listened as ideas cropped up. One thing was certain. They'd have to return to the borderworld and do their damnedest to open a channel of communication with the guardian. If Moira had guessed right, and the thing behind the lines was on their side, the journey would be uneventful. If not, the odds of tricking it into releasing them a second time would grow much more complicated.

Viktor elbowed him. "Any last thoughts, mate?"

"Other than some of us have to return to the borderworld? No."

Viktor nodded. "We did a good night's work, people. We'll figure out the mechanics of the best way to approach the guardian after we've had a decent rest."

Conversation rose around them, and Viktor turned to Leif. "Goes double for you on the rest front. Will you be here or in the sea?"

Leif glanced at his pod. They were on their feet and clearly waiting for him. "In the sea. We'll be back aboard in the morning."

"Excellent. Thanks for your help tonight."

"I didn't do much of anything."

"Oh, but you did. Us standing together is symbolic to everyone."

Leif extended a hand, and Viktor shook it. "Symbolic and I hope to hell prophetic we'll come through our trials with at least some survivors."

"We have to." Viktor's usually pleasant manner dropped away, showing the man beneath. Harsh. Somber. Determined.

Clacks and bleats rose from his restive pod, and Leif loped to them, avoiding the temptation to keep an eye on Moira. More than keep an eye. He ached to sit and talk with her, hold her, kiss her. Leif redirected himself fast. He couldn't be in two places, and now was a time for him to retreat to the sea with his kinfolk.

UNSEEN THREATS

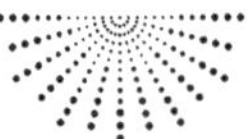

Moira had spent the morning working alongside Tessa and Ketha rearranging provisions in the galley. Karin was trying to grow seedlings in raised beds located in a small alcove behind the galley, but at least so far none of them had germinated.

"I'm going to take another look at the garden," Moira told the other two Shifters.

Ketha angled a glance her way from where she knelt in front of open cabinets. "Good idea. I hadn't exactly forgotten about them, but last time I looked, things were pretty quiet."

"Maybe a shot of magic?" Tessa raised a dark brow. Her black curls were bunched into a leather thong tied low on her neck.

"You've been reading my mind." Moira pushed to her feet, stretching out muscles that had stiffened from her stint crawling around on the floor. "Geez. How long have we been in here, anyway?"

"Hours, but at least it will be easier to find things. I'm not sure what Karin had in mind when she arranged supplies from Invercargill, but her system wasn't working for me." Ketha placed the remaining sacks of dried food inside a drawer and began the process of closing everything up, standing once she was done.

Moira came behind her brandishing a sharpie and scrawled enough on each cupboard and drawer front to identify its contents.

"Good idea," Tessa said. "We know where stuff is, but this way everyone else will too without opening everything."

"It is a most excellent idea, one I should have thought of." Ketha rolled her golden eyes. "At least this project has kept me away from my glass. I swear, that thing is more addictive than I remember."

"Nah. That's not it." Moira folded her arms beneath her breasts. "You're desperate to know more."

Ketha screwed her face into a serious expression. "I am. Damn but I miss our library. If we had access to it, we could dig up source documents to verify Aura's account of the beginnings of the world."

"We could, but what would we gain?" Moira played devil's advocate, mostly to move Ketha out of being mired in the way she'd always done things. That world had been dead for a long time and wasn't likely to ever return.

"She's seeking a mental comfort zone," Tessa spoke up. "It's been in short supply ever since we left Ushuaia."

"Try since the Cataclysm trapped us there." Moira did her best to rein it in, but bitterness seeped beneath her words.

"What if we do something wrong?" Ketha shoved her hands through her hair, moving the dark locks shot with red and gold behind her back. "If we approach the horse goddess in a way that's not pleasing to her, she may ignore us. Or kill us on the spot."

"As long as you brought it up, the whole horse thing has me damned nervous," Tessa said. "Is Eiocha related to the Kelpies?"

"I don't believe so," Ketha mumbled, "but it's a good question."

Moira considered her interaction with the unnamed energy in the cave. "I don't believe we can apply anything like our usual standards to the ley lines' guardian. From what I saw, the energy source has been closeted caring for the lines for so many thousands of years, even speaking has become difficult. It seems to understand, though, so perhaps its ability to communicate will return."

"I still wish we knew more," Ketha muttered.

Moira rounded on her. "We marched into battle against the Cataclysm with an incomplete information set and made it work."

"By accident. It was happenstance Vik and I chose that moment to make love, defying the prohibition against Vampires and Shifters having sex."

"Was it truly accidental?" Tessa got to her feet. "Zoe and Aura and I kicked it around, and we decided the goddess's hand was at play."

"That's lovely and lyrical"—Ketha shook her head—"but I think we got lucky, and there's no way to sort out if I'm right or if divine intervention played into our victory that day."

"You're wasting mental energy," Moira said.

"It's how I solve problems." Ketha sounded prickly and defensive.

Rather than answering, Moira crossed the room to the door into the small garden area with its raised beds. A quick glance lifted her spirits. "Look! We have seedlings. Finally."

Tessa and Ketha hurried to her side, crowding into the small space. "I'm taking this as a good omen," Ketha said. Nurturing magic flashed from her fingertips as she encouraged the rows of tiny, unfolding leaves to keep growing.

Moira checked the drip system and made a few adjustments. She turned to face the other two women. "We've had a hard go of things for a long time, but we're reaching the endgame. Now isn't the time to pussyfoot around. We have to play this part fast and hard. Like we're sure of ourselves and know what we're doing."

"Fake it till you make it?" Ketha looked askance at her.

"Something like that."

Tessa tipped her chin upward. "I don't know about you two, but every single thing we've faced has scared the crap out of me. From avoiding Vamps in Ushuaia to all the nasty shit we've run into on this voyage." She shrugged, a small motion that underscored her words. "No matter what, I keep going. I don't have any expectations. I'm taking this day by day, or hour by hour when the going gets really tough."

Moira stepped close and hugged her. "That was perfect. It's exactly what I'm trying to do."

"Me too, but that doesn't mean I like it," Ketha muttered, adding, "We need to get something going for lunch. It's past noon."

Moira let go of Tessa and returned to the kitchen, closing the door on the baby lettuce and spinach plants. Noon. Where were the sea Shifters? She'd managed to make it through the entire morning without thinking about Leif. At least, not too much.

What she'd actually done was redirect herself when her thoughts segued in his direction. Tessa turned on one of the ovens. When she caught Ketha's questioning glance, she said, "We had plenty left over from breakfast. I'm going to heat it up."

"I'll head to the bridge," Ketha said. "It's almost my shift anyway."

"Here." Tessa cut a square of room-temperature breakfast casserole and put it on a plate.

Ketha made a face. "Not particularly hungry, but I suppose I should eat."

"Yes. You should. Before you get lost in your scrying mirror again." Moira sent a pointed look Ketha's way.

"Maybe Zoe and Aura had luck with the cards, and they'll need an assist from my seer magic."

Moira folded a hand around Ketha's arm. "If they do, be sure to eat first."

Mumbling something that sounded like, "Yes, Mom," Ketha snatched up the plate and trudged out of the galley.

Tessa slid the remaining breakfast into the waiting oven. "Do you suppose we should make something to go with it?"

"Like what?"

"Some kind of quick bread? Whatever we don't eat can show up again at dinner."

Breath whistled through Moira's teeth. "Sure. It's a good plan. Do you need help?"

"Not really. It's kind of a one-woman job." Tessa narrowed her dark eyes in speculation. "We don't talk much, but then you've always kept to yourself—"

"Really?" Moira's temper surged. "You're going to criticize me for—"

"Back off, sister." Tessa held up a hand. "You're touchy as a scalded cat and about as approachable as your bondmate."

"Watch it. Do not dig yourself in deeper. What do you have against vultures?"

"Nothing." Tessa shook her head. "We shouldn't argue. We have enough problems without creating internal dissension."

Moira's quick spurt of anger guttered and died. "You're right. We're all jumpy. I'm sorry. Vultures aren't warm, fuzzy birds. But all the bond animals can have sharp edges. What are you bonded to? I don't believe I ever knew."

"A mountain cat, like Juan and Aura." She slapped her forehead with a palm. "Juan's cat."

Moira waited, but Tessa didn't say anything else. "What about Juan's cat?" she prodded.

"It was one of the first bond animals. It's very old. Karin's wolf is too. Maybe they'll know something about Eiocha or whoever is guardian for the lines."

"Someone mentioned querying the bond animals last night, I think." Moira chewed her lower lip but couldn't force the memory to center field. "Anyway, it's a good idea. I'm as worried as the rest of you."

The ship canted to one side before righting itself.

Tessa blew out a tight breath and widened her stance. "It's been a while since we hit a stretch of bad water."

"I have a feeling we'll be dealing with a whole lot of wave action before we reach Wrangel Island." Moira did a few quick calculations. "I'm thinking maybe nine more days."

"At what speed?"

"Good point, sweetie. I was calculating between twelve and thirteen knots. If Vik and Juan have to slow the boat down, it could take longer."

The deck tilted again. This time in the opposite direction. Tessa pulled a mixing bowl out of a cupboard; Moira found a wooden spoon and dropped a bag of biscuit mix next to the bowl.

"I'll stay until we get the biscuits in the oven," Moira said and poured the mix into the bowl to its halfway point.

Tessa added water, stirring until she liked the consistency. "What do you think?" She tilted the bowl so Moira could peek at its contents.

"Looks great. Let me get a baking sheet."

The motion of the ship had become more pronounced. Moira plunked the cookie sheet next to Tessa and walked to the galley door, pushing it open to allow a view out the windows lining the larger dining room. Water splattered the glass, but she couldn't tell if it was from waves or rain or both. The plan had been to skirt the Philippines to the west, but they should be past there and about even with China by now.

The gray she associated with storms filled every window without a hint of sunshine. The weather hadn't ever grown truly warm as they'd figured it would crossing equatorial waters. She drew herself up short. Her mind was wandering, mostly because she didn't want to have to add one more hardship to the already-daunting list facing them.

"Well?" Tessa called from the galley. "What's it look like out there?"

Moira let go of the door and turned her hands palms up. "Like a storm, but we already knew that. If you don't need me, I'm going to find Juan—and his cat."

"Let everyone know lunch will be ready in about half an hour."

"I'll do that." Moira's gaze darted away. "Sorry I was prickly."

"You don't have to apologize. We're all on edge, and I figure it will do nothing but grow worse as we get closer to the fissure." She thinned her lips into a line. "Remember how darkness got its claws into Daide?"

"Of course." Moira nodded. "What about it?"

Tessa scrunched her eyes into worried slits. "I feel it. Evil. Darkness. All around us hunting for a way in. It backed off after Antarctica, but it's back again."

Moira resisted the urge to pepper the other Shifter with questions. Instead, she settled on, "What type of magic runs strong in you?"

"I'm an empath, rather like Zoe."

Moira cast her magic in a full circle, hunting for the evil Tessa felt but not finding it. "Does your cat feel the darkness too?"

Tessa nodded, and Moira turned her attention inward to her bondmate. *"What do you sense?"*

"Not what she does, but it doesn't mean it's not there."

"You were talking with your vulture," Tessa said.

It wasn't a question, so Moira didn't bother denying it. "Yes, and neither of us are tuned in to the vibrations bothering you."

A startled look flitted across Tessa's freckled face. Magic sparkled where she formed a ward around herself. Her nostrils flared as she settled the protective circle into place. "Everyone should do this," she said. "It must've selected me because it saw me as a weak link. With me warded, it will transfer its attention to someone else."

"None of us has enough power to maintain warding twenty-four/seven and still fight whatever awaits us in eastern Siberia."

The scent of cooking biscuits sent Tessa scurrying toward the oven, mitt in hand. She drew out the pan and set it on a countertop before twisting to face Moira. "No. We don't. Which means we'll have to figure out a kind of early-warning system. Maybe if we frustrate this thing enough, it will give up."

Moira opened her mouth to tell Tessa she was being ridiculous. Evil never went away. It grew cagier, tried harder. But Tessa wore such a determined look, Moira nodded and said, "I'll let people know about lunch."

The ship lurched, and Moira grabbed onto a countertop. Scooping a hot biscuit off the tray, she made her way out of the kitchen and tackled the stairs, clinging to the rail so the next wave wouldn't send her ass over teakettle to the bottom.

She had faith in the ship. It was sound, and between Viktor and Juan, they possessed the skills to pilot it. Evidence of wickedness lurking in the wings was damned unsettling, though. No wonder Ketha's glass wasn't overly cooperative, or the Tarot cards.

The biscuit was almost too hot to eat, so she worked at it from the edges inward.

She'd finished it by the time she hit Deck Four. Having two hands helped a lot as she pulled herself up the remaining risers. She stopped at one of the large windows outside the bridge and stared out at twenty-foot swells beneath a gray sky thick with thunderclouds.

No wonder the ship was rocking and rolling. Had the men predicted this storm with their instruments, or was it spawned by the same magic that had Tessa in its gunsights?

After taking a deep, steadying breath, she walked onto the bridge. Viktor was at the helm. Juan stood near the bank of instrumentation writing in a small notebook. Aura, Ketha, Karin, and Zoe sat huddled in a tight circle off to one side. Recco and Daide stared out the windows as if they were hunting for something.

Everyone was so deep in what they were doing, no one noticed her at first. She cleared her throat, not wanting to startle anybody. "Um, lunch is ready."

"Figured as much when Ketha showed up with leftovers from breakfast," Viktor said. "How are those calculations coming?" he asked Juan.

"Slow." The Argentinian cat shifter must have been asleep when

Viktor summoned him to the bridge. His normally neat hair hung past his shoulders in tousled curls.

"Did you anticipate this storm?" Moira asked. Tension tightened her gut as she waited for the answer.

"Of course not." Viktor's words were terse. "I'd have warned everyone to batten down their cabins."

"Has to have been spawned by magic." Karin looked up. "We were trying to sort that out."

Moira licked dry lips. "This gets worse."

Every set of eyes in the room zeroed in on her, but she was familiar with being the center of attention in troubled situations. "Evil targeted Tessa," she said without preamble. "Good thing she mentioned it because we determined it was focused specifically on her."

A strangled sounding gasp emerged from Ketha. "Did she ward herself?"

"Oh yeah. First thing she did once what was happening became clear, but no one can ward themselves all the time. None of us have enough magic for that." She stopped to suck in a breath. "We figure since she blocked whatever wanted her, it will switch things up and target someone else."

Daide turned from where he'd been staring out into the storm. "Do you mean like the time darkness overran me?"

"It's exactly what she means," Karin answered his question. "Damn it. Whatever's out there is strong if it has enough juice to gin up a hurricane-force storm and threaten Tessa."

"Do you suppose something new came through the fissure?" Zoe asked, sounding rattled.

Juan slapped a hand down on a nearby table. "One thing's for certain, our instruments are worthless for predicting the course of this storm. My barometer's rising when it should be dropping like a stone."

"How far are we from Wrangel Island?" Aura asked her husband.

"Eight or nine days if the weather clears." Juan scanned the instrumentation again.

"And if it doesn't?" Moira spoke up.

"Could take double that. Or we might not get there at all," Juan replied tightlipped.

Worry nipped at Moira. "Where are the sea Shifters? Is that what you were watching through the windows?"

"Welcome to problem number six hundred," Aura mumbled.

"Huh?" Moira walked closer, not understanding. Remaining upright was hard, so she dropped into a nearby chair.

"We haven't heard from Leif or his pod since last night," Ketha said. "I had no idea there might be a problem until I got up here."

Fear clawed at Moira's belly, and the biscuit congealed into a doughy lump in her stomach. It was a stupid question, but she asked, "Have you tried telepathy?"

Karin sent an incredulous look skittering her way. "Right out of the box. We started trying to raise them around ten."

"Sea kicked up a couple of hours after that," Recco said. He'd turned from the window but still gripped the railing running beneath it. "Seems like more than a coincidence to me."

Moira unclenched hands that had balled into fists all by themselves. "We have to do something. Help them."

"How?" Karin nailed Moira with her copper gaze.

"It's impossible if we can't locate them," Zoe reached across to touch Moira's leg.

Ideas tumbled through her mind. Most departed as fast as they entered when she booted them to make room for ones that had a better chance of being helpful. Thinking on her feet and making decisions on the fly were second nature, but she didn't have much to work with.

"Can we use the lines to locate them?" she asked.

"The ley lines?" Ketha clarified. At Moira's nod, she added, "How? We can't touch them, or we'll end up fried to a cinder like Rowana."

"We have to go back to the cave with the lines!" Moira's bondmate screeched.

"I heard that," Karin said. "Please tell your vulture it's brave but foolish."

"And you tell that puerile wolf-bitch to keep her opinions to herself."

Moira winced and muttered, "Sorry, Karin."

Karin made a sour face. "I didn't hear whatever you're apologizing for."

Grateful the vulture had switched to a more private communication channel, Moira retreated to running odds and options. The only one that had any chance of success was her vulture's idea of returning to the cavern.

Where were Leif and his pod? Had they been captured? Were they already dead? A particularly rambunctious wave almost tumbled her from her chair. Worry grew until her throat thickened with tension. She couldn't give up because the cards were stacked against her. Not if it meant abandoning Leif to whatever was holding him against his will.

"Moira."

She looked up at the sound of Karin's voice. "Uh-huh."

"It's possible they decided to leave—"

Moira lurched to her feet, clinging to the table. "Stop right there. He would never do that."

"We don't think he would," Daide said, "but in truth we don't know our sea kin all that well."

"Maybe he made peace with Poseidon," Zoe cut in. "Seems unlikely, but one of the scenarios we tossed around before you got here was Poseidon discovered how faithless his consort is and dumped her."

"It's possible." Recco moved to his wife's side and wrapped an arm around her shoulders.

"Aye, 'tis." She leaned into him.

"I know Leif. He'd never leave without telling us," Moira insisted.

"Which means he's in big shit trouble, and we're a bunch of assholes for not doing more to help."

"Honey, we have enough problems," Ketha murmured.

"No. Right now we only have one—if you don't count the storm —and it's locating Leif and the other dolphins and whales," Moira said.

"We have to leave now," the vulture cawed. *"Now. Why are you standing around talking?"*

"What do you have in mind?" Karin asked, not bothering to modulate the disapproval laced into her words.

"I'm going back to the cavern where we found Amphitrite. Alone, if I have to. I'm hoping to use the magic in the lines to trace what happened to Leif and his pod." Moira squared her shoulders and looked around the bridge.

"I'll go with you," Aura said.

"Not without me." Juan left the instruments. "I'm not doing much good here anyway. Besides, my cat's been giving me nine kinds of hell. It knows the guardian."

A slender flicker of hope kindled deep in Moira. Maybe all wasn't lost after all.

"I don't agree with that plan, mate." Viktor's tone was cold.

Ketha went to him, bent, and said something into his ear.

Moira didn't want to waste any more time. "Come on." She gestured to Juan and Aura and left the bridge. If they followed her, great. If not, she was prepared to go by herself. If she'd been the one missing, Leif would have gone after her. It was the kind of man he was.

How could she offer him anything less by way of consideration and have a prayer of living with herself?

Footsteps clattered down the risers behind her. "How are we going to do this?" Aura demanded. "None of us teleport very well."

"Not a problem," Juan cut in. "We turn things over to the animals. They know where to go."

9

GIVE ME BLOOD

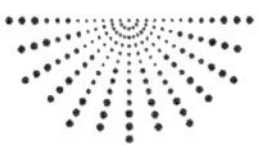

Few Hours Before

Leif and his pod swam through the night, talking and planning. Rather than return to the borderworld where they'd come face to face with the guardian, the group consensus was to search the ocean bottom for one of many openings leading to subterranean ley lines. Prior to his trip to the cavern, he'd always assumed the lines stretching beneath the ocean floor were primary.

Perhaps they were for his kind. It might have been the reason he couldn't understand Eiocha—or whoever he'd run into on the borderworld. He, Lewis, and two of the whales had burned through far too much time attempting to come up with a logical explanation of how the lines could exist beneath the sea and in some obscure borderworld, while circling Earth at the same time.

They'd finally decided the general laws of physics and magic didn't apply in this situation. Splitting into small groups, they'd begun swimming a grid, crisscrossing the ocean bottom. It was time consuming, but at least the sea wasn't so deep here as to make the task impossible.

"Over there!" Lewis bleated in dolphin-speak.

Leif took stock of his air. He had maybe five minutes left, which would be enough if Lewis had located a portal. Lynda swooshed past, clearly responding to Lewis's summons. Everyone else was too far away. They'd wait to see if Lewis truly had found something, or if it was another false alarm.

Several had cropped up over the last few hours.

Leif switched direction, swimming fast. Soon they'd be out of time. He didn't want to create needless worry for those aboard *Arkady*. If this latest gambit didn't work out, he'd return to the ship while his pod continued to search. Sand churned up from the bottom by small fish and other creatures turned the water murkier by the second. It was a common tactic meant to obscure their presence from predators, and Lewis cruising past had no doubt alarmed them.

Leif blinked several times to spread the thick, fatty tears dolphins secreted to protect their eyes. A glowing arch faded in and out of view. He stared at it, confused. He'd never seen its like, and it felt out of place. Wrong, somehow.

"Lewis!"

But the other dolphin didn't answer, no matter how many times Leif called his name. Neither did Lynda, and she'd have spoken up if she heard him—or if she knew where Lewis was. The archway was clearly visible now, pulsing with a warm, silvery glow.

All the other sea life had fled, which added to the creeping wrongness assaulting him. He should leave. Look for the rest of his pod. Alert the ship. But if he didn't go through the portal, Lewis and Lynda might be lost forever.

A series of notes trilled, swelling around him. Tantalizing, bittersweet, they drew him toward the gateway. More than anything, it reinforced that he was swimming into a trap, but who the hell had laid it? Squeals and bleats joined the notes, but he couldn't make them out. Was it Lewis and Lynda? Or some other entity mimicking the dolphin language?

The time for hesitation was over. He had to do something. Certainty intruded that if he left this place, he'd never find it again.

He might locate this spot, but the gateway would be gone, and Lewis and Lynda lost forever.

Resolute. Determined. He flicked his tail a few times and swam through the shimmering portal. Magic pricked his hide, but it felt warm, welcoming, which had to be an illusion. He had a very bad feeling about what waited within, but he had to do what he could to save his dolphins. Thousands of sea Shifters had died, mostly on his watch. His gut twisted into a hard, bitter knot.

The silvery light flashed once and extinguished, leaving him in pitch blackness. He navigated by echolocation, sending high pitched sounds to bounce off what turned out to be a narrow, twisting tunnel with a definite downward cant. The water warmed as he swam.

His heart beat faster. No way out. The tunnel was far too narrow to turn around, and swimming backward uphill was nearly impossible. The water level fell until the channel developed a definite layer of air. He exhaled through his blowhole and sucked in whatever passed for atmosphere, half expecting it to be poison.

It wasn't. He filled his lungs with air. It solved one problem, but not the mystery of who'd constructed the gateway guarding this passage. Or what had happened to his sea Shifters. Two more twists, and the channel leveled out, opening into an enormous undersea cavern.

If he'd been in a different mind space, it would have been beautiful. The air sparkled with motes of silver and gold, and cunning rock formations rose from the still, dark waters, spiraling upward as far as he could see.

He honked and bleated, calling for Lewis, for Lynda. No one answered. Awkward in his dolphin body, he invoked the magic to shift. It glistened around him, turning the air iridescent, but he was still a dolphin. Blowing air, he tried again. The shift took him, but painfully slowly. Each part of him ached, burned, and writhed as if a million knives jabbed his flesh.

Did his magic not work here? Would he turn into a screaming, howling mass of protoplasm that wasn't a dolphin, but not a man, either? Breath shuddered between his clenched teeth as he willed himself to complete the transformation. Too much of him was human to try going back. That would be a sure recipe for disaster. He grunted, determined not to scream his pain into the gleaming air. Still glowing with gold and silver motes, it mocked him with its perfection.

A thought crashed over him. If it was this hard to shift, how the hell would he ever leave this place? His human lungs could never hold enough air to swim through the corkscrew tunnel and an additional hundred fifty feet to the ocean's surface.

Leif forced himself to remain centered in the moment. The pins-and-needles jabs were lessening. When he took stock, he had arms, legs, a trunk, and a head. Panting with effort, he finished off the transformation. As soon as it was done, the pain ceased abruptly, and he stroked for the nearest shore, determined to locate the other sea Shifters. There didn't seem to be another way out of this cave, which meant they had to be here somewhere.

His mind was slow, sluggish. The same song that had enticed him from the sea bottom was back. Alluring as any Siren's summons, it promised peace from his trials. No need to travel north. No need to address the demons holding the fissure open so more of their hideous ilk could invade—and destroy—what the Cataclysm had missed.

Desire to lay his burdens aside swelled within his breast, overpowering in its intensity. He shook himself where he trod water and pulled a primitive ward around himself. Drawing magic hurt, but not quite as much as shifting had. Determined not to give in to the unknown singer, he headed toward shore. It was farther than it looked, and weariness dragged at him.

It took an ungodly amount of effort to keep his warding in place. Clearly it offended the keeper of this place. Finally, when swimming was beginning to feel beyond him, his toes touched rock and then sand. He slogged through water thicker than any salt water had a right to be and pitched onto wet sand, gasping like a landed fish.

Minutes ticked past as he lay there, trying to find the strength to get up and keep going. He had to find the other dolphins, but it would take forever to search the shores of this pool. It was enormous. So large the other side stretched beyond his vision.

"No!" He screeched and brought both fists down on the sand. He hadn't come this far to throw his life away. He'd come to find Lewis and Lynda.

The dirt he lay on rose around him, forming tendrils that turned into something hard as they wrapped around his prone form. Understanding leapt to the fore, and he scrambled to his feet, snapping off bits of stone that were growing thicker. Blood flowed from his abraded flesh where the dirt had tried to hold him in place.

Goddammit! Was this what had happened to Lewis and Lynda? They'd laid down and been subsumed by the hungry sand? Sand determined to feed itself from their energy?

Places where his blood dripped turned into smoking holes where the sand drank it down hungrily. Tendrils rose around his feet, clearly desperate for more of him. Leif took off at a trot. Standing still spelled death in this place. He drew magic over his ears to block out the escalating music and scanned the shore as he ran.

It didn't matter if he'd chosen an impossible task. He'd go down fighting. Not let this place absorb his essence. Maybe because he was thinking again, he reached for the other sea Shifters with magic, shifting to his third eye to see more clearly. The solution was so simple, he dunned himself for not coming up with it sooner. Ley lines shimmered, looking healthy as a whale down here. Even better, he felt the distinctive pulse of other dolphins through one glistening strand.

Breath shuddered from him. They were alive. He hadn't figured things out too late after all.

Leif turned back the way he'd come, moving fast. Lewis and

Lynda were behind him and not very damned far from the place that had nearly turned into his tomb. He girded himself for what he'd find but wasn't prepared for two oblong lumps in the sand.

He tripped over one before he realized what it was. Falling to his knees, he dug frantically, scraping dirt, sand, and rocks off Lewis's prone form. As he cleared debris, shock vied with horror. The same vine-like rocks that had almost trapped him wound around Lewis, holding him to the ground. They'd dug into his flesh, so blood dribbled, pooling around him.

Thank all the gods the vines hadn't punctured any major vessels, but protrusions stuck into his abdomen, into his lungs, into his groin. Fury filled Leif, and he roared his angst until his outraged howls filled the cavern. At least the fucking Siren thing shut up.

Heedless of pain, Leif shot magic through the bands that held Lewis captive. Rock shattered with a sharp, cracking sound and fell away, forming small piles of rubble. Once all the sharp bits piercing Lewis were gone, Leif grabbed his hands and dragged him to a sitting position. The dolphin Shifter's head lolled. Leif blasted him with magic.

"Goddammit! Wake up. We have to rescue Lynda." Leif used the harsh bleats and clacks dolphins employed to depict extraordinary danger.

He got through because Lewis groaned. "What the hell happened to me, mate?"

"Doesn't matter. Wake up. Something wanted us right where we are, but we are not giving in to it."

"Where's Lynda?"

Leif pointed at an oblong hump in the dirt. "Under there. Help me."

Without waiting for Lewis to reply, Leif clawed dirt off Lynda's tomb. His fingertips were abraded. Blood flowed from them, delighting the sand. It jumped beneath his hands, anxious to soak in the crimson drops.

Lewis dragged himself to Lynda's other side, mimicking Leif's motions. "I must be daft. Hallucinating," he mumbled. "The dirt can't be drinking your blood."

"Oh yes, it can. What the fuck do you think it was doing to you? Look." Leif had cleared enough dirt off Lynda to expose her torso. The same bits of rock had impaled her, sinking into the soft flesh of her stomach, breasts, and hips.

Lewis made a gagging sound. "Poseidon's balls, mate. I am so fucking sorry. This was my idea. I was the one who fell for the trap."

"Never mind that. Help me." Leif summoned magic to snap off the horns that had dug into Lynda's flesh. Because two of them were at work, it went far faster than things had freeing Lewis.

Between them, they dragged Lynda upright and walked her in a circle until she came around. "What happened?" She looked from Leif to Lewis. "I don't remember anything."

"You followed me." Lewis's words held shame. "I was wrong."

"Stop. You can beat yourself up later. Right now, we need a way out of here." Leif paused. "Shifting hurt. A lot, but we can't leave as humans."

"I never shifted," Lynda said. "Last I remember, I swam in here, but then everything kind of folded in on me."

"It was the same for me." Lewis shook his head. "What is this place? I've never heard of anywhere in the sea where the dirt drinks your blood."

"Ewww. I need to hear what happened, but not right now." Lynda shuddered and dragged one foot off the dirt, stamping it back down. "Damn it. The fucking sand just bit me."

"We have to keep moving," Leif said. "What trapped us is sentient. We thwarted it, but it hasn't given up."

"Let's shift and swim out of here," Lewis urged.

"Not as easy as you might think," Leif countered. "I had a hell of a time shifting to human, and for all I know the way in here was crafted with magic and no longer exists. Come on. We'll walk as we think through our options. It should at least slow the thing that wants to drill through our skin."

"Ley lines look good here," Lynda ventured. "I just peeked."

Leif switched to his third eye and scanned the lines crossing the cavern. "They do indeed. It's how I found the two of you. Look over there." He pointed.

"Rocks and dirt," Lewis muttered.

"Use your third eye." Lynda shot a pained look his way.

"Tell me what you see," Leif instructed, not wanting to influence the other two.

"A cluster of the lines bend, and they all come together before they disappear through the wall," Lynda replied.

"Lewis?" Leif elbowed him.

"Aye. I see the same thing. It's odd. I've never known them to bunch up like that."

"Nor have I," Leif agreed. "But they're not shimmering or glittering or trying to lure us. I'm thinking maybe it's a way out of here that won't entail shifting. At least not until we're clear of the magic powering this place."

"I want to know what's behind luring us in here to drain our blood," Lewis said. "I thought only Vampires did that."

"Many of the gods were bloodhungry," Leif replied. "Toutatis, Esus, and Taranis for starters. Let's save the philosophical underpinnings for if we manage to extricate ourselves."

"Those were Celts, weren't they?" Lynda asked.

"How's your magic holding up?" Leif asked, ignoring her question.

"Not bad."

Leif kicked sand closing over one foot aside. Something had clearly figured out they were leaving and was determined to stop them. "Whatever snared us won't go down without a fight," he told the other two. "Listen closely. When I give the word, we'll draw magic and teleport to the other side of the wall as close as possible to the spot the lines all come together. I have no idea what we'll find there. Maybe ocean. Maybe nothing."

"Maybe we'll uncover whoever set the trap I fell for," Lewis cut in sourly.

"It's possible," Leif plowed on. "Regardless. Be ready to shift if we're in the ocean. I have no idea how far it will be to the surface, and if we remain in our human bodies, we might drown."

"Got it," Lewis said, sounding determined to redeem himself.

"Why can't we shift and take the tunnel?" Lynda asked.

"It is another option. Maybe." Leif considered it. "I have a funny feeling, instinct more than anything, we'd never find the passageway again. I felt magic prick as soon as I swam through the portal."

"I did too," Lewis said. "Tried to turn around, but something wouldn't let me. That's when I knew I'd made a mistake. I called to both of you. Told you to turn back."

"Never heard you," Lynda said.

Leif hadn't either, and it clinched his decision to go with teleporting through the wall. They closed on it quicker than he anticipated, but physical properties in this place were fluid. The air thickened with static electricity from proximity to so many ley lines.

He herded them as close as he dared. At least the attack on his bare feet ceased as they neared the lines. Maybe malevolent energy couldn't coexist so near the clean purity of the lines.

"Ready?" he asked the other two.

"Aye," Lewis said.

"Yup," Lynda replied.

Leif held out his hands. Lewis grasped one, Lynda the other. "Open your magic to me, and let me guide this."

He sensed glowing channels as his Shifters followed his directions, gratified their magic was in decent shape. Unless something truly unexpected popped up, they'd be out of here fast.

"If we end up in the ocean," he told them, "I'll cut my connection to you. Shift immediately."

Leif drew magic until it bubbled and boiled around them. He didn't want to underestimate and end up stuck in endless rock and dirt. Who knew what the other side of the cavern wall looked like? Since this whole shebang was probably magical illusion, the far side of the wall was anyone's guess.

He let power fill him until he was certain he had enough for almost anything and cast a teleport spell. The pool fell away as did the cavern. For long moments, they were suspended in a familiar, black, airless void. The space between Earth and the borderworlds.

Leif urged his casting to locate the nearest point, be it borderworld or Earth.

Light flashed, brilliant white, and they rolled out into the place he'd apprehended Amphitrite. "Yes!" He let go of Lynda and Lewis and fist-pumped the air, a decidedly human gesture.

Ley lines stretched in both directions, glowing, healthy ley lines, so the guardian had continued restoring them.

"Where are we?" Lynda turned in a full circle.

"A borderworld. It's the same spot I went with Moira and the whale."

"Which means we have a way back." Lewis danced a jig, kicking and stomping dry, dusty dirt. "Woohoo! The surface isn't trying to eat me."

More light flared, and magic pummeled Leif. He dragged a protective ward across all of them, ready for anything. "Look sharp. Something's headed our way."

"It can't be any worse that what we escaped from. Unless it decided to follow us." Lewis twisted to face the spot throbbing with power.

Leif readied defensive magic, letting it build as he tossed a growing ball of destruction from hand to hand. He'd lob it at whoever had the temerity to show up here. If he got lucky, he'd nail Amphitrite, returned to the scene of her thievery. He wouldn't kill her, but the blow would hurt—a lot.

Moira tumbled through a rip in the ether, followed by Juan and Aura. Leif extinguished the demolition balanced between his fingertips so fast it burned him.

"What the hell?" Moira scrambled upright and faced them, hands on her hips. "What are you doing here? Why didn't you—"

Leif held up a hand. Steam rose from where he'd stopped himself from killing her on the spot. "We just got here."

"Aye, we were trapped," Lewis said.

"Trapped, but not here?" Aura strode forward with Juan next to her.

"Yes," Lynda said. "Lewis and I would be dead, but Leif rescued us from a bloodsucking horror that—"

"Later." Leif made a chopping motion. "Apologies for any worry our absence caused. Have you seen any of the other sea Shifters?"

Juan shook his head. "If we had, we might not have followed Moira's lead and launched the cavalry."

Warmth fluttered deep in Leif's chest. Coming after him had been Moira's idea. He glanced away, hoping no one was looking closely enough to see either his delight or the confused welter of emotions running through him.

"So long as we're here," Aura said, "shall we attempt to sort out who the guardian is?"

"We'd planned to return to the boat," Leif said, "but it's a good suggestion."

"Exactly." Moira nodded sharply. "Since half a dozen of us are present, we shouldn't waste the magic it took to get here."

Leif raised his head and met her gaze. "You land Shifters don't teleport well. How'd you get here without one of us?"

"Our bond animals." Moira tightened her lips into a line. "My vulture was most insistent."

"As was my cat," Juan said. "Viktor pitched a fit, but I left before he could order me to remain."

"He wouldn't have," Aura said. "Ketha was on top of it." She rubbed her hands together. "This place is fascinating, like something out of the olden tales. Where shall we begin?"

"We begin here. I'm going to shift." Moira drew shadows about herself and shucked her clothing. Leif did his best not to look, but the curves of her body were visible as she undressed. They drew him like a lodestone, heating his blood with need.

Magic pulsed, bright and strong, and Moira's vulture formed. Cawing, it flew toward the far end of the cavern.

"Should have asked her what she had in mind," Aura said. Switching to telepathy, she repeated the question.

Caws, screeches, and delighted vulture sounds filled the cave. Leif smiled, eager to discover what Moira had unearthed.

10

GUARDIAN

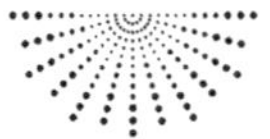

Moira couldn't have held her vulture back if she'd wanted to. If she hadn't cooperated, her bondmate would have forced a shift amid shredding clothing. Far better to salvage what she'd worn so she didn't freeze on the airless trip back through the void between worlds. She could count a handful of instances over the half century since she'd bonded with the bird when it had plowed ahead, heedless of anything but what it wanted.

She'd known her bondmate was headstrong, but she'd dreamed the vulture when she was only a child. If there'd been a choice point somewhere along the way—an opportunity to select a more tractable partner—she'd never hunted for it. Being bonded was a lot like falling in love, the attraction hot and instantaneous. Once the vulture had materialized in her dreams, Moira never looked back.

At least she'd shucked her clothing before wings and feathers formed, and she flew straight and true through shiny veils, one after another draped across the far end of the cavern. Shimmery with rainbow-hued light, the veils were gossamer thin and incredibly beautiful.

She wanted to savor finding Leif alive, but events were moving at breakneck speed. Anything as prosaic as her probably one-sided

109

attraction to the dolphin Shifter had no place right now. It didn't help that he was buck naked and twenty shades of gorgeous, but she shouldn't let that divert her.

The vulture cawed and shrilled and cooed, more of a variety of sounds than Moira had ever heard from the creature. The veils came faster now, one layered atop the next. Her wings made a zinging, whooshing noise as she bypassed one after the other. Ley lines glimmered above, below, and next to where she flew, their energy palpable, but not threatening. They cast a fey light over everything, adding to the impression she'd fallen into fairyland.

She wanted to ask her bondmate where they were going, but she'd find out soon enough. In the distance, a horse whinnied, harsh and strident. The vulture shrieked and flew faster.

The thrum of hoofbeats, faint at first, grew louder. With a thunderous rip, reminiscent of burlap sacks shredding, a graceful ivory horse appeared. Suspended above the ley lines beneath its hooves, it galloped through air. Moira's vulture executed an aerial flip and ended up clinging to the horse's withers, talons digging deep enough to stabilize its perch.

"Old friend," the vulture cawed in a very ancient form of Gaelic.

"Well met, indeed, old friend," the horse responded in the same language.

Moira had to stretch her language skills to understand. Even with the filter provided by her bondmate that allowed her to interpret things lost to her when she was human, the conversation was next to unintelligible.

"You carry another within you," the horse went on. "How curious. What is she?"

"Too long a tale, but one I shall share presently. You met her. 'Tis who showed you how to mend the lines."

A sharp whinny was followed by, "That one? Better than the thieving bitch who crept in here and hid from me while damaging my children." The horse twisted its long neck and rubbed against the vulture's feathers, the gesture simple and poignant as they hovered above the rock-strewn surface.

Moira longed to ask how they knew one another but didn't want to interrupt what was clearly a heartfelt reunion. Had her bondmate been part of the world's beginnings, right along with Eioha? Bond animals never talked about things like that. They knew all about you, but you only understood the parts of them they deigned to share.

She hung back, watchful, not intending to be pushy but hoping her bondmate would address the fissure. Would Eiocha—if that's who the horse was—help them? If Moira understood her correctly, she'd referred to the ley lines as her children The lines extended over the entire globe, crisscrossing its length and breadth, which meant there had to be lines on Wrangel Island.

A different footfall pattern raced toward them, not hooves but paws. Big ones. Moira wasn't surprised when Juan's mountain lion leapt through the veil nearest them, landing lightly between two vertically placed lines scant inches from Eiocha's churning hooves.

With a low, purring growl it stretched its neck until it swiped a tongue over one of the horse's front legs.

If their situation hadn't been so desperate, Moira would have smiled at what was looking a lot like old home week. Clearly, this trio had known one another since the dawn of time and were thrilled to be reunited. Magic glistened and shimmered around horse, vulture, and mountain lion, colors shading from white to blue to green to red to violet and back again as they vocalized their joy.

"Moira?" Leif's voice rumbled through her mind, tentative, questioning. Not wanting to interrupt but too worried not to reach out to her.

"I'm fine. Reassure Aura that Juan is too."

The horse had settled to ground level between two lines; they'd spread to make room for her. Close up, her mane held silver strands mixed with the ivory ones, and her coat glowed as if lit from within.

Wide and liquid, her eyes shaded from blackest night to a deep blue that reminded Moira of the ocean.

Juan wove between her legs, rubbing against the horse in the way cats have where their bodies appear fluid, boneless. A deep, throaty purr rumbled from the mountain lion, the sound both threat and promise.

Moira dragged herself back from what felt like a flight into whimsy, except it wasn't. Not really. The mountain lion would stand against evil just as it always had, dragging Juan into its battles much as her vulture had pulled her along on its headlong flight a few minutes before.

Aura was next to emerge from behind the veils. Unlike her mate, she walked slowly, deliberately, her cat a tawnier shade than Juan's. Moira watched as Juan moved away from Eiocha and licked Aura's nose. Tonight was a time for Shifters to take to their animal forms, at least here in this cavern.

The horse bent her long, graceful neck until she was at eye level with Juan and Aura. "You are mated?"

"Yes, Goddess." Juan's cat inclined its head and narrowed its green eyes to happy slits.

The horse looked as if she were considering its words; Moira girded herself for an outburst of jealousy. Who knew what this bunch had been to one another once upon a time? Close, but how close? Was Aura in danger?

Apparently, the same thought crossed Aura's bondmate's mind. The cat drew back its upper lip showing its fangs.

"*Do something,*" Moira shouted to her vulture. "*We do not need any more enemies.*"

"*Awk, child. You don't understand.*"

"*How could I?*" Moira countered. "*You rarely tell me anything.*"

The vulture focused their shared attention on the horse. It had exposed its squared-off teeth, mirroring Aura's mountain lion. "*He was mine first,*" Eiocha announced. "*But everything was mine first. Lovers left me. Children left me. Friends left me until all that was left was the most important task of all. Holding the world's magic together. Keeping it safe from those who would harm it, but my job has grown much harder."*

A sorrowful whinny was followed by, *"What has happened in the world? Why can others, like the one claiming to be queen of the sea, enter my realm and steal from me? Such events have never occurred before."*

"Tell her," Moira urged her vulture. *"Everything."*

"Yes," Aura cut in. *"Maybe, if she knows, she'll help us."*

"Who are you?" Eiocha's equine brow creased in confusion. *"My old companions, yet not."*

"We are bonded with humans," the vulture replied. *"Please do not ask how it happened, for such is a very long tale. If we survive—"*

"What do you mean if we survive? Is there any question? Any doubt? How could there be?" Eiocha's mind voice grew shrill.

"How long since you've set foot on Earth?" Juan's cat asked.

Before she could respond, Leif, Lewis, and Lynda parted the nearest veil amid a shower of silvery sparks. "May we join you?" Leif asked.

Eiocha angled her neck to one side, regarding him. *"I remember you. You were here when the other one—the sea queen, except she couldn't be anything so grand as all that—stole from me. Were you part of her scheme? Answer honestly. I will know if you lie to me."*

Leif bowed until his forehead nearly touched the ground before straightening. "It's a great honor to meet you, Eiocha. I am a dolphin Shifter, alpha to my pod. My sea name is…" He trilled a series of notes. "The power thief is Amphitrite, and for many a long year, she was a goddess, but she repudiated her rightful role and has embraced evil."

"We are dolphin Shifters as well," Lewis said.

Eiocha tossed her head. *"You asked how long since I walked the Earth. Many thousands of years. At first, the lines required my presence, but after a time, I grew used to my solitude."*

The vulture laid her head along the horse's neck. *"Bad things have happened in the world, old friend. Very bad things. Earth may be doomed.*

"You must tell me." Eiocha stamped her hooves on the ground.

"A spell went sideways," the vulture replied, *"opening the door to great evil. A courageous group of Shifters fought the wickedness and altered its course, but not enough."*

"We sail toward northern waters." Juan's cat stepped in. *"A hole between worlds must be closed. Malevolent forces are pouring through. They will strip what's left of goodness from Earth, rendering it uninhabitable for any save demon spawn."*

Moira couldn't remain silent any longer. *"Will you help us?"* she demanded.

"Who was that?" Eiocha shook her head until her mane danced along the length of her neck.

"My human bondmate," the vulture replied, adding, *"The one who showed you how to repair the ley lines."*

"Aye. Her. I haven't forgotten," Eiocha muttered. *"I do not know how I could help. I have not left this world for so long, I'm not certain I even could."*

"Your ley lines," Moira persisted. *"They circle Earth."*

Juan's cat stood tall, tail twitching. *"You are the Guardian."* It growled low. *"You have no choice. Caring for Earth was tasked to you. While you may choose the how and why of that caretaking, nonetheless, it is your job."*

"But I've done my job," she insisted. *"Caring for the lines means magic will never die."*

"Oh but it will. Die, that is." Moira couldn't seem to keep her mouth shut, but she wasn't about to stop now. *"If we can't close the gateway to Hell, everything good on Earth will wither and perish."*

"Surely you must be mistaken." Eiocha tossed her head.

Moira didn't contradict her. She'd said enough.

"I was happy. So happy you came to see me. At last. After all these long years of being alone." Eiocha dropped her head low, as if holding it up were too much trouble.

"I was happy to see you too—" the vulture began.

"I think not." The horse shook herself until the vulture let go and flew in circles.

"How can you say such a thing?" the vulture demanded. *"You overstep yourself."*

Moira felt her bondmate's temper rise and searched for a way to intervene.

"You were here with the human you say is linked to you. Granted, you appeared in her form, but since she exists within you, I assume the opposite holds true as well. Hence, you were here but held silence. No well met, old friend then." The horse turned until one laterally placed eye skewered the vulture. The eye had developed a red cast.

"We were in a hurry." Leif stepped closer. "We are part of a larger group. Our companions would have worried needlessly, risked themselves if they thought we were in danger—"

Aura's cat growled low in its throat; hackles raised the length of its spine. *"With all due respect, Goddess, you don't understand the nature of the Shifter bond since it came into being after you left Earth."*

"Your manner does not match your words." Eiocha's tail swished from side to side. *"I find all of you unspeakably rude. I once counted two of you as friends, yet you forsook me. Aye, you are here now, but only because you want something. So long as magic showed up when you required it, you never thought of me at all.*

"Leave me. Go now while I'm feeling generous."

The vulture cawed her outrage, wings beating a staccato tempo inches from the horse's head. *"Look to yourself, Eiocha. If no one made the effort to visit, it's because none of us had any idea where to find you. Friendship runs two ways, and my heart is heavy because today I lost someone I once held dear."*

"If you choose not to aid our cause"—Juan's cat picked up the banner—*"we may fail. If we do, your time tending magic on this borderworld will come to an end along with all of us."*

"You'll fail on purpose." The horse squealed its dismay. *"To thwart me. Leave before I change my mind."*

"We're going. Thank you for your time and consideration." Leif bowed again, and he, Lewis, and Lynda turned and walked through the veils. No longer shimmering, the fabric hung like tired rags.

Moira had a whole lot she wanted to say, starting with reminding Eiocha she'd done her damnedest to hold them in the cavern on their first trip to her domain. Before she had a chance to confront the horse, her bondmate wheeled and flew after the dolphin Shifters.

Juan and Aura ran lightly beneath them.

The vulture landed next to where Moira had left her clothes. She took it as a sign her bondmate was ceding their shared form to a human body. When shifting required almost no effort, it meant the vulture was troubled.

As she dressed, she asked, *"What's wrong?"*

"What's right?" the bird shot back. *"I know her. I handled this badly."*

"I'm not seeing how." Moira tried to understand her bondmate's point.

"Eiocha always needed coddling, reassurance of her spot at the center of everything."

Moira bent to lace her boots. *"But we told her she could play a major role. She grew angry. Accused us of failing on purpose—to make her look bad."*

Back in her human form and dressed, Aura called, "Ready to go?"

"Yes." Moira hurried to where everyone was bunched in a tight circle. "Before we leave, is there anything we can say or do to fix what just happened?"

"My cat says it's a lost cause," Juan snarled through tight lips.

"Not precisely what my vulture believes, but we can dissect this back on *Arkady.*"

"I have to round up the rest of my pod," Leif said. "Depending on where we emerge this time, if the rest of you don't need me, I'll locate them before I come back aboard."

"They're probably hunting for us," Lynda said.

"My guess too," Leif agreed, "but I still have to track everyone down. Shouldn't take long."

"We want to hear what happened to you." Moira turned a worried look his way.

"Not sure I totally understand the thing that first lured us, and then would have eaten us, but—"

"It's part of what doesn't want us to get to Wrangel Island," Aura spoke over him. "We need every detail to protect ourselves."

"Leave. Leave. Leave!" The words echoed off the walls, so loud Moira jammed her hands over her ears. She resisted an urge to shake her fist at the imperious horse goddess. She'd bet her last spell Eiocha was terrified and covering with projection and threats.

The more Moira thought about it, the surer she was that she skirted close to the truth. Eiocha's words rumbled through her mind. *Lovers left me. Children left me. Friends left me until all that was left was the most important task of all. Holding the world's magic together.*

Maybe, after tens or dozens or hundreds of abandonments, the goddess was done putting herself forward. That was why she'd run away, hiding on an obscure borderworld under the guise of it being the most important task of all.

Even if I am right, what good will it do us?

None, she answered herself. *Eiocha dismissed us.*

"Moira?" Leif's voice held a question.

"I'm ready. Let's go."

Power surged around them, carrying them out of the cavern. The ley lines' magic was strong, so strong Moira ended up sprawled on *Arkady's* wide quarterdeck in the blink of an eye.

What a difference from their last exit from the same borderworld.

She'd tumbled through a torn place in the ether. Neither shimmery nor glistening. When she stared at the hole, it dripped red before it snapped shut as if it had never existed.

Blinking, she wondered if she'd been hallucinating. "Did you see that?" she asked Aura.

The blonde cat shifter nodded solemnly. "If I didn't know better, I'd say the portal was sealed with Eiocha's tears, although I have no idea what that might mean."

Juan helped Aura to her feet. Moira pushed upright. Leif and the two dolphin shifters weren't there, but she hadn't expected them to be.

"I'm off to make peace with Vik," Juan announced.

"Would you like company?" Aura asked.

Juan wrapped his arms around her and kissed her forehead. "Thanks for the offer, but this might go better if I'm by myself."

"Okay. I'll be in our cabin showering."

Juan kissed her again and turned, taking one of the outside staircases and trotting upward two steps at a time.

Aura leveled her green gaze on Moira. "We really fucked that up."

"Not my take at all."

"What do you mean?"

"If Eiocha is such a prima donna that looking cross-eyed at her is all it takes for her to turn on us, maybe we don't need her for an ally."

Her vulture squawked, but Moira couldn't interpret what it meant.

"Is your bird agreeing or dissing you?" Aura asked.

"In this instance, I don't know. It did say it should have known better and handled things differently."

"Mmph. We can pick everything apart later." Aura's shoulders slumped. "I'm discouraged, although I'm doing my damnedest to argue myself out of it. Before a couple of days ago, I hadn't thought about that myth in years."

"Maybe it's not the correct prophecy for our circumstances?" Moira furled her brows.

Aura screwed her mouth into a forced smile. "There is that rationalization to consider, but you may be onto something. I'll see if I can't find another prophecy that's a better fit." She trudged through a nearby side door.

Moira watched her go and charted her own course. What she needed was a heart-to-heart with her bondmate, but whether the vulture would cooperate was a huge unknown.

Magic sparked nearby, filling the air with the fresh scent of the sea as dolphins and whales materialized on deck. Water sluiced down their bodies, pooling around their sleek forms.

She waited until Leif formed in the middle of a shiny, golden sphere that broke apart around him. "All present and accounted for?" she asked.

"Yes." He smiled, and her heart gave a funny little hitch. "Lynda was correct. They were hunting for us and not willing to give up until they were certain we were safe."

"I'm glad everyone is okay." She turned away, warmed by the sea Shifters' tightknit brotherhood and ashamed how much she craved something similar. When she went inside the ship, no one called after her, but why should they? They had each other.

She walked slowly down the corridor to her cabin and was all the way inside, closeted behind a closed door, before truth crashed over her. If she felt alone, it was her own fucking fault. Much like Eiocha, she'd always kept to herself. Even through the decade in Ushuaia, she'd held herself aloof from the other Shifters. For the first couple of years, even though it was irrational, she'd blamed them because she was stuck in Argentina. Once she'd finally moved past that, it was late in the game to build bridges, so she'd fit in as she could.

Sitting gingerly on the corner of her berth, she dropped her head into her hands. Crying was stupid, but tears came anyway. Maybe when she was done indulging herself, she could do something useful to redeem today's fiasco.

Something that might convince Eiocha to become their ally.

A TIME FOR TRUTH

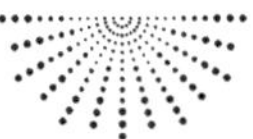

*L*eif watched Moira leave out of the corner of his eye. She seemed upset, but their time in the borderworld had been disconcerting. Enough to trouble anyone. The language of the sea rose and fell around him as his pod celebrated being reunited. The sounds were peaceful and soothing except for where a whale faced off against Lewis.

"You almost got our alpha killed." Accusation sharpened the whale's words.

Leif paid attention. How would Lewis handle things? He was slated to take over as alpha if disaster struck. Had the pod made a solid choice for his successor?

Lewis faced the whale squarely. "Aye, and myself along with him. Lynda too. I feel quite the idiot for being taken in by a cunning illusion." Lewis stood straighter. "You're right to chastise me, but no matter what you say it won't be as harsh as I've been on myself."

"Good you see it that way," the whale grumbled before lumbering inside the ship.

Leif smiled to himself. Lewis would be a good leader if circumstances placed him in that role. Knowing when to accept blame was a gift and a skill, as was acknowledging when you were wrong. His thoughts turned to Eiocha. Talk about a mirror opposite. She cast blame in a wide net, unwilling to view herself as anything other than perfect.

Too bad. She might have become a most excellent ally, but not if they had to mollycoddle her every step of the way. His dolphin had a few choice words about the exchange in the cavern, mostly regarding what they did to younglings who viewed themselves as the center of the universe.

Before his pod could pepper him with more questions about his time in the cave with the bloodthirsty sand, he slipped inside the ship, stopping by the clothes locker. He needed a breather to sort through today's events, but first he'd stop by Moira's cabin to check on her. He might have been wrong about her being upset, but it wouldn't hurt to make sure she wasn't blaming herself—or her bondmate—for Eiocha's hostile reaction to them.

Clothes had never mattered to him, not even when he spent more of his time in his human form, but he took care the colors didn't clash. If Moira was upset, he didn't want to make things worse by showing up at her door looking like a court jester.

He finger-combed his wet, tangled hair and inhaled briskly. Court jester be damned. His real reason for paying attention to the black trousers and shirt, topped with a red jacket, was he aimed to make a good impression, not a slipshod one. Admitting the truth to himself was important, even if that truth started and stopped with him. When he realized he was lingering over the clothing locker longer than necessary, he zipped his coat partway and hurried down the corridor, stopping in front of Moira's door.

Feeling somewhat foolish, he stopped to listen. A muffled sob met his ears, followed by two more. Leif drew back, shrouding himself with power so she wouldn't detect his presence. Not only was she troubled, she was troubled enough to be crying. He didn't know how land Shifters reacted to adversity all that well, but she didn't strike him as the crying type.

Should he move on by? Approach her at another time? One

where she was feeling more balanced? The longer he considered it, the less willing he was to intrude on her grief or her guilt or whatever the hell she was feeling.

Thank the goddess no one chose this particular slice of time to walk down Deck Three's corridor. It would be difficult to explain why he was standing outside her door, cloaked in magic like some arcane peeping tom.

I am such a fucking coward.

He hurried to the far end of the hall and stared out a porthole, collecting his scattered thoughts. He'd suspected she was troubled; it was why he'd come this way. Yet presented with evidence she was indeed distraught, he'd run like a skittish minnow being chased by a shiver of sharks.

Thoroughly disgusted with himself, he released the magic blanketing him, strode quickly to her door, and knocked once. If she didn't want to answer, a single knock wasn't overly intrusive.

A jolt of magic buffeted him, but he'd expected her to at least check who stood outside her door before responding. The next part happened fast. The door flew open, and a Moira with red-rimmed eyes faced him, elbows akimbo and hands on her hips.

"Crap on a cracker," she muttered, "what's gone wrong now?"

Understanding kicked him in the guts like an ornery mule. He'd never shown up on her doorstep before. Of course, she'd assume some new disaster had struck.

"Nothing new. Just the same old menu of insoluble problems."

Moira flipped her hands palms up. "So, why are you here?" Her words were followed by a wince. "Jesus. I'm sorry. That was rude even for me."

"A good question, though." He tamped back a soft smile. Damn but he liked her. She had mettle. Grit.

"Are you going to answer it?" She swiped the backs of her hands across her damp cheeks but didn't offer any explanations for her appearance.

He respected her for that. She owed him nothing. Better to stick with what was real than to pretend they were anything other than two of the last few Shifters in the world fighting for a common goal.

"You seemed upset when you went inside. I stopped by to see if you wanted to talk about our go-round with Eiocha. It was harsh and not the outcome we'd hoped for."

A complex array of emotion flickered across her expressive features, but he wasn't certain how to interpret any of them. "It was kind of you to worry about me, but—" She chewed on her lower lip.

Before she told him to go away, he hurriedly said, "Not kind, self-serving."

"Huh?" She creased her brow into a welter of lines.

"Whenever one of my pod lives through something difficult, we talk it through until the unpleasant emotions that went along with it have found at least partial resolution. Juan and Aura have each other. I have my pod..." Leif faltered, not sure where to go from here. He'd painted himself into a word corner and was reluctant to add the obvious, which was that as far as he could see, she had no one to confide in.

A tear welled. Just one, sliding down Moira's right cheek. Leif chided himself. "Sorry. I'm sorry. I'm making a botch of this. I wanted to offer support, but now I've only made you feel worse." He looked away. "I'll go."

A harsh, bitter laugh erupted from her, sounding a whole lot like something that might have come from her vulture. "I'm the rude one. You extended yourself, and I'm standing here like a critical bitch, hunting for something I can glom onto to push you away."

He angled his head to one side. "Why? Do you dislike me that much?"

Breath hissed from between her teeth, and she shook her head. "It's not you. I push everyone away." Moira stood back and gestured him inside. "I understand if you'd prefer to leave, but I don't want to have this conversation in the middle of the corridor, either." She waited, not looking at him.

Leif scanned her with magic, trying to be subtle. He didn't want to make things worse. What he found surprised him. Pride. Humiliation. Resignation. Self-loathing. He'd known she was competent and smug, but he'd never have guessed at the negativity running beneath it.

He stepped through the door, pulling it closed behind him.

Moira retreated to a crumpled duvet, the spot she'd probably been sitting on when he interrupted her descent into misery. He glanced around the room, wondering where to settle. It didn't seem prudent to stand; that made it look as if he were anxious to get this over with and leave. But he couldn't sit too close, either. He settled for turning the cabin's desk chair toward her and sinking into it. He waited, giving her time and space to proceed at her own pace.

She studied hands she'd clasped together in her lap. "Sorry. I'm not usually this tightly strung."

"I didn't stop by for an apology." He tried to catch her gaze, hoping she'd take it as an invitation to talk about what was troubling her.

"I'm not sure where to begin." She raked curved fingers through her black hair, tugging the curly strands into a rough bun behind her neck.

"How about if you don't worry about making sense and trust I'll be able to sort through this?"

She glanced up, regarding him speculatively. "You sound like an alpha."

"Oh, and how's that?"

Moira shrugged. "Wise. Kind. Even-handed. Supportive. Not that I have any firsthand experience with alphas, but it's how I've always imagined one would be."

He nodded her way. "Yes. I try to be all those things. Sometimes I succeed better than others, but sometimes I fail monumentally."

"Oh honey, we all do." Moira clapped a hand over her mouth. "I am sorry. That was way too familiar. Damn it. From one extreme to the other."

Leif waited. Not prodding, but hoping if he projected a quiet acceptance, she'd say enough to clarify which extremes she meant.

"On top of everything, I'm not making a whole lot of sense. Christ! I'm a sorry mess."

He longed to move to her side, gather her into his arms, and cradle her head against his chest. She was suffering, and he wanted to spare her, but the world didn't work like that. Moira had to find her own way through whatever was tormenting her.

Moments slid by. Misery sheeted from her in palpable waves; he battled feeling helpless. Maybe this had been a bad idea since both of them were tiptoeing around whatever the real issues were.

"I can't help much if I don't know more," he said at last. "Was it Eiocha's refusal to even consider assisting us that's bothering you?"

"Yeah. That was the beginning." Moira clacked her teeth together. "My bondmate was as furious as I've ever seen it, which didn't help matters since our moods overlap."

"My dolphin wasn't any too fond of Eiocha's highhandedness, either," Leif cut in, hoping she'd feel vindicated that her vulture wasn't the only pissed off bond animal.

"Like I said, Eiocha was the lynchpin that got my mind rolling." Moira squinched her eyes shut before opening them and regarding him. Pain swam across her face, distorting its beauty into something harsh.

"Keep going," Leif urged. "Nothing is ever as bad as we imagine it to be."

"This is," she mumbled, "but you're correct. Cutting through a whole lot of fancy words, the bottom line is I'm a lot like her. Watching some of my less savory traits mirrored in her hurt. A lot."

"I'm not seeing any similarities. And before you tell me I'm wrong, I'm not trying to be kind. She's a millennia-old goddess; you're a Shifter. She has infinite magic. You're like the rest of our kinfolk, which means you have to take care how you deploy power, or it runs dry."

"Of course, there are many ways we're different," Moira replied.

"I was homing in on similar personal styles. We've both kept to ourselves. We both push people away if they get too close because we're afraid."

"Of?" Leif leaned closer.

"Of the inevitable pain when they disappoint you. Easier not to get involved in the first place."

She looked so lost and so vulnerable, Leif moved to her side and held out his arms. He gave it fifty-fifty she'd bolt, but he had to try. He couldn't stand by and allow her to suffer.

Moira's eyes sheened with tears, and she stiffened. "Do not feel sorry for me. I don't want your pity."

He lowered one outstretched arm until his hand settled on her shoulder, hoping to convey through touch what he was failing to get across with words. "It's not pity, Moira. I care about you."

"But I'm not a sea Shifter."

"Does that mean I can't care about what happens to you? Where is it written my compassion starts and stops with my pod?" He squeezed her shoulder gently. It would have been simple to prod her with subtle magic, just enough of a push to make her want the comfort of his arms, but he resisted.

She had to come to him on her own—or not at all.

Moira scooted closer, and he scooped her against him, holding her tight and murmuring in his dolphin tongue. That way, she'd never know he was saying he loved her, that he'd move oceans to protect her from everything wicked in this world and others.

Slowly, tentatively, she threaded her arms around him, but she held herself stiffly, as if allowing herself to accept comfort was foreign. From what she'd revealed about herself, it probably was. He switched to Gaelic. "It will be all right, Moira. Nothing is ever quite so awful in the light of day."

She leaned into him, finally relaxing into his embrace. "I was horrible those first few months in Ushuaia. Furious. Frightened. Blaming."

He smoothed her hair and pulled her head against his chest with one hand. "It's human nature to look for a scapegoat."

"I'm scarcely human, and I understood the other women would never have gone on that trip to Ushuaia if they'd had any inkling what was about to happen. Even though my rational mind knew that, it took a long time to get past being angry. I wasn't really one of them to start with. They'd all put down roots in Wyoming, where I was just another Shifter passing through."

"Wasn't Zoe there on some kind of limited teaching assignment?"

Moira nodded. "But she'd been there for months, bonded with the others..."

"Whereas you were used to working alone." At her nod against his chest, he went on, "Nothing wrong with that. We all find our own niche. The way we can be most effective."

She tightened her hold where her hands crisscrossed his back. "Thanks, but I'm not proud of how I was. I could have done better, and I tried to make up for my piss-poor showing by doing more than my share of work supporting the humans with magic to keep crops growing."

Leif didn't doubt it for a moment. "You've always been a hard worker."

She snorted. "Blessing and curse. I've filled in with work when I should have paid more attention to the people around me. Who they were. What motivated them."

"You can't go backward."

"What if moving forward is nearly as difficult?" She tilted her head enough to meet his gaze.

"You know the answer. You keep going because you have to."

"Of course. Wanting to turn the clock back ten years to a time when I picked my challenges, rather than having them stuffed down my throat, is nothing but a waste of energy. It diverts me from where I should be paying attention."

"Those arguments between our heads and our hearts are never easy."

"That's not the worst of it." Her mouth twisted into a bitter moue. "No matter how they come out, part of me loses. Speaking of losing, what was the bloodsucking horror Lynda referred to?"

Her question wrenched him back to the oddness he'd faced. "I don't know. Something lured us into one of the strangest places I've ever been. The dirt was deadly. It rose around me and dug into my body, feeding from me."

Moira disentangled herself from his embrace. The spot she'd been curved against him felt cold and empty, and it was hard not to draw her back into his arms. "You mean like a plant wrapping shoots around you?"

"More or less," he replied. "If the plant then poked those shoots through your skin."

A shudder tracked from her shoulders downward. "That's wicked, but these weren't plants."

"No." He inhaled raggedly. "When I located Lewis and Lynda—and I had to use magic to find them—they were already buried."

"As in not visible?"

"Exactly. They were nothing but long, raised lumps of sand. I tripped over Lewis before I understood the hump was a shallow grave. I dug like a madman, fighting dirt that wanted to shackle me. When I got him uncovered, he had stone shards poking through his flesh. He's damned lucky none of them punctured something vital."

"No. He's lucky he had you."

Leif shrugged, pleased by the compliment but uncomfortable too. "Regardless. Once I severed the bits of stone holding him in place, both of us went to work freeing Lynda. Even after we were upright, though, we had to keep moving. If we stood still, the sand drilled into our feet."

"Did you have to employ magic to break the stone shackles?"

He nodded. "Why? Do you know what manner of being captured us?"

"The only stone monsters I know about are golems, and they always report to a master." She shuddered again. "Jesus, but that's creepy and horrible. Lost forever in a magical net while some fell creature grows strong draining your blood. It's like Vampires raised to the tenth power."

It had been eerie, which was why he'd avoided thinking about it. "All of us will have to be exceptionally cautious. Lewis knew he'd made a mistake as soon as he swam through the gateway—"

"What gateway?"

"Oh that's right. I didn't tell you that part. Precursor to Lewis's misstep was a decision we'd made to swim a grid along the ocean floor hunting for an alternative way to access the ley lines. We'd separated into groups, and I was with Lewis and Lynda. We'd blown through hours, and I was almost ready to order everyone back to the ship when Lewis flashed past, trilling he'd found something.

"It felt wrong to me. Really wrong, but—"

"Sorry to keep interrupting, but what did the thing that snagged Lewis's attention look like?" She regarded him with an earnest expression.

He drew an archway in the air. "Like that. Maybe six feet tall, glowing, inviting. As I drew closer, musical notes began. That was when I became truly wary, but by then Lewis and Lynda were gone. This will sound odd, but I felt certain if I left to alert others in the pod, the gateway would wink out and I'd never find the spot again."

"Not odd at all," she murmured. "It's how magic works. So you swam through. What happened then?"

"Power pummeled me, feeling wrong, but by then I was swimming through a downward twisting tunnel. Not the kind of thing where a dolphin can turn around." Reliving the experience made his stomach clench uncomfortably. "I came out in a large pool and knew I had to shift to find my dolphins since they weren't in the water. Shifting took a long time and hurt like crazy."

"Something was subverting your magic."

"My take on it too," he agreed. "Anyway, we got out of there by teleporting through a spot where many ley lines converged. It led straight to Eiocha's lair."

Moira's eyes widened. "Aw shit."

"What?" Leif hunted for what she was reacting to.

"Do you suppose the golems were her creations? That they answered to her?"

He started to reply it wasn't possible, but the words died in his throat. "I have no idea. I don't know enough about the horse goddess to extrapolate about her motives."

"Maybe not, but I bet my vulture does. Let me ask it."

12

TOO MANY FEELINGS

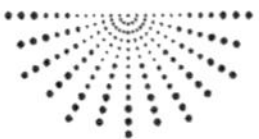

Moira turned her attention inward. *"Have you been listening?"*

"So now you accuse me of spying on you?" the vulture retorted.

"For fuck's sake, get over yourself. Eiocha may have been your friend, but she turned on you. What else is new? The world's not a nice place anymore."

"Vultures don't do nice," her bondmate informed her loftily, sounding surly.

Moira inhaled sharply and blew it out. Having Leif right next to her was doing odd things to her body and addling her brain. Being in his arms had been ambrosial, but she hadn't trusted herself not to push him onto his back and plaster her mouth over his. He'd stopped by to check on her, not be ambushed by a sex-starved woman.

She tried a different tactic with her bondmate. *"Do you have any idea what manner of being wraps stone tentacles around you and drinks your blood?"*

"I've been thinking about that," the vulture replied, proving it had indeed been paying close attention to her conversation with Leif. *"It*

133

has to be some iteration of golem, but I can't envision Eiocha as a golem-mistress."

"Why not?" Moira pressed, mining for details.

"Because they require an ongoing infusion of power, and Eiocha always had a short attention span."

"What happens when you forget about them?"

The vulture squawked. *"They wither to dust. That was a stupid question."*

"No questions are stupid when I'm trying to get my mind around something. So far, you haven't come up with much. From what I saw of Eiocha, if an entire golem army died, she'd simply make another and never look back."

"She felt different than my memories," the vulture muttered.

"What's your bondmate's take?" Leif asked. "I feel the magic from you two talking but didn't want to be rude and listen in uninvited."

"May we include Leif?" Moira asked.

"Why not invite his dolphin too?" The vulture's tone was unreadable, but something lay behind it.

"Sure," Moira said. *"Go ahead. I have no way of communicating with it."*

"What's going on?" Leif placed a hand over hers.

Moira turned her attention his way. "I'm not certain. When I asked about you, my bondmate said to include your dolphin."

"Makes sense. They relate to one another differently than they relate to us."

"If that's true, why would your bondmate require an invitation?"

"The animals have a complicated social structure—one I've never fully understood—but we face bigger problems. I'd already alerted my bondmate, so we're all present."

A squawk that could mean anything reverberated through her breastbone. Maybe the dolphin would mitigate the vulture's foul mood. Or make it worse. She had no idea how one animal would play off the other. It occurred to her the storm buffeting the boat was gone. Maybe it had been part of the enchantment luring Lewis…

She turned toward Leif. "A whole lot of loose ends here. One you're not aware of is a squall blew through, but it didn't match up with any of the instruments on the bridge, so it had to be a magical storm. That was one of the reasons I took a stand about going after you and your pod. I was concerned there was a relationship between the storm and us not being able to contact any of you."

"Thanks for caring." He smiled crookedly, and her heart beat faster. "Did your bondmate have an opinion about the stone shackles?"

"Not beyond them being an iteration of golems, but she ruled out Eiocha as their mistress."

"Why?"

Moira shook her head. "Not much of a reason, really. Something about the stones requiring too much attention."

Leif turned his hands palms up. "Not buying it. If they withered for lack of attention, she'd make more. She didn't strike me as being overly attached to anything." He tilted his head. "Our bondmates are deep in a discussion."

Moira focused inward but couldn't locate her vulture. "That's odd. How come you can sense them, and I can't?"

"Because my bondmate rarely closes the channel between us. I never figured out if it's sloth on its part, or if it finally trusts me after five hundred years."

She smothered a snort. "Vultures never trust anyone. It's not in their natures."

"Good you don't take it personally when your bird carves out a private spot."

"There's a saying you end up with the bond animal that's a perfect fit for you. I never wanted to scratch the surface of that expression too closely. I'm prickly and hard-headed and a loner. Might be why the vulture showed up in my dreams. And why I never told it to go away."

He squeezed her hand. "Dolphins are only cute and endearing on television shows like *Flipper*. In the ocean, they kill intruders and ask questions later. Vultures are intensely loyal. They'll do damn near anything to protect their family flocks. You're being unreasonably hard on yourself."

"Viewing the world through an accurate lens isn't a bad thing."

"No, it's not," he agreed. "So long as your execution is balanced. Do you ever rattle off a list of pleasing traits? Or do you stop with ones designed to drive a wedge between you and everyone else?"

Heat rose from her chest over the top of her head. He had her number. She wore her faults proudly, like a banner proclaiming *this is how I am, take me or leave me.*

She reached inward, hunting for her bondmate, but the vulture wasn't there. "Our animals are still talking, huh?"

Leif tilted his head. "Mmph. Now mine is gone too. They must have retreated to their borderworld."

"Any idea why?"

"The main one that comes to mind is they couldn't solve the problem and are conferring with some of the older animals."

"We should join the others." Moira felt mildly guilty for taking any time for herself.

"We should," he agreed. "Are you feeling more composed?"

A smile started in her heart before it turned the corners of her mouth upward. "Very much so. Thank you. I'm surprised you knocked at all. You must have heard me crying with your dolphin's ears."

"I did, and I almost left. Not because I didn't want to offer what support I could but because I didn't wish to embarrass you or be intrusive."

He laced his fingers with hers. When she met his blue eyes, twin fires burned in their depths. Was she reading the signals right? Taking a chance, she leaned closer, hoping for a kiss.

He smoothed his fingertips over her mouth. "You have the most beautiful lips." His words were low and lined with unmistakable longing.

Moira tilted her head and closed her mouth over his, the kiss light, experimental. He groaned and captured the back of her head with his hand, holding her in place as he returned her kiss.

No going back now. She'd ached to kiss him for weeks, and she savored the feel of his lips against hers, biting, sucking, teasing. Following little nips with more kisses to heal the sting. He licked the seam between her lips, and she opened her mouth to his tongue, sparring with it. When he withdrew, she followed his tongue with hers and explored the inside of his mouth. Something about tongue-kissing him felt raw, intimate. She could tell by the way he touched her—tentative and intense wrapped up together—how important the interaction was to him. Unlike most men, he didn't take physical contact lightly, and the perception pleased her. She ended up sitting in his lap, arms wrapped around his neck and breasts pressed into his chest. Her nipples pebbled, and her breath hitched with wanting him.

His cock swelled where it pressed into her side. She longed to reach between them and grasp the length of that hot hardness, but he was from a much earlier era, one where women weren't so bold. She didn't want him to view her as a slut.

Leif lifted his mouth from hers. The fires in his eyes had grown into a raging inferno, and he cooed to her in his language, followed by, "Thank you for that. You kiss like an angel."

A vigorous squawk announced her vulture was back. When had it returned? Reluctantly, she turned her attention inward waiting to hear her bondmate's assessment of Eiocha and stone shackles and whatever else the bird had come up with.

"Back to the real world and all its problems," Leif murmured. "I suppose I should be grateful we stole even a scant handful of minutes to be together, but I would have liked more."

His words cheered her. They held an old-fashioned note that

hearkened back to when the world was a simpler place and survival was measured in centuries not weeks. "I would have too," she said.

"According to my dolphin, the consensus seems to be the Cataclysm altered the ease with which the ley lines hold and transmit magic." Leif narrowed his eyes into a thoughtful expression. "Because of how tightly bound Eiocha is to the lines, the Cataclysm changed her too."

Moira thought back to her bondmate's assessment about Eiocha not matching up with its memories of her.

"Your mind is busy," Leif observed.

Moira blew out a tense breath. "I get the part about the Cataclysm changing Eiocha. Hell, it changed all of us, and not exactly for the better, but the lines had power to spare when she booted us out of her lair."

"My read on things," the vulture shrilled, *"is something is feeding wickedness into the lines, has been for some time now. Because of her connection to the lines, Eiocha has been absorbing the wrongness a little bit at a time."*

"What about the sand that turned into stone and did its level best to kill me?" Leif asked.

"We couldn't figure that out," the vulture replied. *"Not with any level of certainty."*

"My dolphin claims it's more likely the work of demons loosed through the fissure that are doing everything in their power to make sure we never reach northern waters."

That explanation resonated for Moira and chilled her to the marrow of her bones. Tessa had felt darkness targeting her and rebuffed it. About the same time, they'd sailed into an unnatural storm, and the sea Shifters' alpha was threatened. Another unsettling thought surfaced.

"When we were trying to reach you and your pod, I understand why you and Lewis and Lynda didn't answer, but what about the others?" Moira asked.

"I'm guessing they either didn't hear you or chose not to respond because it might mean Viktor would order them back to the boat." Leif thinned his mouth into a tight line. "Not that they'd have abandoned their search for me, but it would have put them in an awkward position of refusing a direct order from a Shifter in an authority position."

"I'm not concerned if they chose not to answer." Moira spoke slowly. "What worries me is if they never heard us calling. We have to come up with a foolproof way to communicate when we're not all in the same location."

"Give me a moment. I'll find out." Magic flared around Leif as he employed telepathy. He drew his brows together.

Moira waited. She should be beyond reacting to new manifestations of evil, but she wasn't, and she licked at dry lips.

The shining nimbus around Leif faded, and he steepled his fingers together. "That's curious. The whales heard; the dolphins didn't."

"Is your magic species-specific?"

"Not the way you mean. I'm wondering if the whale we left in northern waters has been working behind the scenes to strengthen his kinfolks' sensitivity to magical manifestations." Leif stood and extended his hands, drawing her upright.

She held onto him, savoring the heat from his hands and not wanting to ever let go, but she recognized it for a diversion. Easier to get lost in desire than give in to her trepidation about what form of wickedness would strike next. She offered him a crooked smile. "I bet everyone is on the bridge—except us."

"You'd be correct." He held her against him for one delicious moment before letting go. "See you up there." He turned and slipped out the door, letting it close behind him.

Moira stood over the sink and rinsed her face to erase the last traces of her tears. She wanted to hide the evidence of her meltdown. No one would ever accuse her of being the brittle link that let them all down.

The vulture screeched, the sound blasting through her mouth and filling the cabin.

"What now?" Moira didn't bother with telepathy.

"He kissed you. It's a contract. Why didn't he wait and accompany you to meet the others?" the vulture demanded.

Moira shut eyes that still felt hot and gritty. "It was only a kiss," she said and opened them to stare at her cabin.

"There's no such thing. Not for those like him." The vulture lowered its voice from a shriek to something slightly less shrill. *"His dolphin is plenty worried. He's supposed to mate with another sea Shifter, but none are left who don't share his bloodlines."*

The meaning in her bondmate's words sank in. "You and Leif's dolphin discussed him and me."

"Of course. Why wouldn't we. Choosing to mate is a momentous—"

"Stop right there," Moira growled. She'd never tried to bend her bondmate to her will—much less stand up to it—and had no idea if it were even possible. "I have no expectations. I like him, sure, but it was just a kiss."

She quieted her mind, burying her longing for Leif deep, and went on the offensive. "I've taken lovers before. You never opened your beak about any of them."

"None of them were Shifters. I knew you'd never consider joining your life with theirs."

"What if I had?" Moira persisted. Her gambit was working. The vulture's attention had been diverted from her and Leif to her and the other men who'd shared her bed.

"I'd have severed our bond."

Dismay beat a tattoo through Moira. Before she could demand how the vulture could even consider such a Draconian move, the place her bondmate lived within her was suddenly empty.

"Coward!" Moira shook her fist at the air. "Drop a bombshell like that and hightail it out of here." She fully expected the bird to dive back into her head, but it didn't.

She dried her face and found fresher clothes. If choosing the wrong mate was all it took for her vulture to abandon her, maybe she'd picked badly when she was young. Other Shifters made stupid mistakes, but she'd never heard of their bond animals leaving in a huff.

Ready to go, she shook off the desolation that had settled over her like a shroud. Talk was cheap. In her heart of hearts, she didn't believe her bondmate would desert her. A disquieting thought lodged in her brain; once there, it refused to leave. If being old and magical meant you were more susceptible to the wickedness permeating Earth, maybe her vulture wasn't immune.

Despite its threats to abandon her, a fierce protectiveness filled Moira. She'd do whatever she needed to ensure her savage, sharp-tongued bondmate didn't succumb to evil.

Moira hurried up three flights of risers to the bridge. Several sets of worried eyes settled on her, and she nodded pleasantly. "Sorry. I hope you weren't waiting on me. Don't worry about catching me up. I'll do that myself from context."

"The storm bought us a couple of days," Aura informed her.

"You must mean set us back," Moira said.

"No. I just went through my calculations a third time." Juan rolled his green eyes. "Maybe *Arkady* got caught up in a time warp, but we're only about six days from Wrangel Island. It's welcome news, but I expect the weather to do nothing but worsen the farther north we travel."

"The whale that got sucked through that portal with Ketha is only a few hours away." Leif sounded jubilant, as well he might at the prospect of a reunion with the whale who'd served as seer for the sea Shifters.

"Six days isn't very long," Viktor said in a tone so devoid of inflection Moira wondered what was on his mind.

"So are we going to sail full steam ahead into whatever trap the demons have laid to snare us?" a whale boomed.

"They've had plenty of time to come up with something to trip us up," Lynda agreed.

"We need a plan," Leif broke in before more of his pod weighed in with gloom and doom predictions. "Except it's tough to forge a battle strategy against something we've only guessed at."

"I could teleport," Lewis said. "Have a little walkabout and report back."

"No," one of the whales thundered. "If anyone does that, it should be one of us."

"It's actually a decent idea," Viktor said. "It would make sense for one of us to go along."

"If by one of us, you mean land Shifters, your ability to teleport isn't up to snuff," Leif said flatly. "You burn through too much magic, and you'd alert whoever's waiting for us. Might mean we wouldn't get back."

"I have a decent handle on teleporting." Moira took a step forward and then kicked herself. Just because she'd managed a couple of clumsy teleport spells didn't mean she had any subtlety.

Karin angled a pointed glance her way. "Not the best idea I've heard."

"Okay. You come up with something better," Moira met Karin's keen copper eyes. After her vulture's abrupt announcement, she wasn't in the mood for being told no.

"Enough, you two." Ketha's tone was sharp. "The thing that pulled us through our standoff against the Cataclysm was sticking with our assigned roles. Granted, we had a plan then." She dragged her grimoire out from beneath her seat. "The book helped us last time, and I still believe in its ability. Who will work with me to coax answers from it?"

Words wanted out, but Moira sat on them. Last time, Ketha hadn't solicited aid from any of them. Her book had spit out what they needed without any additional prodding. Times had changed, and a barrier stood between them and easy access to magical accoutrements—like the book—that had provided support before.

A raucous squawk rattled from her before she could squelch it. "Sorry. My vulture is feeling frisky today."

Moira turned away, striding to the far side of the bridge, determined to regain the upper hand. *"You came back, huh?"*

"Never mind your hurt feelings..." The vulture rattled off a series of squeals and honks while conversation rose and fell behind her. When she was certain she'd picked up the gist of her bird's insights, she flipped back to face everyone and stepped into their midst.

"Apologies for interrupting, but hear me out. I don't have a clue where my bondmate comes up with its information, but I've never known it to be wrong. The Shifter spell that launched the Cataclysm provided a convenient smokescreen. Wickedness used it as a steppingstone to gain a significant toehold on Earth, but even with most magic-wielders trapped much as we were in Ushuaia, evil didn't fully take over. If we can figure out why, determine what barriers have thwarted demons and their ilk, we'll have what we need to win."

"That's a damned esoteric message," Viktor grumbled.

"Magic is esoteric by nature," Ketha replied, "but I'd like more direction locating whoever's been standing on the sidelines sabotaging evil. Maybe they'd help us."

"Any information would help at this point." Karin nodded tersely.

"Aye, at least it provides a starting point," Zoe muttered.

"Back to teasing out a battle strategy from my grimoire." Ketha tapped its cracked cover with an index finger. "I could still use a couple of volunteers."

Magic crashed through the bridge, bright and smelling of the sea. The whale who'd been dragged to a borderworld with Ketha tumbled through a split in the ether and thence to his feet. Water pooled from his long, straw-colored hair, but his eyes flashed merrily.

He bowed in Leif's direction. "Greetings, Alpha."

"Greetings, my friend. It's good to see you and sooner than I expected."

"I hold knowledge to add to our effort. What initially appeared to be an ill wind contained elemental data."

"You're talking in riddles." Viktor eyed the whale.

"If whatever dragged Ketha and me through that gateway knew they'd handed us the key to their destruction, they'd have left us alone." The whale grinned.

Someone tossed him a towel.

Moira wanted to drag the information out of him, but that was Leif's job. Why wasn't he urging his Shifter to talk and talk fast? Instead, Leif had crossed to where the whale stood and clasped hands with him. Relief to see the whale streamed from him, so stark it was impossible not to share his joy.

The edgy, antsy annoyance that was her usual go-to place ebbed. She was happy for Leif. He was right to take advantage of every scrap of joy that came his way. Who knew how many more scraps of anything they'd have? She edged closer to Ketha and bent low, speaking near her ear. "If you need help, anything at all, let me know."

"Thank you. I appreciate it."

"Don't just appreciate it. Use me. I'm not attached like you and Aura and Zoe and Karin. I'm willing to take chances."

Ketha turned her golden eyes on Moira. "We all have value, and it has nothing to do with whether we're mated or not. Don't you ever forget it."

The whale tossed the soaked towel aside and said, "Listen up."

Moira straightened and faced him, anxious to hear what he had to say. Even if it was a half-finished picture, they could add it to all their other incomplete snapshots and hopefully weave the mess into a whole that made sense. That would shape their actions over the short span of days between now and their last battle.

The words *last battle* held an ominous note, but they also promised closure. No matter what happened, she'd be done with endless looking over her shoulder, with bottomless catastrophe chasing. Of course, she might also be dead, but the fear she'd always harbored about the way of her ending dropped away. Living the way she had since the Cataclysm hit was no life at all.

Hiding in shadows wasn't her style. If she went down, she'd go down hissing spitting, cawing, fighting back. Maybe with Leif by her side, but she wasn't going to worry about it. Like she'd told her bondmate, they'd shared a kiss, nothing more.

Now, if I can just get myself to believe that, I'll be golden.

13

STRATEGIES

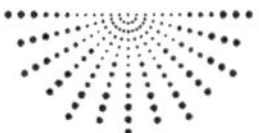

*L*eif felt dragged in incompatible directions, but his role as alpha to his people had to come first. He'd wanted to walk upstairs with Moira, but if he'd entered the bridge with her by his side, his people would have assumed he was claiming her as his mate. The alpha's mate was always second-in-command, had been from the beginnings of time. Placing a non-sea Shifter in that role wouldn't go over well. He was fairly certain his people would wish him well in terms of finding a mate, but no one would accept Moira's word as his.

No. They'd treat her more like a consort or concubine than a mate, which would hurt her feelings. The deeper he dug, the more problems cropped up. He was falling in love with her. It was about the only part he was clear on. How their attraction would play out, where it would lead, remained cloaked in mystery.

Maybe it was better to walk away; certainly, walking away was the prudent path. Sadness welled. How could he forget that amazing, delicious kiss? Forget how she'd felt in his arms? No, forgetting wasn't possible. The best he could hope for was setting his emotions aside. It would be better for everyone. Each path with her as his mate posed new problems, not the least of which was how

147

they'd handle children. Sea Shifter babies were born in the sea with the entire pod in attendance.

I have to stop this right here. Before I get so lost in wanting her I miss something critical. Something that might avert disaster for my pod.

He constructed a metaphorical vault and swept his confused places inside, sealing them over with magic. He'd receive enough speculative glances once he joined the others. Best to give nothing away. As if they didn't face enough complications, ones that made him wonder what their small band would look like a fortnight hence. At the end of everything, once they were done on Wrangel Island, he'd take stock of what was left. Assuming he was still alive.

Nothing was certain. Not his survival, nor Moira's.

Whichever spell they summoned to seal the fissure might damage Earth or the oceans. They could end up as trapped on Wrangel Island as the Shifters had been in Ushuaia. Minus the Vampire problem.

Maybe. For all he knew, Wrangel Island was crawling with Vamps.

As long as he was lost in what-ifs, a line out of Tolkien cropped up. Something about Frodo saving Middle Earth, but not for him as he faded into the Gray Lands along with the Elves. Tolkien had known about magical beings. He'd been one of the few humans who saw their auras…

Oh for pity fucking sakes. Thank all the gods no one's close enough to read my mind. We need something real, not the ramblings of a long-dead novelist.

Leif pasted a neutral expression on his face and trotted onto the bridge. Everyone nodded his way, but no one asked where he'd been. In a flash of insight, he understood his pod didn't want to address the issue of their alpha pairing off with anyone other than another sea Shifter, either. Sometimes the best strategy for a problem you couldn't solve was to ignore it and keep moving forward. He'd taught them that.

Multiple conversations flowed around him, but everyone was

hunting for a way to address what lay in wait on Wrangel Island. He was aware of Moira's unique energy when she entered the bridge about ten minutes after him. The urge to go to her and clasp her hands was overpowering, but he rode herd on it.

He listened while Ketha urged a consultation with her magic book and Moira's vulture offered decent advice. The thing that diverted his attention away from Moira was when his missing whale showed up sooner than he'd anticipated, and with what might be promising news.

He hurried to the whale and gripped his arms, Viking style. Because they were so few and he'd experienced each death in his pod as a personal failure, he valued those who were left—probably more than he should. For a fleeting moment, he wondered how he'd react to still more deaths and stiffened his spine. The odds of all of them making it through what lay ahead were close to zero.

He had to face facts, accept them, and be the best leader possible.

The whale let go; Leif took a few steps back, offering space for his story to emerge. If they'd been in the sea, the pod would have gathered in a circle, and whale song would have spread through the water to whale Shifters swimming hundreds of miles away.

Except every single whale Shifter was here in this room.

Leif rebuked himself. Now was a time for happiness, not sorrow. His pod was whole again. Maybe not forever, but for now. He snuck a glance at Moira. She'd been hunkered next to Ketha, but she straightened. Encouragement spilled from her as she waited for the whale to begin.

Aura had a clipboard balanced on her lap, the slip of notebook paper divided into columns. Maybe she'd find a prophecy to match up with the whale's recitation. Leif hoped so. He was hungry for any good omens that came their way.

"Listen up," the whale intoned and waited while side conversations died away. "Ketha and I ended up on a borderworld. I suspect Poseidon was behind our abduction, but we'll never know for sure. We were fortunate to arrive before our abductor, but we felt him closing fast and had to make some swift decisions. Ketha left immediately in wolf form for the animals' world. I activated a teleport spell with no idea where I'd come out."

The whale extended a hand, and Boris gave him a tumbler full of water. "Thanks." He drank noisily, not bothering to mop up water running down his chin.

"I ended up swimming among icebergs. I knew I was on Earth because of the atmosphere and the specific salinity of the ocean. The thing I wasn't certain of was where, so I poked around hunting for something familiar. Didn't take long before I found the ruins of Anadyr, a small town in northeastern Siberia. So long as I was close to Wrangel Island, I did a small reconnaissance."

"You took quite a chance," Leif murmured.

"Not really. We may be shy of whale Shifters, but I found a pod of Orcas and swam along with them." A smile softened the harsh planes of the whale's broad face. "They were delighted to see me. All species are frightened of dying out, and the presence of an elder whale gave them hope they weren't the only ones left."

"How'd they survive the Cataclysm?" Lewis asked.

"They were young when it hit, and they'd been playing in a protected cove well north of the Arctic Circle. For whatever reason, the water there never developed the poisonous aspect it did elsewhere, so they had food, but they couldn't swim beyond a certain perimeter. Once the barrier lifted, they didn't leave right away."

"Probably wondered if it was a trap," Lynda murmured.

"They said as much." The whale nodded her way.

"The Cataclysm was horrible to live through," Moira spoke up, "but it did much of its damage in subtle ways by making us wonder if we were the only ones left."

"Indeed," Karin said. "Many a day we talked about friends and family back in Wyoming, wondering what had become of them. In truth, we still have no idea."

"Exactly," the whale agreed. "Using the Orcas as cover, I swam quite close to our objective. There is a gap in the ether, but it's not pumping out demonkind as I feared it would be. I watched for several days. During that time, a handful of goblins and sprites emerged, but they're more annoying than dangerous."

He stopped to take another drink. "The hole is guarded. The keeper appears weak and harmless, although I'm certain it's a disguise, and it's unlikely the creature is human. Poseidon showed up once. Amphitrite twice. Not together, mind you. The man—or whatever he is—spoke with them. Here's where things get interesting, though. My mythology could be stronger, but other entities I'm almost certain were gods also materialized. On those occasions, the gatekeeper vanished, as did the gap. The place appeared to be one more stretch of Arctic beach, indistinguishable from the rest."

"Surely some magical residue remained," Karin said.

"My thought as well," the whale said, "yet when I tested with my own magic, I couldn't discern a thing." He shrugged. "My take on this is some of the gods remain. I have no idea if they're still sorted into pantheons, or if they gave up on that nonsense and are simply themselves."

"Could you explain what you just said?" Boris got to his feet.

The whale nodded. "As an example, Diana, Artemis, and Arianrhod are one and the same. Virgin huntresses who control the moon and tides. One is from the Roman pantheon, one the Greek, and the other Celtic. Three names. One goddess. They allowed the split to encourage more people to worship them."

"Fascinating. Thanks." Boris sat back down.

"Anyway," the whale went on, "my guess is the gods got wind of a weak place in the ether, one allowing demons access to Earth. They aren't overly worried—since it's not the way of gods to concern themselves with what they view as mortals' affairs—but they are checking."

"If the creature manning the fissure were strong enough, it

wouldn't have to vanish when Zeus or whoever drops by," Leif muttered.

"That's one interpretation," Ketha said. "Another is whatever we face is maintaining a low profile so it's at full strength when we arrive. It is a piece of welcome news some of the gods still remain."

"Hopefully, they're not as faithless as Poseidon and Amphitrite," Leif muttered.

"Or Eiocha," Moira cut in.

"How often did the ones you thought were gods stop in?" Viktor asked.

"Other than Poseidon and Amphitrite, only twice while I was there, so we can't count on them showing up when we need them." He scanned the room with his wise, ancient eyes. "I was hoping some of you would know how to communicate with whomever remains of the deities."

"You brought up an important point about them not paying much attention to humankind," Moira said.

"But we're not human," the whale protested.

"To them, we are," Karin said.

"It is how things used to be, but their attitudes may have changed since the Cataclysm," Ketha spoke up.

"'Tis unfortunate each topic brings naught but more unknowns," Zoe muttered, her brogue thicker than usual.

Leif offered her points for astute observation and hunted for a unifying concept that would weave the disparate threads of their conversation into something useful. There had to be one if he dug deep enough.

"It seems apparent our lieges have gone separate ways," the whale went on. "There should be a way to deepen that divide and turn them against each other."

"Is there any chance at all someone could have detected your presence and underplayed the fissure's strength?" Leif asked.

"I don't believe so. Otherwise why would Poseidon and Amphitrite have shown up separately? And why would the gatekeeper only disappear when someone I didn't recognize showed up?"

"Did you see any dolphins?" Leif asked.

"I did. And sharks. And quite an array of smaller fish. The ocean is recovering faster in the Arctic than around Antarctica. Or maybe things have improved in southern waters over the months since we've been gone."

"What are you thinking?" Viktor asked.

Leif exchanged a pointed look with *Arkady's* captain. "The ship is a dead giveaway. We need a way to approach Wrangel Island at full strength without the boat. It's easy for us. We'll just take to our sea forms. Sounds as if we'll fit right in."

"I can fly," Moira said.

"As can I," Viktor tossed in.

"It's a big island," Juan said. "I wonder what the back half looks like. The side opposite to the fissure."

"How do you suppose it looks this time of year?" Viktor asked. "Probably blanketed in pack ice."

"I have an idea." Aura looked up from where she'd been writing on her clipboard. "It involves the faeries. At one point, they said they were willing to help."

Understanding crashed over Leif. "You want them to build a channel, like they did for Ceridwen from Malaita to that borderworld."

"Yes, but this would be easier since the passageway would be entirely on Earth, from a spot on the Siberian mainland to the island. It fits in with a prophecy too, one where the faeries crawl out from beneath their hills and barrows and break free from their dependence on the Fae."

"Possibly a win all around. It could work." Karin sounded excited, which wasn't like her.

"How can we reach them?" Daide asked. He smiled. "I remember the little green faery. She claimed me for hers until I tried to teach her arithmetic. After that, she decided I was too much trouble."

"No. She decided you lived too far away to contemplate. She did appear mollified when I reassured her I'd take care of you for both of us." Karin smiled fondly in Daide's direction.

"Locating the small folk shouldn't be difficult," Leif said, relieved to have a project that was doable, an action plan that might yield results. "I'll teleport to the British Isles. If I bounce off a borderworld, I can be there fast."

"Take me," Moira said. "The only way I'll get better at teleporting is if I practice, and this is one trip where I don't see any downside if I'm clumsy or use too much magic."

They were good arguments. Regardless, Leif started to tell her thanks, but no. The words stuck in his throat. He wanted the time with her, particularly since it might be the only time alone they'd ever have. He wasn't nearly as convinced as the whale that the fissure—and its guardian—didn't have some ugly tricks up their sleeves. One of the soundest strategies had always been to appear innocuous—until your target drew close enough to kill. Predators had practiced a variation of that technique forever.

He nodded in Moira's direction. "While we're gone," he told the others, "raise Poseidon. Flatter the hell out of the old bastard. It might be enough to get him back in our court."

"Same with Eiocha," Aura said. "She could be a valuable ally if we approach her on a better day."

Grateful to have the beginnings of a plan falling into place, Leif wove through the crowded room to where Moira stood. "Dress warmly," he told her, "and meet me outside on Deck Three as soon as you can."

"Thanks for giving me a chance." She met his gaze in her forthright way.

"Don't make me sorry." He turned aside to issue a few last-minute instructions to Lewis. He'd been harsh with Moira, but he couldn't risk her seeing too deep into the crazy patchwork of emotions roiling through him. Part of him wanted to lock her in her cabin until the confrontation on Wrangel was over. Another wanted to walk away and never look back. Yet another hoped they'd forge a path together, something new where land and sea Shifters had a future as mates. Sorting through options had never been a problem for him before, but it was now.

"What can I do to help?" Lewis asked.

"Make sure Poseidon knows his consort offered herself to me—and that I was horrified and refused. It's the truth, and he'll figure that out quick enough once he hears it. If he doesn't know already."

"I'm not at all sure I can raise him, but I'll try. And after that?" Breath whistled through Lewis's teeth. "I do not like him, but I can't let it show."

Leif dropped a hand onto the other dolphin's shoulder. "The reason you don't like him is you believe he forsook us."

"He did. It's not some errant fantasy."

"The Cataclysm made us all a little crazy. Listening to thousands of whales singing their pain and death must have cut deep. Try to join with his grief. His sense of loss."

"Got it. I'll do my best."

"I know you will." Leif squeezed his shoulder and let go.

Lewis leaned closer. "Be careful. Who knows what's lying in wait in the U.K."

"I'll be fine. It's like going home for me. I'll return before you've even had a chance to miss me, but hopefully not before you've had a go at Poseidon." Leif sprinted out of the bridge, glad to be moving. They'd talked long enough.

He stopped by the cabin he'd selected when he began spending more time on the ship and added a warmer jacket and over-pants. The trip would be chilly, but if he didn't use a borderworld to speed things along, they'd be gone longer.

He sketched out a few equations, checking his calculations. They were sound. Nothing left but to meet Moira. If she wasn't there, it would give him the best excuse possible to leave without her. He'd never promised to wait. The push-pull of wanting her versus suspecting his attraction was a minefield waiting to explode left him with a queasy, uncomfortable sensation.

Like he was dabbling in something forbidden.

I am, unless the rules change.

He left his cabin and set a quick pace for the nearest door. Moira stood hunched into a parka, facing away from him. He crossed the open deck to where she stood. Slowly, she turned and said, "I'm ready."

Concern seared him. She looked terrible. "You don't have to do this."

"Yes, I do." Her expression twisted into something grave and determined. "Running away only makes it harder to face the thing that sent you scrambling with your tail between your legs. The borderworlds give me the heebie-jeebies, but we won't be there long. And I keep telling myself there's no way we'd end up stuck there."

"But there is. It's not a very big chance, but it exists. The energy on other worlds is unpredictable. I've never had it trap me, but I've come damned close." He forced a calm, exactly as if he were training an inexperienced sea Shifter. It was a comfortable spot, one he'd been in many times before, and it allowed him to push his longing for the woman standing next to him aside.

"If you come along, you have to pay close attention and do what I tell you as closely as you can manage it."

"I can do that. Do you have a plan mapped out?"

He nodded. "We'll visualize the Highlands north of Inverness. Open a channel to your magic, and I'll send you an image." At her nod, he went on. "An object can exist in several planes at once, and time is fluid. You have to believe you can be here and other places simultaneously."

"You sound like my physics professor."

The words made him smile. "I never went to anything like a university, but that sounded like a compliment. Half the battle with anything magical is believing you can do something. Once you believe in yourself, everything else falls into place."

She kept her dark eyes glued to his face. He stared back, never wanting to look away. She had beautiful eyes, like luminous, black pools with silvery flecks floating on their surface.

"Your task is to visualize us growing closer to the image I just sent your way of the crumbling castle perched on moorlands. Pay attention to how I weave fire and air together. If things go well, we'll trade roles on the return trip."

She smiled gamely. "If I can learn how to do this so it doesn't drain my magic down to nothing, I'll be delighted."

He closed his hands around her upper arms, holding on. "Remember you can exist in more than one form and more than one place. Through our journey, hang onto your sense of my hands on your arms."

"But our bodies will be different."

"Aye, and also the same. Don't try too hard to make sense of it. Just accept the magic same as you do with power you're familiar with."

"Solid advice. I understand how you ended up alpha."

"Save the compliments for after we get back. Hold your magical center open. I'll join with you, and we'll be on our way."

He drew familiar power and let it sheet through him, feeling his molecules separate yet remain together. It was an odd sensation, one that took getting used to. He was amazed any of the land Shifters could teleport at all, but they did it clumsily, inserting a surfeit of power in spots where delicacy would have served them better.

The ship's familiar deck fell away, replaced by the chill, airless void that flowed between worlds. First stop would be an uninhabited borderworld where they could bounce their energy, reflecting and augmenting it to send them winging for northern Scotland. Because the space-time continuum was flexible, their trip would happen between motes of time. At least in theory, they could return before they'd left, but he'd never had things happen that way.

Moira wasn't fighting him. She'd listened and was doing exactly as he'd instructed. Her trust pleased him beyond words. He longed for her, ached to open his heart to her, but it wouldn't do either of them any good.

Their trajectory slowed as they neared the borderworld. The air thickened, but not by much. "Breathe as deep as you can," he instructed, "and then we'll be off again."

"Fascinating," she managed through shallow, panting breaths.

"What's fascinating?" He bound the borderworld's energy to his bidding and sent them flying back into the void.

"Watching you manipulate magic. Feels like I'm back in Shifter school." Her last words were lost in a rasping cough as breath eluded her.

"Don't talk." He switched to telepathy and tightened his grip on her arms. *"We'll be there soon."*

The enchantment of the British Isles drew him like a beacon. Home. With its rich greenery and nurturing waters. He could show Moira where he'd grown up—

Leif redirected himself fast. They'd locate the faeries, pitch their case, and determine how to proceed. No room for anything beyond planning for the upcoming battle. None at all.

Breathing became easier, the air piquant with smells from perpetually damp greenery. This part had been easy. Now, if they could just get the faeries to cooperate…

"I was thinking the same thing," Moira murmured.

"You've been inside my thoughts?" He winced and brought them down lightly on a muddy moor.

Her face split into a shy smile. "You were joined with my magic. It creates a two-way street." She reached up and placed her hands over where his still rested on her shoulders. Her skin was warm, silky, enticing. "We shared a kiss. It was wonderful, and I care about you, but kisses aren't contracts. We have a job to do. Let's get Aura her supernatural work crew."

Maybe it was a mistake, but he bent forward and kissed her lightly on the forehead before he raised his mind voice and called the faeries.

"Is that all it takes to lure them?" Moira was still smiling.

He shrugged. "We're about to find out." He let go of her, taking his time moving his hands from beneath hers, and upped the ante on his magic.

1 4

THE FAIR FOLK

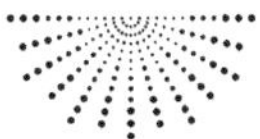

*O*oira fought against happiness that threatened to overrun her. Being with Leif soothed her soul and inflamed her by turns. He exuded a quiet competence that made her believe good would prevail in the end. She could not let her guard down, though. Not for more than a few seconds, anyway. It would be far too easy to lose her focus, and she needed every angstrom of perceptiveness she'd cultivated over the years.

Others among the dozen Shifters she'd been trapped in Ushuaia with had their roots in the U.K. Not her. She'd passed through here a time or two, mostly lecturing on various aspects of her trade. Her long-ago Shifter kin had hailed from more southern climes in the Carpathian Alps where the mountains spanned Central and Eastern Europe. Prime hunting territory for vultures. She'd always realized her family tree was an anomaly. Most Shifter groups sported various animal bondmates, but all her relatives had been bonded with vultures.

Maybe that was another reason she'd never looked back when her bondmate appeared in her dreams.

Her magic was still joined with Leif's. What she'd gleaned from his thoughts was that he was drawn to her and ambivalent as hell. It

161

was why she'd made it clear the kiss they shared didn't mean she expected a lifelong commitment from him. Magic hummed along her nerves, and the air thickened with the scent of honey and flowers. It took her a moment to recognize it as the smell of mead.

Did that mean the faery folk were about to show up? Or would it be the Fae instead with their clouds of fair hair, silver eyes, and robed elegance? Up until her stint on the borderworld linked to Malaita Island, Moira had never laid eyes on faeries or Fae. They'd only existed in the realm of magical history books.

The air took on a glistening, shimmery aspect, and beings popped from a series of gleaming gateways. They all glowed as if lit from within. Moira counted two dozen or more, tiny with quick-beating wings and wands and swirls of hair in pastel shades. She hunted for the green-haired female who'd claimed Daide but didn't see her. Nor did she locate the redheaded male from before.

"Looks like a different group," she murmured. "Hope they've spoken among themselves."

Leif looked askance at her. "There are thousands of them. The odds aren't good, but perhaps some of the Fae will materialize. They number far fewer."

As if his words were prophetic, regal creatures floated through portals that shimmered in the still air. Two, a male and a female, walked purposefully toward where she and Leif stood. Silver hair reached their knees, and each wore a slender golden circlet around their brow. Robes the color of old cream were embroidered with runic markings in a bevy of colors and sashed with pure white.

Leif bowed low. Moira mirrored his actions, wondering if perhaps a curtsey wouldn't be in order—if she could figure out how to execute one without falling over her own feet. Her vulture cooed, sounding more like a morning dove than a raptor. Who the hell were this pair? Not much would bring her bondmate to heel.

Leif straightened but kept his gaze downcast. "Oberon. Titania. You honor my humble presence."

"I remember ye." Oberon's expression didn't let on how he felt about the memory.

"Of course you would. I stole fish from your royal pools." Leif spread his hands in front of him. "Can't we ever move beyond that? I wasn't much more than sixteen. I apologized. I worked for you for a full year to repay my folly."

"Aye," Titania spoke up, her voice reminiscent of silvery chimes. "All has long since been forgiven. The world has turned into a far harsher place than 'twas then."

Oberon pinned his consort with a pointed glance. "The answer is still no. Shifters are not our concern. Our own people require our attention."

A faery flew toward them, his lower lip stuck out in disapproval. "Amithra made a bargain. She is very irritated ye stand in the way of us honoring it." Before the king or queen could chastise him, the faery went on. "Evil that attacks *any* magic will eventually hurt us too. If we do not assist those on the front battle lines, who will be left to fight for us?"

"We will fight for ye," Oberon replied in a stern tone.

The faery shook his head until waves of iridescent hair shrouded his form. "Won't be enough," he intoned. "By then, wickedness will have established an unshakeable toehold."

"It may happen anyway." The chimes shading Titania's words darkened to a minor key, bringing to mind every sad thing in the world.

"Aye." Another faery flew near. "No one to fault but us if we walk away."

"Ye already helped the Shifters," Oberon said in the same tone he might have adopted to humor a child. "Ye made certain the wolf found her human body again." He dusted his long-fingered hands together. "Ye did a good thing. Nothing further is needed."

"We do not agree," the faeries said in unison, sounding like a hive of angry bees.

"Furthermore"—the faery with the iridescent hair flew in a tight circle—"we don't report to ye. Ye only think we do."

Moira looked sidelong at Leif. How would he finesse his way through this? On the surface, it appeared impossible to accept aid from the faeries without angering the king and queen—and probably the remainder of the Fae as well. She wasn't clear if the dark and light halves of Faery even spoke to one another, but that wasn't particularly important at the moment.

She moved closer to him, offering silent support for whatever lead-in he selected.

Leif spread his arms wide; faeries settled along their length, starting with his shoulders. "I am touched you stand willing to help. Let me tell all of you—Oberon and Titania as well—what we have in mind. We will not place you in any danger. All we need is a channel similar to the one your kinfolk built for Ceridwen—"

"That upstart bitch," Oberon snarled.

"Aye, she had no right to any of our people's magic, yet she shanghaied Fae and faeries, using them for her own nefarious purposes," Titania broke in.

"The only reason ye got us back is because of this Shifter and his companions," the faery who appeared to be their spokesperson pointed out, bouncing up and down on Leif's outstretched arm.

"'Tis true!" another faery piped up. "I was there. Both these Shifters were too. They were part of the larger group that freed us."

"Ye should be grateful." Yet a third faery shook a finger beneath Oberon's nose.

"And ye should keep a civil tongue in your head even though I'm not technically your liege," Oberon retorted.

Moira wasn't certain, but the king of Faery seemed to be struggling to maintain a straight face. He was fond of the little folk; that shone through loud and clear.

"We may have assisted a single wolf Shifter," the spokesman said, "yet 'twas a small boon in comparison to what the animals from their borderworld offered us in return. Our freedom."

Moira schooled herself to hang onto a neutral expression. It wasn't easy since she wanted to cheer. Events had developed a decidedly rosy turn, and she considered nudging the flow along with a wee bit of subtle magic. A tempting notion, but not a smart one. If Oberon and Titania felt protective of the faeries—and it appeared they did—best to let this play out on its own.

To reduce the temptation to intervene, she focused on Leif. Damn but he looked even more appealing with a dozen faeries balanced along the lengths of his arms. He'd be an amazing father, with just the right combination of tender and tough to keep his children in line.

His children, she chided herself. *His. Not ours.*

Moira gave herself a firm mental slap. This wasn't a world to add children to, not unless a whole lot changed. What had Leif said about not encouraging his pod to procreate? He'd been afraid the younglings wouldn't survive.

"Ye can't stop us from helping," one of the faeries was saying.

"Ye should be there too," another cut in.

"Aye." A female with violet hair flew close to Titania. "Ye'll never forgive yourself if ye miss the decisive battle. The one that finally ousted evil from Earth and allowed us to take it back for our children and our children's children."

Titania smiled faintly. "That was a pretty big speech."

The faery puffed out her chest. "I'm only small in stature. Nothing wrong with my brain."

Oberon swept a hand downward; a gleaming curtain shading from blue to violet to gold and then silver formed a barrier around him and his queen.

"Could be good," Leif whispered near Moira's ear. "They're conferring."

A whirr of wings caught her attention. Moira glanced up to see the green faery headed their way. "Sorry, sorry," she panted once she'd drawn even with them. "I was clear across the land near the sea on the other side."

Moira held out her arm, and the faery landed lightly, wings beating so fast they were a blur. "My name is Moira. I'm guessing you're Amithra. We never got around to formal introductions last time."

The green-haired faery smiled. "Aye. 'Tis my name indeed." Her expression turned serious. "Names hold power, Shifter. Ye must never speak mine where an enemy might hear."

"I'll take great care that doesn't happen," Moira assured her.

"Did I get here in time?" Amithra asked the faeries, her brow drawn into a mass of worried creases.

"Time isn't relevant. We do not require permission to offer our aid," the male with iridescent hair said.

"Of course we don't." Greenie shot him an annoyed look. "But even ye have to admit it makes things easier."

The faery's wings had slowed. Intricate patterns were inscribed on each, the left different from the right. Moira wanted to stroke them but refrained. For all she knew, wing touching was off limits.

"How long have they been like that?" Greenie angled her head toward the colorful barrier surrounding the king and queen of Faery.

Another faery shrugged. "Not long. Ye know how they are. It could be days afore they surface."

"We don't have days," Leif said.

"Tell us everything," the green faery urged. "Maybe by the time ye're done, they will be too."

"Isn't this something they need to hear as well?" Moira asked.

"Oh they'll hear ye, right enough," another faery piped up.

Moira felt Leif's particular brand of power as he built a ward encompassing them, the faery folk, and Oberon and Titania. She scanned with magic and didn't pick up any fell forces, but it paid to be cautious. Once he was satisfied, he began speaking.

"None of us knows what the next few days will bring. A seer amongst us foretold a portal in the northlands."

"Do ye mean the one allowing bad things access to Earth?" Amithra raised an eyebrow.

Leif nodded. "The same. How is it you know about it?"

"We can feel it," a crimson-haired male faery perched on Leif's wrist said. "It showed up suddenly, out of nowhere, and has been growing."

A sensation like a lock and key finding one another skated across Moira's mind. The faeries already knew about the fissure and recognized it as a threat, which made things easier.

Leif scanned the gathering of small, earnest faces. "The Shifters some of you met on Malaita plan to close the gateway once and forever. Our biggest problem is demonkind has guessed what we're up to, and they've had time to plan for our arrival."

"Ye must surprise them," Greenie said.

"Our assessment as well," Moira agreed.

"One huge problem is we're all aboard a ship. It's a good-sized vessel, not one where we can sneak up on the gateway unnoticed," Leif said.

"Ye could swim," the iridescent faery pointed out.

"And ye can fly." Greenie turned to look Moira in the eye.

"True enough," Moira replied.

"That strategy works for fourteen sea Shifters and the two land Shifters who take bird forms," Leif clarified. "Thirteen other land Shifters take forms that don't lend themselves to either flying or swimming long distances in polar waters."

"If we're to have any hope of success, all of us must join our magic right next to the portal at the same time," Moira added.

"Oh." The crimson-haired faery's mouth rounded into understanding. "Which would explain the need for a passageway."

"What passage?" Greenie demanded. "What'd ye talk about before I got here?"

"Our thought was to anchor the boat near one of northeastern Siberia's deserted towns and travel to the gateway via a channel like the one you constructed for Ceridwen."

Moira waited, barely breathing.

Was such a thing possible? She'd thought it would be simpler since a borderworld wasn't part of the equation, but that might make it harder—or impossible—if the faeries required some element of a borderworld's magic to finesse their tunnel-building.

The undulating curtain around the king and queen of faery fell away. Oberon stepped forward. "We offer aid freely and willingly, without expectation of a boon in return."

"Aye, we are agreed." Titania stood tall and regal.

"We shall bring an army of Fae with us," Oberon said.

Cheers broke out among the faeries, all of whom took to the air zipping and diving as they whooped and hollered in Gaelic.

Leif dropped to one knee and bowed his head. "Thank you. All of you. If I survive this battle, I shall devote myself to repaying your generosity."

"Nonsense," Titania retorted. "In the name of all that's holy, man, get up off your knees. If ye survive, ye'll live the life ye were meant to."

"You have my thanks as well," Moira murmured.

"We must leave." Oberon sounded almost cheerful. "We've an army to raise."

"Do you know where—?" Moira began.

"Aye. Do ye think us deaf and dumb?" Titania rounded on her, silver eyes blazing with indignation. "Ye'd have to be naught but a mortal not to feel poison pumping though the ripped place."

"Apologies. I just wanted to make certain—"

"Young Shifter—for ye are indeed young," Titania said, "trust we will request information if any is required."

Moira's vulture chose that moment to commandeer her vocal chords. Squawks mingled with cooing as the vulture heaped praise on the queen of faery.

Titania smiled and patted Moira's hand. "Your bond animal is wise. Ye'll grow into its wisdom given a few more years."

Moira smiled back through gritted teeth. The only other option was telling Titania to piss up a rope, which wasn't wise. Never antagonize a brand-new ally.

"Hurry along, dear," Oberon said. "Ye can correct the young Shifter later." He drew a glowing doorway next to him and stepped through. Titania leapt after him.

Moira stood still until the opening winked out, resisting the temptation to shake her fist at the glittering rectangle.

"She can be annoying"—Greenie landed on Moira's shoulder —"but she means well."

"Doesn't matter," Moira said. "They agreed to help."

Leif moved closer to her and the faery. "Will it be possible to construct a passageway to accommodate the thirteen land Shifters who can't fly? We never finished that conversation."

"A wee bit harder without a borderworld to borrow magic from," Greenie said, "but not impossible."

"We should return with ye," the faery with iridescent hair said. "That way, we could get started. How long do we have?"

"Maybe five days," Moira replied.

"Awk! We should have started long since," the crimson-haired faery screeched.

"We'll be fine, Piotr," Amithra said. "Ye worry overmuch."

"Fine?" he sputtered. "First we have to create foundations and make certain the whole thing won't collapse beneath its own weight. Once that part is done, we—"

"We will make it work," she told him and angled her head to look at Moira. "We should get moving soon, though. No time to waste."

Moira considered how to proceed. Bringing the faeries back to the ship wouldn't help any of them. "Do you know where we'll leave the ship in northeastern Siberia?" she asked Leif.

"I've been thinking about that. Anadyr is too far, and not precisely a straight line."

"Straight lines are much better," Piotr said.

"In that case, we'll aim for the coastal area north of Pevek," Leif said. "It has a harbor where we can drop anchor, and then we'll launch rafts to get to the tunnel's starting point."

"Ye'll have to help," Amithra said. "'Tis a verra long way for us to teleport. 'Twas how Ceridwen trapped us. She knew we couldn't return easily on our own."

"How many are coming?" Leif asked.

"All of us," Piotr said.

"Gather close. Find a spot to latch onto Moira or me. Once you're there, hang on. This will be clumsy since we'll bounce off a borderworld."

"Easier for us. We'll resupply our magic as we pass through," the green faery said.

"Do whatever you want, but don't let go. Got it?" Leif's words were lined with steel.

Nods went around the circle of faeries. Leif wrapped his arms around Moira. Faery hands clutched her arms, shoulders, legs. Wherever she had a spot good for grabbing. Their energy felt nurturing, reassuring, not unlike Leif's.

"I'm counting backward from ten," he said. "When I reach one, we'll be gone from here."

Moira pushed her magical center open and felt Leif's essence pour into her like warm honey. She welcomed the feel of him, lapping it up like ambrosia. The moorlands fell away, replaced by the airless space between worlds. Surrounded by faeries, she found it easier to breathe. Maybe their wings trapped air.

They passed through the borderworld in the blink of an eye and fell through blackness, but not for long. A desolate vista, ice-coated rocks and an empty beach took shape. Waves crashed on a deserted shoreline. No vegetation. No trees. No seabirds. Maybe they'd sensed incoming magic and gone to ground. The whale had said sea life was making a recovery, but you couldn't prove it by this bleak stretch of real estate.

The spell Leif had secured around them frittered away, and

Moira was grateful for her many layers of cold-weather clothing. She'd been sweating in the U.K. Not here.

Seemingly oblivious to the icy wind, the faeries flew this way and that, chattering amongst themselves. "We will be ready when ye find us," they said in unison.

"If you get into trouble, summon me," Leif told them. "Use telepathy. Or teleport to the ship. It won't be far."

"We will," Amithra said. "Leave us so we can begin."

Leif smiled crookedly. "Looks as if we've been dismissed."

"It does indeed." Moira leaned into him, ready when he circled her with his arms and his magic. She didn't want the time with him to end, but they had news to impart and needed to get back to the others.

Leif draped them in magic that had a slightly different feel to it, and the rocky beach dropped away. Unlike crossing immense distances, this spell felt small, intimate, warm. Plenty of air here, which told her Leif hadn't taken them to the place between worlds.

They came out in an unfamiliar building, but at least it was out of the wind that had scoured the beach north of Pevek. "Where are we?" she asked.

"In Anadyr. The whole point of you coming was to learn to do this yourself." He skewered her with his deep blue gaze. "I couldn't turn you loose when we had all those faeries to transport, but you will teleport us back to *Arkady*. I'll be next to you, but you'll have control of the spell."

She smiled softly. "Learning was important, but mostly I wanted to be with you."

Ignoring the crux of her words, he said, "Talk me through how you'll do this, and then make it happen."

She extricated herself from his embrace, standing straight. He'd challenged her, and she wasn't one to back down from a test of her abilities. "Our magics aren't precisely the same. You're better at manipulating water than me, but how about if I mix fire with air to get us going? I can temper the mix with earth, inserting it where you used water."

"Let's see how it goes."

She reached for him, but he shook his head. "I touched you to ensure my magic would bring you along. Trust I'll take what I need from your spell."

Moira reached deep to the accompaniment of approving clucks from her bondmate. *"For Christ's sake, stop sounding like a chicken."*

"I'm delighted you're expanding our horizons," it shot back.

Moira narrowed her consciousness to her spell. It wasn't intuitive. When she'd teleported before, she'd thrown everything but the kitchen sink into her casting. This was a far more elegant deployment of her power, one that wouldn't drain her to bedrock. When the place Leif had dropped them disintegrated, jubilation filled her, but she didn't focus on it. Her entire consciousness revolved around visualizing the ship and bringing them out within its confines.

"Breathe," Leif suggested. It was the first word he'd spoken, and she recognized she'd been holding her breath, perhaps in anticipation of there not being any air, but more likely because she was nervous as hell.

She inhaled raggedly. It helped her concentration immensely. Moments later, they tumbled into an empty cabin. She redirected her magic, letting it zing wide to make certain they were on *Arkady* and not some other ship.

Leif grabbed her and swung her around so hard her feet left the deck. "You did it." He sounded as excited as she felt.

"I did, didn't I?" Unbalanced, she fell against him, triumph racing through her. It wasn't so much a matter of needing strong magic, as of making the best possible use of the power at her disposal.

He crushed her against him right before he slashed his mouth over hers, kissing her with the intensity of a drowning man who finally got his head above the waterline.

Moira opened her mouth to his kiss, drinking him in. They

needed to head to the bridge, but five minutes one way or the other couldn't possibly make any difference. They'd earned this time together.

Deserved it.

Regardless, she craved the man in her arms with a force that stole her breath and weakened her knees. A raucous wail rose from her bondmate, the cry of a vulture on the make for its mate. Moira would have told it to stand down, but she was too busy, too lost in Leif, to let anything get in the way.

15

MATING CALL

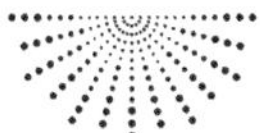

*L*eif wanted to drag Moira into his arms when she disclosed she'd come along not only to learn but because she wanted to be with him. Despite how tempting she was and how desperately he wanted her, the timing wasn't right. If she'd been paying attention to how he manipulated power, she needed to test her skills now when the learning was fresh. Not later when she'd have to dredge important parts out of memory.

So he'd pushed hard, and she'd succeeded.

He felt almost giddy by how well she'd done. Because he'd been so delighted and proud of her, he'd let down his guard and swung her off her feet. When she stumbled against him, he'd stopped thinking and kissed her. The feel of her in his arms, pressed the length of his body was incredible.

So enticing, he never wanted to let go. She threaded her arms beneath his, hooking her elbows and splaying her hands across his back. Even though he couldn't see them, she had beautiful hands with delicately tapering fingers, fingers that were kneading his back and shoulder muscles, leaving trails of heat in their wake.

He ran his hands the length of her spine until he cupped her high, rounded ass. She made a little mewling noise and let him draw her closer still. Breath hitched in his throat, and his cock thickened where it pressed against her belly. He wanted her with a lusty directness that set fire to every nerve, every sinew of his body, but they had to get a whole lot of things squared away first, not the least of which was the upcoming battle.

She darted her tongue into his mouth. He sucked on it, delighting in how sweet she tasted. As if she'd been drinking the faeries' nectar. Where her breasts were crushed against his chest, the nipples formed stiff peaks. He wanted to reach between their bodies and caress her breasts, rolling the nipples into points of delight with his fingers and his tongue. Just before he dipped his achingly swollen hard-on into the mysteries between her legs.

His cock jerked where it was sandwiched between their bodies, perilously close to release, which wasn't a surprise. He'd ignored the sexual part of his nature for years. Long before the Cataclysm, he'd focused on his people to the exclusion of anything personal.

Yes, he wanted to come, but coming wouldn't make a dent in his desire for Moira. The feelings he'd longed for in his youth when he'd hunted far and wide for his one, true mate, were upon him. His dolphin's bleats and clacks reinforced his knowledge that the woman in his arms was the one for him. At least his bondmate wasn't giving him a tough time because Moira wasn't a sea Shifter.

How could he explain their customs to her? That the courtship period came after the mating?

Reluctantly, he broke their kiss and cradled the side of her face in one hand, running his thumb over the pronounced line of her cheekbone. She gazed at him, eyes liquid with longing and splotches of color decorating her face.

"I know," she said. "Horrible timing and all that. We need to find the others." Her generous mouth turned upward, forming a wry smile. "I'm surprised no one's battered down the door. Surely, Karin and Ketha have had their magical antennae out, awaiting our arrival."

"Don't forget my whales." He flicked the upturned corner of her mouth with his tongue. "The time for declarations is all wrong, but I've fallen in love with you. I'm delighted and humbled, but also worried one—or both—of us won't make it through the battle at the gateway."

She nodded, her expression turning solemn. "We'll do the very best we can. If the goddess wills it, we'll live long enough to explore our attraction."

He shook his head. "Not how we do things. Sea Shifters declare our love, mate, and then enter into a lifelong courtship period."

"Sounds delightful since courtship is when you treat one another like precious gems." She'd slid her hands beneath his clothing and ran her calloused fingertips along his ribs. "I hate to let go of you, but we have more urgent concerns."

"Does that mean you'll agree to be my mate?" Leif pressed, needing to know.

A shadow crossed her face. "I'd love to say yes, but we'll revisit this after the battle." She was watching him closely and must have picked up on his disappointment because she added, "Nothing can get in the way of our complete and total concentration defeating the demons who would claim Earth for their own."

Moira's nostrils flared, and she went on, "From listening to your whale, I was hopeful it wouldn't be as bad as I feared, but—"

"The fact that all of Faery knew about the fissure blew that theory out of the water," he finished her thought.

"Something like that." She ran her tongue over her lips. "I want a future with you as badly as I've ever wanted anything, but I cannot let that interfere. Nor should you be thinking about me right now."

"You're wise as well as beautiful." He hugged her close and then let go. She tugged her arms from beneath his, and the spot where she'd been pressed against him felt hollow, bare. His entire body thrummed with wanting her, but this was no time to announce a mating, particularly not for him. His pod would fear his senses had deserted him.

"Thank you for the compliments. Most would describe me as a

cold, overbearing bitch." She cocked her head to one side. "It appears our presence has been discovered."

He picked out energy approaching from above. Juan and Aura and a whale. No way to erase the scents of desire from the cabin. He grinned, feeling mischievous, and gripped her hand. "Come on. We'll take a shortcut to the bridge."

Squandering magic wasn't his style, but he drew enough to teleport them from the cabin, that turned out to be on Deck Two, to the bridge. They stepped out into gray light streaming through the bridge's glass wall. Viktor eyed them from his spot at the helm.

"What'd you find out?" he asked without preamble, but Viktor wasn't one to waste words on superfluous things like greetings.

"Looks as if we'll have help from Faery." Moira unzipped her jacket and slid out of it, draping it across a chair.

Ketha clasped her hands together. "What a relief. I'm so glad. I was afraid they'd forgotten, or now that we were closer to the actual skirmish, they'd get cold feet."

Juan and Aura pounded through a door with a whale behind them. "There you are." The whale looked exasperated.

Aura favored Moira with a pointed glance. "I could have sworn you were down on Deck Two, but before we got there, I felt your energy emanate from up here."

Moira shrugged. "Magic does funny things sometimes."

Aura regarded her through narrowed eyes but didn't say anything more.

"Tell us about this assistance from Faery," Viktor urged.

"Yes, I want to hear too," Aura chimed in. "Do I get my tunnel?"

"Yes, plus an entire Fae army." Leif sent a sunny smile her way, hoping to lessen the sting of deceiving her with his rapid teleport maneuver. He undid his jacket to counteract the warmth of the bridge. His cock had subsided, so no need to keep the bottom half of his anatomy swathed in clothing.

"Where will we leave the ship?" Juan asked.

"Pevek has a harbor, right?" Leif looked from him to Viktor.

"Yup, a decent one," Viktor agreed, "but it's quite a way from Wrangel Island."

"We left the faeries on a deserted beach a few miles to the north," Leif said. "They're on the spit of land that sticks out southeast of the island."

"So we'll launch Zodiacs to reach them?" Juan asked.

Leif nodded.

"Hopefully, *Arkady* will be far enough away to escape notice," Viktor muttered. "It's not as if the sea lanes are crowded with vessels."

"They never were in that part of the world," Juan mumbled, adding, "We'll have to bring a fuel can along. Not sure a loaded raft can get that far and back again."

"The humans will remain aboard *Arkady,* right?" Leif asked.

Juan made a face. "We hadn't actually gotten that far yet. Some of them will want to help."

"Yeah, but if none of us return, it will take all nine of them and then some to pilot *Arkady* out of here," Viktor said.

Leif walked to where Viktor stood. "If none of us come back, it won't make any difference how many humans are aboard. There won't be anywhere for them to run or hide."

Viktor cracked a bitter smile. "I suppose I haven't fully accepted that."

Ketha draped an arm around her husband. "It's a prudent warrior who goes into battle anticipating success. If you visualize failure, you can tip the scales in unforeseen ways."

"Not quite the right venue for estate planning, eh?"

Ketha leaned toward him and kissed his cheek. "No, it's not. You love this ship, but if we lose against evil, it's doomed right along with every other remnant of our old life."

Leif thought about the humans. "Anyone who wishes can offer aid," he said. "Who are we to tell our human companions they have no value in a war where magics clash?"

"They'll get in the way," the whale argued.

Leif twisted to face him. "You have no way of knowing that."

The whale inclined his head. "I defer to my alpha, but if it turns out they're an impediment, I may flatten them myself."

"If they turn out to pose a liability, I don't think you'll have to," Leif replied. "They're smart enough to keep out of the way. The plan is simple," he went on. "Sea Shifters, Viktor, and Moira will approach the island as animals."

"Where we'll stick out like sore thumbs," Moira cut in. "I didn't see anything living in the spot where we left the faery folk."

"That part can't be helped," Leif said. "Maybe we should take the faerie tunnel along with most of the land Shifters. As I assess the plusses and minuses, it seems better if we all show up at precisely the same moment, magical guns blazing."

"Will the tunnel accommodate all of us?" Aura asked.

"I don't see why not," Moira replied. "The one on Malaita did. If not, we can retreat to plan A, which is twelve land Shifters take the tunnel along with any Fair Folk who wish to fight."

"When is this Fae army going to show up?" Ketha asked. "How many can we count on?"

"I have no idea how many. Oberon and Titania went to gather them." Leif frowned.

"What's wrong?" Moira asked.

"Nothing, but we need to craft a battle strategy that doesn't include them—in case they don't show up on time, or at all."

"Kind of difficult to plot a course when part of your cohort's not here," the whale seconded. "Won't matter overmuch. It's not help we'd planned on. If they get there, we'll welcome their aid. If not—" he shrugged.

"They knew about the fissure." Leif eyed the whale and saw surprise register.

"How?" the whale asked. "It's a long distance from their homeland."

"They sensed evil leaking through," Moira answered.

"Which suggests this undertaking will be far harder than any of us are counting on." Leif aimed his words at the whale.

"We need everyone included in this discussion," Viktor said.

"Agreed. How do you want that to happen?" Juan asked.

"Dining room in an hour, so it coincides with dinner. Did anyone make anything?"

"Not yet, but it's easily remedied." Ketha loped out of the bridge with Aura and Moira behind her.

"Shall I alert the pod?" the whale asked.

"Sure. Thanks." Leif told him. He'd rather have gathered his people, but the whale needed time to rethink the threat they faced.

The whale left by an outside door, probably heading for the quarterdeck to shuck his clothes and shift.

"What did you really think about your sojourn in fairyland?" Viktor asked.

Leif weighed what to say. The only ones on the bridge were Vik, Juan, and himself. "Why do you believe I've left things out?" He met Viktor's forthright gaze. The raven Shifter's green eyes glittered like uncut emeralds.

"Because you're like me. You play with the endgame in mind and ignore the little parts you deem unimportant."

"Fair enough." Leif hooked a foot beneath a stool and dragged it close. "At first, Oberon and Titania took a stand and told the faeries they couldn't honor Amithra's bargain."

"Who's she?" Viktor broke in.

"The green-haired faery who freed Ketha in exchange for escaping Ceridwen's clutches."

"Got it. Go on." He thinned his mouth into a tight line. "I'm having a hell of a hard time believing you laid eyes on two mythical figures from storybook land, but what changed the king's and queen's minds?"

"Several things," Leif replied. "Apparently the faeries don't answer to them. They made it abundantly clear they were free agents, which could fit in with Aura's prophecy about them leaving their hills and barrows and breaking free from the Fae." He creased his brow, remembering the flow of events. "What really seemed to get to them, though, was one faery who challenged their refusal. She asked what if this were the decisive battle to save Earth and they missed being part of it? Missed being included in history?"

"I can see where that would be a seductive argument," Juan said.

"It drove them into consultation mode," Leif went on. "While they were closeted behind a magical barrier, we explained to the faeries what we needed. Before we were quite finished, Oberon loosed his ward and announced he wouldn't miss the upcoming battle for the world. Not quite those words, mind you, but you get the drift. On the heels of that statement, he said he'd be bringing a host of Fae with him.

"He and Titania left after that, and Moira and I shepherded the faeries into position to begin constructing the tunnel."

"Do you know Oberon well?" Juan asked.

Leif bit back a snort, but part of it emerged anyway. "You might say so. I stole from him as a youthful prank and spent the next year one step up from an indentured servant. If you're questioning how reliable he is, he's as good as his word. The part that's lacking is his sense of time."

"What do you mean?" Viktor asked.

"It's not Oberon's fault," Leif replied. "Not really. Time flows differently for immortals. He appeared to be delighted to be off in search of troops. I imagine things grow dull when your existence is always the same."

"Dull, huh?" Juan made a sour face. "Couldn't he have done something to stave off the Cataclysm before it spewed so much poison?"

"Probably not. Magic tends to be species specific, and it was Shifter magic that broke the world. It's rather like asking if a Russian chess master can pilot a submarine."

"Apples and oranges," Viktor muttered. "Besides, Ketha was convinced the origins of the Shifter spell gone bad were cloaked in secrecy for ten years. She tried to break through, figure things out, the whole time they were stuck in Ushuaia and only managed it right before Raphael captured her."

"I remember," Juan said. "I also remember finally getting out from under that old fucker's thumb. Things moved pretty fast once he was out of the way."

"Fast in some ways," Viktor agreed. "Back then, we were convinced we'd solved the problem, and we set sail to see what was left of the world."

"I wondered how you ended up on *Arkady*," Leif said. "You'd already faced several unexpected setbacks when you rescued my pod and me."

"It's one way to put it." Viktor's words held a sour note. "By then, we'd determined we couldn't retreat to Ushuaia unless it was to wait out the end of the world."

"So we kept going." Juan glanced from Leif to Viktor. "Part of me believes this last battle is nothing but a sham. Even if we win, some other manifestation of evil will crop up to taunt us."

"Maybe so," Leif said, "but we have to fight the battles that are put in front of us. Just because it's not the last or the hardest or we don't know doesn't excuse us from doing our damnedest to succeed."

"Did you leave anything else out concerning Oberon and his consort?" Viktor asked.

Leif was able to look him in the eye and say, "No. The last piece is about the faeries. Some were concerned they wouldn't have enough time to build the passageway. It's harder when they don't have a borderworld's magic to leverage."

"Do they have a way to reach us?" Juan asked.

"Telepathy," Leif replied.

Juan made a face. "Of course. One of these years, I'll get used to magic being part of the weave of everyday life."

"You've only been a Shifter for a few months," Leif said. "Cut yourself some slack."

"*Si, amigo*, but I was a Vampire for a long time. Never warmed to it."

"I'm not seeing that as a cause for complaint." Leif smiled, but it held grim edges. "Never met a Vamp I liked, and they were thicker than fleas a few hundred years ago when it was much easier to find victims."

Viktor had been studying the bank of instruments. "We're closing on our objective. Is there anything more we can do to get ready?"

"Beyond crafting a battle plan?" Leif raised one brow.

"Yes. Will I need to secure the ship?"

Leif shook his head. "Demons have no use for ships."

"Everyone should be in the dining room by now," Juan cut in. "I'll go down and make certain, so I can round up any stragglers."

Leif waited until Juan left. "I hope these next few days bring us success. If I don't make it, knowing you has been a privilege."

Viktor extended his hand, and Leif clasped it. "Don't think like that, mate."

"I have to accept reality," Leif countered. "I was living on borrowed time when your veterinarians rescued me. I'm grateful for every added moment of life. As alpha, I will put the lives of my pod over my own. It's hardwired into my makeup."

"I can see how you're linked with the other thirteen here," Viktor said, "but did you have a connection to your entire pod when it numbered in the thousands?"

Leif nodded.

"How could you keep them straight?"

"I never questioned how. It's part of being their alpha. I probably shouldn't say this, but land Shifters lost an elemental part of being Shifters when they moved away from reporting to an alpha."

"Eh, I haven't been a Shifter long enough to recognize the fine points." Viktor cracked a wry smile. "My raven reminds me of that all the time. Ready to go downstairs?"

"Yes. I want to get this next part over with. Parceling out tasks is never easy."

"Some jobs are harder than others," Viktor said.

"And inherently more dangerous," Leif agreed, "which is why I solicit volunteers whenever I have time. People work harder when it's a task they've selected, rather than one that's been foisted upon them."

"I like you." Viktor punched his shoulder lightly. "And I don't speak those words lightly."

"The feeling is mutual, land Shifter. Shall we?" Leif angled his head toward the door.

Viktor made a few course adjustments and then followed him out of the bridge.

Leif's mind was busy, running a million directions at once as he trotted briskly down several sets of risers. The foul magic that had stirred up the last storm was absent, but probably far from gone. A creeping wrongness scuttled up his spine. He was edgy and might have imagined something harsh lurking on the sidelines, plotting its next attempt to sabotage them getting close enough to Wrangel Island to challenge the gateway's guardian.

He raised his mind voice. *"Lewis?"*

"Right here, Alpha."

"Did you reach Poseidon?"

"I did. Mission accomplished. The expression on his face was worth having to breathe the same air."

Satisfaction began in Leif's feet and spread through him. *"Thank you."*

"For once, the pleasure was all mine. See you in the dining room."

16

I WALK IN FRONT

oira was huddled in the smaller dining room with all the other Shifter women. One of the things they'd decided the night before was she'd teach them what she'd learned from Leif about leveraging their magic to teleport. The plan was for Ketha, Aura, Zoe, and Karin to then explain the technique to their mates.

"What am I doing wrong?" Zoe muttered when the shimmery air around her broke into motes of shiny brilliance and fell to the deck.

Moira chewed her lower lip, thinking. "You're empathic. Maybe if you downplay that piece."

Zoe spun her hand in a circle. "Could ye say a wee bit more?"

"It's not an intuitive mixture, particularly the fire aspect. Perhaps your magical nature is working at odds with the spell."

Karin frowned. "Magic doesn't operate like that, though. It blends with whatever direction we shape it."

Moira bit back exasperation and rolled her shoulders amid cracking joints, which told her she'd been sitting far too long. "Fine. You come up with something useful for her. Granted this wasn't exactly smooth at the beginning, but everyone's managed to teleport to the bridge and back again."

187

"Except me." Zoe sounded glum.

Moira walked to her side and gave her a quick, hard hug. "You'll figure it out. Believing in your ability is half the battle."

"Sure and ye're not telling me aught I doona already know." Zoe's brogue was more pronounced than usual, reflecting her distress.

The dining room door flew open, and Leif strode in. "How's it going?"

Moira was happy to see him. They'd spent the previous evening glancing at one another and looking away just as rapidly. He'd retired to the sea to firm up details with his pod after their strategy session.

"Pretty well." Moira gestured for him to come farther into the room. "Maybe you can help us figure out why Zoe is having difficulty."

He quirked a curious brow. "Only her?"

"Aye, 'twould be sad but true." Zoe flexed her fingers; little jolts of leftover magic flared from them. "Mayhap one of the rest of you could work with Recco. Surely, he'll have more facility than I do for this maneuver."

"You can't give up." Leif moved close and dropped a hand on her shoulder. Moira felt him scan her with magic. A knowing smile tugged the edges of his mouth, a mouth Moira wanted more kisses from.

"What'd you find?" Zoe demanded.

"You know that point midway into the spell where you add earth?" At her nod, he went on, "Skip that. Add water. Visualize the Irish Sea. Go ahead"—he stepped back—"try it now while I'm here."

Moira backed up as well, offering room for Zoe to work. The coyote Shifter shut her eyes, chanting softly, and worked her hands in the intricate patterns that were part of her magic. Moira stilled her breathing, willing Leif's suggestion to do the trick. Zoe was demoralized, as well she might be given the other ten of them had managed with very little difficulty. When you became too discouraged, magic often deserted you, almost as if it was saying it wouldn't believe in you if you refused to have faith in it.

The air around Zoe took on the same glistening aspect it had her other half dozen tries, but this time she vanished without fanfare. One moment she was there, the next gone.

"How'd you know what to tell her?" Ketha asked Leif.

He shrugged. "She has a lot of water in her makeup, probably might have become a sea Shifter if one of the sea creatures had staked a claim to her first. Since the path Moira described wasn't working for Zoe, I suggested the one I use."

"Probably a worthwhile lesson," Karin said, adopting her thoughtful, scientist tone. "Since I'll be teaching Daide."

"And I'll be coaching Juan," Aura noted. "It's important to have a fallback strategy when the primary one fails."

Magic flashed bright out of the corners of Moira's eyes. Zoe tumbled into a crouch and sprang to her feet, squealing, "Yay! I did it! I canna believe that worked. 'Twas so simple with a wee bit of alteration in the directions." She covered the distance to Leif and threw her arms around his neck, kissing both cheeks. "Thank you."

"You're quite welcome." Color rose to his stubble-covered cheeks.

A hot, quick jab of jealousy stabbed Moira. Zoe had a mate. She needed to take her hands off Leif. Right now. Moira jammed her jaws together and balled her hands into fists to keep herself from hooking her fingers around Zoe's arm and pulling her away from Leif.

Zoe let go, still beaming.

"It appears our work here is done," Karin said, looking satisfied.

"Yeah, but this was the easy task," Ketha reminded everyone.

"You are such a killjoy," Tessa mumbled.

Ketha sent a grim smile skittering her way. "No matter how diligently we prepare, we'll wish we'd done more."

"At least this is an enemy we can come face to face with." Leif's words were lined with bitterness.

"As opposed to the Cataclysm?" Moira asked.

"Something like that," he replied.

"We managed to lure it into open combat," Ketha said, "but it took ten years to figure out a way."

"Unfortunately, it wore different faces in different parts of the world," Karin added.

"Which was why we only thought we defeated it," Aura tossed in. "Victory was sweet while it lasted, though."

Zoe elbowed her. "You're a historian. You should know victories are never permanent."

Aura narrowed her eyes to slits. "I do know that. Sorry to say, defeat can develop a life of its own. Doesn't seem fair, does it?"

"Nothing that happens is fair." A stern tone lined Leif's words. "Even if we emerge victorious from closing the fissure, it's far from a guarantee. Evil has always been here. We can slow it down, stymie its progress, but that's the best we can hope for."

"Earth is changed," Moira murmured. "We're still finding our way." She swallowed around a thick place in her throat. "I hope we're offered a chance to make a life for ourselves because if we can't staunch the flow of demonspawn, the planet is done for."

"If that happens," Leif said, "we might consider relocating to a borderworld. It would be a one-way trip, though. If we remain very long, the will and desire to leave will desert us."

"I'd wondered about that." Ketha scrunched her features into a frown. "Being an expatriate beats fighting a string of battles until one finally kills you."

"This discussion is premature," Leif said. "It's one we'll only have if we lose." He tossed his long, tangled hair over his shoulders. "And we're not going to lose. Got it?" Amid a chorus of *got its*, he went on, "My pod is ready to practice battle drills with you."

"Give us half an hour," Karin said. "Should be long enough for us to give Viktor, Juan, Recco, and Daide a crash course in this method of teleporting, which won't deplete their magic."

"Yes. That way, we'll be ready for anything, including the faeries' tunnel not being finished or not having enough magic for all of us to use it," Moira said.

"Half an hour?" Ketha glanced Leif's way.

"That will work. We're drawing even with the Kamchatka Peninsula. Some of the eastern coves will provide a perfect practice location."

"Tell us where to meet you," Aura said.

Leif grinned; it transformed his face into something so striking, Moira couldn't have looked away if she tried. Her heart gave a funny little hitch.

"You only just now learned to teleport effectively." Leif pointed out. "Meet us outside on Deck Three, and we'll all go together. That way we won't waste time tracking down stragglers."

Ketha trailed curved fingers through her unbound hair. "Recco and Daide will want to join us. Maybe Vik and Juan could take turns since one will need to man the helm."

The deck canted to one side and then back. Moira waited to see if it was an isolated wave, but it happened again. "Damn it. Looks like the water's getting choppy."

"I'm not surprised," Leif said. "The wind was picking up, but this feels like a natural phenomenon, not something formed by magic."

"Not much we can do about it," Karin said. "We'll see how things look in thirty minutes and if we need to alter our plans, we will." She headed out of the dining room with the other women strung out behind her chattering excitedly.

Moira hung back, craving a few private moments with Leif but not wanting to appear too forward. "How's your pod doing?"

"Their spirits are high, but they want to get their teeth into the battle." He turned and looked right at her in his direct way. "When you were certain your life was numbered in days, any event is worth looking forward to. Even one where some of your kin might not make it through."

"I suppose that's true enough." She thought back to her years in Ushuaia, many of which she'd spent buried in denial, and cleared her throat. "It was only during the last few months in Ushuaia, when I couldn't ignore the worsening air and tainted water, I let myself contemplate my death."

"You're a fighter."

"Correction. I used to be. Once I got done feeling sorry for myself and blaming the other women because I was stuck in Argentina, I moved to full-on ostrich-dom."

He tilted his head. "I'm not understanding. What is it ostriches do that reflected your situation?"

"Put their heads in the sand." She smiled softly. "I don't imagine they really do that, but it's been an urban myth for a lot of years."

He dropped his hands onto her shoulders, keeping his touch light. "I would spare you pain and unpleasantness if I could."

"I appreciate the thought, but I never did the kept-woman routine very well—or at all."

He moved a hand from her shoulder to cup the side of her face. "Another word choice I'm not familiar with, but I can pick it up from context. Wanting to spare you misery exists in a whole different universe from locking you in a tower." His eyes crinkled at their corners. "Although, I admit to a fleeting desire to sequester you in a cabin until the battle is over."

Heat from his palm seared her and made her long for more. She leaned into his touch. "Do you still?"

"Yes and no. Being near you makes me happy in ways I never thought would grace my life."

Moira understood. "And being happy like that makes you afraid. At least, it makes me afraid. I want to cling to the feelings I have when we're close to one another, but I want to run away from them at the same time because I worry they'll interfere with some crucial little detail. I'll forget something, and it will mean someone dies or is hurt. And then, I'll have a hell of a time forgiving myself."

"Precisely. I still blame myself so many of my pod died, even though it's irrational and there was naught I could do to prevent any of it."

"Do you think we'll get another shot at Poseidon and Amphitrite?"

"I do. They're part of whatever's behind the fissure." The softness left his face, leaving harsh planes; a muscle flickered beneath one eye. "If it's within my power, I want to seal them inside. They picked evil. Let them parlay with the devil for the rest of their days. Being immortal means they'll have a long time to contemplate their choices. At least Lewis made certain Poseidon knows about his consort's loose morals."

"When did that happen?"

"While we were gone rounding up the faeries."

Moira rolled her eyes. "Serves the old bastard right. How'd he react? Or did he already know?"

"From Lewis's description, I'm fairly certain it was new information. Poseidon hung around just long enough to test Lewis with a truth spell—"

A rush of strong magic sent her twirling out of Leif's arms, hands raised to call magic. "What's coming?" she cried.

"Not sure. I don't recognize it." He pushed in front of her, between where she stood and the unusual sensation. Magic crackled, turning the air electric. Little blue lightning bolts danced around them, and the stench of ozone burned her nostrils.

Moira moved to the side, so she stood next to Leif. "I need to see what we face."

"But I can't protect you as well."

"We'll protect each other." Moira sent her magic outward, sensing, seeking. What the hell was racing their way? She switched to her psychic view; the ley lines glowed as if supercharged with the far lines so brilliant they seared her corneas.

"Smart." Leif stood shoulder to shoulder touching her, but at least he'd given up on shoving her behind him.

"Not sure about smart, but something's activated the lines..." Realization crashed into her. "Has to be Eiocha. The question is what she wants."

"I came to the same conclusion. We won't have to wait long to find out."

The bright, glowing place came closer in surges that moved in and drew back, but each successive wave ended up nearer than the last. The distant sound of thundering hooves grew louder, clinching her impression Eiocha was almost upon them. The horse goddess wanted something, but what?

Leif threaded an arm around her and dropped his other hand to his side. Moira had nearly forgotten about the defensive magic she'd summoned, and she loosed it, watching it fritter into shimmery motes that settled to the deck.

A deck that was rocking and rolling from side to side with far more fury than before. Waves crashed against the hull, making a hollow, booming noise that reverberated in the pit of her stomach.

A glowing hole ripped through the air over by the windows, and Eiocha jumped through. Her silvery-white hide glistened, and her eyes were a lighter blue than they'd been in her cavern. She pranced to where they stood, sashaying on hooves big as dinner plates.

Leif bowed low. "Goddess. You honor me with your presence."

Moira bowed too. The temptation to blurt something like, "Why are you here?" was strong, but she rode herd on it.

"Where is everyone else?" the horse asked in Gaelic. *"I sense many yet see only you two."*

"Spread throughout the ship." Leif lifted his head. "Do you need us in one place?"

Rather than answer his question, she replied with one of her own. *"Have you crafted battle plans?"*

"They're in process," Moira replied.

"And easy to alter at this point," Leif broke in. "Have you come to stand with us?"

The horse tossed its head and whinnied. *"My old associates, the king and queen of Faerie, paid me a visit. They convinced me this battle was worthy of my time, that wickedness will commandeer my children, my ley lines, if the tide doesn't turn in our favor."*

Words crowded at the back of Moira's throat wanting out, but she swallowed them. They'd told Eiocha much the same thing, but the horse goddess had ignored them. Apparently, messages from those she considered peers carried more weight.

The ship canted to port before snapping back to starboard. Moira might have stumbled except for Leif's arm still holding onto her. Eiocha tossed her head. Power boiled around her, flaring bright white. Moira switched away from her psychic view to save her third eye from blindness. By the time the dining room swam back into focus, a tall, regal woman draped in a long, white dress stood before them. Silver hair fell to deck level, but the goddess's eyes were the same, a rich and varied blue.

Moira blinked in surprise.

Eiocha stood straighter. "I can take many forms. This one will be more convenient, as I doubt my horse would fit through most of this vessel's passageways. 'Tis also a convenience to converse without expending magic."

"What the hell?" Viktor exploded through the dining room door, the old Remington tucked under his arm.

Leif hastily inserted his body between Viktor and Eiocha. "All is well. This is Eiocha, guardian of the world's magic."

Viktor engaged the rifle's safety. "But I thought she was a horse." He strode forward, one hand extended. "I'm Viktor Gaelen, captain of this ship."

Eiocha angled her head but didn't take his hand. "The other one gave you my name. I would hear an apology for pointing a weapon in my direction."

Viktor settled the rifle's stock on the heaving deck. "I apologize if I trampled on your toes, but keeping this ship as safe as I can is my job. I felt a great deal of magic burst from this quadrant of the ship and hurried to investigate."

The goddess crossed her arms beneath her breasts. "I didn't ask for an explanation, mortal, but an apology."

Annoyance flickered across Viktor's features. He bowed, but not very much. "Apologies."

"Better. If we are to be allies, we will have to find acceptable ways of working together."

"Allies?" Viktor exchanged a pointed look with Leif.

"Indeed." Leif smiled pleasantly. "Eiocha has come to offer aid in the upcoming battle."

"Where is everyone?" Eiocha repeated her earlier query. "No time like the present to launch a practice session."

"We're all meeting one deck up outside," Leif told her.

"Excellent. One of you will show me the route."

"Right this way," Moira swept past her and started for the dining room door.

"Stop right there. I walk in front," Eiocha said, her tone pointed.

Moira ground to a halt and turned. "Please don't take this as disrespectful, but it's far easier for you to follow me than for me to trudge behind you barking orders."

"Not orders, my dear. Suggestions."

Moira pinched the bridge of her nose between her thumb and forefinger. When she dropped her hand to her side, she said, "I appreciate your offer of aid. We could use it. But we cannot worry every single word or suggestion will be met with disapproval from you if you believe we didn't treat you with adequate respect. Or violated some tradition you honed back in two thousand B.C."

"Everyone on this ship is an equal," Leif said. "We have different magics, different methods of deploying that magic, and differing roles. Regardless, no one has more value than anyone else."

Eiocha looked down her patrician nose at them. "Did you outline that structure when you requested aid from Oberon and Titania?"

"We didn't have to," Leif replied. "And we didn't request their aid. The faeries made it clear the king and queen would be remiss to ignore a decisive battle, so they decided to raise a Fae army and meet us at the gateway."

"We're developing battle tactics on our own," Viktor said, "since it's impossible to make plans with someone who's not present. We figured when they showed up, we'd deploy everyone as best we could to maximize their various magical abilities. See you all soon. I need to get back upstairs."

Viktor scooted around them and left the room at a quick trot, the rifle tucked beneath his arm.

Moira balanced from foot to foot to compensate for the ship's motion. She envied Viktor, who maintained his balance seemingly without effort. "We're late to meet the others," she said, eying Eiocha. "Are you coming?"

Moira was a veteran dealing with paternalistic coworkers, who thought women had no place beyond shuttling from the bedroom to the kitchen on a ball and chain. Without waiting for Eiocha to respond, she turned and left the room as briskly as she could manage given the motion of the ship.

She was halfway up the stairs, clinging to the railings, when she felt the goddess's energy behind her. In a way, she felt sorry for Eiocha, transplanted into a world she didn't understand, but she'd catch on.

She had to. No choice.

The battle was nearly upon them, and they had no space to mollycoddle anyone. Not even an ancient goddess.

17

HUBRIS

*L*eif watched the interchange between Viktor, Moira, and Eiocha. Had it only been him, he'd probably have complied with the goddess's demands, but his life spanned a time when magical beings paid homage to deities. Apart from Karin, all the land Shifters were young, still working through their first hundred years or so.

Worry bit deep that they'd have a hell of a time forming an effective unit when they came face to face with the fissure—and its denizens. He and his pod were used to working together. All of them were past masters of many battles, whereas the land Shifters weren't warriors. They sprang from a variety of modern disciplines, mostly in the sciences but some in the humanities like Aura with her Ph.D. in history.

Educated, but not particularly battle-tested. The educated part boded well. At least the women could think on their feet.

His thoughts transferred to Viktor, Juan, Recco, and Daide. Their time as Shifters was measured in months. Perhaps their ten years as Vampires would offer them a fighting edge. Absent that, all four men had mates to protect, which would help.

Another concern intruded. If Oberon and Titania had taken the time to hunt down Eiocha, who else had they invited? When they'd said they were bringing a Fae army, Leif hadn't batted an eye. Fae would do as their lieges instructed, but the gods were as likely to pull together as to get into a pissing contest over who was running the show.

He thinned his lips into a line and inhaled briskly. Naught to do but move forward. He'd always been one who liked to have all his ducks lined up, but this was one instance where he'd have to abandon his need for control.

"*We have a problem,*" a tinny voice blasted into his mind.

Leif's eyes widened in time to hear a second voice add, "*Ye said to let you know.*"

Eiocha, who was mostly out of the room, turned beneath the doorframe until she faced him. "And who was that?" she demanded, still using Gaelic.

"The faeries we left near the gateway. They were supposed to build us a conduit from the mainland to our objective."

"*Did ye hear me?*" faery number one demanded.

"*Yes. What kind of problem?*" he replied.

"*We almost get the passageway completed, and something blows it up. We've started over twice now. How much more time do we have?*"

Eiocha's nostrils flared, reminiscent of her horse form. "*What is this something? Can you identify it?*" she asked, jumping into the conversation.

"*Who are ye?*" the faery demanded.

"*It's all right,*" Leif reassured the faery. "*It's Eiocha. Oberon and Titania told her about—*"

"*Oooh, the horse goddess,*" another faery squealed.

A chorus of excited shrieks followed.

Eiocha smiled, looking regal and pleased. "*My subjects. Not all have forgotten me. I will be right there, and I shall ensure your next passageway remains standing.*"

"Thank you, Goddess."

"Return as soon as you can, please," Leif eyed Eiocha.

She nodded. "I will do the best I can. How important is this tunnel?"

"Very. We'd hoped to use it to transport ourselves to the gateway."

"But you can swim, and—"

"Most of the land Shifters just learned to teleport. They're clumsy, and all that magic would be a dead giveaway. No point in showing up only to have demons mow us down with magic they've been holding at the ready."

"I see. This shouldn't take long. The fair folk are adorable, but their power has always been weak as dishwater." Eiocha screwed her face into a thoughtful expression. "The one stealing from me, who calls herself queen of the seas, will she be at the gateway?"

"I expect so."

"Good." A feral smile turned Eiocha's beauty into something grim and foreboding. "I have a score to settle with her."

"That makes two of us."

"What did she do to you?" Eiocha raised one silver brow into a question mark.

"Stood by while thousands of my people died. Sea people, who were ostensibly her subjects."

Eiocha crossed the distance between them and gripped Leif's shoulder hard enough to hurt. "She will pay for her sins."

The air flashed once, a brilliant blue, and the goddess vanished.

Leif rubbed his shoulder. He'd seen her grab him with fingers, but it felt as if she'd pounded a hoof down on his collarbone.

"Where are you?" one of the whales demanded.

"Coming," he replied and ran for the doorway. He made a quick stop at the clothes locker and zipped a parka to chin level. If they spent the next few hours outside in the howling, subzero wind, the jacket would be essential.

He pushed through a door to find everyone gathered in small groups on the broad, open expanse of deck, but not too near the sides since spray slopped over from vicious waves.

"Where's Eiocha?" Moira had to scream to be heard over the roar of the wind.

Leif gestured for all of them to come closer. Once everyone was near, he said, "The faeries put out a distress call. Something is sabotaging their tunnel-building. Eiocha went to help."

"Not good news about the passageway," Ketha said.

"We can all teleport," Karin spoke up.

"Not a good idea," Leif and Lewis said almost in unison. After exchanging an amused look, Leif continued, "Too much expended magic in the same spot will be like hanging out a banner that announces our imminent arrival."

"Aye, we need the passageway," Lewis concurred.

"Do you believe Eiocha can fix the faeries' problem?" Viktor asked.

"She has enough magic, and the ley lines jump to her command," Leif replied. "If anyone can do it, she can."

"Means we won't be able to practice with her, but that might not be a bad thing," Moira said.

"She should be back quite soon," Leif said. "We do need to practice group maneuvers, so we don't end up hurting one another by mistake." He glanced Viktor's way. "Does the fact that you're here mean you can join us?"

Viktor nodded. "Yeah. Boris and Ted are manning the helm along with Sasha. This isn't bad as weather goes. *Arkady's* sailed through much worse." He grinned rakishly. "And I can always teleport back to the ship if they need me."

"They can't use telepathy. How will they contact you?" Leif asked.

Viktor fished in a parka pocket and pulled out a two-way radio. "The old-fashioned way, mate."

"Does everyone have enough warm clothing?" Leif scanned the

group. Seeing nods, he instructed, "Form groups with one sea Shifter in each. The sea Shifter will control the teleport. We'll all come out in the sandy cove with caves. My pod knows it well, since we've sheltered there."

He gathered Moira, Ketha, and Viktor close. "Ready? I'll open my magic to you, so you can watch how I do this. Consider it a continuation of this morning's lessons."

Summoning a modest spell, he visualized the spot where he wanted to bring them out and launched the casting. As he'd hoped, the beach was protected, compared with *Arkady's* open deck, where the ship was anchored in the Bering Sea. Once all twenty-nine of them were present, he motioned them into a cave. It felt almost balmy out of the wind.

"We have very little time and much to accomplish," he began, selecting his words carefully. "Whatever structure we decide on may well get blown out of the water once Eiocha or Oberon and Titania show up. If they do materialize, we will have to at least try to blend in with their lead."

"Why?" Juan asked.

"Seems they could blend with us just as easily," Karin muttered.

"No, they can't," Leif said. "They're used to being obeyed without question. You weren't there when the faeries began cooing over Eiocha. She was thrilled and delighted to offer her aid." He sucked in a breath. "I understand this grates on your twenty-first-century sensibilities, but flattery is the ticket to working with the gods."

Amid grumbles, Leif kept talking. "If no one has any objections, I'll orchestrate this practice session and our initial appearance at the fissure. My pod is used to working together, and we have a communication system in place. How do the rest of you feel about teaming up with a sea Shifter and fighting in pairs?"

"Can we do trios?" Viktor asked. "That would allow Ketha and me to join with a sea Shifter. I'll fight better if my mate is where we can lay eyes on each other."

"Works for me," Leif said. "I'll see everyone outside in five minutes. We'll square off against one another. Whoever you group up with is who you'll be fighting with at the fissure, so pick carefully."

"Can I fight alongside you?" Moira had scooched close.

"I'd be honored." He headed outside with her striding next to him. He'd been hoping to find a way to keep an eye on her, but it cut both ways. Better to be worried with her right next to him, though, than trying to catch sight of her if she was in another group.

THE DAY WORE ON. The sun was hidden behind thick cloud cover, but it had moved well past its zenith. He and Moira had fought against Viktor, Ketha, and a whale, and then switched to Juan, Aura, and Lewis as opponents. They were improving at coordinating their offensive maneuvers while keeping a solid defensive ward in place.

During a breathing spell between drills, he said, "Our warding is critical. Even if it means we miss a shot or two."

Moira rolled her shoulders back. "I figure they'll bait us, try to turn us against each other because that's how evil operates."

"Good point, and one we didn't cover." Leif took advantage of the lull in the action to raise his voice and yell, "Prioritize your wards. No matter what. You may not get to take a shot, but maintaining our safety is paramount."

"How's everyone's magic holding up?" Viktor shouted. "Because mine is fading."

Leif trotted over to him. "Open your psychic view and latch onto the power in the Earth beneath you. We can use it, the other side can't, which gives us an advantage."

"Land Shifters, over here." Ketha cupped her hands around her mouth.

Viktor was concentrating hard, his forehead a roadmap of wrinkles, when he broke into a broad grin. His eyes snapped open. "Christ! It's like hitting the mother lode."

Leif slugged him in the shoulder. "You still need to guide your power, not squander it, but there's more right beneath your feet now that the ley lines are close-to-fully charged again." He turned his attention to the others. "Next skirmish, practice running wide open. Pull power into you and give the enemy everything you've got."

"We'll become conduits," Karin said.

"Exactly. This is a technique we'll use when we get into the thick of things and have to maximize our effectiveness."

"It would help if we had some idea how many we'll face," Moira muttered.

"Doesn't matter," Leif said. "Our strategy is to shut the gateway. Once it's been annihilated, we'll deal with whatever's still on our side."

"I thought you wanted to make certain Poseidon and Amphitrite were trapped on the wrong side of the gate," Moira said.

"I would love it if things happened that way, but I'm not going to stand on ceremony waiting for them to show up."

So long as everyone was still milling around, pulling power from the ley lines, he went on, "Our battle plan is to hit the gateway hard and heavy. The minute we have boots on the ground, we will pull as much destructive magic as we need to obliterate it."

"Demons will be trying to swarm through," a whale said.

"We'll have to ignore them," Lewis added. "Unless they're right in our way, and then we blow them to smithereens, hastening their journey back to Hell."

"This is why maintaining our warding, no matter what, is so critical," Leif said. "They will be doing their damnedest to kill us, but we have to get that gateway closed."

"Makes sense," Moira said. "It will limit how many of the enemy we have to deal with. Only the evil on this side of the gate, not the infinite number of wicked spirits who live in Hell."

Leif clapped his hands together. "Back at it, folks."

This time, he left Moira to extract power from the ley lines and get used to how it felt running through her body. He worked his way from group to group, fine-tuning their efforts. By the time he'd looked in on everybody, light was fading from the day. It was time to return to the ship.

He was worried Eiocha wasn't back yet. Meant the fix she'd been convinced would be easy hadn't been all that straightforward. He made his way to Viktor and drew him aside. "What would you think about finding a spot to drop anchor after we're back aboard?"

"We can do that. There are ports the length of Kamchatka. Why?"

"I want to give Eiocha and the faeries the time they need to construct a bombproof tunnel. Also, we made good progress today. At least one more skills-training day would add to everyone's confidence."

"I agree," Viktor said. "In truth, I'm surprised we've done as well as we have today, and that trick of yours to augment my magic when it gets low was little shy of inspired. In terms of possible ports, Ivashka or Ossora could work to drop anchor. They're past the midway point of Kamchatka, heading north."

"Excellent." Leif scanned the groups, which were winding down. "I'm going to call it. We'll employ the same groupings we used to get here to teleport back to the ship."

His throat was raw from inhaling the cold, damp air and all the talking he'd done, so Leif switched to his mind voice. *"Back in your transport groups, everyone. We'll teleport back to Arkady. Take showers. Warm up, and we'll meet in the dining room in an hour."*

He walked to where he'd left Moira, but she wasn't there. Ketha tapped him on the shoulder. "If you're looking for Moira, she and Tessa teleported back to the ship. She asked me to let you know and said she'd see you at dinner."

Anxiety soured his stomach. He could see her getting frisky with her brand-new magic, but now wasn't the time for showing off. They were too near the fissure to let their guards down for as little as a minute.

He tried to tell himself it would probably be fine and shepherded Viktor and Ketha back to the ship. They'd barely rolled out onto the ice-coated deck when he bolted to his feet and scooted inside. His first instinct was to hustle to Moira's cabin and assure himself she'd arrived safely, but he sent seeking magic in an arc instead. It was faster and would cover all the possibilities, like the bar and the bridge, in case her cabin wasn't her first stop.

His sweep didn't locate her, so he switched to looking for Tessa. He didn't expect to find her, and he didn't. He'd just reversed direction to head back out onto the pitching, heaving deck when Moira's distinctive energy pinged back at him. She was outside.

Why the hell had it taken her so long to get back here? It wasn't as if you could take wrong turns teleporting.

He shouldered the door open and almost ran into a distraught Moira with Juan on one side of her and Aura on the other. "Slow down, sweetie," Aura was saying.

"You don't get it." Moira turned anguished eyes on the mountain cat Shifter, "I lost Tessa. One minute we were together, and the next she wasn't there. I returned to the beach where we practiced, thinking something had gone wrong with her casting. I was certain I'd find her there, but I didn't."

She inhaled shakily, and her eyes sheened with tears. "Where the hell is she?"

Wind howled and screeched, wrenching the door against its stops. Leif yanked all of them inside and pushed it shut. He wanted to tell Moira she'd been a fool, but it was a waste of words. She already blamed herself. Nothing to be gained by pounding her into the ground.

"She could be anywhere," Leif said, holding onto a neutral tone and not asking why the hell Moira had broken the protocol he'd established to keep all of them safe.

"I don't understand."

"Do you need us?" Juan asked.

Leif shook his head. "No. Get warmed up." Hooking an arm

around Moira, he half-dragged her one flight down and into the nearest cabin so they'd have a spot to sit.

She slumped onto one of the two beds. "I was stupid. How could I have misjudged so horribly? I got back here fine. Twice. Why didn't she?"

"She doesn't have your magical ability," Leif said, "but beyond that, evil marked her. They had the feel of her energy, which made it easy for them to snag her. When we teleport, it's not anything like selecting a road. It might be closer to routes airplanes pick, but not even much like that, either. You leave the realm of physics and enter a buffer zone, for want of a better term. It's not a borderworld, but nor do the rules that govern Earth apply. This is why you must have an endpoint to visualize. If you lack that, you can get lost in the buffer zone and never find your way out."

Moira had drawn her knees up and wrapped her arms around them. "It's useful to know how things work, but will the knowledge help us get her back?"

Leif didn't want to tell her Tessa could be anywhere by now, depending on why her teleport spell had been interrupted. An idea percolated. It was a long shot, but he needed to check in with the faeries, anyway.

"It's possible Eiocha can track her through the ley lines." He leveled his gaze her way. "Remain silent. You didn't make any friends today when you challenged the horse goddess."

She mimed dragging two fingers across her mouth and hunched into a dejected heap at the edge of her bunk.

"How are things going?" Leif extended his telepathy to the faery who'd reached him earlier.

"How would you expect?" Eiocha replied. *"We just finished. This structure will last the ages."*

"I'd expect nothing less from your outstanding magical ability." Leif laid it on thick and watched spots of color spread across Moira's cheeks. Good. She was embarrassed, but it meant she was developing an understanding of the value of ass kissing.

"I'll be on my way back soon."

"It will be a pleasure to see you. We will be dropping anchor to allow us another practice day."

An approving whinny rippled through the telepathic channels.

"While you're on your way back here, we seem to have lost one of our number. Her name is Tessa, and she's a mountain cat Shifter."

The whinny turned into equine laughter. *"Aha! I wondered if you had dual motives in play. As it happens, I felt a significant disturbance in my lines. I shall investigate, but I bet I find your missing Shifter. She will come with me, correct? No hysterics? No lack of respect like that one this morning?"*

"I'm certain she'll be so grateful, she'll worship you forever," Leif replied.

The connection blanked out, and Leif turned his attention to Moira. Tears rolled down her face. "If anyone can find Tessa, it's Eiocha," he said in an effort to comfort her.

"I hope so. I have to mend my ways. If it was me lost in the ether, Eiocha wouldn't lift a hoof to help me, and I don't blame her. Once she's back, I'll apologize. Sincerely and profusely. My vulture is giving me hell, along with a bunch of tripe about how I have to stand proud, but this is one place it's wrong. If it abandons me over this, I'll find a way to keep going."

Leif moved across the cabin until he sat next to her, taken aback. "Surely your bondmate wouldn't do something like that." He tried to wrap an arm around Moira to console her, but she squirmed out from under it.

"You must have things you need to do. Things way more important than coddling me." She swiped at her wet cheeks with the backs of her hands. "I'll be fine. I'm strong."

"Are you certain you wish to be alone?"

She nodded, sadness and guilt streaming from her in waves. "Quite certain. You should be with the others processing our practice session."

"What will you do?" He draped a light truth spell between them, hopefully light enough she wouldn't notice it. He was worried she'd go off half-cocked in search of Tessa, and he couldn't allow her to do that.

"Go to my cabin. Get cleaned up then join everyone in the dining room. I'm not used to playing nice with others, but I'll figure it out damned fast." She got to her feet, swaying with the motion of the boat. "And I'll be praying to the goddess for Tessa's safe return." A muffled sob followed her words. Before he could make another attempt to soothe her, she fled out the cabin door.

He released his spell. At least she'd told him the truth.

Leif struggled upright, fighting the canting deck, and stopped by the clothes locker. Two of the whales were there. "Do you want to go hunt for Tessa?" one asked, looking worried.

"I reached Eiocha. She'll use the ley lines to locate her. Or she'll try."

"Brilliant!" One of the whales clapped him on the back.

"That's one word for it. Desperate is another." Leif squared his tired shoulders. "I considered going after her, but it wasn't wise. We're too close to the gateway, and our enemy was hoping we'd split forces. It's why they grabbed Tessa."

"Which is why you're the alpha," a whale said. "See you in the dining room."

Leif left his parka in the locker and trudged toward his cabin. The expression on Moira's face, haunted and desolate, wouldn't leave him alone. He reached for his dolphin, relieved to find his bondmate close. "Can you talk sense into that vulture of hers?"

"I'm trying, but it's very stubborn."

"Will it break the bond with Moira?" Leif held his breath and walked into his cabin.

"Maybe not. It seems to love her, but it's hard to tell. Let me do what I can."

"Thank you."

Leif pushed everything aside but the upcoming battle and stood under the shower with the water turned as hot as he could stand it. Before he was done, the rumble of the anchor chain reached his sensitive hearing. They'd made port, wherever it might be.

18

BROKEN BONDS?

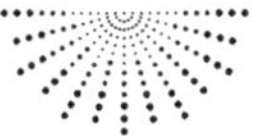

oira raced headlong down Deck Two's corridor, taking a back staircase that came out close to her cabin. She ducked inside without seeing anyone while her vulture shrieked threats in the background. Too tightly strung to sit, she paced from one side of the small space to the other and back again.

She wanted to launch herself into the ether to look for Tessa but recognized it as foolhardy. Leif had outlined why she needed a destination, and the only place she knew to try was back on the beach where they'd trained. She'd already gone there and found it empty.

No point in wasting magic to go back. Tessa wouldn't be there this time, either.

Her palms itched with wanting to draw magic and teleport out of her claustrophobic cabin. She clasped them behind her back to lessen the temptation. Her jaws ached from grinding her teeth, and she opened and closed them to reduce the tension drumming through her.

She couldn't do a damned thing to address Tessa's disappearance —or her own guilt that she'd urged the mountain cat shifter to join her foolhardy plan. Delight had shone in Tessa's dark eyes as she'd

213

agreed to what surely felt like an adventure—but something easy and safe.

"Nothing is safe," Moira muttered. "And I'm the worst kind of fool." She raised her mind voice in Gaelic, invoking every goddess she could think of to guide Eiocha's hand and bring Tessa back safely.

"Not your fault," her bondmate cawed. *"The other one, she made her own decisions, and—"*

"Shut up!" Moira screeched. "Just shut up. Of course this was my fault. It was my idea, and it turned to shit."

"It isn't the way vultures operate," her bird informed her in a patronizing tone that grated on her nerves.

"Oh really?" she retorted acidly. "Then what is?"

"Every bird takes responsibility for itself."

"Are you trying to help? Or do you just need to be right?" Weariness washed over her in waves, and she sank onto one of the bunks, steadying herself with a hand. The boat's motion had improved, which probably meant they'd sailed into a sheltered area where they'd anchor for the night.

"I am always right."

Moira sucked air to the bottom of her lungs, blew it out, and did it again. Here it was. The confrontation she'd seen coming with her bird for years. She'd sidestepped it many times, smoothing the rough waters between them, but she couldn't do that anymore.

"What happened to the last Shifters you bonded with?"

"What do you mean?" the bird sputtered, clearly caught off guard by her question.

"It's a simple enough question," she replied. "You're old. I can't be the first Shifter you've bonded with. What happened to the others? Did they die?" Moira tucked her hands under her and scooted so her back rested against the wall. In years past, she'd never have had the moxie to question her bondmate about its past.

"I am not bound to answer such queries."

"No," she agreed. "You're not, but my guess is when your bonded one fell shy of your impossible standards of perfection, you broke the bond, spent years nursing your anger, and then tried again. But the next Shifter eventually did the same thing." She stopped to let her words sink in before continuing. "The Shifter bond was designed as a partnership, which means both of us have inherent value, not that one of us gets the final say on every single issue."

The bird remained silent, so Moira pressed on. "We're only a few days away from a battle that may well kill us all. This is a very bad time for you to decide you're finished with me, but if you're going to leave, do it cleanly and go. I'm not going to engage Draconian measures to hold onto you." Breath rattled through her teeth. "I don't have the energy."

"Tessa disappearing isn't my fault, either."

"I never said it was. I take full responsibility for that unfortunate event."

Part of her recoiled from the stand she'd taken. This was even stupider than trying to teleport back to the ship with Tessa. She could duke it out with the bird after the battle. Going into the fight without her bondmate would cripple her, cut her available power by some unknown quantity.

"You're telling me to break our bond."

"No. I'm not. What I'm saying is we have to develop a more equitable balance of power if we're to remain bonded. I'm done stuffing my opinions because I don't want to offend you, or because what I have in mind won't measure up to how you believe vultures should act." She swallowed around a thick place in her throat. "I love you. I've loved you from the first time you appeared in my dreams, but even the hardiest love has limits."

Moira shut up. She'd said enough.

"I have to think about this."

"Well, don't think too long. I need to know if you'll be by my side in the upcoming battle."

"You will be weak and vulnerable without me." The bird's sanctimonious tone was back in spades.

"You think I don't know that?" Words forced their way past her partially occluded throat. "For all the time you've spent linked to humans, you've never bothered to learn anything about their customs because you viewed your bondmate as inferior. The bond we share is not unlike a marriage. Breaking it is just like a divorce, and divorces hardly ever happen at auspicious times."

The place within her where the bird dwelt developed the vacant feel that meant it had departed for the animals' borderworld. Sadness welled, displacing anger. She really did love her bondmate with all its crassness and idiosyncrasies, but it had to love her the same way. And it didn't. It only offered acceptance when she acceded to its wishes. Mostly, its lack of tolerance hadn't gotten in the way when she spent the majority of her time in her human form in a world where most had no idea magic existed.

The Cataclysm sounded a death knell for that world, and once she'd segued into a reality where every day brought new reminders of her magical roots, she'd had more and more run-ins with her bondmate. Where the other women's animals had been warm and loving, hers remained chilly, critical.

Moira pushed to her feet and undressed, draping clothing over the room's only chair. She felt numb and depressed as the shower pelted her with first hot and then cold water. She stood under the icy spray for as long as she could stand it to clear her head, before turning off the taps and grabbing a towel.

It was time to put on her game face and head for the dining room. She'd have to alert the others that her vulture might abandon her. They needed to know she wouldn't be at the top of her magical game and plan accordingly. After the debacle with Tessa, she'd be damned if she'd put anyone else at risk.

She finished drying herself and sopped up as much water as she could from her long hair before bunching it into a bun. Goose bumps lined her arms, and she dressed fast, layering warm items atop one another, and stuffing her feet into a pair of thick woolen socks and her Arctic Pac boots.

She'd be devastated to lose her bondmate, but while she'd been in the shower she'd come to terms with her part in things. Relationships never failed unilaterally, and every time she'd swallowed her opinions, deferring to her vulture, she'd pounded one more nail into the coffin. So much bad water had flowed under the bridge, she didn't hold out much hope for them finding a way through, but she'd done the right thing.

Finally.

Each time she'd cosigned the vulture's actions, even when she knew it was wrong, a little part of her died. The bird had a great deal to do with the harsh, bitter, my-way-or-the-highway woman she'd turned into. One who did a damn fine job pretending she didn't need anybody or anything. The vulture heartily approved of that stance, but look where it had led her.

Moira stood straight and left her cabin. She might not have much time to savor her freedom from the overbearing bird, but she'd make the best of whatever the goddess saw fit to offer. Done with feeling sorry for herself, she sent her magic in a wide arc, hunting for Eiocha.

Had the horse goddess returned? If she had, was Tessa with her?

Breath rasped in her throat as she searched for the goddess's distinctive feel. She'd get the apology part over with right away. The shimmery flow she associated with Eiocha was, indeed, moving closer. She hadn't yet returned but was on her way.

Moira dug deeper, working to see past Eiocha's robust magic. It wasn't easy since the goddess's power overshadowed almost everything, but she thought another's magic skimmed along next to the goddess's.

Hope kindled.

"Please, please let it be Tessa." She spoke the words to the empty corridor, pelting to its end and down one flight to Deck Two. The smell of food and the murmur of voices reached her.

Moira hurried into the larger dining room and joined the small group huddled around a table spread with platters of food. She felt guilty she hadn't helped with this particular meal, but she wouldn't have been much more than a liability in her frame of mind. Her stomach was still twisted into a knot, but she needed to eat.

Eiocha's signature magic was nearly upon them. Moira turned away from the food and faced the spot where she felt certain the goddess would emerge. The air bubbled and glistened, forming a silvery gateway. Breath clotted in her chest and breathing became a chore. Her hands knotted into fists, nails cutting into her palms.

Eiocha burst into the dining room with Tessa clinging to her back. Breath whooshed from Moira, and she felt the hot bite of tears as relief coursed through her. Her next moves surprised her. Spontaneous and unchoreographed, they were nothing like her norm.

She ran to Eiocha and fell to her knees, head bowed. "Thank you, Goddess. I haven't adequate words, but thank you from the bottom of my soul for rescuing my companion. Heartfelt apologies, too, for my behavior this morning. It was inexcusable."

Moira remained on her knees, head lowered, willing to accept whatever censure fell from the goddess's lips.

"It's all right, child. No harm done. Get up and greet your friend."

Tessa slid from the horse's back, happiness streaming from her.

Moira straightened, unashamed of the tears rolling down her cheeks. When she held her arms out, Tessa barreled into them. "I'm so sorry," she said. "I got distracted by something shiny and realized too late I'd been suckered into a trap."

"Same thing that happened to Rowana and me on South Georgia," Karin said.

All the women had formed a tight circle around them and were exchanging hugs and kisses and offering thanks to Eiocha, who'd morphed back into her human form.

The goddess clapped her hands briskly. "Enough. Shall we eat afore the food grows cold?"

After one more hug, Moira let go of Tessa and returned to where she'd begun filling a plate. Her heart was full, but the exchange with

Tessa highlighted exactly what was wrong with the relationship between her and her vulture. Tessa apologized for her role in the failed teleport episode, but Moira had as well. Both of them accepted responsibility for something that hadn't worked out.

Neither blamed the other.

Moira hoped the vulture had been watching, but the odds were thin since she couldn't feel its presence.

Leif caught her eye as she glanced about the room hunting for a table with an empty spot. He patted a place next to him, and she nodded, stopping to scoop up a glass of wine before making her way to the table where he sat with Viktor, Ketha, and two whales.

"That wine is a grand idea," Viktor said. "I'll go find us a bottle."

"Be sure to bring glasses," Ketha said. "Moira has one, but none of the rest of us do."

"Eh." He winked at her. "We can pass the bottle around, seaman style."

Ketha snorted. "Do as you wish, but I'd like a glass."

Moira settled next to Leif and took a sip of what turned out to be a decent Syrah, rolling it around on her tongue.

"I'm happy for you," Leif said near her ear.

"Thanks," she replied. "I can't recall when I've been so relieved to see anyone, and I mended my bridges with Eiocha."

"I noticed." He touched her hand, and then went back to his dinner.

She ate methodically, welcoming the warmth of food in her belly. Leif sitting beside her felt right, comforting and exciting by turns, but he wouldn't even consider joining his life with hers once she wasn't a Shifter anymore. The thought was like a splash of cold seawater, but it reinforced her resolve.

A quick scan told her most everyone was done eating. She rose to her feet and walked to the front of the room. "Could I have your attention?" She raised her voice for emphasis and waited until the side conversations faded.

"Thank you. This won't take long, and I guess tonight is my time to apologize. I know the timing couldn't be worse, but it's possible my vulture will break its bond with me."

A wave of surprised gasps rolled through the room, followed by "Why would you think that?" and "You must be overreacting. That's unheard of."

Karin started toward her, but Moira shook her head and the wolf Shifter retreated to her chair.

Moira extended the flats of her hands and drew them downward, hoping for silence. "My bondmate and I have had problems for a long time. I circumvented them by always agreeing with it, but today after Tessa disappeared and the bird kept harping about it not being my doing, something snapped."

Everyone's attention was riveted on her, so she went on. "I suspect it's broken bonds with other Shifters. My bird is very old, so I can't be its first bondmate. When I asked it pointblank what happened to its other mated ones, it refused to answer."

Moira stopped to take a measured breath. "I'm bringing this up not for sympathy but because if my bondmate abandons me, I have no idea what will happen to my magic. I don't want to be a liability on the battlefield, and we may have to plan around my weaker magic."

"No worries, child." Eiocha surged to her feet. "You will fight alongside me, and I will ensure the ley lines provide what you require." She hesitated. "I have known your bonded one for a very long time, and it's added a new dimension to the word stubborn."

Touched by Eiocha's candor and generosity, Moira said, "Thank you. That's all I had to say. We need to move on to planning for the battle." She strode back to her seat, avoiding the stricken look on Leif's face. She'd been correct about her no longer being mate material if she wasn't bonded with an animal.

Sadness rolled through her in a wave with sharp claws, but she pushed it aside. Hard to lose something she'd never had except in the most distant of dreams. She'd come to terms with whatever choice her vulture made, and Tessa was back. Those two things and the battle were important. Everything else paled in comparison.

"I have news about the passageway," Eiocha trotted nimbly to the space Moira had just vacated at the front of the room. "Afore I begin, might there be any mead aboard this vessel?"

Viktor stood. Something about the goddess encouraged standing before addressing her. "I'm afraid not. We do, however, have scotch whiskey, Irish whiskey, vodka, bourbon, and a credible selection of wine."

"Irish whiskey."

"I'll run and get it." Ketha slid from her seat.

Eiocha nodded. "About the passageway—"

"Begging your pardon, ma'am, er Goddess." Boris rose, keeping his gaze downcast.

"I give you permission to speak, mortal."

"Might there be any chance you could address us in English? It's the one language everyone here understands." Bobbing his head, he sat, still looking at the floor.

"Aye, I know all languages," Eiocha said in stilted, archaic English. "No more interruptions unless I solicit your opinions." Her nostrils flared, and she gazed about the room. "The passageway is in place. It begins where you left the faeries and extends to within a few feet of the fissure. I have anchored it with ley lines, which will infuse magic into its weave and ensure naught disturbs it."

Ketha trotted back into the dining room and ducked into the kitchen. When she resurfaced, she handed a glass full of amber liquid to Eiocha before making her way to her chair.

Eiocha inclined her head and sipped the fragrant brew. "Some of the fair folk wished to be included in the battle. I moved them to a nearby borderworld where 'tis warmer to await our arrival. I returned the rest to Scotland. Since I was near the fissure, I did a wee bit of scouting."

The whale who'd been stranded in northern waters rose. Rather than talking, he waited for the goddess to recognize him. She rolled her eyes. "Aye. What is it you would add?"

"I did much the same, Goddess, when I ended up near the fissure. I will be interested to see if your observations match up with mine, or if things have changed."

"I shall find that interesting as well. The fissure is a busy place with much coming and going. Demons, wicked sprites, a griffon or two, Harpies." She made a small shrugging gesture. "I thought I caught sight of Tantalus and the Minotaur. Even a few Vampires, although their power appears to be waning."

"When I was in the same spot a few weeks back," the whale said, "the place was very quiet. Is there still a guardian who sits at the gate?"

Eiocha nodded. "Several guardians working in shifts. The uptick in activity isn't surprising. They are gearing up much as we are. Never underestimate underdogs. They can be hellishly tenacious."

Moira stood, unsure if she should raise her hand or just wait.

"Aye?" Eiocha glanced her way.

"Why are creatures from mythology walking the Earth again?" She smiled faintly. "I suppose my question encompasses you as well as Oberon and Titania."

A thoughtful whinny emerged from Eiocha, and Moira could almost see her flick an imaginary tail. "I do not know, but my first guess is we are starting over." She took a measured breath. "Long ago, in the beginnings of the world, good battled evil and won. Evil has been trying to wrest the upper hand back for thousands of years. The Cataclysm changed things, gave evil hope they might gain the toehold they'd been hoping for. So, creatures like the Harpies and Tantalus are working like the demons they are to seize what they feel should have been theirs all along."

"Thank you." Moira sat back down.

"'Tis as good an entry point as we are likely to get to crafting battle strategy," Eiocha said. "Fill me in on how your drill went today, so we can build on it."

Leif stood and outlined their activities. The consensus once he'd finished was everyone would be up early the following day for more practice, this time with Eiocha overseeing their efforts. Assuming things went well, they'd sail to Pevek that night with plans to launch their offensive the day after.

No point in waiting. The longer they put things off, the more time their enemy would have to grow stronger.

Moira drained her wine glass and stumbled to her feet. Weariness dragged at her, and she longed for her narrow bunk and a few hours of blackness when nothing could bother her. She was out the door and heading for the stairs when Leif caught up and hooked a hand beneath her arm.

"You've had a rough day. Feel like talking?"

People streamed around them on their way to their cabins. Moira waited until everyone was gone. While she waited, she drank in Leif's beautiful, kind eyes, his classically handsome features, and his broad-shouldered build. Desire stirred in her belly, but she shut it down fast.

"Not much to talk about," she said. "Tessa's back, and I did what I should have done long ago with my bondmate."

"Which was?" His blue eyes never left her face.

"Told it I was done taking shit, that relationships were two-way streets and respect had to flow both ways."

He tightened his hold on her arm. "I asked my dolphin to talk with your bondmate."

"Aw, that was kind, but unnecessary. My vulture has a nasty habit of not listening to anyone."

"Moira." The way he said her name was part entreaty, part prayer, and she wanted to hear him say it again.

"It's all right. My timing standing up to my bondmate is abysmal, but this would have happened sooner or later."

He dropped his other hand on her shoulder. "No matter how this works out, I love you. I want you as my mate."

She leaned into him, resting her head on his shoulder. "You need another Shifter as a mate, but I appreciate the thought."

"No. I need you. We'll revisit this after the battle—assuming we're both still alive." He kissed her forehead and let go of her.

The places his hands had rested on her body felt empty. It was hard not to wrap her arms around him and drag him into the nearest cabin, but that would add a layer of complexity neither of them needed. "See you in the morning." She smiled, hoping he'd recognize how much he meant to her without her having to say the words.

"I'll look forward to it." He stood aside, and she felt his gaze on her as she climbed the stairs.

19

DECLARATIONS

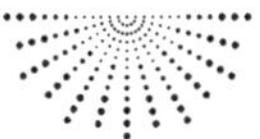

*L*eif loped from one group to the next, making suggestions and fine-tuning how people deployed power. Their human contingent had been content to remain aboard *Arkady*, keeping it safe from harm. All recognized they'd be out of their depth in a battle of clashing magics.

He'd tried not to hover near Moira, but he'd kept an eye on her no matter where he was on the field. She had strength. To watch her, he'd never have guessed her bondmate had threatened desertion. His dolphin had returned from attempting to talk with the vulture more pissed off than he'd ever seen it.

"Faster!" Eiocha yelled. "Mix fire in faster. Don't think about it. Do it until it becomes second nature." She'd been alternating between her horse and human forms. Leif suspected she'd have stuck to the equine one were it not for the necessity to issue orders.

A whale, Juan, and Aura jumped to her command. Magic prickled Leif's scalp, making the fine hairs on the back of his neck stand on end. The air was overly saturated with the trappings of power. They were pulling magic faster than either air or earth could absorb it. The excess sparkled in untidy clumps, some on the ground, some floating in the still air.

Yesterday's storm had blown through. While it was still bitterly cold, so cold Leif flexed his fingers and directed a flow of magic to keep them functioning, there was no wind. Viktor had chosen well, anchoring the ship near Ossora. The deserted fishing village was tucked between two protective spits of land. Never a densely populated region, at most it had hosted a couple thousand people.

No one was left. Perhaps they'd taken one of the ancient trading routes back to the Russian mainland at the beginning of the Cataclysm. Or maybe the town was littered with corpses. No one had taken the time to check. The rocky shoreline where they'd established their training ground was a few miles outside the village proper.

Eiocha sidled to where Leif stood and motioned for him to follow her off to one side while the groups continued to lob power at targets she'd set for them. He felt her magic settle around them, so she must not want to be overheard.

He turned so he faced her and bowed. "Thank you again for helping us, Eiocha."

A garbled snort blew past her lips. "You say it as if I had a choice, dolphin. I can move to a borderworld if things go to hell here, but it isn't my first choice."

"Might be hard to leave your ley lines behind, eh?"

"That and other things." She narrowed her eyes. "My roots date to the world's beginnings. It's not easy to leave everything you've always known behind, but that wasn't why I drew you aside."

Leif waited, curious what Eiocha wanted. Was she disappointed in everyone's magic and going to suggest another few days of practice?

"No easy way to ask this," she muttered, "but what are the chances corruption has reached the animals' world?"

Leif's eyes widened. He hadn't anticipated that question, or anything remotely connected with it. It wasn't hard to connect the dots and follow her reasoning, though. "You're concerned the vulture Shifter may have fallen prey to evil?"

Eiocha nodded. "I'd thought to ask Moira, but she appears to be holding up well under the strain, and I didn't wish to flog her with her bondmate's perfidy." She creased her high forehead into thoughtful lines. "I've spoken privately with Juan's mountain lion. According to its memories, there are only a handful of instances where the Shifter bond was severed. There may have been a few others, but it's a rare enough occurrence to be notable."

Adopting his usual, methodical approach to problems, Leif ticked points off on his fingers. "First"—he extended a forefinger—"none of the other bond animals are having problems. Second, according to Moira, her vulture has always been cantankerous."

"Aye, I heard her well enough when she shared her suspicions about it breaking other bonds, but it's difficult to believe. Furthermore, I've known that vulture for a very long time. Granted, it's highhanded and imperious, but it never mentioned jettisoning bondmates. Furthermore, why wouldn't the other bond animals have censured it if such were the case?"

"Perhaps they did. We'd have no way of knowing. It's not the sort of thing our bondmates discuss with us. If it has broken bonds before, I can't imagine it sharing that fact—with anyone." He rolled tension from his shoulders. "Are you concerned about sabotage from within the animals' ranks?"

"It did occur to me. The enemy we face is bad enough without a subtle disruption hammering us from inside our magic."

"If poison was spreading within the bond animals, my dolphin would have alerted me."

"For sea Shifters or land Shifters as well?" She folded her arms beneath her breasts.

"For everyone. My bondmate attempted a conversation with Moira's vulture."

"And?" Eiocha arched a silvery brow.

Leif shrugged. "I don't have details other than it didn't go well."

Eiocha leaned closer as if she feared being overheard even through her warding. "Should we sever that bond afore the battle?"

"No. It's Moira's decision. If I had to guess, in her secret places she's still hoping her bondmate will make an effort to become a partner, not just a taskmaster."

"Unlikely. It's one of the oldest bond animals and as prone to change as me, which is to say not very." She chuckled wryly, amused by her own joke.

"But you did change," Leif pointed out. "When we visited you in your cavern with the ley lines, you refused to leave the place you'd been for millennia. Yet, here you stand."

"Point taken. I will keep the vulture Shifter next to me during the battle just in case I'm onto something about her bondmate—and to shore up her power if it becomes necessary."

Eiocha waved a hand, and the magic surrounding them dissipated. "The group has done well today. Far better than I expected. While I'd love to have another few days to hone our skills, every day we tarry is a day our enemy grows stronger." She shut her eyes for a moment, lashes brushing her cheeks. When she opened them, she looked ancient and harsh and foreboding. "We're close enough to the fissure," she went on, "I feel nascent evil. It pricks me from all sides like an insidious cold that refuses to retreat."

"Have you heard from Oberon and Titania?"

She shook her head. "Nay, and it worries me, but neither have they put out a call for aid."

"We will do what we can with the talent available. Poseidon and Amphitrite did their best to kill off everything in the sea, yet they failed. I have to believe good will rise above wickedness."

She trained her changeable eyes on him. "Aye, dolphin Shifter, believing in our cause is a first step, but..." She tossed her head, chin jutting at a defiant angle. "We do what we must. 'Tis why I am here and not cowering in my cave letting others fight my battles. If you want the truth, Oberon shamed me, as did his consort."

Compassion and understanding flooded him. "Regardless of the reason, I'm glad you're here."

"Thank you, Alpha. We should orchestrate a final round where everyone runs their magic fully open, and then we shall return to the ship."

Leif turned to the groups, an idea forming in the back of his mind. At first, he dismissed it as indulgent and ill-advised, but the more he thought about it, the more it wouldn't leave him be.

"I think you should," his dolphin spoke up.

Leif swallowed surprise since his bondmate rarely forwarded an opinion on anything. *"Let's see how I feel about it after we're done here,"* he said.

"Some actions require doing, not thinking," the dolphin observed.

Leif reached the nearest group. Zoe, Recco, and Lewis were adding fire as Eiocha had instructed, and their targets had almost been obliterated. "Great work!" Leif clapped Lewis on the shoulder. "Last exercise. Give it everything you've got. Open a conduit to the ley lines and blast away. Not for long. We don't want to squander magic. Get a feel for running full throttle, and then shut it down. When you're finished, return to the ship."

"Sure and I'm not feeling ready," Zoe mumbled.

Leif gripped her hand hard. "None of us will ever feel ready, but we have to do this. The longer we wait, the stronger our enemy grows. If we take another week to hone our abilities, we may pass a tipping point where we can't win no matter how skilled we are."

Recco wrapped an arm around his mate, and she leaned into him. He met Leif's gaze and nodded, silently urging him to leave them. Leif moved to the next group with the same message. The last practice round was over in the blink of an eye. Ready to teleport back to *Arkady,* he located Viktor and Ketha.

Before he could open his mouth to ask what happened to Moira, Ketha said, "It's all right. This isn't a repeat of yesterday. Moira went back with Eiocha."

Maybe it was just as well. Leif had some thinking to do. Moira's absence afforded him space to do it in. He shepherded Viktor and Ketha back to the ship. "Good choice of a port," he told Viktor.

"Thanks. This little part of the Bering Sea has always been the banana belt of the Arctic."

Ketha snorted. "Banana belt? It can't be more than ten degrees."

"Yes, darling, but there's no wind. Imagine how much worse it would feel with windchill added in." Laughing, he tucked a hand beneath her arm and led her inside the warmth of the ship.

Leif trailed after them. Everyone would gather for a meal, but tonight would be a time for mates to spend what might be their last night together, for friends to say whatever had been left unsaid. They'd travel through the night. By morning, they'd be at Pevek and launch the Zodiacs, heading for the faeries' passageway.

By this time tomorrow night, who knew how many of them would remain?

Lewis rolled from his teleport spell and walked to Leif. "We'd planned to spend a bit of time in the sea. Will you join us?"

"Let's eat with the land Shifters, and then we'll retire to the sea for a while."

"I'll let the pod know." Lewis nodded briskly.

"We won't remain with the others for very long, but it's important to break bread together." Leif understood why his pod wanted to take to their sea forms. They'd be doing much same thing as the land Shifters: saying what might be final goodbyes.

"I get the part about making an appearance at dinner. See you inside." Lewis slipped through the nearest door into the ship.

STARS WERE out by the time he returned to *Arkady*. His pod was still swimming, recalling happier times, but he'd come to a decision about the problem he'd tackled earlier. No one knew what tomorrow would hold. Because he owed it to them, he'd told his pod what he planned, and they'd given him their heartfelt support.

Water pooled around him on the chilly deck bathed in moonlight. He hurried inside and ducked into the first empty cabin he found, using its dusty towels to dry off. He snatched an equally dusty robe off a hook and wrapped it around himself. Maybe what he planned was ridiculous. He'd probably wake Moira, but he'd take his chances.

He was going to tell her how he felt again, and that he longed for a future with her. What happened next would be up to her. It had surprised him his pod hadn't pitched twenty-seven kinds of fits. She wasn't a sea Shifter. In truth, she might not be a Shifter at all much longer, but they hadn't cared. Leif had told them he loved her, and they'd wished him well.

He pushed his dripping hair over his shoulders. The salt smell of the sea rose around him, tangy and welcome. So he wouldn't create puddles in her cabin, he directed a small stream of magic to finish drying himself. Leif hesitated, standing in the empty cabin. Maybe this wasn't a good idea, but damn it, he had to try. Worst thing that would happen is she'd send him away. Waiting wasn't making things easier, so he pushed resolutely into the corridor and strode to her cabin. Not bothering to send magic ahead, he tapped on her door.

Footsteps rustled from within, and she pulled the door open a few inches. Her long, thick hair hung around her in messy curls. Her dark eyes held a haggard expression, and her face was blotchy from tears. She wore a robe twin to his, except hers was light blue.

"Did something happen?" she asked, swallowing visibly. "I know I look like shit, but I'm not in that bad a shape. Do you need me for something? I can be dressed in a flash."

"May I come in?"

She drew her brows into a thin line. "Um, sure. I guess so." Moira pushed the door open wide enough to admit him and backed into her cabin. The duvet was crumpled into a heap at the bottom of her bunk, and the desk held sheets of paper covered in finely-written script.

"What were you working on?" he asked.

She shrugged. "It's how I solve problems. I write things out over and over, refining them with each pass. I used to use a computer program to do it. Mathcad was way faster than my hand calculations." She plopped into the desk chair and waved an arm at the bunk she didn't ever sleep in. "Have a seat, unless you weren't planning to stay long. In that case, tell me why you're here."

Leif tightened the robe's belt and perched on the edge of the bunk. "How's the problem solving coming along?"

"Not well." She screwed her face into a bitter expression. "Everyone will know soon enough. My vulture plans to sever our bond, but it's waiting until after the battle." A tear leaked from one eye, and she brushed it aside. "I suppose it's decent of it to stick by me for now, but I suspect one of the animals in the borderworld threatened sanctions if it abandoned me on the verge of the most important battle in Earth's history."

Compassion filled him. "I'm so sorry."

Another tear followed the first. "Don't." Her voice held anguish. "I can't talk about it. Hell, I can't even think about it. I have to keep moving forward."

"Is that what were you writing about?"

"I was trying to sort out what I'd have left for magic." She held up a sheet covered with calculus equations. "Turns out I won't be in quite as bad a place as I'd feared." One corner of her mouth turned down. "I will miss flying. I'd become quite fond of it. The one thing I couldn't get a handle on was what impact this would have on my lifespan."

"Maybe another would bond with you." Leif tried for a supportive tone.

"Even if another vulture showed up, I'd never take a chance on one. A raven maybe. Or an eagle, like Rowana's... No more vultures."

"I'm not feeling too kindly disposed toward them myself about now," he growled.

She swiped at her damp cheeks. "Damn it. I can't stop crying. I don't get it. This is a relief—or it should be. If I hadn't wanted to force a choice, I'd never have stood up to my bondmate."

Leif fought fury at the vulture. If it showed up once it was no longer linked to Moira, he'd throttle the damned thing for causing her pain. "Tears serve a purpose. They're cleansing and will help clear your head for tomorrow." He hesitated, not sure how to approach the reason he was in her cabin.

Perhaps she'd been inside his head because she scooted her chair closer to where he sat and said, "You didn't stop by here to console me about my bondmate. Are there new developments? Something I need to know before we reach the gateway?"

It was as good an entry as he was likely to get. "Nothing new." He rested a hand on her knee. "I love you, Moira. I want you to become my mate. I'd planned to wait to formalize my request until after the battle, but tonight may be the only time we have together." Breath hitched in his throat, and he offered up a prayer she felt the same, that she wouldn't turn him away.

More tears rolled down her cheeks, and she shook her head until hair fell around her face. "You're only saying that because you fear many of us won't survive the battle. I won't be a Shifter anymore afterward. I'm not the right mate for you. Besides, your pod would never support such a pairing."

"Oh yes, they would. They encouraged me to speak with you."

Her eyes widened, kindling with hope, but then she drew back. "The wisest course would be to wait, see if we survive tomorrow and whatever comes after."

He wrapped his hands around her waist and pulled her into his lap, so she lay across him. "If one of us dies, wouldn't you want to have spent tonight in my arms loving me? We may not get any other chances."

A host of conflicting emotions crossed her expressive features. He smoothed a thumb across her lips, loving the feel of her skin beneath his touch, silky and smooth. She didn't push him away. Desire ignited. It had been there all along, but he'd kept it under wraps.

Taking a chance, he lowered his head and closed his mouth over hers. After an initial hesitation, she kissed him back, opening her mouth to his tongue. He explored the inside of her mouth, while she sparred with him, exchanging sucking his tongue for biting his lips with little sharp kisses.

She threaded her arms around him, gripping his back with her fingers. He rolled them onto the bunk so they lay on their sides, mouths still pressed together and bodies straining against one another. Her nipples turned into hard peaks where they pressed against his chest, and he thrust his hips, craving the feel of her belly against his erect cock. She angled a leg across him and ground her nub against his thigh. Heat from her seared him, and he slid a hand between her legs.

She made a hungry, mewling noise and writhed against him. Desire spilled from her, feeding his own hunger.

Leif forced his mouth from hers. He was breathing fast, and every cell in his body wanted to rip her clothing aside and plumb her as quick and hard as he could, but that wasn't the way he wanted her their first time.

"Are you sure?" he asked.

She smiled crookedly, her eyes dark pools of lust. "Yes. I'm sure. The mystery is why you'd want me. Not only am I not a sea Shifter, I won't be a Shifter at all."

"It doesn't matter. It's you I want. We'll figure out the rest as we go." He didn't add his concerns about the morrow. He didn't have to. She knew the stakes as well as he did.

Catching the end of the sash holding her robe together, he flicked it to undo the bow. When her robe fell open, he pushed it aside. Breath caught in his throat as he gazed at the vista of high, firm breasts tipped with coppery nipples. Shapely ribs led to a slender waist and flared hips. A carpet of spiky curls nestled between her beautiful, long legs. The musk of her arousal mingled with the scents of her magic, bayberry, pine, and wild things.

He traced the lines of her body with both hands. "You are so beautiful. So unbelievably lovely." He filled his hands with her breasts, rubbing the nipples with his fingers. She arched her back, moaning low in her throat as he encouraged her nipples to grow longer, harder.

She moved until she could snake a hand beneath his robe and curve it around his cock. The feel of her flesh against his was heady, and when she tightened her grip on him and explored his shaft with her fingertips, it took all his willpower not to come. He mixed in a jot of magic to mute his arousal.

"I want to see you too," she said.

Because he didn't want to let go of her breasts, he directed a thread of magic to untie his robe. Once it was free, he shrugged out of it, letting it pool around where they lay entwined.

"You've seen me naked plenty," he reminded her. "Every time I transitioned from dolphin to man."

"Yes, but then I had the good grace to look away—most of the time."

"And now?" He smiled because it felt so good to have her in his arms, bodies pressed together.

"Now I'm sorry I was so polite before. You're incredible." Letting go of his cock, she ran her fingertips from his shoulders down one arm. From there, she pinched his pebbled nipples and then moved her hand lower, across his stomach and hips. Wherever she touched him, his body heated until every cell was on fire with need.

He flipped her onto her back. Starting with the hollow in her throat, he ran his mouth down her breastbone until he hit nipple level. He took one of her breasts into his mouth, sucking hard. She groaned and grappled for his cock again but couldn't reach it.

He lashed his mouth from breast to breast. Joining his magic to hers, he felt her arousal spin higher and higher. She was panting, head thrown back as he pleasured her. Before she came, he slithered lower, licking her belly, until he latched onto her nub, alternating sucking with swirling the tip of his tongue around her distended flesh. She gripped his head. Her hips thrust against his tongue as he urged her higher still. He slid fingers inside the hot wetness of her body in time to feel her muscles clench and release as orgasm streamed through her. Because he was linked to her magically, it was harder than hell not to come.

Leif had moved beyond choreographing his next moves. The need to be inside her surpassed everything else in the world. As soon as the spasms from her climax quieted, he knelt between her legs, one hand wrapped around his achingly hard cock.

She spread her legs, curling them around his waist, and settled her hands on his hips, drawing him forward. Her skin had developed a lovely rose cast, and lust flowed from her in waves. He wanted everything. To look at her forever. To plumb her until he was dizzy with heat. To go back to suckling her distended nipples.

She grinned up at him. "We may get to all those things. For now, I want you inside. It's been a really long time."

"For me as well." He stopped, hovering at the opening to her body, the head of his cock seated at her entrance. "No going back, Moira, my heart, my love. Once we're done, you shall be my mate."

Her smile softened, and her eyes turned molten with desire. Thrusting upward, she captured the first inch of him."

He sank into her. As the heat from her body surrounded him, the rest of the world dropped away. Always before when he'd made love, he'd withheld his semen. Not tonight. He'd gift Moira with his seed, and it would seal their mating. He waited until he was fully encased, allowing her to stretch around his girth. She writhed, pushing with hands on his hips to encourage him to move.

"Once this gets going, it will develop a mind of its own," he warned her.

"Music to my ears. Come on. My first orgasm was an appetizer. I want the real thing."

He supported himself on his arms and bent low, kissing her while he withdrew from her body, swirled the head of his appendage around her opening, and sank back inside. Her breasts jutted into his chest, and sensation ratcheted through him. To be making love with Moira was like a dream. He'd imagined being inside her just like this so many times, he almost couldn't believe it was finally happening.

Around the dozenth stroke, he stopped thinking. He moved her legs so they draped over his shoulders and held onto her hips as he drove into her. Her body tightened around him, upping the ante on his pleasure. She was close to release. He felt it in her magic and in the tension of her vault.

He wasn't sure how much longer he could hold on, so he wove a streamer of magic around her clit, snugging it to rub against her engorged nub. She arched her back and melted around him in a flood of heat. No more need to hold back. Two more thrusts and semen juddered from him. He came for a long time, drowning in pleasure.

Somehow, he ended up lying on top of her with her arms and legs wrapped around him and her crooning to him in Gaelic. He wanted to scream his triumph to the skies. Moira was his. They were mated.

"I love you, darling," he murmured into her ear.

"I love you too. There, I said it." She dragged her head back to look at him. "I hope to hell you don't regret this. It would be hard to bear if I lost you too."

Feral protectiveness ran hot. "The only way you'll lose me is if I die in battle. You are mine, my heart, my love."

She drew his head down next to hers on the pillow. "You've made me a very happy woman. We should try to sleep a little."

"Yes. Morning will come all too soon." He held her close and spun spells to ensure she rested. "I'll watch over you. Now and always."

Her breathing slowed, and she relaxed against him.

Leif cleared his mind. No point worrying about what came next. They'd face tomorrow when it happened. For now, the woman he craved more than life itself loved him back. It was more than enough.

"*Sleep,*" his dolphin said. "*I will wake you when it's time.*"

20

BATTLE CRY

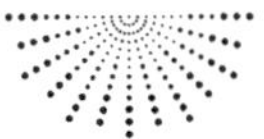

oira zipped her parka all the way up and buried as much of her face as she could in its folds. They'd reached Pevek at dawn. After a quick meal where everyone wore grim expressions and choked down food because they needed it to fuel their magic, not because anyone had an appetite, Juan and Viktor had readied two rafts.

No one had said much, either on the ship on in the rafts. They'd fight in the groups they'd practiced with and deal with whatever presented itself. Sleet sheeted from the sky, bitterly cold and stinging when it hit her face. Wind scudded by, turning the gunmetal surface of the sea into whitecaps that sent water over the pontoons. A couple of inches coated the floor of the raft, turning to a slushy, slurry of ice.

Bringing two rafts had been a last-minute decision. The sea Shifters had originally planned to swim but carting along bags of dry clothes to keep all of them warm enough to fight would have overloaded a single raft holding fifteen land Shifters.

The rafts were burdened as it was, riding low in the water, which exacerbated the problem of waves crashing over the sides. Beyond the foul weather, a hideous stench had done nothing but

239

grow worse. She didn't understand why the wind didn't blow it away. Instead, it bore down on them in a choking miasma that tied her belly into a painful knot.

One minute it smelled like a charnel pit, replete with rotting bodies. The next like roadkill that had sat so long, maggot-riddled flesh sloughed off the bones. She resisted gagging, and the food she'd consumed earlier settled into a heavy, indigestible lump in her gut.

Eiocha was the only one who'd used magic to travel to the faeries' portal. She'd left before them, ostensibly to gather the fair folk who wished to lend a hand today. Still no word from Oberon or Titania. It was hard not to worry whether they'd show up, but Moira was used to working with what she had.

The previous night with Leif had heartened and revived her. She loved him, and his unconditional acceptance of whatever form her magic ended up taking allowed her to dismantle her barriers. They'd fallen asleep in each other's arms and made love one more time just before dawn.

It would be a cruel twist of fate if she'd finally found a man to love only to have the small slice of happiness ripped away later today.

I can't think like that, she chided herself, knowing she had to focus on sealing the gateway. If they couldn't manage it, evil would continue to pour through its portals. Whoever was left on the good side of the aisle would end up leaving Earth for a borderworld.

Once that happened, the world she'd always known would die.

Viktor angled the raft toward a sandy spit coming into view through the storm. Eiocha was in horse form, stamping her front hooves. A bevy of color sorted itself into a phalanx of faeries. It looked to Moira like all of them were there. Their valor made her chest tighten with emotion. They understood this was a battle for everybody. No one got to sit this one out.

The second raft chugged alongside of them, and both Zodiacs ran aground. Moira waited, exiting the raft when her turn came.

Eiocha cantered over. *"Hurry,"* she urged. *"Oberon and Titania are already there, and they've sustained serious losses. They need us."*

A frantic cry rose from the faeries. Sorrow and worry were rolled into their anguished shouting. The king and queen of faery might not be their lieges, but they adored them and didn't want them harmed.

Leif gripped Moira's hand, and they followed Viktor and Ketha to a glistening slash in the gunmetal air. Fairies scuttled into the portal, chanting to enhance their magic that had built the enchanted tunnel.

Time slowed, seconds turning into minutes, as they slogged through the passageway. Moira felt the magic anchoring it to the bones of the Earth. Resolve straightened her spine. She would not allow evil to triumph. Earth was helping them. It needed their support, so darkness wouldn't overshadow its goodness.

"Ready yourself," Leif murmured next to her ear. "This will go fast once we emerge."

She held tighter to his hand, giving it a hard, fast squeeze, before extricating hers to free it for fighting. "Magical battles never last long."

"It seems so," he agreed, "or maybe they go on forever but when we're in the thick of them, time advances differently."

"Thank you for last night. I'll treasure it always."

He draped an arm around her shoulders, drawing her against him as they trudged through the passageway. "I'll treasure you, protect you with everything in me."

Alarm rattled through her. "No. You're alpha for your people. They must come before me."

"You don't understand. You're my mate, which means you're part of my pod now too. I feel the linkage the same as with my whales and dolphins. If you extend your magic, you'll sense the connectedness betwixt us."

She leaned into him before ducking from beneath his arm. "I'll sort that part out later. For now, loving you is the best thing that's ever happened to me." She didn't add anything further. Her fears about the outcome of the battle had no place here.

Visualize winning, she instructed, her mind voice stern. Winning was everything, no matter what the cost.

Magic altered around them; it took more effort to move forward. They'd emerge at the fissure very soon. Panic threatened to engulf her, and she gulped air to calm herself. Now wasn't the time to second guess anything. They were here because they had no choice. She narrowed her focus to the dirt beneath her boots and steadied her breathing, sucking each breath to the bottom of her lungs. The stench had vanished when they entered the faeries' tunnel, but she had no doubt it would return.

As if her thoughts held Aura's prophetic ability, the tunnel's incandescent walls shuddered to nothingness. Rot and decay hit her like a wave, along with the clash and cries of battle. She joined Viktor and Ketha, the Shifters she'd practiced with, and directed power outward.

"Wait until we're closer and have a clear shot," Viktor shouted.

Moira scanned what lay in front of her. It was so surreal, she blinked and switched to her third eye, but nothing changed except ley lines, which came into view. Glowing beneath her feet, they formed an interlacing network. A few feet away, a gaping, throbbing hole rimmed with what looked like blood, pulsed as if alive.

Twisted, hideous creatures poured through the hole. Some with a single eye in the center of horny foreheads, others with three red eyes scattered in no particular pattern. Demons with scales, cloven hooves, and forked tails joined squat, swarthy goblins. Giants carting cudgels entered the fray. Harpies flew above, screeching their war cries. Foul magic flowed from them, emitting a rancid hypnotic quality. A griffon burst from the hole, followed by a tall, beautiful man with clouds of black hair and eyes the shade of raw emeralds.

Oberon and Titania sat astride winged white steeds. In front of them, ranks of Fae fought with magical swords and power jetting from upraised hands, but they were no match for the monsters rushing through the gateway. Wherever a Fae fell, the ley lines wound gleaming tendrils around him, forming a protective barrier. Moira hoped the strands offered healing for those not mortally wounded.

Three more goblins marched through the ever-widening scar across the landscape. It looked as if someone in Hell had issued orders, and every single foul denizen was on the move.

"The gateway!" Leif cried. "We must seal it now. Everyone to me."

Moira buried her terror deep. She'd been rooted in place because the reality stretched before her was too much to take in. Eiocha thundered past, faeries clinging to her wide back. Flanked by Viktor and Ketha, Moira ran after her. Fell creatures sent dark magic crashing against her warding, the blows so stout they nearly knocked her to the ground, but she kept going.

Their progress toward the hole felt like it was happening in slow motion, as if they swam through an oily, dank residue that stuck to her feet and kept her from moving forward. She shook her head to clear the darkness pummeling her and eroding her thought processes.

"Ley lines," she panted, forcing out words. "Got to hook into them."

With difficulty, she focused her third eye on a shiny line. It brightened beneath her attention, and clean, pure power surged through her feet.

"Thanks," Ketha gritted. "It's like I got stuck in a bad dream."

The gateway loomed. The beautiful dark-haired man stood in front of it, the griffon next to him. With its eagle head and lionesque trunk and legs, it drew her attention like a lodestone until she wrenched her gaze from its magic.

The man held up his arms, and the fissure quieted. "We can come to terms." His voice was low and musical, imbued with compulsion the likes of which Moira never dreamed existed. The urge to run to him and fall at his feet was so intense, she took a step in his direction before stopping herself.

Who the hell was he?

Eiocha planted herself right in front of him. Amid a bright flash of white light, she claimed her human form. "Tantalus." She tossed out his name like a curse.

"Eiocha, most lovely of goddesses." He bowed low. "So pleased you remember me."

"Save your false compliments."

He crossed his arms over an impossibly broad chest. Flowing robes fell open, displaying his perfect body. "No need to be so cross. Your time on Earth is done. It's finally our turn. I offer you a small portion of land where you'll be most comfortable." He made a disapproving face. "'Tis far more than you and yours did for us."

Tantalus.

Moira raked through her memory banks and came up with the half-human son of Jupiter who'd not only stolen from the gods, but who'd killed and dismembered his son, serving the unfortunate lad up in a stew. Furious at being fed the flesh of their own, the gods had exiled Tantalus to Tartarus, where he lived in constant hunger and thirst.

She balled her hands into fists. If the myth was true, how had he escaped?

What a stupid question. All of Hell is on the loose, why not him?

She narrowed her eyes, paying close attention to Eiocha. The goddess had draped power around her faery escort, and they stood close, forming a ring around her.

"No bargains," Eiocha cried in a clear, ringing voice. "If you weren't worried about losing, you'd never have offered one."

"Fine. Have it your way." Tantalus waved a lazy hand, and the fissure came to life again, disgorging a giant, who'd apparently been trapped in the liminal space behind the gateway.

Two Harpies divebombed Eiocha, but her warding held, deflecting the magical arrows aimed her way. Oddly beautiful with their women's heads and bare breasts and thickly plumed bird's bodies, poison spewed from their clawed hands. Their eyes were hammered silver, spinning like pinwheels.

Ketha wrapped an arm around Moira's shoulders, forcing her gaze downward. "Don't look," she hissed.

"Everything in this fucking place wants to mesmerize you," Moira muttered.

"Yeah, right before it kills you," Ketha sneered. "Makes their job easier if you don't fight back."

Ketha's words redirected Moira, and she gathered power, balancing it between her hands, waiting for when Eiocha would clear the path between them and the gateway.

She and the other Shifters arrayed in front, beside, and behind her had moved closer, spreading into a single line, while Eiocha talked with the fallen half-god. Not that Tantalus viewed himself in that light.

Leif had been working his way through their ranks. He drew near, talking low. "At my signal, give this everything you have."

"Last chance." Tantalus leaned toward Eiocha, oozing a raw sexuality that made the air shimmer with lust.

Desire thrummed hotly between Moira's legs. The part of her that had wanted to throw herself at Tantalus's feet changed direction. Now she wanted to jump into his arms and wind her legs around his waist, so he could plunge into her body. A shudder racked her. She might be aroused, but it felt sick, wrong. She experimented until she found a weave that muted Tantalus's sinister come-fuck-me vibes.

"I feel it too," Ketha said, her tone sharp.

"You'd have to be dead not to." Moira extended power until it included Ketha. "This should help you disregard his seductiveness."

"Thanks." Ketha blew out a jagged breath. "I figured we'd be fighting, not sitting ducks for whatever he's dishing out."

"Look at the demonspawn." Moira jutted her chin at the collection of abominations, many of whom were stroking erections. "They're in thrall. Apparently, his spell snared them too."

"So long as they're beating off, they're not hammering us." Viktor smirked.

"Small favors, eh?" Moira kept her gaze on Eiocha.

"First chance, or last or middle." Eiocha tossed her hands skyward. "You weren't worth much as a lover two thousand years ago. I don't imagine you've improved with time." She brought her arms down until both index fingers pointed right at him. "Move aside."

"Or?" Tantalus sounded amused.

Red-tinged lightning bolts left Eiocha's outstretched hands. They blew Tantalus backward before they augured into his chest. Blood spurted, and he clutched at his wounds.

The blood flowed faster, geysering onto the ice coating everything. "Why aren't I healing?" he screeched, clawing at himself.

The griffon padded lazily to where he lay and pecked at the wounds, tilting its head back to swallow the blood. Tantalus tried to bat the creature away, but it sank its beak into his chest, chewing and swallowing as fast as it could tear strips of flesh from its erstwhile associate.

Moira snorted. "No loyalty in the nether world."

"Why would there be?" Viktor countered. "Friendships require generosity, empathy."

"You're not healing," Eiocha yelled over Tantalus's screams, "because my magic overshadows yours. It always did. You're only half a god. I won't repeat the mistake we made last time where we didn't kill you and merely locked you away."

"What does that mean?" His imperious tone had morphed into a high, thin wail, riddled with fear.

Eiocha shrugged. "What do you think it means? Your creature will finish what I began." Dusting her hands together, she moved aside.

"Now," Leif shouted and ran for the fissure, power blazing from his hands.

Moira linked with Ketha and Viktor. They repeated their actions from the previous day and let magic from the ley lines roll through them. It strengthened their destructive power as they planted themselves right in front of the fissure. Magic blasted it from all sides. Shifter power married with Fae magic into a pulsing canopy that coated the opening from top to bottom and side to side.

Dark power bombarded them, but their wards were holding so far. The air thickened, the stench of sulfur adding to the rot and decay already present. A horned demon pressed against the fabric they'd plastered across the gateway. Its horns punctured the weave, and Oberon flew forward on his winged steed. Bending he sliced a shining, silver blade across the horns. They fell to the ground, amid howls from the demon who was trapped in Hell, minus his horns.

Moira hoped the fucker would bleed to death or be banished or whatever the hell happened to demons who'd been dehorned.

"Give me more," Oberon bellowed. Magic billowed from him as he added another layer across the gateway. His working glowed a faint blue, and he chanted in an ancient form of Gaelic.

Titania flew near, adding her own sheet of sealant over the hole. At least it had stopped pulsing. She slid from her horse and joined Eiocha off to one side of the fissure.

"Everyone!" Eiocha screamed. "Draw fire, mix it with earth and let's finish this."

Moira called fire from the Earth's core. It jumped to her bidding as if it understood how high the stakes were. She directed heat and smoke to sear the fissure, burning it from the inside out. The net effect of their combined magic was formidable, and the edges of the gaping hole began to draw closer.

"Keep it coming," Leif cried.

She felt him inside her magical center. When she reached a little farther, she felt the other sea Shifters too, just as he'd said. Despite her grim surroundings, she smiled faintly. A family. She had a family after long years on her own. Maybe the departing vulture wouldn't leave as deep a scar as she feared.

Her breath came fast. Drawing this much magic was hard work. Whenever she gulped air, it was so tainted with evil, it burned her lungs and made her eyes water, but she had to breathe.

The fissure continued to fold in on itself. Moira asked for earth power and threw it after the fire in great handfuls, as much as she could heave. Around her, Shifters were panting like racehorses who'd been ridden hard. When the opening had been reduced to a small rectangle, Eiocha nodded to Oberon. He slid from his horse and joined her and his consort in front of the fissure.

Eiocha placed the flat of her hand in the center of what was left of the portal to Hell, chanting in harsh tones. Oberon laid his hand over hers, and Titania followed suit. With the three gods joined, they exhorted the rent between worlds to not only close forever, but to trap whoever remained within its folds.

The words were simple, punitive, uncompromising.

Smoke rose from where Eiocha's palm was flattened against the fabric they'd made with their combined magic. Her face contorted with pain, but she didn't move her fingers. Moira wanted to send healing energy but was afraid anything she added would dilute sealing the portal.

The skin on Eiocha's hand blistered. Bone showed through, but the goddess didn't move.

Leif ran to where the gods stood and focused a beam of magic above where their hands were joined. Power flared blue like the sea, and the wound scarring the frigid air vanished.

Moira felt like cheering, but she didn't have either breath or energy. Magic still ran through her like high voltage electricity, leaving her wrung out, drained.

Eiocha tried to move her hand, but Oberon held fast. "I shall heal your hurts."

"No time," she protested. "The gateway is sealed forever but look around you." She pointed with fingers where bone showed through charred flesh.

Moira followed the line of Eiocha's singed fingers. Hell's minions had sloughed off Tantalus's sex spell and begun to fight again while the gateway was closing, their blows bouncing off the Shifters' wards. Fury rained from them as they charged, clearly having identified the Shifters as a weak link in the chain of magical beings who'd thrown a clod in their plans to take over the world.

"Damn, but there are a lot of them," Viktor muttered.

"Be grateful there aren't more," Ketha countered.

Moira refocused her power. "Take out one at a time," she yelled. "It's efficient, and eventually, none will be left."

A bloodcurdling screech was followed by, "Noooooo."

Heart pounding, Moira bolted toward the scream, but Viktor hauled her back. "We keep to our groups." His tone was grim.

"What happened? I have to know what happened." Moira twisted until she saw Zoe lying on the ice-coated ground, a black arrow protruding from her chest. Recco was bent over her, his face twisted into a mask of pain and fear.

Resignation beat a gritty path through Moira. So far, they'd gotten off cheap. Apparently, their run of fair weather had just ground to a halt.

Eiocha ran to Zoe and bent, patting the ground. Shining lines jumped to her call, winding around Zoe's inert form. Her coyote hovered above her, visible in the chill air. Moira recalled Rowana's death. Her eagle had shown itself when the Shifter died, so the presence of Zoe's coyote had to be a harbinger of doom.

I cannot think that way. I have to believe she'll survive.

Moira gave herself a robust mental slap, so she'd have the will to keep fighting.

Eiocha whinnied, the sound contorted by her human vocal chords, and two faeries ran to her, throwing their small bodies across Zoe, presumably to potentiate the ley lines' magic.

"We need your attention here not there," Ketha said, her tone sharp and riddled with anguish.

"Got it," Moira bit off the words. If the ley lines couldn't cure Zoe, there wouldn't be much she could do, either. Focusing on a particularly loathsome goblin carting a bow and a quiver of black arrows, she loosed magic to stop his heart. Before he'd even fallen to the ground, she picked another target.

Now was a time to fight, not to think or to mourn. Both of those would come later.

21

OLD SCORES SETTLED

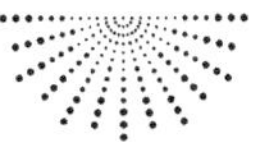

*L*eif was relieved he'd guessed right when he inserted his power into the mix at the fissure. Blending magic with the gods was always a crapshoot, but the gateway had been not just shut but annihilated. He'd been poised to cut the flow of his magic fast if it had clashed with the gods' and pushed the fissure farther open. He expelled air through his teeth. They'd accomplished their first step, but they were a long way from done. When Zoe fell to a goblin's arrow, his magical center went on high alert. That one of theirs had been hit after the gateway was sealed was a bad omen.

Ridding themselves of the portal to Hell should have lessened the demonspawns' power, but it hadn't had much effect.

Recco knelt next to his mate, hands around the arrow's shaft. A cudgel whistled past Leif's head, *thunking* against his warding. He spun to face a giant. Formed from stone, they were impervious to most magics, but nor could they heal themselves. Leif focused his third eye, hunting for the giant's heart. They were never in the same spot. Whichever dark mage created this abomination had formed it to their own specifications.

Harpies flitted past, spewing poison, but it slid off his ward unable to penetrate it. He needed to get to Recco and Zoe. To hell with the giant. It swung its cudgel. Closer now, a blow from it could do more damage. Leif ducked, intent on out-maneuvering its clumsy efforts.

Oberon was back on his winged steed. Flashing hooves connected with the giant's head, severing it from its neck. Leif jumped sideways to avoid the hefty stone orb. It hurtled to the ice next to him, wide fissures spiraling out from where it landed.

He glanced up intent on thanking Oberon, but the king of Faerie had moved on. Leif skidded across the ice to where Recco squatted next to Zoe. Her coyote glided above her, whining softly.

"How is she?" Leif asked.

Recco shook his head. "I want to remove the arrow, but it punctured one of the big vessels feeding her heart. It's all that's keeping her from bleeding to death."

Ley lines had threaded around her ankles and wrists. Another, larger line was snaking around her torso. At least they weren't burning her where they touched her. Perhaps Eiocha's summons had a modulating influence. Grabbing hold of the lines had signed Rowana's death warrant, but they weren't harming Zoe. Not that he could see, anyway.

Karin ran to them and then dropped into a crouch. Power flared as she scanned Zoe's inert form. After a lengthy pause, her eyes fluttered open. "Sure and 'tis you. I'd know your magic anywhere." She coughed; blood bubbled from her mouth.

Recco blew out a tortured-sounding breath. He knew what the blood meant.

Karin thinned her mouth into a grim line. "Zoe. I have to get the arrow out, and then I'll use magic to repair the aorta."

"Not a sure thing, eh?" Zoe rasped around more blood, turning her head to spit out a mouthful.

"No. Not a sure thing at all, but if I do nothing, you'll bleed to death slowly. The main things holding you on this side of the veil are the lines."

"I'll help," Recco gritted. "Tell me what to do."

Zoe clutched at his hand. "If I doona make it, I love you."

Her coyote howled once, a desolate, mournful sound.

"I love you too," he told her, "but goddammit it, you will survive. You have to."

"Do you need me?" Leif asked Karin.

She shook her head. "No. Too many cooks. Go kill something." She addressed Recco. "Watch out for the Harpies. They're soul snatchers, and Zoe is vulnerable since she's so near death."

"Will my magic kill them?"

"No, but if you make them miserable enough, they'll leave us alone. Aim for their wings. They don't like it overmuch when they can't fly. Strengthen your warding so their poison doesn't touch you. They immobilize their prey with poison and then suck out your soul through your mouth."

"What a nasty image," Recco muttered. Power flared around him as he added to his ward and draped it around Zoe as well.

Leif bent and kissed Zoe's forehead. "You have courage, coyote Shifter, and you are well loved. Your bond animal is watching over you."

She trained her dark eyes on him, the pupils so dilated, they covered her irises. "I will do my best." Her words slurred.

"No one can ask for more than that." Leif straightened and took in the field. At least twenty varieties of demons ranged over the frozen tundra. He tallied over a hundred goblins, giants, demons, and things he didn't have names for, before he quit counting. This far north, no trees grew. At least there wasn't much to hide behind beyond columns of ice and rock.

The Shifters and Fae were killing one abomination at a time. They should have made more of a dent in the demon population than they had. A creeping wrongness beyond the evil that permeated this place jabbed him. He knew that energy source.

Recognized it.

After checking on Moira, who was well shielded and killing

methodically, Leif ran toward where he felt evil squatting in a concentrated mass. It wasn't in plain view but hidden behind invisibility spells. Was this a secondary gateway into Hell? One far more subtle and closed to all but a select few? Was that why the Harpies were still here? Out of all the creatures, they had ways to teleport back to the island in the Aegean they'd called home for millennia.

Heedless of running through his magical stores, Leif trained a prodigious blast at the suspicious spot. It shimmied, skittered first to one side, and then the other. He hit it again, harder this time, and it fell aside. Amphitrite rose to her feet, offering him a sunny smile.

"Ye always were too smart for your own good," she crooned.

"Where's Poseidon?"

Her face twisted into a derisive grimace. "That old bastard? He's a craven. A coward. He wanted nothing to do with anything that smacked of a fight. Or with me. Told me I was a faithless slut and that he might look me up later. Ha! I told him not to bother." She tilted her head, adopting a seductive pose. "Now that I'm free, dear boy, your reasons for turning me down have gone away."

Leif decided to play along for a short time. She'd never dealt in artifice, and maybe he could get information out of her. "A second portal?" he narrowed his eyes. "Who would have guessed?"

She stood tall, hands on her hips. "That other one was too large. Too obvious. Tantalus was convinced we needed a superhighway, while I argued for a back alley."

Leif didn't bother telling her about Tantalus's demise. If she'd been paying attention, she'd know. "Who else was behind this portal-from-Hell plan of yours?" He moved slightly closer, smiling.

"I know what you're up to," she snapped.

Leif shrugged. "You want to share my bed. Lovers hold no secrets—"

Eiocha galloped up, back in horse form. One of her front legs showed scarring from where she'd been burned, but it didn't seem to bother her.

"You!" Eiocha tossed her head, whinnying. The word came out garbled but understandable.

"There's a second portal," Leif told her. "It's behind Amphitrite."

"I never corroborated your second portal idea." Amphitrite sounded nervous.

"Doesn't matter." Eiocha steamrolled toward the other goddess. Rearing back, she drove her hooves into Amphitrite's chest, shoving her to the icy ground.

"I am your liege." Amphitrite must have been addressing her words to him. "I command you to protect me." Leif felt a flutter in his magical center. Once upon a time, he'd been linked to her and Poseidon, but that had been before the Cataclysm. He'd taken care to dismantle his connection to both sea gods once they'd let his people die in droves.

Leif stood back as Eiocha reared again, and then brought her powerful front feet down on Amphitrite's chest to the accompaniment of cracking bones. Not that the goddess couldn't heal herself, but Eiocha had no intention of offering her a chance. He'd lost his chance to pry information out of Amphitrite, but sealing the portal was more important.

"Find the portal," Eiocha screamed into his mind.

Leif extended magic, hunting for another fissure, this one small and well concealed. While he searched, Eiocha continued to flatten Amphitrite with her hooves. The sea queen grunted and cried piteously. Leif enjoyed every squeal. Amphitrite couldn't suffer enough to suit him.

"Help me. I'll give you anything you want." More words burbled from Amphitrite's crushed lungs, but Leif tuned her out.

One place soaked in his power, not giving it back. He probed deeper, pushing ice aside until a small throbbing opening, not unlike the entrance to a womb, grew visible.

"Got it." Eiocha punctuated her words with a ferocious equine scream. Bending, she closed her squared-off teeth around

Amphitrite's head and dragged her to the opening, pushing the broken body through with her hooves.

Light flashed, bright as a hundred suns, and Eiocha stood panting, hair straggling around her face. She held a hand out, and Leif took it. Together, they invoked the casting that would shut this portal as well. Maybe because they'd had practice, they dispatched this affront to the Earth in far less time.

"We can't kill her," Eiocha said around gasping breaths.

"We don't want to since sea Shifter power is linked to both her and Poseidon. What we've done is better than killing," Leif replied. Revenge was sweet, goddammit, and he'd relish every second.

Eiocha let go of him and flexed her burned hand. Flesh was starting to grow back over the naked bones. "That was satisfying. Where's her scoundrel of a consort?"

"She said he'd deserted her."

"All the better. One less problem for us. He'll be far weaker without her by his side." Eiocha inhaled deeply. "No rest. We're not finished yet."

As if to validate her observation, the three Harpies flew close, black ichor spewing from their extended talons. Leif poured power into his warding. Eiocha faced the Harpies squarely. White magic shooting from her hands surrounded their poison, turning it a sickly gray. The disgusting mix dribbled to the earth, creating smoking holes where it landed.

"You think to challenge me?" Eiocha tossed her head much as her horse would have.

"Only one of ye, *sister,*" the Harpy in the lead called back.

"Aye, ye must sleep sometime, and when ye're least expecting it —" another Harpy mimed drawing an index finger across her throat.

Eiocha grunted derisively. "I was never sister to any of you. You're weak. All of you. Not enough souls to snatch and feed yourselves. You think you can sneak up on me? My ley lines will make short work of you if you dare disturb my rest." She made shooing motions. "Go away."

The trio circled but didn't leave. Eiocha ignored them. "At least this additional portal explains why we've made so little progress."

Leif did a quick check of his pod—and Moira. All were immersed in killing demons. He hunted for Zoe but couldn't locate her. "The coyote Shifter?" he asked Eiocha.

She frowned. "Alive, but very weak. The arrow contained poison. It's complicating the wolf Shifter's healing."

A small group of faeries ran toward them. "Fae need you. The ice woke up."

Eiocha held out her arms, and the faeries jumped into them. "Say more, little ones."

Leif left them, running to where he could see what was happening. He didn't realize how far he'd gotten from the main battlefield, perhaps half a mile. He gritted his teeth. Amphitrite's location hadn't been accidental. She'd lured him away from the others, thinking to weaken their offense.

And she'd damn near succeeded.

He ran toward where Moira, Ketha, and Viktor had formed an outward facing circle, each of them killing whatever crossed their line of sight. "I found Amphitrite, and a second portal. Eiocha and I sealed her within it."

Moira skinned her lips back from her teeth. "I'm glad she's dead."

"Not dead," Leif corrected her, "but contained forever. I hope."

"A second portal, eh?" Viktor cut in.

"No wonder more demons kept piling up," Ketha grunted as she sent power to kill a squat little sprite with a horn in the middle of his forehead and clawed feet.

"Thank the goddess for the ley lines," Moira said. "If it weren't for them, we'd have run out of power an hour ago."

Leif didn't point out they'd barely been here for an hour. Time passed differently with this much evil afoot.

Lewis raced toward him, killing a trio of hissing, spitting

demons that rolled in front of him. Another approached from behind.

Leif focused a beam of power to flatten it. When the no-name monstrosity caught fire, Lewis glanced over one shoulder. "Thanks, mate. We have another problem. At least this one isn't linked to Hell, but we woke something."

Leif thought back to the faeries' message about the ice waking up. "Do you know what it is?"

Lewis made a face. "You're not going to believe me, but I believe it's either Scylla or Charybdis."

"If one is here, the other would be as well." Leif had met the two supernatural sea monsters a time or two. They lurked in the western Mediterranean Sea, luring boats and sailors to their doom.

"How'd they end up here?" Moira asked.

"The Cataclysm, how else?" Ketha replied.

"They probably thought this would be as safe a place as any to wait out Armageddon," Viktor muttered.

"What did it look like?" Leif asked Lewis.

"Six heads and—"

"That's Scylla," Leif interrupted him. "Take me to her. Perhaps she'll remember me."

Lewis took off at a quick pace. Leif followed him, racking his brain as he tried to remember something that might placate the ancient sea monster. As he threaded his way through demon bodies, an idea took shape. He grabbed one of the fallen goblins and slung it over a shoulder, wrinkling his nose at the noxious smell. Black blood dripped down his shoulder, staining his clothes. Bugling blasted his ears, probably from a pissed-off Scylla.

Lewis turned, leading them behind an icefall. Twenty-foot-tall fluted columns of blue-white ice rose in free form sculptures that were beautiful in an esoteric kind of way. Eiocha had beaten them there, along with Oberon and Titania. Scylla lay on her belly on the ice, twisting her six heads this way and that. Magical netting held her in place, and her fury at being restrained was palpable. Two of her six mouths opened, bugling again. A sea serpent's body trailed behind her six stalky necks. Twelve feet long, her trunk and tail were covered with black-and-silver overlapping scales.

Leif tried for an upbeat note. "This is Scylla—" he began.

"We know quite well who she is," Oberon cut him off.

The monster opened one of her mouths and roared, thrashing her tail from side to side.

Leif dropped to a crouch, holding out the dead goblin. "I bring you an offering. Do you remember me?"

Scylla trained one set of eyes on him. In olden days, she'd worn a girdle of baying dogs' heads, but no more. Steam hissed from the head facing his way. "Aye, wee dolphin Shifter. Of course I remember. Tell these cretins to release me."

"What did you do to frighten them?" Leif eyed her, hoping she'd answer.

"Naught. I did naught but emerge from where I have been asleep these many years past. Something bad came. It sullied my waters." Six sets of jaws opened and clacked shut. "It killed Charybdis, my heart, my sister, my love."

Genuine pity stirred through Leif. "I'm so very sorry."

"Aye, she and I were formed together. We've always been together. And now, I am alone. Once she died, I swam and swam. For weeks, or mayhap 'twas years. I ended up here and hid myself, hoping for death, yet here I am."

"Sheathe your magic," Leif ordered. "She will not harm us."

"Why harm ye?" Scylla's head nearest him asked.

"Aye," another chimed in. "There's food enough to last me a year. I smell the blood and rot."

Eiocha cut the flow of her power, and the silvery netting around Scylla fell away. Leif remained in his crouch, and the monster slithered to him, laying one of her heads on his lap. He stroked the sharp scales, not knowing what to say to comfort her.

Some losses cut too deep for words to have any effect.

"A favor?" the head on his lap asked.

"If it's within my power."

"Help me carry food into my grotto. It's just behind me."

"Of course," Leif said.

"I'll help as well," Lewis cut in.

Scylla twisted the head nearest him to examine who'd spoken. "Another dolphin Shifter?"

Lewis bowed. "Aye, ma'am."

The head in Leif's lap leaned into him much as a cat would have. "One more favor, since ye're in a generous mood."

Leif waited. Oftentimes, like with quests, subsequent requests grew more difficult to fulfill.

"Leave the rest of the demons alive." Interest lit her coppery eyes, turning all six sets to small fiery orbs. "Killing them will be fun. Much better than living off what's already dead."

"You'd have to be certain not to let any escape." Eiocha walked close.

Steam sprayed from Scylla as several heads brayed laughter. "Goddess. Ye doona know me at all."

"You've done us a tremendous favor." Leif found a spot of skin beneath a scale and scratched, hoping she'd enjoy the sensation.

Scylla arched the neck attached to that head. "In that case, dolphin Shifter, the last request is for ye to return each year to visit me."

"Done. It would be my pleasure." With a final scratch, he got to his feet. To his surprise, Scylla started to sing. Unlike the Sirens, her song was primitive and discordant, but lovely in an untamed way.

"Come on." Lewis tapped him on the shoulder. "Let's get this carrion-moving project off the blocks."

Leif grinned. Once they'd carted some bodies near the icefall, they could leave. Scylla would pick off the remaining demons, except the Harpies. They'd depart on their own if they hadn't already. While he and Lewis dragged carcasses to the spot Scylla indicated, Lewis said, "I've been talking with my bondmate."

"And?" Leif quirked a brow.

"It knows a dolphin or two that would be delighted to bond with Moira." Excitement streamed from Lewis. "Don't you see, mate? She'd well and truly be one of us."

"I like the idea," Leif said carefully, not at all certain how Moira would feel.

"There's a but hanging about." Lewis eyed him.

"Yes, there is. She's just been treated very badly by one bondmate. She may not be in a rush to dive back into another bond." He blew out a breath. "Don't mention this to her. I will, but later. Once we're back on *Arkady* and have had a chance to rest and breathe a bit."

Scylla had been watching as they piled carcasses. When the stack was so high they had to swing the next one to toss it on top, Leif said, "Enough, my lady?"

"Aye. In truth, 'twas enough a while back, but I'm enjoying your company. Doona forget your promise."

"I won't."

"I'll come with him to visit you." Lewis bent and stroked the head nearest him.

Scylla slithered to the stack of dead demons and tugged one out of the bottom of the pile, tearing into it with two of her heads. It seemed a good time to leave her to her meal, before she thought of more promises to bind him.

Leif headed for where he'd left everyone. Lewis trotted alongside.

"Do you know how Zoe is?" Leif asked.

"Weak, but she'll survive. Karin and Recco moved her into the faeries' tunnel to take advantage of the strong earth magic inside. Also, it's warmer."

Eiocha and Moira waited for them near the entrance to the passageway. Everyone else was already gone. Demons milled about, looking lost with nothing to take aim at. True to Leif's prediction, the Harpies were nowhere to be found.

"Why aren't those bastards still fighting?" Leif asked, angling a pointed look at a group of red-scaled demons with horns and hooves.

Eiocha skinned her lips back, managing to look both feral and pleased at the same time. "I cast an obfuscation spell. They know we're here, but they can't find us."

"We'll meet half the group where we beached the Zodiacs," Moira told him and Lewis.

"Aye, the others are on their way back to the ship. Karin wanted to get her patient out of the weather," Eiocha said.

"Did Oberon and Titania gather up their fallen Fae?" Leif asked.

"Of course," Eiocha snorted. "Not that they wouldn't have anyway, but…"

Leif nodded. The king and queen of Faery wouldn't have left their fallen companions to turn into food for Scylla. They'd give them heroes' burials back in the U.K.

"We did well," he said. "Far better than I'd hoped."

"Aye, that we did," Lewis agreed. "Very few casualties, and we accomplished our goal."

"You two are so bloody understated," Eiocha cut in. For once, she was smiling, and it lent an otherworldly beauty to her austere features. "We won. We saved Earth from darkness."

Leif didn't want to put a damper on her enthusiasm, but after losing thousands of sea Shifters to the Cataclysm, he didn't feel like he'd won much of anything. He'd survived and saved a few of his pod.

"Darkness isn't gone," he muttered.

"Nay, but we reestablished the balance point where we hold the upper hand." Eiocha nodded briskly. Power flashed from her hands, and the passageway morphed into view. "Hurry through," she instructed. "I shall seal it behind us, so none of the demonspawn can use it as an escape hatch."

Lewis ran ahead, kindling a mage light to illuminate the passageway.

"I want to hear about Scylla." Moira gripped Leif's outstretched hand, and they entered the tunnel. "And I have news. I guess."

Something about her tone alerted him it might not be good news. "What?"

"While I was waiting for you, my vulture popped up. It changed its mind."

"So now it's not breaking your bond?" Leif asked to make certain he understood.

"Yeah."

"You don't sound very happy."

Moira glanced his way. "I'm not. I don't trust it anymore, and I don't know what to do."

"No need to do anything right this minute. We can talk about this after we're back." He almost told her about the dolphins who wanted to bond with her, but the timing was terrible. That information would have to wait. He didn't want her to think he was pushing her toward being a sea Shifter. He'd told her he loved her no matter what she was, and he'd stand by his words.

This transit of the tunnel went far faster than entering it from the other end. Magic was like that sometimes, plus they weren't battling evil. They emerged onto the rock-studded spit of beach where they'd landed hours before. Light was leaching from the day.

Two Fae stood straight, silken robes drawn tight around them and silver hair falling to waist level. Amithra and Piotr rose from where they'd been crouched drawing pictures in the sand. Amithra's green hair was streaked with black blood. She hurtled to Moira who lifted her into her arms.

Piotr ran to Leif and Lewis, crimson hair streaming behind him. Lewis lifted the faery, swinging him in a circle until he squealed with delight.

"We won!" Amithra beamed, her small face wreathed in smiles.

"That we did." Moira hugged her tight.

"We waited for ye," one of the Fae said, "to extend thanks from Oberon and Titania."

"Aye," the other Fae spoke up. "They hope ye will visit them."

Leif bowed. "Please tell them we'd be delighted, and that they are welcome anytime no matter where we are."

"Will ye remain traveling aboard the ship now that the quest has been dispatched?" the first Fae asked.

"I don't know," Leif replied. "We haven't gotten that far yet."

Moira hugged Amithra and set her down.

"Do ye want kisses?" The faery grinned mischievously.

Moira smiled back. "No, little one. Not yet, anyway. Can I take a rain check?"

"What's that?" Amithra placed her hands on her hips.

"It means, may I save your offer and take you up on it in a hundred years or so?"

Amithra clapped her chubby hands, clearly delighted with the idea. "Of course. Ye know where to find me."

"Put me down," Piotr demanded.

Lewis set him next to Amithra and extended a hand. Both Fae clasped it, along with the faeries.

Leif and Moira did the same. "We should go," he said, glancing at the group fifty feet down the beach standing around the Zodiac. "They're waiting for us."

"My condolences on your lost companions," Moira said.

"Thank you. We shall see them to their rest once we return home."

Light formed around the Fae and faeries; magic swelled replete with the rich scents of heather and gorse. The air shimmered and grew liquid. When it quieted, Leif, Moira, and Lewis were alone.

Turning, they walked to the Zodiac. "Ready to go home?" Juan asked.

"More than ready," Leif said and bent to untie the raft from its anchor point on the beach. Juan herded everyone aboard, and Leif slogged through the surf, jumping over the pontoons and into the Zodiac.

A dolphin swam alongside. Lewis slapped his tail against the raft and said, *"See you back on the boat."*

"Would you rather swim?" Moira asked Leif.

"No. My place is next to you."

Juan quirked a blond brow. "Oh-ho. Looks like Vik will be officiating at another wedding."

"The sooner the better," Leif said and gripped Moira's hand. "So long as the lady is in agreement."

She gifted him with a warm smile that didn't require words, and well wishes flowed as the raft cut through the darkening sea.

22

UNEXPECTED GIFTS

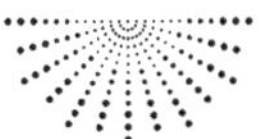

Moira stopped by to see Zoe as soon as she left the raft and was encouraged by how quickly the coyote Shifter seemed to be regaining her strength. Karin and Recco had settled her in the lab, where Karin constructed a healing canopy.

"How's she doing?" Moira asked Karin.

"Excellent." Karin beamed. "She nearly died from the combination of poison and the arrow, so it'll be a few days before she's up and about."

"Whatever was in those ley lines helped a lot," Recco said. "We'll have to figure out how to tap into that power source and direct in into our healings."

"I'll talk with Eiocha about how best to accomplish it." Karin nodded, her expression serious once again.

Moira didn't want to tire Zoe, so she squeezed her hand, murmuring, "I'm so glad you're all right. I'll stop by tomorrow morning."

"Thanks. Sure and I'll look forward to it," Zoe wheezed. A worried look shadowed her dark eyes. "Your vulture?"

Moira snorted. "Changed its mind. It's not leaving after all."

"Aye, but is that good?"

267

Moira released her hand. "We can talk about it later. Don't tire yourself." Switching her attention to Recco and Karin, she asked, "Will I see you two upstairs?"

"Not me," Recco said. "I'm not leaving Zoe's side."

"I'll stop by the bar in a little bit." Karin smiled, but her copper eyes looked tired. She'd blown through boatloads of magic between fighting demons and healing Zoe. That she was still standing was a testament to her iron will.

Daide strode into the lab. Addressing his words to Karin and Recco, he said, "I'm here to help. Let me know what you need."

"Good to see you, dear heart," Karin replied. "You can take over what I'm doing, and I'll catch a shower before I join the group in the bar."

Daide walked to her and wrapped an arm around her shoulders. "I left you some dry towels."

"Kind of you..."

They were still chatting when Moira left and made her way to her cabin. Weariness dogged her, and she sat on the edge of her bunk. The cabin still smelled like Leif and their lovemaking. The rich, tangy ocean scent filled her with both hope and sadness. Hope because she loved him, and sadness because she still thought he needed a Shifter mate. She was supposed to be showering and putting on clean clothes, so she could meet everyone in the bar for a celebration, but so far all she'd done was visit Zoe and argue with her bondmate.

"I still don't see what's wrong," the bird pressed. *"I assumed you'd be thrilled."*

"At what?" Bitterness lined her words.

"Us still being bonded. What else?"

Getting slowly to her feet, she started stripping off clothing. Everything needed laundering, so she dropped the items in an untidy heap and walked into the small bathroom. It took time to coax all the dried ichor from her hair, but she felt better clean than she had before.

At least the vulture hadn't said anything else.

Moira toweled off and then wrapped the damp terrycloth around her head to soak up water. Her stomach had twisted into a sour knot, and a headache pounded behind one eye. Her bird often had that effect on her. It was like any other dysfunctional relationship where she was expected to swallow crap without satisfactory explanations. She hadn't laid down and let anyone else walk all over her. Why should this affiliation be any different?

She dragged on clean clothes. Stretchy thick, black pants and a silver long-john top with a black vest over it. Once her trousers were in place, she shoved her feet into sheepskin slippers. Resolve moved through her in an inexorable tide. She'd put this to rest once and for all.

"Why'd you change your mind?" she asked her vulture.

"It's better for you if I remain." The bird's normal, supercilious tone grated.

"No," she corrected. "It's not. I don't trust you anymore. What happens next time you get a wild hair up your ass and decide I'm not good enough for you?"

"How about if we cross that juncture when it happens?" Compulsion lined the bird's words.

Moira's mouth dropped open. "Do. Not. Use. Magic. To. Manipulate. Me. Got it?"

The vulture squawked denials, but Moira was furious.

"I'm done. Leave. I dissolve our bond." Because she'd researched the incantation, Moira chanted in Gaelic, determined to end her travesty of a bond with the vulture.

"No!" It squalled into her mind. *"You have no idea what you're doing."*

Understanding slapped her hard, and she broke off chanting long enough to say, "I know exactly what I'm doing. Ha! You've broken one too many bonds and face sanctions for your inability to get along with your bondmates."

She sucked in a breath, waiting for it to contradict her. It didn't.

"If you force me to leave, I'll be exiled."

Moira tried to find compassion. Years of mistreatment, episode after episode where her vulture had run roughshod over everything she held dear, got in the way and rose to taunt her.

"The one you are betrothed to requires a Shifter mate." The bird tried another tack.

She balled her hands into fists. "No. He doesn't." Closing her ears to the vulture's pleas, she returned to her incantation. The one that would rip the bond loose from the spot it dwelt inside her magical center.

"It hasn't been all bad," the bird pointed out. *"We did good work together in Invercargill."*

Damn! Her bondmate knew her like no other. Moira's innate sense of fairness surfaced. "It hasn't been all bad," she agreed. "Problem is there's been far more bad than good." She went back to chanting. Not much more. Another five minutes, and the deed would be done.

A knock at her door was followed by Leif opening it. He took one look at her, shoved the door shut, and asked, "What the hell is going on? Magic is so thick in here I can taste it." He held out his arms, but she shook her head.

"Let me finish. I'm doing what my bondmate couldn't. We'll discuss this once I'm done."

"I'm not leaving."

He sounded so fierce and so protective, it warmed her. "No one said you have to." She picked up where she'd left her incantation. The spell developed its own energy toward the tail end and passed a point where she couldn't have cut it off if she'd wanted.

Moira had no idea how the spell would end. How the world she'd tried to carve out with the vulture would end. All she knew was she had to see this through to its conclusion. A sharp jabbing pain doubled her over.

Leif closed his arms around her, crooning in Gaelic.

Searing agony tracked from her chest to the top of her head.

When it faded, she reached for the place the vulture lived within her and found it altered. Part of her magical center, but no longer shaped to fit the bird's energy. She slumped against Leif, and he held her close.

"I had to do that." Her words were muffled against his chest.

"I know. When trust is gone, no relationship can survive." He kneaded the tight muscles in her back and shoulders.

She tilted her head back and met his blue-eyed gaze. "We don't know much about how the bond animals' culture is arranged, but someone told my bondmate it had to stick it out with me or face sanctions."

"It told you that?" A shocked expression spread over Leif's even features.

"More like I dragged the information out of it." She shook her head. "Never mind. It's over. We'll see where things go next. I thought I'd feel worse, but mostly what I feel is relieved."

"Are you ready to join the others upstairs? I came from there to see what happened to you."

"I am. Tonight is a time for celebration. What we accomplished today was huge, so enormous I don't fully appreciate it yet."

He let go of her and pulled the cabin door open. She walked through and waited for him in the corridor. Hand in hand, they climbed one flight up to Deck Four. The sound of voices and the smells of food reached her before they made it to the bar.

"There you are!" Ketha ran to her and enveloped her in a hug. "Everything all right?"

Moira nodded. "More than all right."

Tessa pushed a glass into her hand. "We're in the midst of toasts," she said, smiling brightly.

"Extravagant toasts," Viktor seconded. "To hear us tell it, we should join the ranks of every hero who graced the pages of a mythology book."

Moira took a sip of what turned out to be whiskey. It burned her mouth and tongue and throat but left a warm glow in her stomach.

She raised her glass. "Cheers! To us all. We deserve warm waters, open fires, and easy sailing."

"Warm waters, open fires, and easy sailing," echoed around the bar.

Someone had brought snacks up from the kitchen. Moira nibbled on cornbread and jam as toasts continued to flow around the room. She was surprised she felt as whole as she did. She'd figured it would take a long time to sort out who she was without her vulture in residence. During a break where Juan had vanished behind the bar to open more liquor bottles, she clapped her hands together.

As eyes turned her way, she stood straighter. "You all may have heard that my bondmate changed its mind." She pressed her lips together. "Problem was, by then I didn't trust it at all, so I cast my own spell and dissolved our bond."

Sharp intakes of breath hit her from all sides.

"It's all right." She held her hands in front of her, palms facing outward. "I still have magic, although I have no idea how much. I told you so you'll know, not so you'll feel sorry for me. Today was a long time coming, and I'm relieved that—"

"But your bird returned to you," Aura protested. "Surely that counts for something."

Moira shook her head. "It only sucked up to me because it's broken one too many bonds, and whoever runs the animals' borderworld threatened to exile it."

"Aw crap. Really?" Aura rolled her green eyes. "That's pretty low."

"That would be my ex-bondmate," Moira agreed. "Self-serving to its core." She snorted. "I feel the same way as if I got divorced from an egotistical bastard."

"On a happier note"—Leif crossed to where she stood and draped an arm around her shoulders—"Moira has agreed to become my mate. Those of you who returned in our raft already know, along with my pod, but the rest of you don't."

"Told you." Juan elbowed Aura, who turned to kiss his cheek.

"I'm getting pretty good officiating at weddings," Viktor strode toward them, hand extended.

Leif shook it; so did Moira.

"Before we get lost in weddings," Leif said, "maybe we could talk a bit about what comes next."

"Good idea." Viktor turned to face everyone. "My preference would be to remain aboard *Arkady,* exploring the world, but I'm sure that life won't be a good fit for everyone."

Boris got to his feet. "We talked about that while you were off jousting at windmills and decided we were happy aboard the ship." A chorus of assent rolled from the other eight humans.

"It's not as if we don't have choices," Viktor said. "We could return to Ushuaia. We were building something viable there with the humans who survived the Cataclysm."

"Or we could return to Invercargill or some other city we haven't checked out yet," Ketha added.

"My pod and I have discussed this," Leif said. "Not in depth, but we'll remain with the land Shifters."

"But it means you won't spend as much time in the sea." Viktor latched gazes with him.

"We were moving away from that, anyway," Leif said. "Our reasons for retreating to the sea vanished after the Cataclysm wiped out most of Earth's population. Plus, Moira's not a sea Shifter, and I'm committed to spending as much time as I can with her."

Lewis leapt to his feet. "She could be," he said.

"Aye." Two whales headed right for her, hands extended as if they meant to lift her bodily off the deck.

"Stop right there." Leif leveled his sharp eyes on his pod members. "She doesn't know about that yet, and this isn't the way I'd have chosen for her to find out."

"Sorry, Alpha." The whales didn't come any closer, and Lewis looked away, cowed by Leif's rebuke.

"What is it I don't know about?" Moira asked. Her tone was even, but she had the squirmy, uncomfortable feeling they'd been planning her future without including her. Not unlike her vulture might have done.

Out of the frying pan, into the fire...

Lewis squared his shoulders, staring down his alpha. "This was my doing, Moira. As such, it's my tale to tell." He took a few steps nearer her. "Please know I meant well. Back when we believed your bondmate was waiting out the battle before leaving, I put out a call. Several dolphins were very interested in bonding with a strong, courageous Shifter. I told my alpha, and he said he'd find the proper time to let you know."

His nostrils flared. "I had no idea your vulture would change its mind or be railroaded into trying to make things up with you. Nor did I have any idea you'd take things into your own hands and break the bond yourself." He bowed. "That took a great deal of valor. Not many would have had the strength to push through what must have been a difficult and painful spell."

The unsettled places inside her receded. Leif and his pod held her dear. It wasn't a bad thing. She cleared her throat. "It's all right. Earlier, on the battlefield, when I sensed the link to all of you, I was overwhelmed by a sense of family. You did what you did because you care about me. How can I fault you for that?"

Leif smiled and hugged her. She hugged him back.

"What about it?" he said low, near her ear.

Emotion threatened to swamp her, and she clung to him before letting go. What she had to say was for everyone, not just her brand-new mate. "I'm humbled and delighted for the opportunity to bond with a dolphin. I'm a Shifter. It's what I was born to be. I had no idea what it would be like to not have an animal form to morph into, but I was trying not to get too far ahead of the curve."

"So you accept?" Leif couldn't contain the eagerness that spilled from him.

"I do. How will this work? Will they come to me in dreams?"

"Nay," Lewis spoke up. "They'll come to you in the sea. You'll merge with them, and it will be just like it's always been."

Excitement kindled. She was thrilled at the prospect of a bondmate who wanted her, unlike the vulture who was only trying to prove its superiority.

"I know that look." Aura laughed. "Before we lose the entire pod to the waters of Pevek's harbor, let's get some closure on our next steps."

"Good idea." Viktor gazed around the room. "What'll it be, folks? Sailing or settling somewhere?"

"They're not mutually exclusive," Karin said from where she'd planted herself near the bar. "We can sail until we find a spot we'd all like to call home."

"Even if we stop somewhere," Recco cut in, "nowhere is it written we have to remain there forever."

"Is the vote to be vagabonds?" Viktor grinned. "Wanderers in the open sea?"

Ayes and yesses surged around the bar.

"Looks as if it's settled." Viktor drank deep from his glass and went to refill it, returning with the bottle and topping off glasses.

Leif turned to Moira and gripped her hands. "Are you certain, darling?"

"Yes. I am."

Whoops and cheers rang from the sea Shifters. Rising as a unit, they streamed out of the bar amid cries of, "See you in the ocean."

"How will that work for me?" Fear joined the excitement churning in her belly. "I can swim, but that water is cold."

"The pod will keep you warm until the bonding is complete," Leif said. "We'll warm the water with magic, and we'll be ringed around you. No harm will come to you. Do you trust me?"

She nodded, suddenly solemn, and followed him out of the bar. They walked down one flight to Deck Three and paused next to the door leading outside. "I will shift and join my pod. Give us about five minutes and then teleport to us."

"What do I use for a destination?" Nervous tension made her voice shrill. What if she miscalculated and drowned?

"Me. Think of me, and all will be well." He kissed her on the lips before racing outside.

Moira waited through what she thought was five minutes before skinning out of her clothing. Too late, she thought about returning to her cabin. If she'd been there, she could have put her clean clothes away, folding them neatly.

An anxious laugh bubbled out. She was scared. Leif had asked if she trusted him. She did, and she put that trust front and center in her mind as she visualized him and activated her teleport spell.

Water closed over her until flippers lifted her, so her head was above water. The pod surrounded her, dolphins close and whales farther out. The patch of water where she floated was indeed warmer than she'd expected.

"Close your eyes," Leif said in the garbled speech he employed as a dolphin. "The new bondmates will come to you."

He supported her body with a flipper, and she shut her eyes, opened her magical well, and waited. Her breathing slowed, and she recognized a trance when it enveloped her. The energy felt strange, but welcome, different from the vulture's harshness.

A dolphin swam through her mind's eye, blue-grey and delicate. It stopped in the center of her psychic view and bowed. *I would be honored to bond with you.*

It faded from sight, replaced by a slightly larger dolphin with more green in its hide. *I would be honored to bond with you.*

The process repeated twice more. "How do I choose?" Moira asked Leif. "They all seem kind and wonderful."

Employ your psychic senses, he said. *Look for the one that glows brightest. That is the one meant for you.*

She wound her fingers around the flipper supporting her and sent magic through her third eye. The four dolphins ranged in a semicircle, waiting for her to choose. It was hard. She was touched by their selflessness, and she didn't want to hurt any of their feelings. She understood the sting of rejection.

Leif must have been in her mind because he said, *"It's all right. We will have children. This isn't their only opportunity for a bond."*

Moira sent her power zinging toward the magical dolphins. The first one who'd approached her glowed in an enticing array of color. Not understanding how she knew what to do, Moira let the magic take her and left Leif's side to swim to the dolphin who would be her mate.

Power raced into her like high-voltage magic, and she felt a shock as her magic blended with the dolphin's. Only moments had passed, but it felt as if they'd always been together. Leif butted her gently from the side, and joy shot through her.

She was a dolphin.

Swimming for the surface, she expelled air and sucked more, inhaling to the bottom of lungs that could remain submerged for a long time. Around her, the pod capered and frolicked. She dove and resurfaced, and then did it again. Swimming wasn't flying, but it was wonderful in its own way.

She felt her new bondmate's energy, gentle but with steel beneath soft edges. *"Thank you for bonding with me."*

"The pleasure is all mine," her new bondmate cooed. *"I can't wait to get to know you better."*

Leif nudged her from the side, stroking her flank with his flipper. *"Do you want to swim with the pod for a while?"*

She slapped the water's surface with her tail. It felt so good, she did it again. *"Yes. I'd love to swim with my pod."*

"Not too long. Somewhere inside, there's a bed with our name on it."

If she'd been human, she would have laughed. Instead, she swam fast. *"Bet you can't catch me."*

"Bet I can."

Water churned around them as the pod joined in a rousing game of chase. Happiness spilled through Moira, but for once she didn't question it. She was exactly where she belonged with her mate and her pod. Tomorrow would bring its own set of joys and trials, but for now she ducked and wove and played until Leif swam close.

"Ready?" he asked once they'd surfaced

"Yes, love. More than ready."

In a blend of teleport and shift magic, she followed him back to *Arkady's* deck. Far more than a ship, it had become their home. No matter what happened next, she had a family—and a mate. Happiness engulfed her as Leif gathered her into his arms.

You've reached the end of the Bitter Harvest series. Thanks so much for reading through to the end. Please leave a review for *Redeemed*. Doesn't have to be fancy. A line or two will do. Thanks in advance! Reviews are really important.

If you enjoy end of the world urban fantasy tales, you might like my Soul Dance series. A sample from *Tarnished Legacy* follows.

ABOUT THE AUTHOR

Ann Gimpel is a USA Today bestselling author. A lifelong aficionado of the unusual, she began writing speculative fiction a few years ago. Since then her short fiction has appeared in several webzines and anthologies. Her longer books run the gamut from urban fantasy to paranormal romance. Once upon a time, she nurtured clients. Now she nurtures dark, gritty fantasy stories that push hard against reality. When she's not writing, she's in the backcountry getting down and dirty with her camera. She's published over fifty books to date, with several more planned for 2018 and beyond. A husband, grown children, grandchildren, and wolf hybrids round out her family.

Keep up with her at www.anngimpel.com or http://anngimpel.blogspot.com

If you enjoyed what you read, get in line for special offers and pre-release special reads. Newsletter Signup!

BOOK DESCRIPTION: TARNISHED LEGACY

Germany, 1940

Half Romani, Tairin's no stranger to hiding her mixed blood from gypsy caravans. What she can't hide is her perpetual youth, courtesy of her shifter heritage. Every few years, she drops out of sight, resurfacing in a new country to join a caravan where no one knows her. She's overstayed her welcome where she is, but Germany is at war, and travel has become all but impossible for everyone targeted by the Reich.

Elliott's clairvoyance is strong, even for a Romani. Seer for all the caravans in Germany, he catches Tairin eavesdropping outside their leader's wagon one night. He should turn her in, but it would mean her execution, and he can't bring himself to do that. Instead, he interrogates her. Her magic is different, but he can't figure out quite what she is.

Any association between Romani and shifters is forbidden, and Tairin shields herself from Elliott's probing. She should leave right now, tonight. It would be easy enough. Shift to her wolf form and run, keeping out of hunters' gunsights. She's on the edge of flight when Elliott suggests a covert task to prove her loyalty. Tairin agrees immediately, kicking herself for being weak where he's concerned. Shifters and Romani have no future together. Zero. Zilch.

She should be smart about this and vanish into the night—before he discovers what she is and destroys her.

TARNISHED LEGACY, PROLOGUE

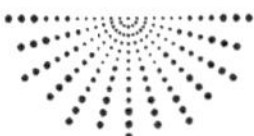

January 1940
Munich, Germany

ELLIOTT BREND MOVED his hands in a circular pattern over three lit candles, the stench of wax made from sheep fat sharp in his nostrils. Patterns danced like mad creatures on the walls of his grotto, and he chanted faster to bring his casting to life.

Darkness swirled, surrounding him. The candles guttered and died, their wicks drowning in pools of grease. Elliott bolted to his feet, hands extended, still working the spell he'd summoned. Fear thickened his tongue, but he couldn't stop now. Partially cast spells would make it possible for the demon he'd apparently conjured to drag him back to Hell with it. Usually this casting brought visions, not an actual entity.

The temperature in the grotto plummeted until ice crystals formed in the air. Wind wailed, thin and menacing. Shudders racked him.

"Why have you freed me? Not that I'm complaining, mind you."

The words echoed around Elliott, chilling him further. "Speak, human. While you still can."

Elliott tried. Instead of words, a breathy croak emerged. He swallowed around his dry-as-dust throat. "F-future," he stammered. "What will happen? Many of the Rom have been captured."

Unholy laughter drove into Elliott's brain like overheated nails. It took all his self-control not to clap his hands over his ears, but if he did that, he'd be lost. His spell would falter, as would his tenuous hold on the demon. He'd be damned if he'd cede the upper hand to it.

Who am I kidding? It already has all the power it needs.

"You scarcely require me for future-telling," the disembodied voice said. At least the profane laughter had stopped. After the briefest pause, it added, "Flee while you can. Or the Rom will die out—here and elsewhere."

"Why do you care?" The words tore out of Elliott before he could stop himself.

"About your people? I don't, but magical energy will keep me on this side of Hell. Along with death. Fear helps too." A low, menacing chuckle punctuated the demon's words. "It's a perfect mix. You can blame the Nazis for my freedom. They provided an ideal medium. Coupled with your drawing spell, it allowed me to pierce the veil."

Elliott gathered power, letting it surge through him. The demon may have ridden in on the coattails of his earlier spell, but he couldn't allow it to remain. Too much evil was running unchecked as it was. Sparks crackled from his fingertips, burning him until his flesh smoked. The incantation, a surefire way to banish Hell's minions, crashed to the rotting wooden floor in a shower of glowing embers.

"Don't waste your magic, human."

"It's not a waste to return you to your proper place," Elliott snarled, wishing he could see the fucking thing.

"Try that last trick again, and you're a dead man."

Elliott sucked in a frustrated breath. He'd suspected the Rom were in serious danger. Signs they'd soon be targeted *en masse*, right along with the Jews, were impossible to ignore. All he'd sought this night was corroboration—and now he had it. He changed the cadence and timbre of his chant, hoping for an end to his spell, the hideous cold, and the abomination that scared the shit out of him. All he wanted now was for it to leave since returning it to Hell was beyond his ability.

"I am not leaving yet," the voice informed him. "You have no power over me, but you've already figured that out. Evil has risen. Rampant. Ubiquitous. As I noted earlier, it feeds me, right along with your magic."

Elliott clamped his jaws together to stop his teeth from chattering. What had he loosed on the world? "You must return at some point." He infused compulsion into his words. "If not today, or tomorrow, then surely soon. The dynamic balance between worlds will fail if you remain on Earth."

Laughter again. This time, it was even more loathsome and obnoxious.

"You haven't been paying attention, *human*. That dynamic balance? It's on its way out." Still laughing, the thing's foul presence receded.

Elliott sank into a crouch, mostly because his legs shook too badly to hold him upright. He wrapped his arms around himself and rekindled the candles with a jot of magic, welcoming their pools of light. Because it was easier than reconstructing what had just happened—and the wickedness now free because of him—he shuffled through options.

The demon's advice—if demons even handed out such things— had been to flee. But where? Austria, Poland, and Czechoslovakia were out of the question. Austria was a German ally. Both Poland and Czechoslovakia had fallen to German occupation a few months earlier. France would soon be under German rule. While his seer skills weren't absolute, he'd seen that particular event clearly.

Even if they could find a favorable location, how would they move the entire Romani population out of Germany? They still favored wagons, so any kind of stealth exodus was out of the question.

He rose to his feet and shambled to a window, gazing out at a moonless night. The elders from all the Rom groups in Germany had assembled a few days earlier, and they were waiting for him to return. Though they dealt in magic, his particular affinity for the darker side of the spirit world unnerved many of his kin.

Should he confess what he'd done?

He'd loosed wickedness eager to sign on with the blood-soaked Nazi regime, but how much worse could things get? He knew what the work camps really were, and so did the other Rom. None of his people fit the Aryan model of perfection, and their nomadic lifestyle was an affront to neat rows of impeccable houses where blonde wives raised blonde children in perfect obedience to the Reich's precepts.

Not much leeway for the Roms' brightly colored wagons or their sturdy horses. Their children who didn't go to school, or the canvas tents where they revealed futures, healed the sick, and fixed whatever was broken.

Bile splashed the back of his throat; he swallowed it down, and it burned all the way to his knotted belly. He still didn't understand how the Reich had mired Germany in such a chokehold, but it didn't matter. What did was ensuring Rom magic survived. It may have provided fodder for the newly released demon, but it also ensured the natural world would continue.

The traveling folk were tied to the world's beginnings in ways that had faded out of time and memory. They'd been run out of countries before and always endured, retooling themselves and keeping their magic under wraps as the world grew more modern.

If leaving Germany were impossible, they'd have to find a way to conceal themselves. The more he thought about it, the more the idea appealed to him. They faced evil, the likes of which the world had never seen. Evil that believed it could kill whomever it wished under the guise of cleansing the gene pool and producing a master race.

It would take gargantuan effort, but he and his kin could leverage magic to sabotage the Reich. Maybe even free the poor sods in those abominable camps. And make damn good and sure Germany went down in flames it would never recover from. Elliott had no idea if the elders would agree, but he'd float his idea. See if their philosophy, *Opré Roma*—Roma arise—was more than empty words.

Even if they don't agree, there's nothing that says I can't gather a few handpicked companions...

He curved his hands into fists until his nails cut into his palms. The more he rolled it around in his mind, the better he liked the idea of small vigilante groups that struck fast and hard, while remaining invisible to the *SchutzStaffel*, Germany's elite corps of political soldiers.

Determination straightened his spine. He dug a warm cloak out of the clothing chest leaning against one wall and wrapped it around himself before striding out of his well-hidden grotto located beneath the city. Part of a deteriorating tunnel system under a crumbling castle, his hideaway dated back to Roman times. He'd titrate what he told the elders until he saw which way the wind blew. Once he had a sense of that, he could make better plans.

Since none of them had stronger power than he did to banish the demon, probably no reason to mention it at all...

He shook his head. Secrecy was a bad idea. He had to live with himself, which meant full disclosure. No matter how much shit he got for his folly.

TARNISHED LEGACY, CHAPTER ONE

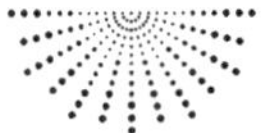

Jairin Jabari prowled from one end of a clearing to the other in a forested glen. Her Rom family group had established a temporary camp here after local authorities ousted them from their previous location inside Munich's city limits. More than a dozen wagons fanned out in a circle, and horses were hobbled off to one side where grass grew thickly. Cars might be faster, but the smoky, noisy contraptions that always required repair had never appealed to Romani sensibilities.

She rolled her shoulders back to quell the creature sharing her skin. Her wolf wanted out, but it was too dangerous. For all their magic, power they scattered about like so much faerie dust, the Romani were superstitious about shapeshifters.

Worse than superstitious. They hated them.

She pulled her thick, black wool cloak tighter around herself and buried her hands in its thick folds. Her leather boots were soaked through, but it was winter. Short days and wet ground meant they never dried completely. Reaching within, she soothed her wolf, agreed its lush double coat and furred paws were far better suited to damp and cold than their current arrangement.

"Promise me," the wolf spoke into her mind.

"Anything, heart of mine."

"Find us an hour when I can run."

Tairin closed her teeth over her lower lip, not wanting false words to fall between her and her bondmate. *"I'll do my best."* Whether *her best* would yield the privacy required remained to be seen.

Something mollified the wolf. Maybe her words. Maybe her honesty. It withdrew to the place where it lived when it wasn't front and center in her mind.

She'd managed to hide what she was from the group she traveled with for the better part of twenty years. Soon it would be time to fade away—to find another country and maybe more Romani traveling companions. As it was, several of the women had made snippy comments about her perpetual youth. Tairin led them to believe she employed a glamour, but no one had the kind of magic to keep something like that going all day, every day, for years.

The sounds of male laughter, boasts, and glasses slapping a tabletop rose from the leader's wagon. He played host to eleven other elders this week. They'd gathered to discuss the evil that had descended on Germany. Elliott, the group's seer, was off doing goddess only knew what. Maybe he'd actually have a vision that would galvanize the Rom into something beyond business as usual.

Not a moment too soon, her inner voice muttered sourly.

If the disaster she suspected were imminent fell out the sky and onto their heads, they'd be rounded up. Herded into the death camps sprouting like cancers across what used to be the Prussian empire.

And that would be that.

She'd find a way through. Her wolf form would see to it. She could join one of many packs that howled their way through Germany's thick forests. But she'd become fond of the Romani after a rocky start. That and shared blood was why she'd traveled with several of their family groups for the past hundred years.

She wove her way into a thick evergreen grove where she

wouldn't have to hide the anger that still filled her whenever she remembered how her people had kicked her out. Looking back was a dead end, yet once she'd begun, it took time to redirect her energy.

She was different from other shifters. And other Romani. Born of a forbidden coupling between a wolf shifter father and a Romani mother, she hadn't been welcome in either camp once her powers blossomed. Her moon blood presaged her first shift, and her life had turned to warmed over crap right afterward. Shifters might have had more tolerance for how strong her magic was if her blood were pure, but it wasn't.

That she could shift at all meant the Rom wanted nothing to do with her.

Tairin took to her wolf form after being rejected by both sides of her kinfolk. She'd lived with local packs in northern Egypt for her first hundred years, give or take a few. Some alphas accepted her; others drove her away. She'd been between packs when a caravan of Romani wagons passing through attracted her attention, alerted her it was time to be human again. As a wolf, she was used to following her instincts without overthinking things. After so long, her animal nature was firmly entrenched.

So firmly entrenched, her first shift back to her human body took days to finesse. A Romani fortuneteller with Runic markings on her face and hands had found Tairin with her arms wrapped around her naked body, crying. After so long as a wolf, speech didn't come easily, so she'd had a ready excuse not to reveal that her tears were relief she still had a human form. Over the days she'd languished part wolf, part human, she'd been petrified she'd never find the purity of either body again.

The woman who rescued her moved her into the back of her wagon. As Tairin regained her very rusty ability to speak, she discovered the Romani group was on the move, traveling through Pakistan, Persia, and Turkey on their way to Romania. The journey had been hard and taken years. She'd stuck with them throughout, helping as she grew stronger. Though her new family wanted to know all about her, the only part she'd revealed was that she had some Romani blood.

She'd never repeated her past mistake about spending years in a single form. Her wolf had warned her it would be folly, but she hadn't listened to it. Nor did she assume her adoptive tribe would be tolerant if they knew what she truly was, so she dove headfirst into relearning Romani magic, remembering her affinity for it.

She'd been such an apt pupil she'd hidden just how potent her power was because she didn't want anyone to guess she was anything other than Romani mixed with human. As she'd developed her skills, she waited for the unknown to rise up and swallow her whole. Surely there was a reason the Rom avoided shifters. A reason why sexual congress was forbidden. Would her use of Romani magic leave her open to some hideous consequences?

Though she'd asked that question and others, taking care to be subtle about it, no answers were forthcoming. The lore books were written in Coptic, an old Egyptian language no one in her caravan seemed to have mastered at anything beyond a cursory level. Tairin spoke Coptic, but she'd never learned to read very well as a child, so translation was beyond her. Over the last century, she'd rectified being mostly illiterate, but her grasp of German and French didn't help decipher the lore books.

She stifled a frustrated sigh. Her current group of companions was the fourth one she'd joined since leaving Egypt. Given the rise of the Reich, it might well be the last.

The sounds of a horse galloping hard drew her back to the circle of wagons. Was Elliott returning? Or was an elder late to the party? She'd thought all were present and accounted for, but she might've been wrong. Tairin sent a slender thread of seeking magic outward. Elliott's energy resonated, making her heart flutter oddly.

The tall, broad-shouldered Rom with his long black hair and deep blue eyes moved with the grace of a large jungle cat. Seer power ran strong in him, and he dabbled in the darker side of Rom magic. Enchantments from Black Magick came easily to her, but she hid that particular ability from her fellows.

Sometimes she'd caught Elliott's gaze on her, sharply speculative. But if he saw through to what she was, he'd never said as much.

Elliott reined his horse to an abrupt halt, its thick hooves churning up clods of mud and stones. "Tairin." His voice rang with command and a surfeit of magic as he dismounted. "See to my horse." He tossed the reins her way and loped toward the wagon where the men held court. His leggy gait drew her gaze. He was so sensual, her body vibrated with wanting to throw herself into his arms. She'd never lain with a man, only with wolves, but she could imagine what it would be like.

Maybe it's time.

Maybe not. I got away with learning Rom magic. I might not be so lucky making love with one.

How would her half-breed blood react to joining with a Romani? She couldn't ask the question without giving away far too much about who she was.

She plucked the reins out of the dirt and sent soothing energy directly into the horse's mind. The stallion had been ridden hard. He needed a cool down, so she vaulted onto his back and walked him at a sedate pace until he stopped tossing his head and his breathing slowed. Some horses sensed her dual nature and resented the hell out of it, but the stallion seemed oblivious.

She'd tethered him near his fellows where he could graze and removed his saddle and bridle before curiosity drew her to the wagon where men's voices droned. Someone had shielded the conversation unfolding within, but she cut through the barrier with ease. Hunkering a few feet away, she eavesdropped shamelessly, wanting to know what would happen next.

Women fared better with the traveling folk than they did elsewhere, but Romani society was still run by men. When she sent her power spiraling outward to listen in on the men, the other women were all in their wagons, probably pretending all was well. The men—beyond the elders—milled about, busy with myriad tasks that needed doing each night. Younger children remained with their mothers. Older boys and girls helped the men do chores. Normally, they'd have set up their tents and wagons in Munich, soliciting local business, but the resident police force had made it abundantly clear they were no longer welcome.

Tension thickened the air. Even though everyone was acting as if tonight was just one more winter evening, they all knew better. Decisions unfolding one thin wall away from her would bind them to a course that might well spell their doom. A hissing snort bubbled up; Tairin smothered it fast before one of the elders heard and came out to investigate.

She swathed herself in invisibility and tilted her head, listening intently.

"You loosed a demon?" Michael thundered.

"How could you have been so irresponsible?" another voice she didn't recognize broke in.

"It's not as if that was my intent." Elliott's even baritone held a calming element. "I cast a scrying spell seeking visions, not one of Hell's minions." He paused for a few seconds, probably to strengthen the spell that lay beneath his words. "I did my damnedest to send the bastard packing. I wasn't strong enough, but we waste time speaking of him. We must decide how to proceed."

"Ye say the demon advised flight?" Stewart's Scottish brogue was unmistakable.

"Yes," Elliott replied.

"When we begin believing anything that emerges from a demon's mouth, we're finished," Michael said flatly.

"Och aye. Still, we canna remain here," Stewart said. "We canna work. We've been banned from the town."

"It won't be any different in Berlin or Heidelberg or Dresden," Elliott said. "The Reich have labeled our kind as undesirables. Our way of life is anathema to them."

"And ye know what happens next." Stewart's words sounded like a dirge. "We join the others. The ones imprisoned by those Nazi bastards."

"Let me say my piece," Elliott cut in. "Then you can decide what's best for your individual groups."

"I'm not certain I want to listen to someone who let a demon loose to feed off the poison spreading across Europe," another elder grumbled.

"Your choice." Elliott spoke clearly, but without inflection. "My path is clear."

"Really?" Michael's single word dripped displeasure. "Last time I checked, you were part of my group, which means you're bound by my decisions."

Elliott cleared his throat. "Nowhere is it written that you own me, nor that I signed on with you for life. Look, men, we have a problem. If we continue to ignore it, the Nazis may well add us to their genocide list—"

"They already have," Stewart broke in. "I, for one, would like to hear what the lad has to say. Listening doesna bind us to action."

"Fine," Michael muttered dourly. "Proceed, but make it quick."

After a period of silence when Tairin held her breath, Elliott began to speak again. "Very well. Escape from Germany is unlikely given our numbers. A few of us might get lucky, but most of us will end up trapped. Neighboring countries aren't a haven. Either they're already occupied, or they soon will be." He inhaled noisily and blew it out. "Our only option as I see it is to hide. If we remain in our groups, they're manageable enough we might be able to pull it off."

"What aren't you saying?" Michael demanded. "I damn near raised you, Elliott. I know when there's more than what's come out of your mouth."

"I'm impressed." Elliott laughed softly. "You do know me, probably far too well. I plan to leverage my magic and do what I can to sabotage the Reich. I'm not certain how it will play out, but if I strike fast and hard, I can catch them off balance. By combining my seer ability and maybe astral projection or invisibility spells, I should be able to determine where my efforts will create the most damage."

"So will ye be doing this on your own, lad?" Stewart asked.

"If need be, yes," Elliott replied. "I admit, it would be better if a small group of us signed on, but this will be extremely dangerous, and I won't ask anyone else to risk discovery—and maybe death—if things go wrong."

"You might have discussed this with me first." Michael's tone held censure.

"When would I have had a chance?" Elliott shot back. "This idea only took shape today, after the demon left me to stew in my own guilt for having offered it free passage from Hell."

"Mmph. The way I see it," Michael said, "we have three choices. Business as usual. Attempt to make our way to somewhere the Nazi scourge hasn't touched. Or conceal our presence."

"That was my assessment," Elliott murmured.

"Ye did well, lad," Stewart said. "Now leave us so we may determine if we all bet on the same nag, or if we separate our fortunes."

Tairin had crept so close, she leaned against one of the wagon's wheels. The sound of scuffling footsteps as Elliott exited the wagon happened fast. Too fast for her to scamper into the forest. Barely breathing, she wound another layer of spells around herself, hoping invisibility would hide her presence. Once Elliott retired to the wagon he shared with three other unattached men, she could make her way to her own bedroll in one of the women's wagons.

Elliott trotted by where she crouched. He moved fast enough, she let herself hope she'd avoided discovery. Listening in on the elders, particularly after they'd shielded their conversation against prying ears, would surely earn her a session with the bullwhip. If not far worse.

For long, tense moments, she thought she'd pulled it off. She was just starting to breathe again when Elliott's heavy tread first slowed and then stopped.

Shit! Crap!

"*Become me,*" her wolf piped up. "*We can knock him down and be gone before he knows what hit him.*"

"*We can't shift that fast.*"

Magic, shockingly strong, probed her perimeter. The gig was up. Elliott might not know it was her, but he realized something was next to Michael's wagon. Something that had no business there.

More power pushed against her invisibility spell, growing in intensity until he punched through. His magic ceased abruptly.

"*Tairin!*" ricocheted through her mind. "*I know it's you. Don't bother denying it. Get over here. Now.*"

She rose to her feet, letting go of her spell as she moved to where he stood twenty yards away. She'd be damned if she'd cower, so she straightened her shoulders and stared him right in the eyes.

"Follow me," he ground out.

"Why should I?" she countered.

He spoke into her mind again. "*You have two choices. Either I call Michael, tell him what you were about, and let him decide what to do with you.*"

"Or?" She feigned bravado she was far from feeling.

"*We go someplace more private, and you tell me what the hell you were doing listening in on the elders' discussion.*" He narrowed his eyes to slits, but switched to speaking aloud. "I might still have to tell Michael. Just so we're clear about that. I owe him allegiance. As do you."

Tairin jerked her chin toward thick timber. "Lead out."

Elliott shook his head. "Nope. You first. I'll be right behind you. And I warn you, if you try anything, I'll flatten you with magic and ask questions later."

She made her way to the grove of pines and firs where she'd been earlier. It was starting to drizzle, so she pulled her hood over her head. Tairin took her time as she worked on organizing which blend of truth might fly better. He'd be able to sniff out falsehoods right away.

His energy pounded against her back as she retraced her steps from earlier. She picked out anger, disbelief, and oddly enough, disappointment. Where was that coming from?

Tairin ducked beneath a low hanging limb and turned to face Elliott. It was dark, but her shifter blood meant she saw quite well in low light conditions. Elliott's dark brows were drawn into a thick, disapproving line.

"Talk and talk fast, sister."

The sizzle of power surrounded her, and she recognized a truth casting. "Was that really necessary?"

"What do you think?" His voice was low, tight with something she couldn't interpret. "I find you swaddled in invisibility spells right outside Michael's wagon. You were obviously listening in. I want to know why."

"That's fair." She let go of her earlier intention of weaving a tale about idle curiosity mixed with boredom. Opening her eyes wide, she netted him with her gaze, trying her hardest not to pay attention to his high forehead, square jaw, and thick, curly hair that almost begged her to sink her hands into it.

"Come on, Tairin." He sounded exasperated. "Talk or you won't leave me any choices. What are you? A Nazi spy?"

Her mouth dropped open. "Awk. Jesus Christ! Oh, hell no." She bristled. "I have eyes and ears. I see what's going on about us. If you must have the truth, I was thinking about leaving, setting out on my own because I could hide myself better that way."

The edges of his magic probed her again. Along with it, his scent rose, tickling her nostrils with bay rum and piquant vanilla. She couldn't help herself, she breathed deep, inhaling the maleness of him.

His power jabbed her when he delved deeper. She rubbed her forehead. "Ouch. Surely that's more than enough. You must've picked up truth in my words."

"I did." Without warning, he closed the distance between them and clasped her head between his hands, pushing her hood back onto her shoulders. Rain pounded from the sky, soaking her.

The intense nearness of him made her knees weak, but she struggled, trying to get away. In all her years with the Rom, the only one who'd touched her had been that first fortuneteller, and the woman had a kind heart. She hadn't suspected a thing, and her touch was aimed at healing, not peeling back the layers of a secret Tairin had guarded for years.

"Stop!" She writhed in his grip.

His scent intensified, and the air around them turned silvery, glistening against the raindrops. Before he could dig deep enough to discover what she was, she wrapped her arms around his neck and pulled his mouth atop hers. The touch of his lips set fire to her blood, and she tightened her hold on him, kissing him as if the fate of the world rested on never letting go. Desire hot enough to set her heart racing sent sensation spilling through her.

After the briefest of hesitations, he buried his hands in her hair and sank his tongue inside her mouth. Something about the way he fell headlong into her embrace made her suspect he'd imagined kissing her just like this.

Whatever works. If this keeps him from unraveling my secrets, it's a small price to pay.

But she was deluding herself. She couldn't make love with him without telling him what she was. He'd never forgive her. More importantly, she'd never forgive herself.

His cock swelled against her belly, rigid with need. What would he look like? Taste like? She ached to wrap a hand around that hardness and drag him inside her body.

Reluctantly, she tore her mouth from his and let go of him. "Sorry," she managed through panting breaths. "I don't know what got into me." She stole a quick glance upward through lowered lids before adding, "I—I'm a maiden. Not a harlot."

"I know." His voice throbbed with yearning. "But you're right that this isn't a good idea. Not with all the problems we face."

She wasn't sure whether to agree, so she held onto a wary silence. Where would this go next?

He let go of her head. "Your magic is strong. As strong as any Rom I've ever come across. Yet you're not full blood."

She licked her swollen lips, anxious to change the subject to something other than her power. "I could help you."

"With what?"

She rotated one hand in a circle. "That plan you described. My magic is potent, and it would complement yours since I'm female."

"Hold on." He shook his head. "I was trolling for men. Women don't go to war."

"The hell they don't." She shook wet hair out of her eyes. Annoyance scoured her nerves, and she stuck out her chin. "Try me. If I don't pass muster, I'll either join the women and sew doilies, or more likely, I'll slip away and wage my own mutiny against the Reich."

His chiseled lips, lips she was having a hell of a hard time resisting, twitched into a smile. "You're on, woman. Feel like a ride?"

"Where are we going?"

"Somewhere we can plan our first offensive."